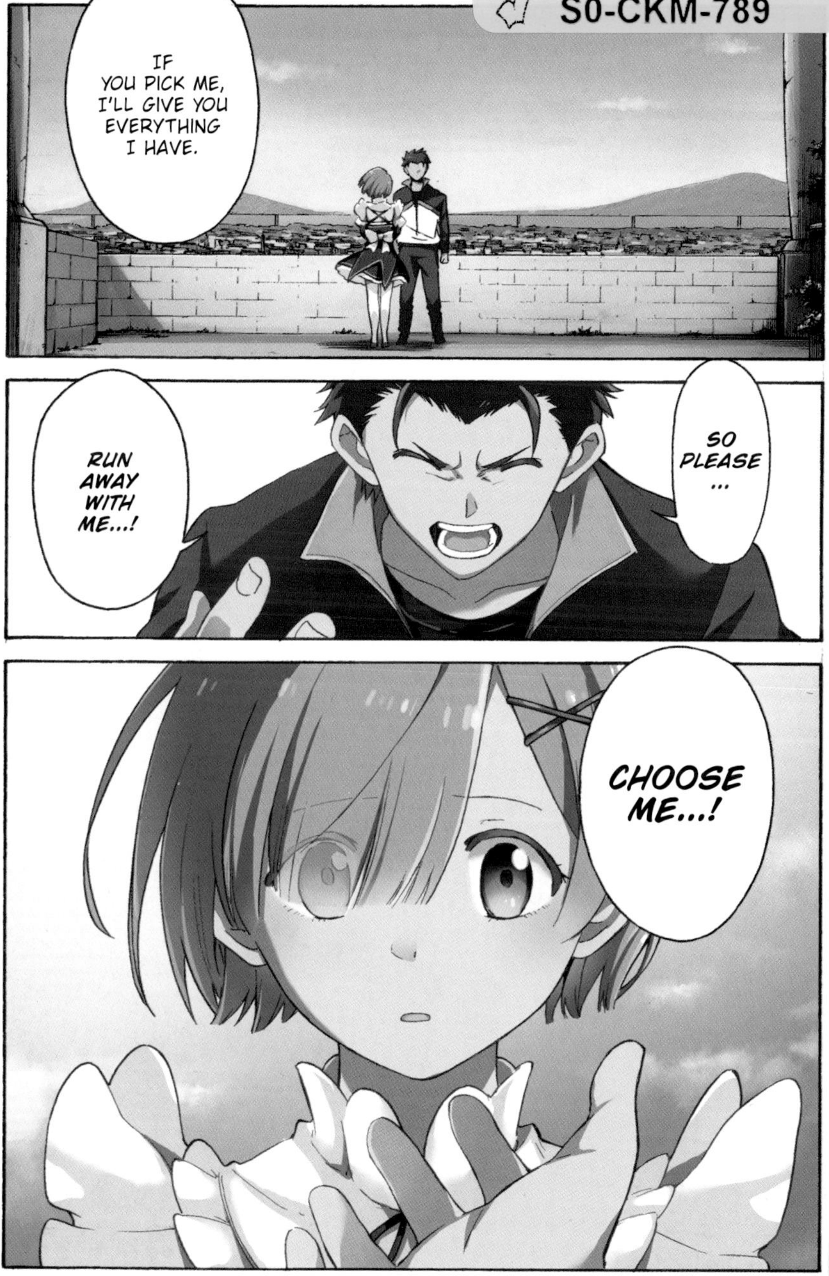
IF YOU PICK ME, I'LL GIVE YOU EVERYTHING I HAVE.
SO PLEASE...
RUN AWAY WITH ME...!
CHOOSE ME...!

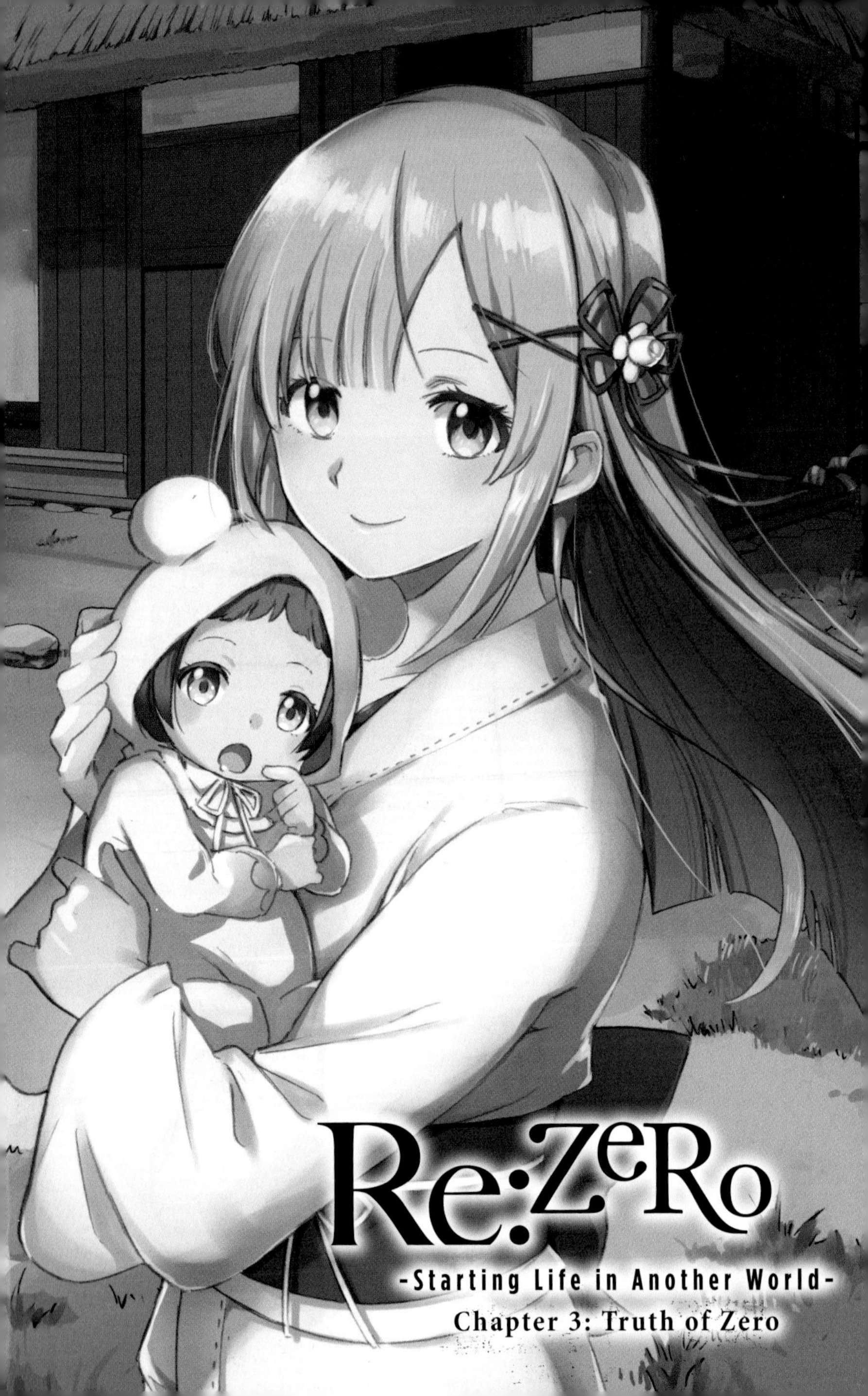
Re:ZeRo
-Starting Life in Another World-
Chapter 3: Truth of Zero

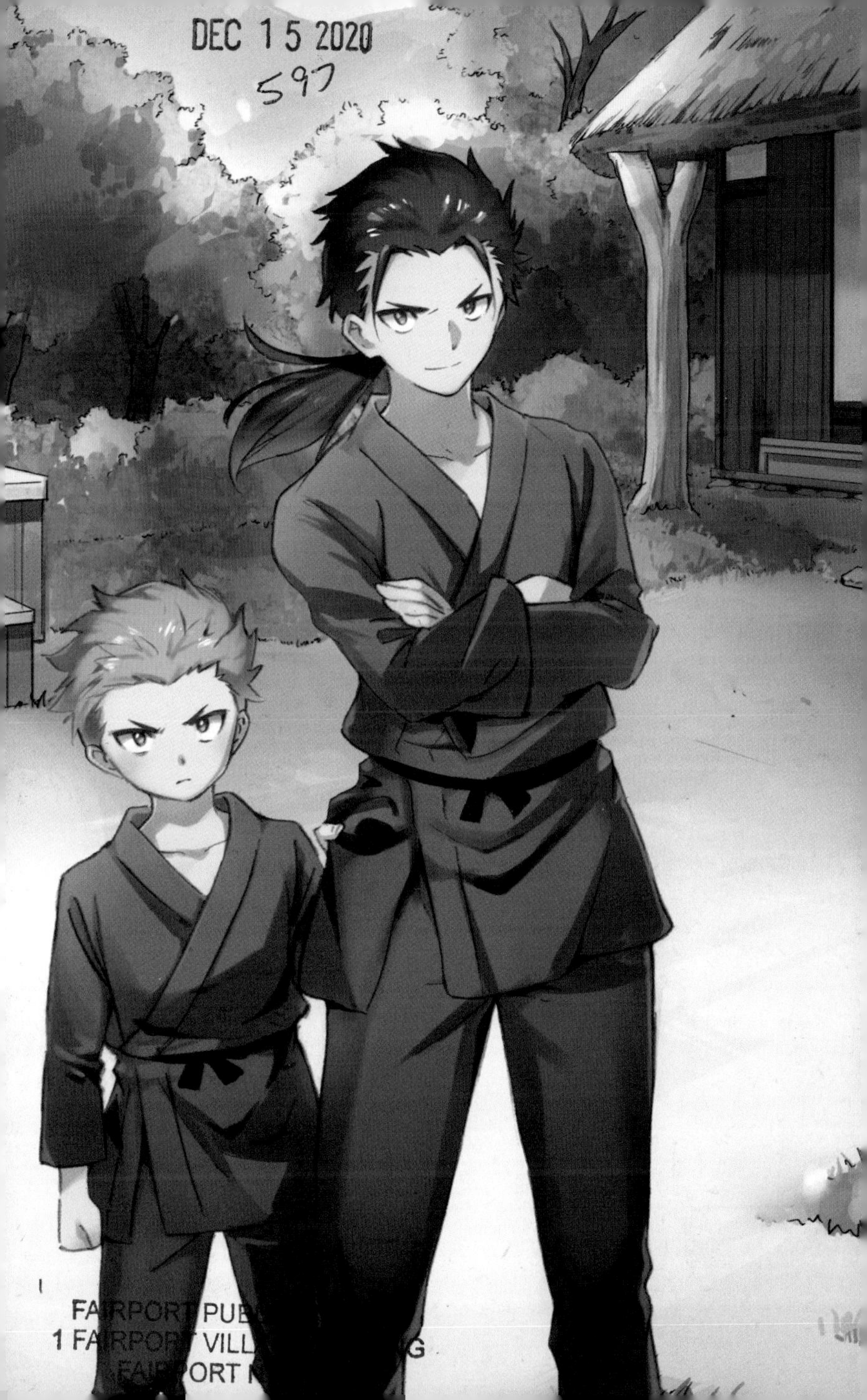

Re:ZERO -Starting Life in Another World-

Chapter 3: Truth of Zero

The only ability Subaru Natsuki gets when he's summoned to another world is time travel via his own death. But to save her, he'll die as many times as it takes.

Contents

005

Episode 50
A Little Time in a
Dragon Carriage

017

Episode 51
Lost Chapter:
Rem Natsuki

049

Episode 52
Let Us Feast

091

Final Episode
To Each,
Their Vows…

135

Special Story
On the Eve of Battle,
Thinking of You

156

Afterword

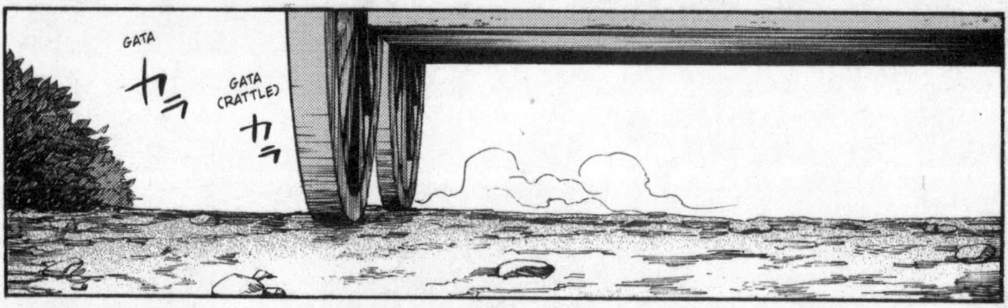
GATA
(RATTLE)
カラ
GATA
カラ

Episode 50
A Little Time in a Dragon Carriage

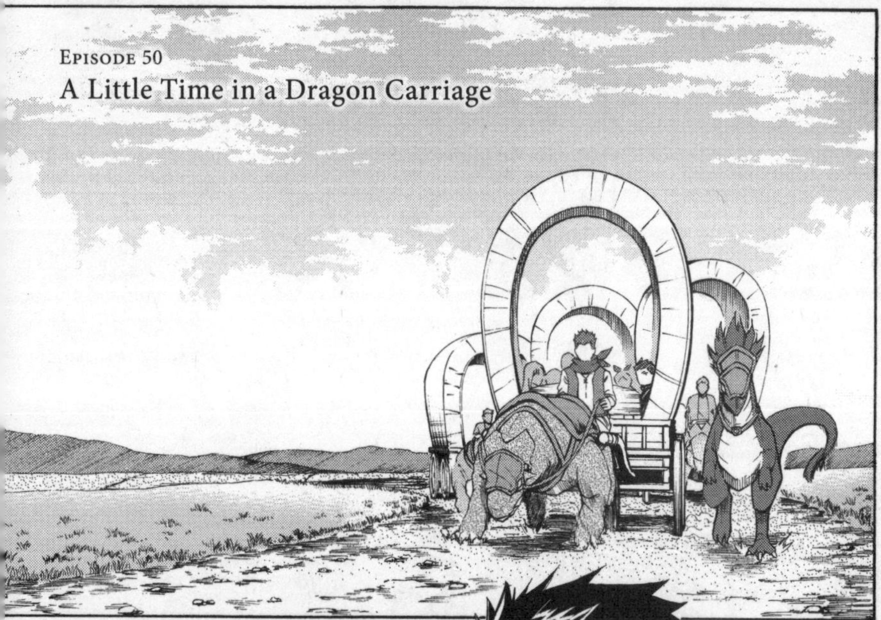

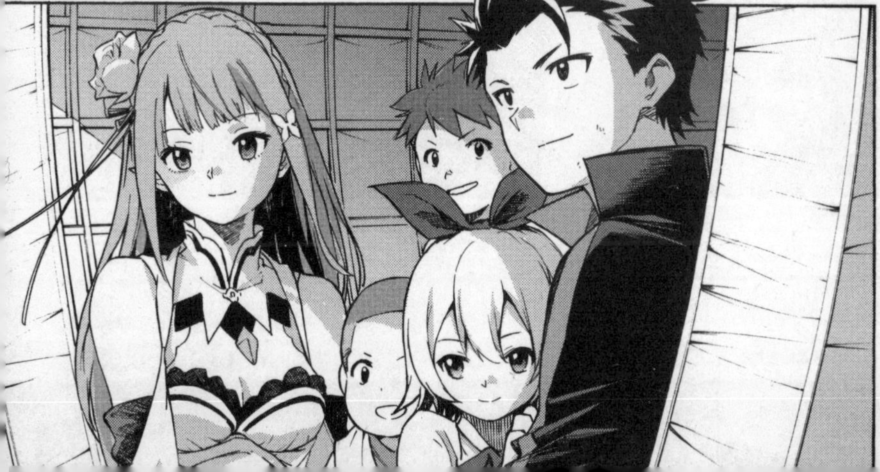

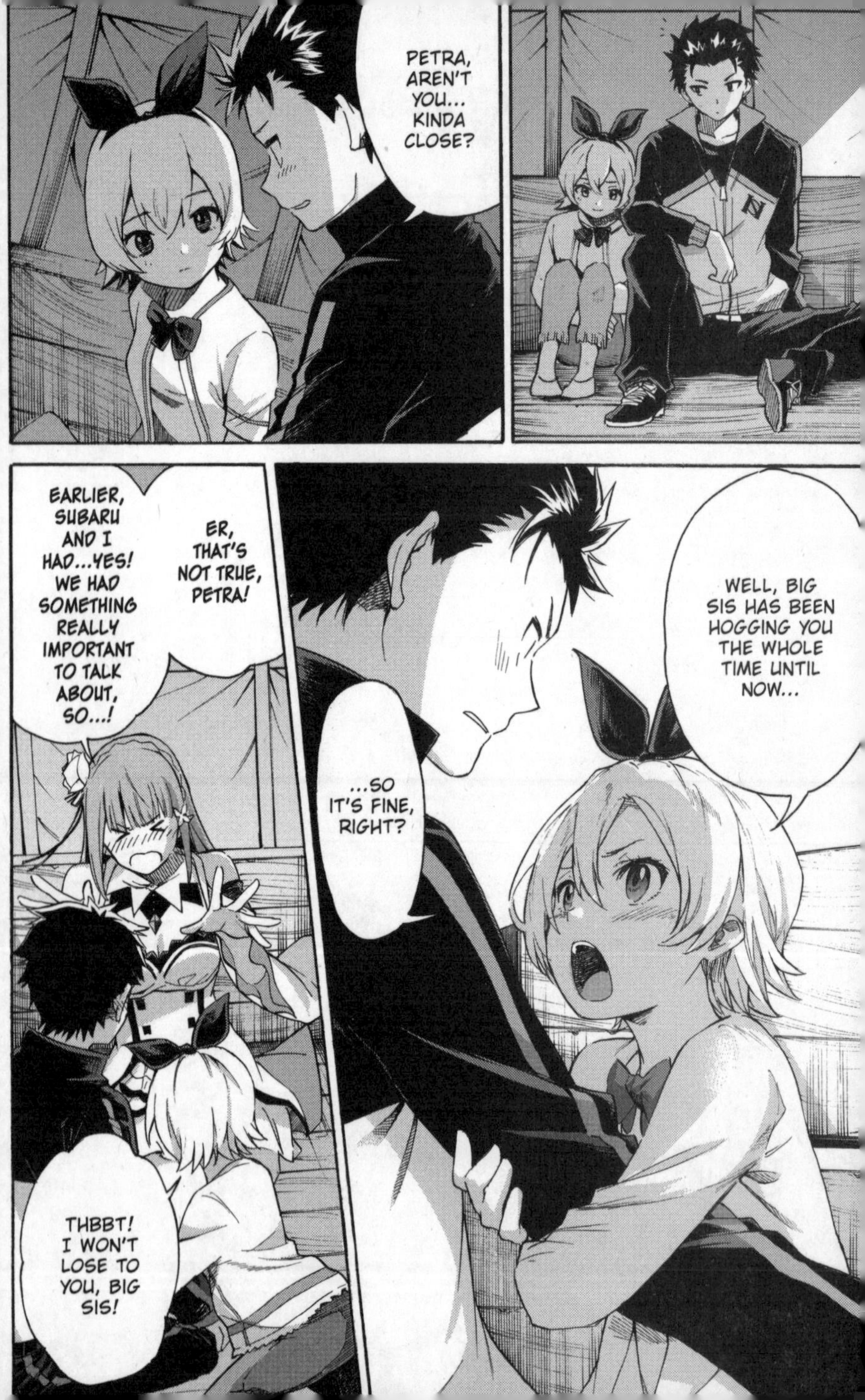
PETRA, AREN'T YOU... KINDA CLOSE?
WELL, BIG SIS HAS BEEN HOGGING YOU THE WHOLE TIME UNTIL NOW...
...SO IT'S FINE, RIGHT?
ER, THAT'S NOT TRUE, PETRA!
EARLIER, SUBARU AND I HAD...YES! WE HAD SOMETHING REALLY IMPORTANT TO TALK ABOUT, SO...!
THBBT! I WON'T LOSE TO YOU, BIG SIS!

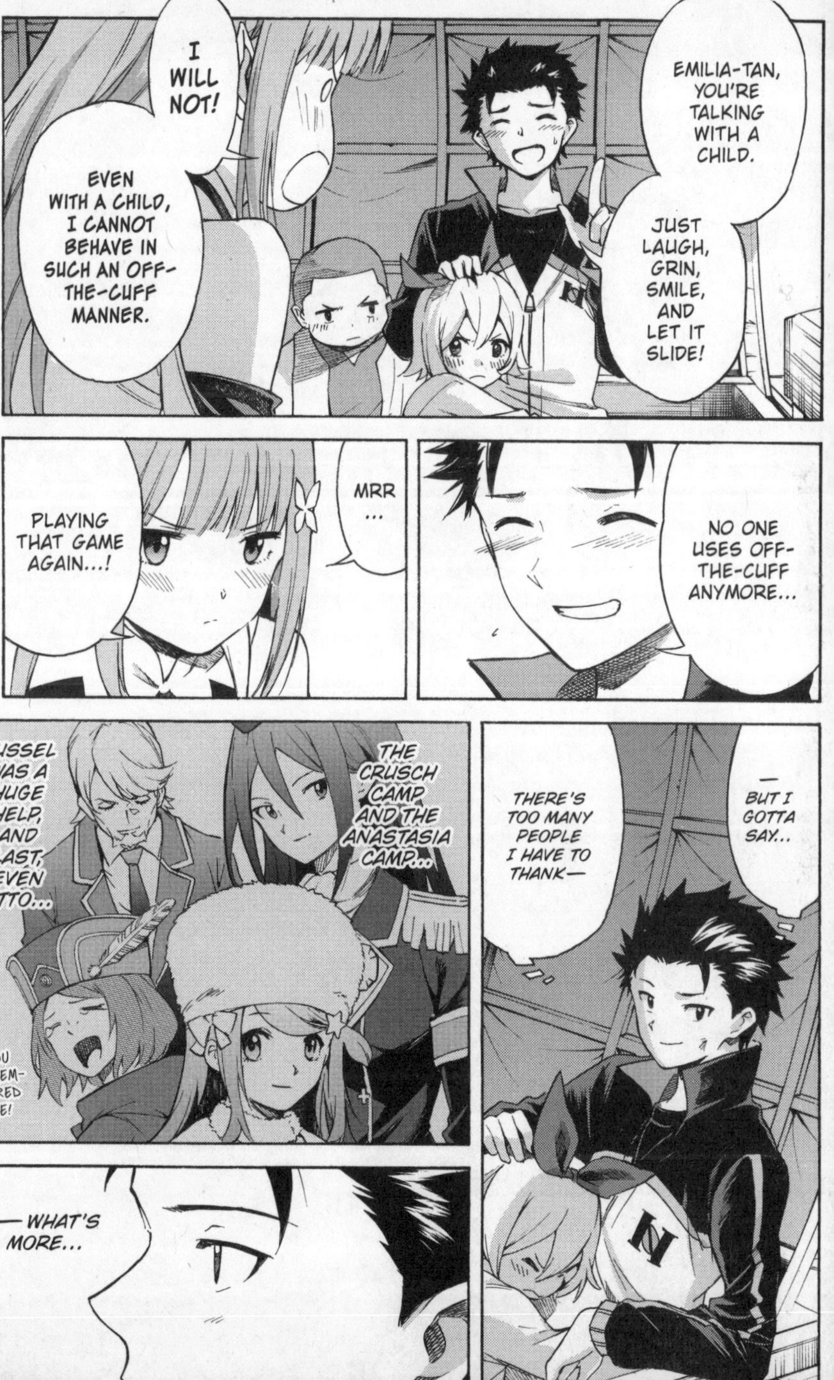

EMILIA-TAN, YOU'RE TALKING WITH A CHILD.
JUST LAUGH, GRIN, SMILE, AND LET IT SLIDE!
I WILL NOT!
EVEN WITH A CHILD, I CANNOT BEHAVE IN SUCH AN OFF-THE-CUFF MANNER.
NO ONE USES OFF-THE-CUFF ANYMORE...
MRR ...
PLAYING THAT GAME AGAIN...!
—BUT I GOTTA SAY...
THERE'S TOO MANY PEOPLE I HAVE TO THANK—
THE CRUSCH CAMP AND THE ANASTASIA CAMP...
RUSSEL WAS A HUGE HELP, AND LAST, EVEN OTTO...
YOU REMEMBERED ME!
—WHAT'S MORE...

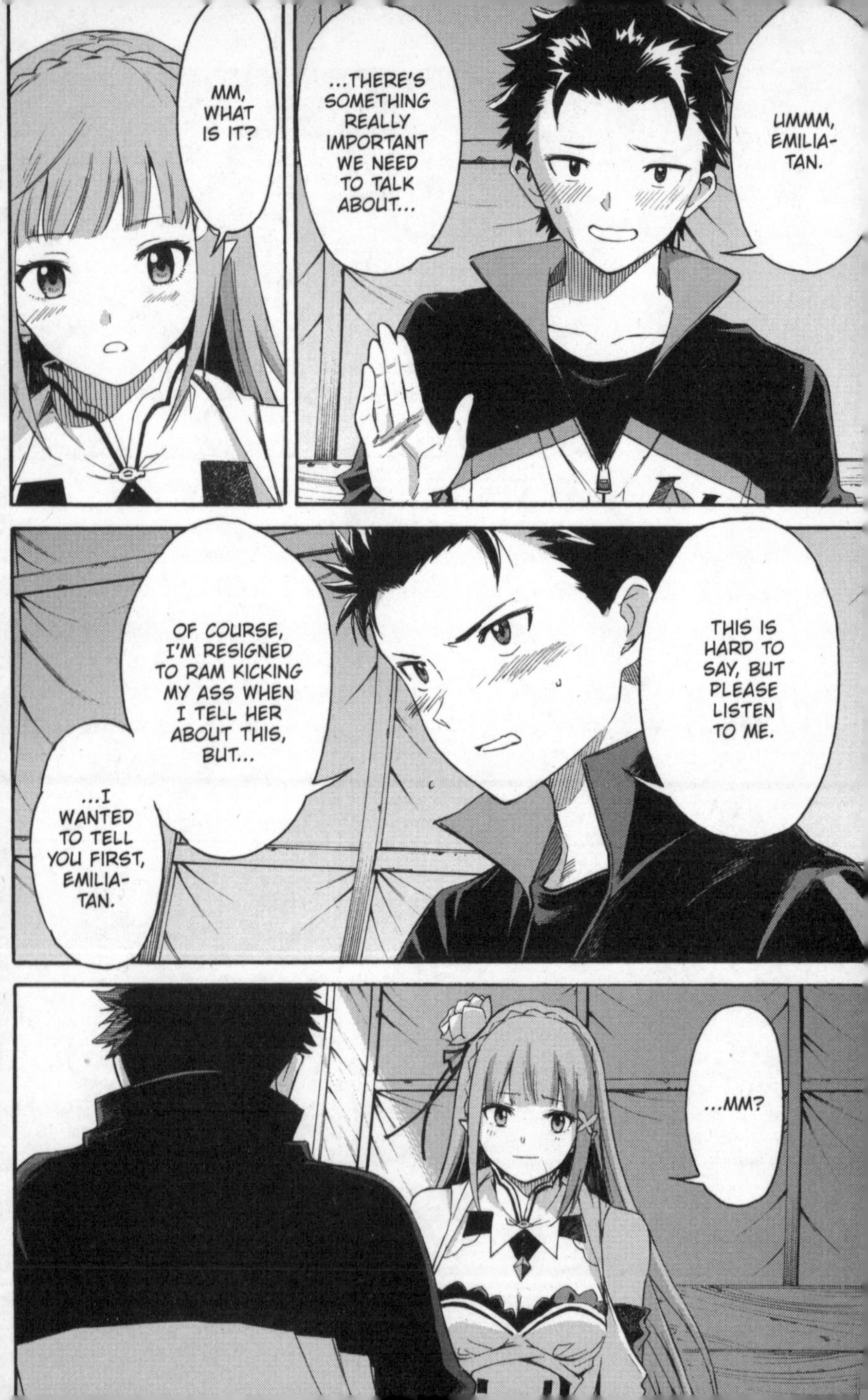
UMMM, EMILIA-TAN.
...THERE'S SOMETHING REALLY IMPORTANT WE NEED TO TALK ABOUT...
MM, WHAT IS IT?
THIS IS HARD TO SAY, BUT PLEASE LISTEN TO ME.
OF COURSE, I'M RESIGNED TO RAM KICKING MY ASS WHEN I TELL HER ABOUT THIS, BUT...
...I WANTED TO TELL YOU FIRST, EMILIA-TAN.
...MM?

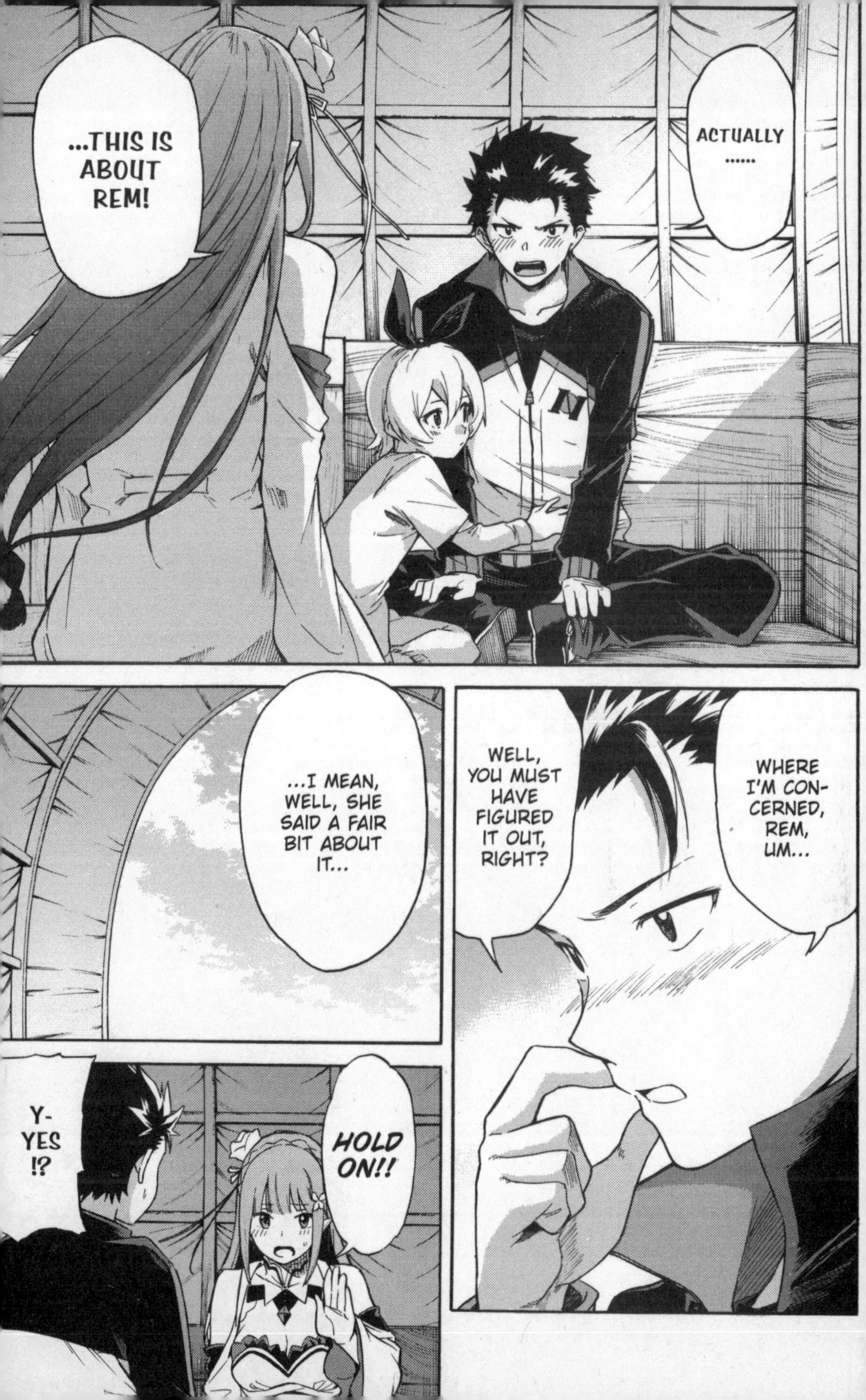
ACTUALLY ......
...THIS IS ABOUT REM!
WHERE I'M CONCERNED, REM, UM...
WELL, YOU MUST HAVE FIGURED IT OUT, RIGHT?
...I MEAN, WELL, SHE SAID A FAIR BIT ABOUT IT...
HOLD ON!!
Y-YES!?

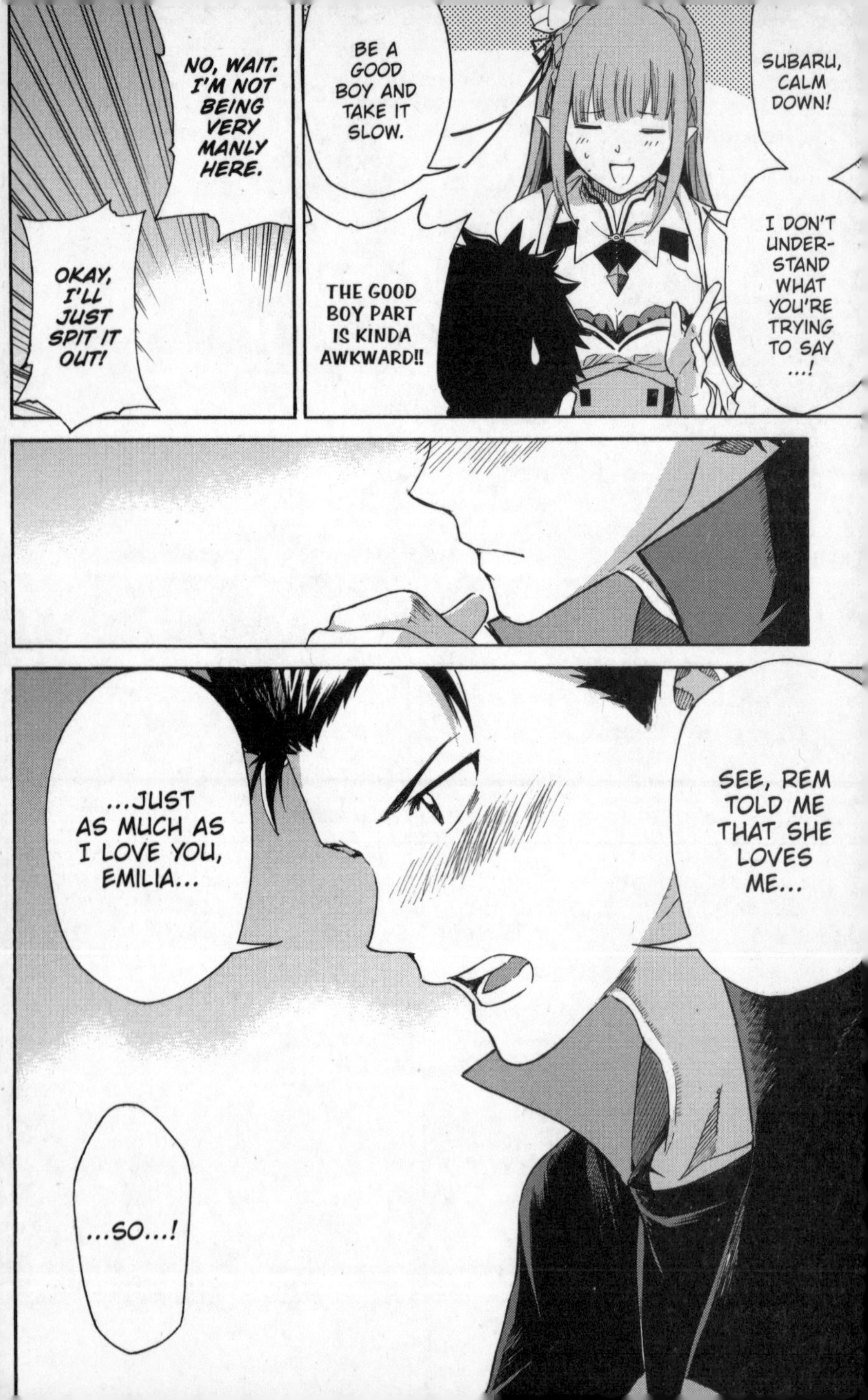
SUBARU, CALM DOWN!
I DON'T UNDER-STAND WHAT YOU'RE TRYING TO SAY ...!
BE A GOOD BOY AND TAKE IT SLOW.
THE GOOD BOY PART IS KINDA AWKWARD!!
NO, WAIT. I'M NOT BEING VERY MANLY HERE.
OKAY, I'LL JUST SPIT IT OUT!
SEE, REM TOLD ME THAT SHE LOVES ME...
...JUST AS MUCH AS I LOVE YOU, EMILIA...
...SO...!

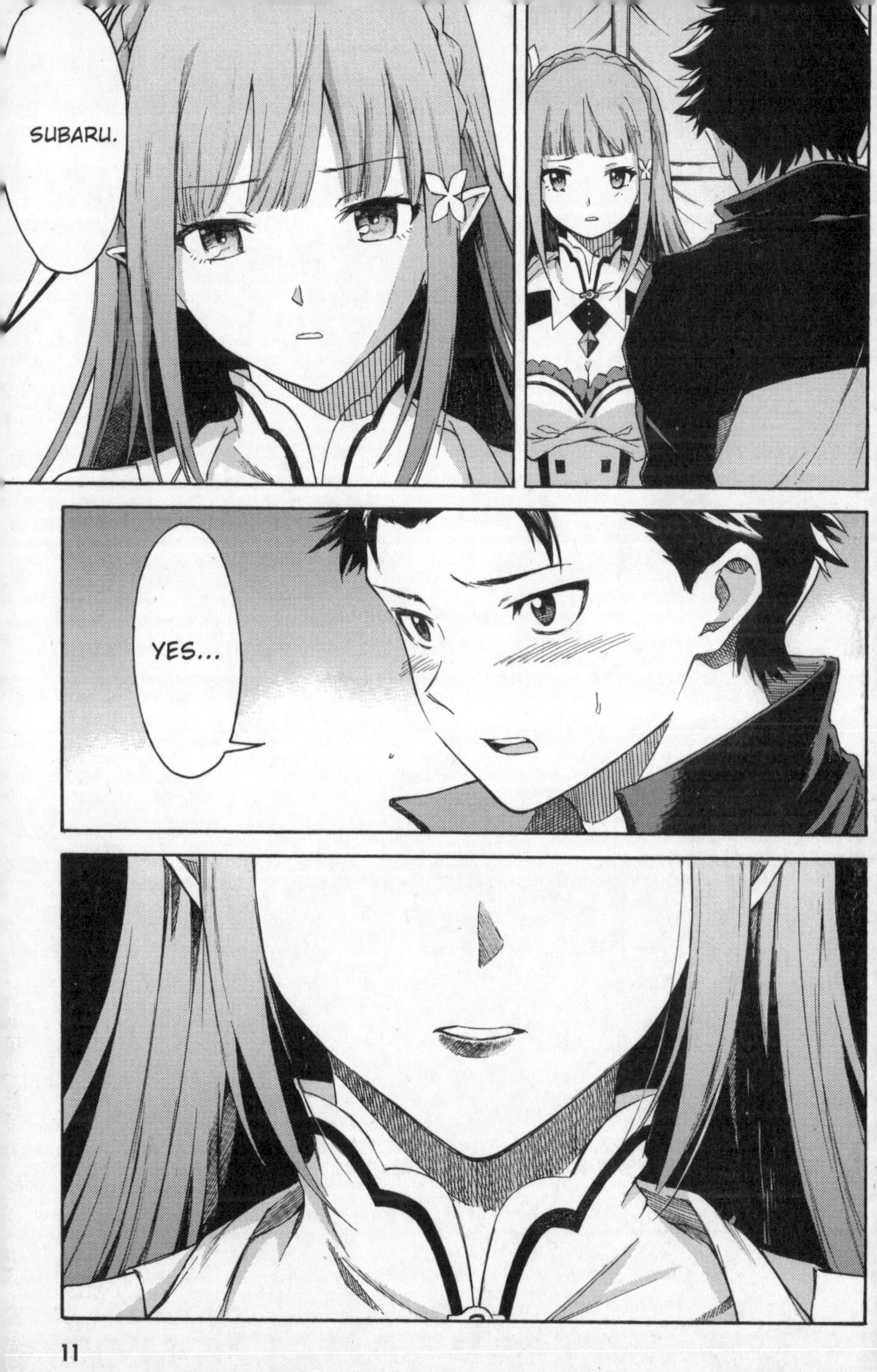
SUBARU.
YES...

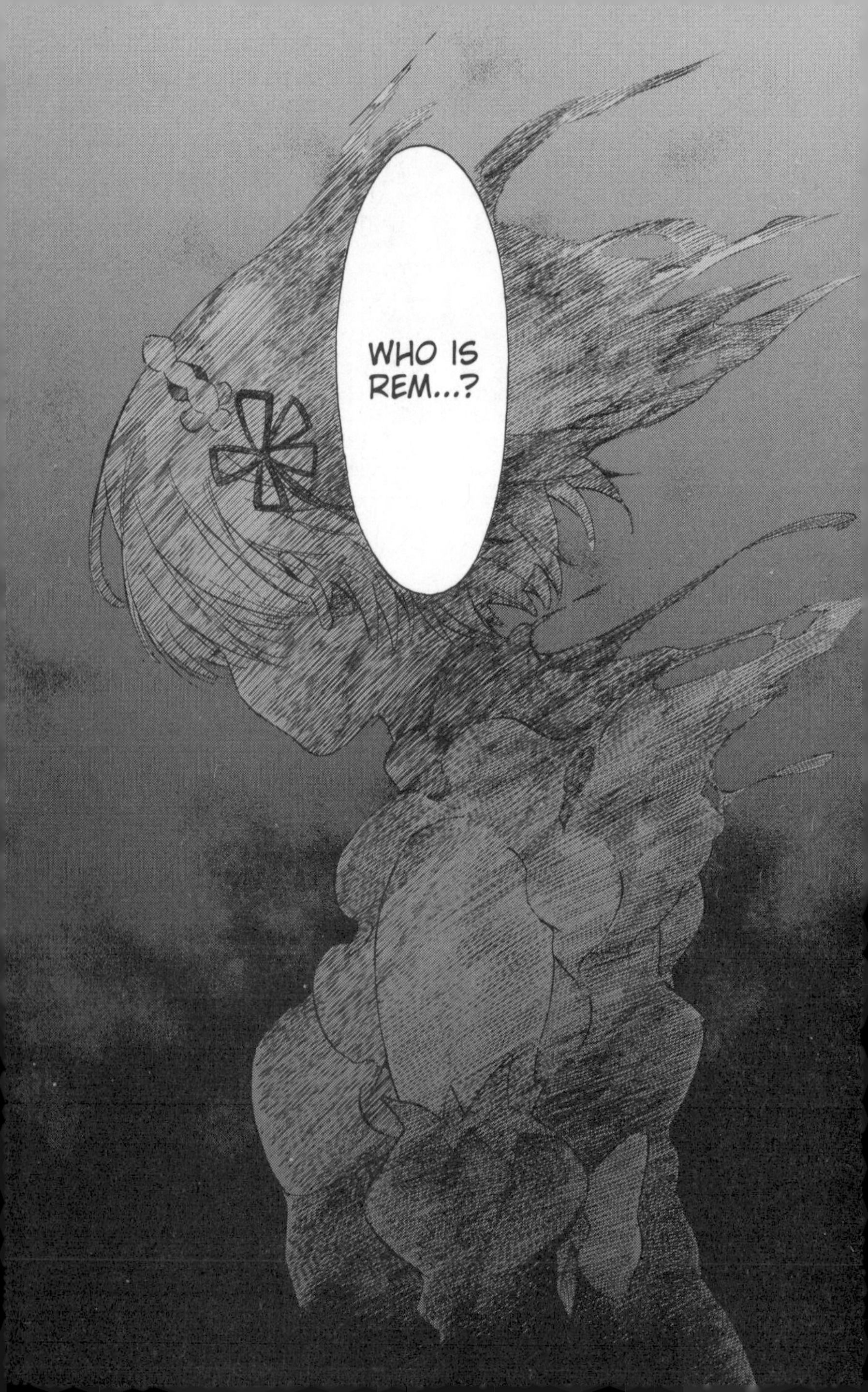
WHO IS REM...?

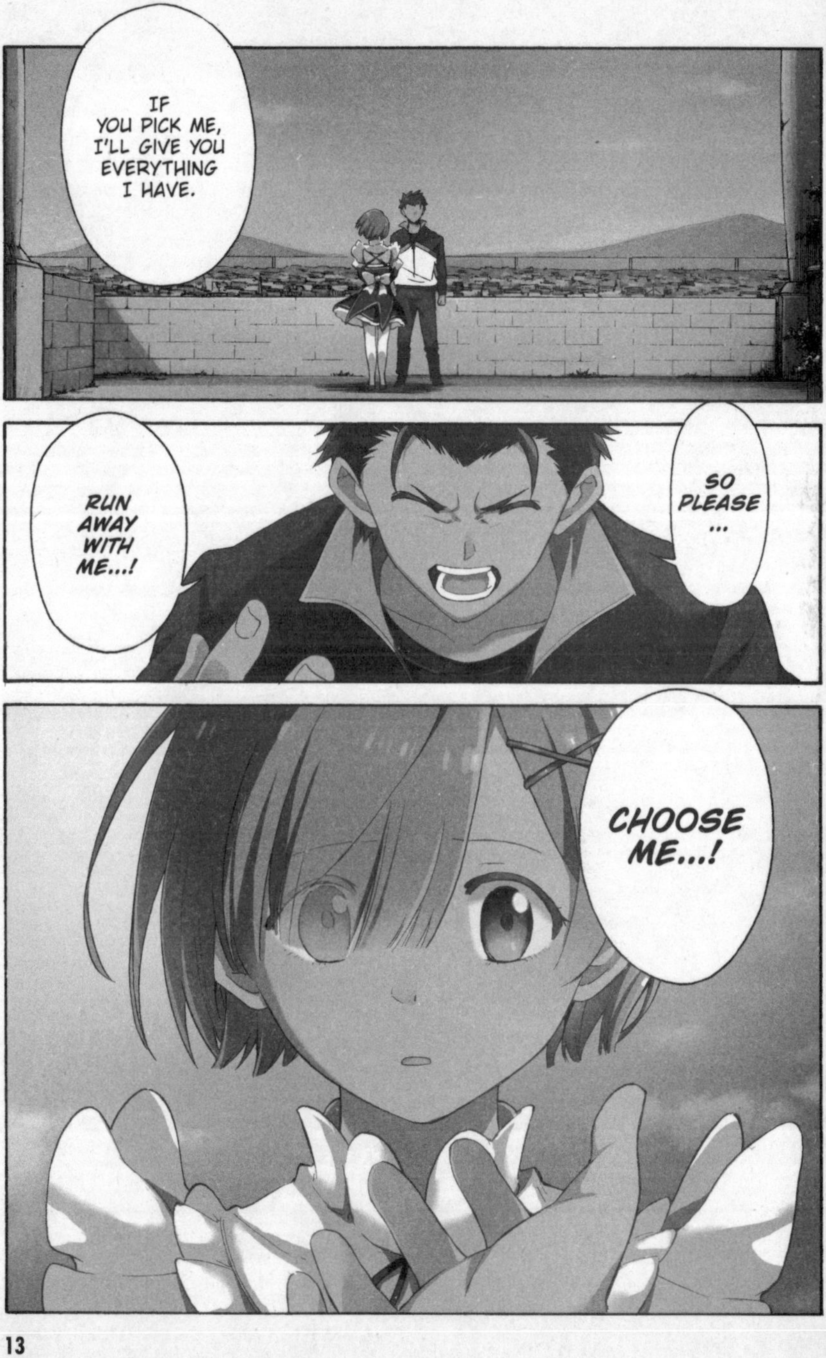
IF YOU PICK ME, I'LL GIVE YOU EVERYTHING I HAVE.
SO PLEASE ...
RUN AWAY WITH ME...!
CHOOSE ME...!

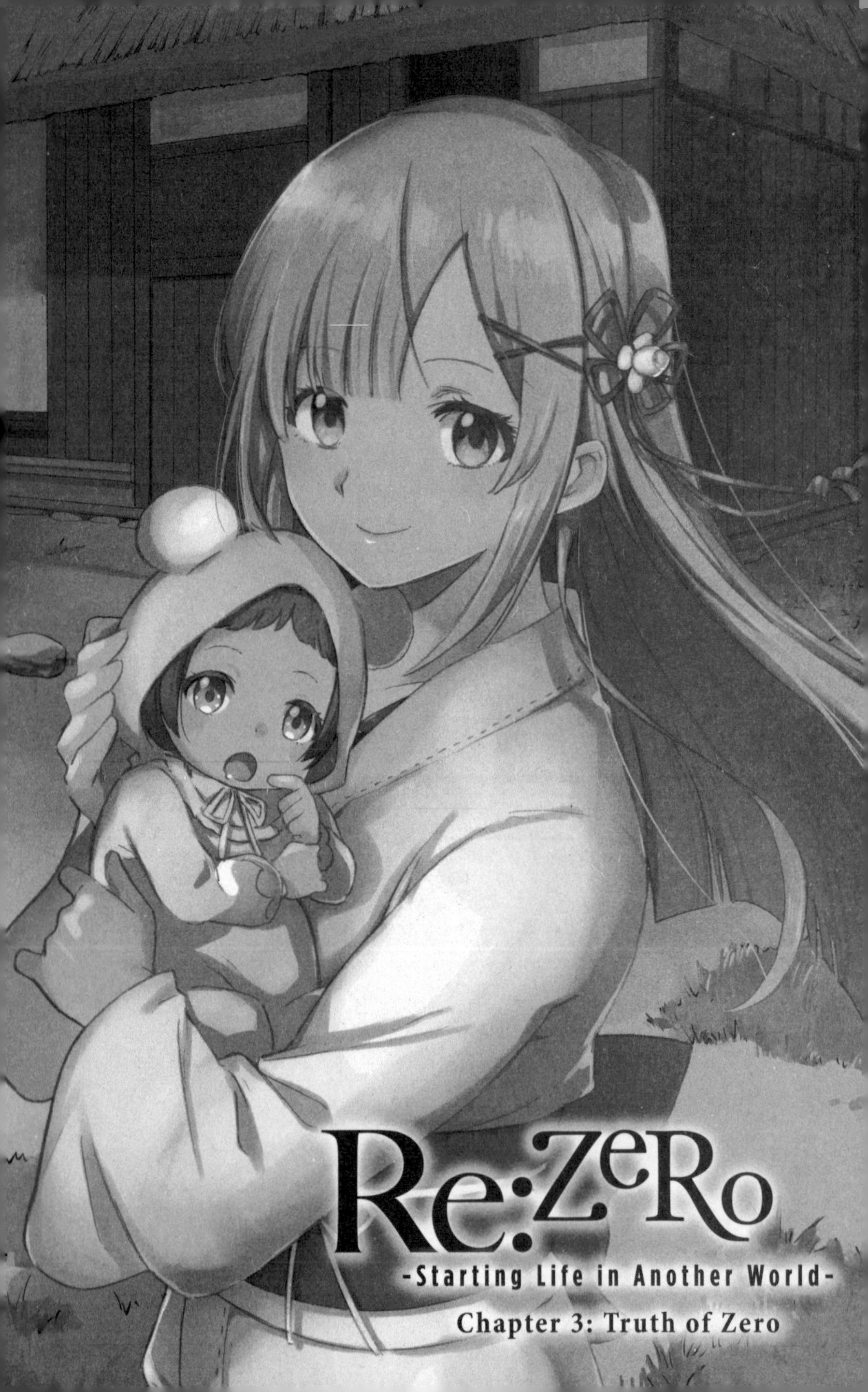
Re:ZeRo
-Starting Life in Another World-
Chapter 3: Truth of Zero

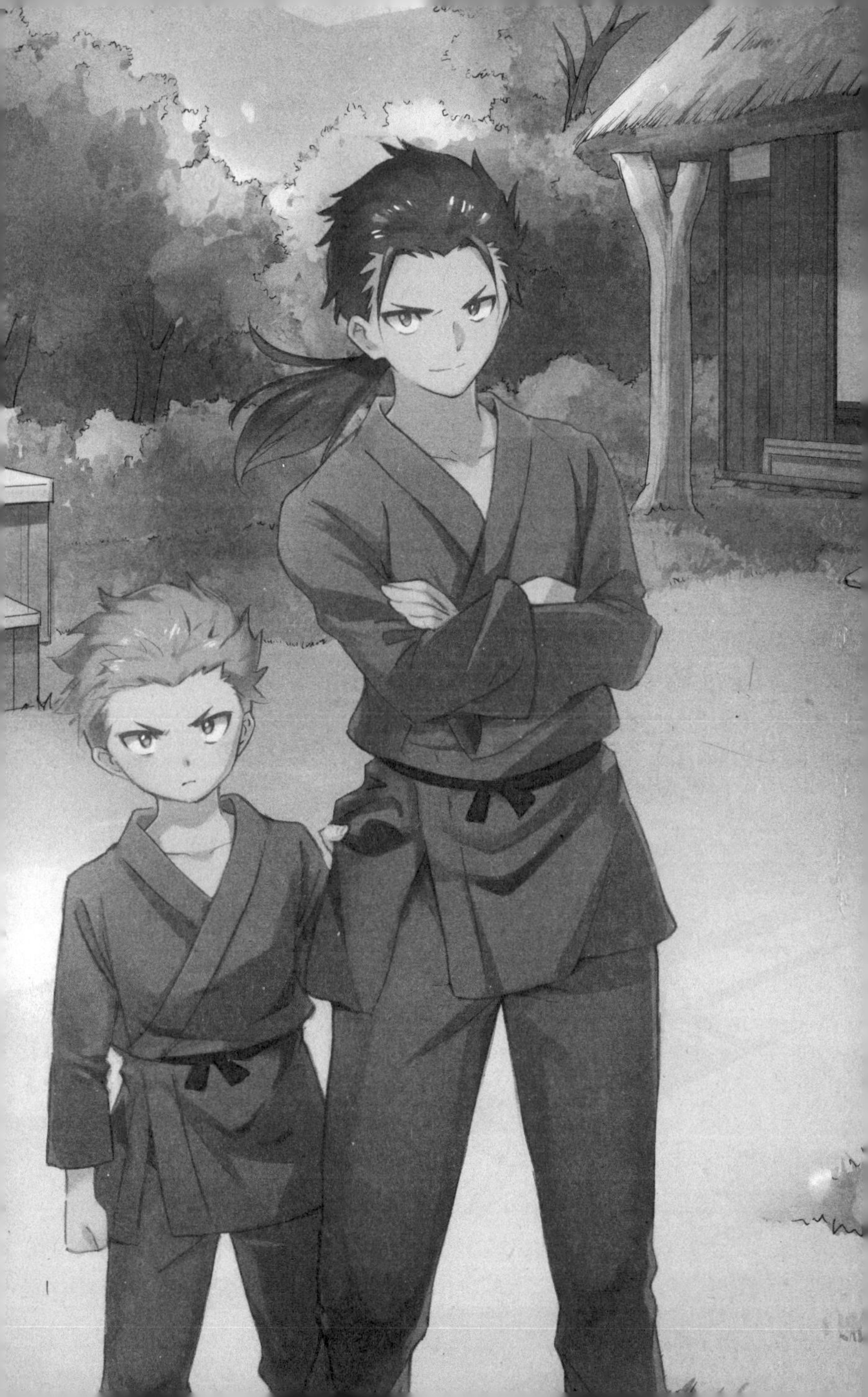

Re:ZeRo

-Starting Life in Another World-

Chapter 3: Truth of Zero

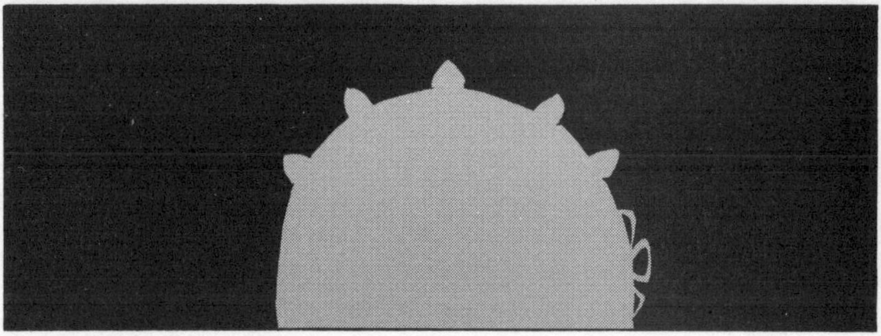

Episode 51

Lost Chapter: Rem Natsuki

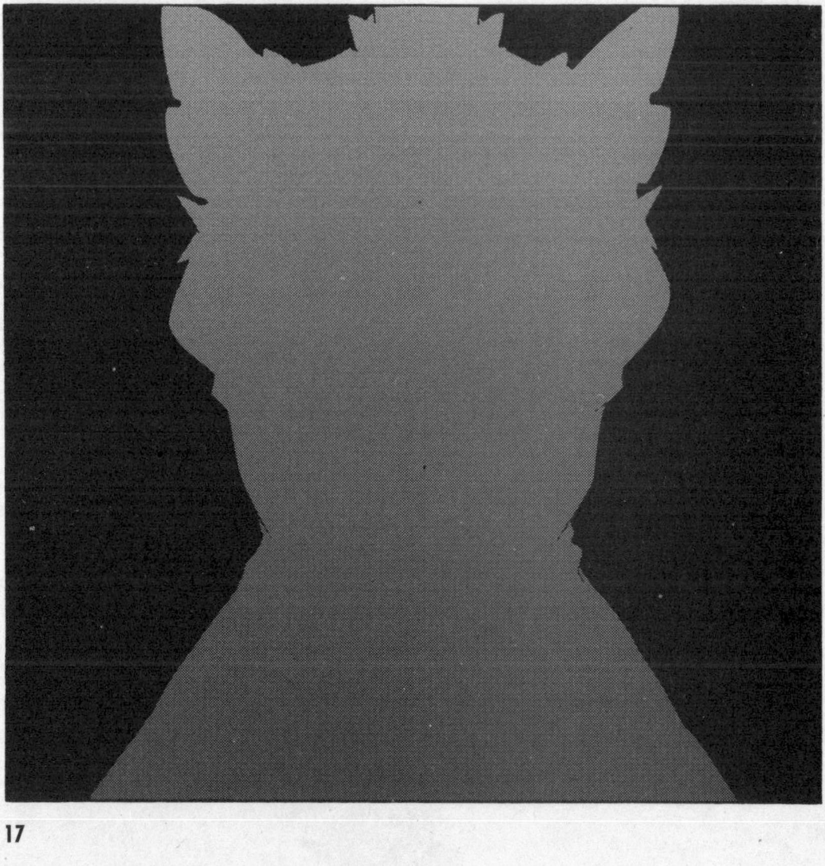

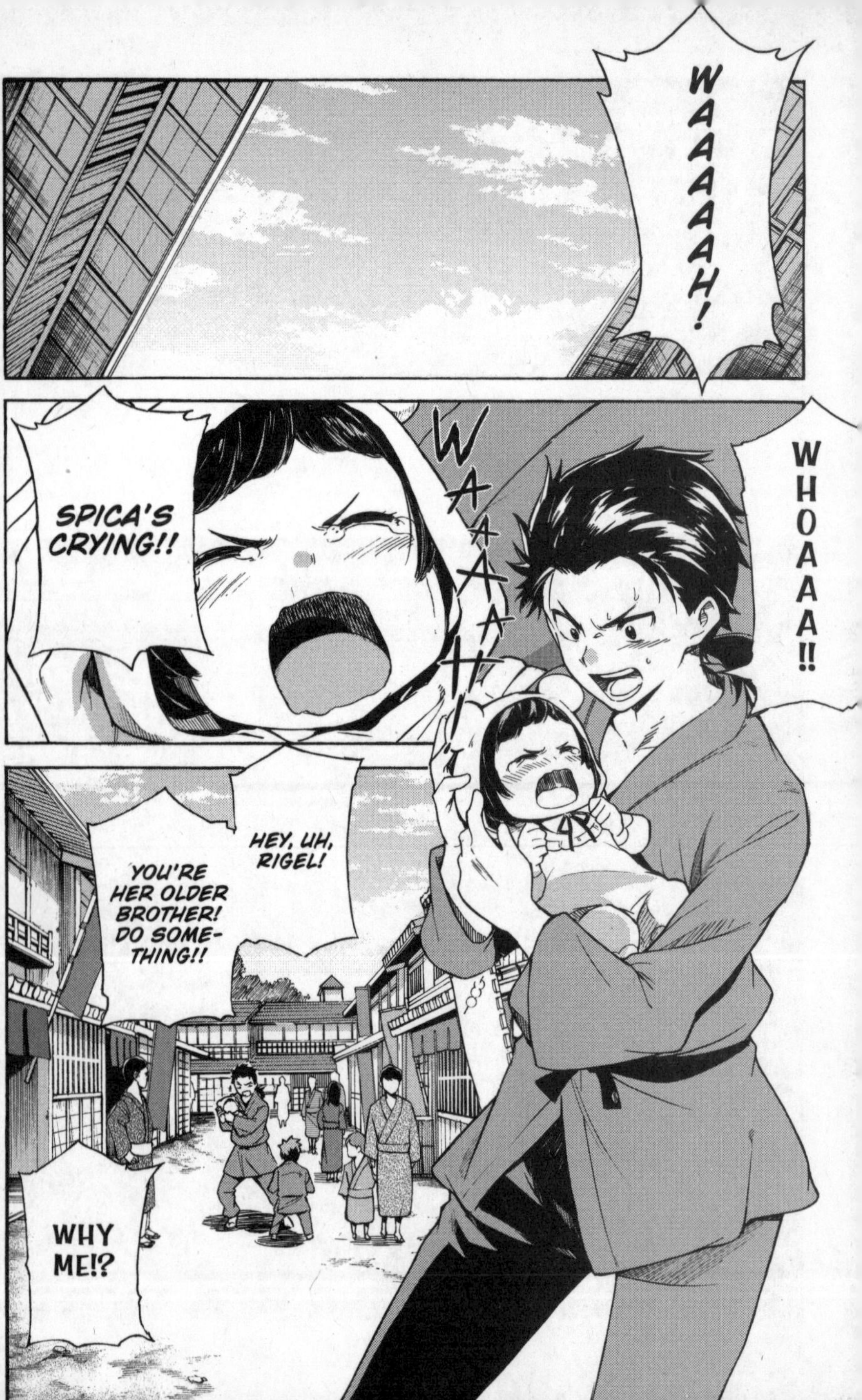
WAAAAAAH!
WHOAAAA!!
WAAAAAH!!
SPICA'S CRYING!!
HEY, UH, RIGEL!
YOU'RE HER OLDER BROTHER! DO SOME-THING!!
WHY ME!?

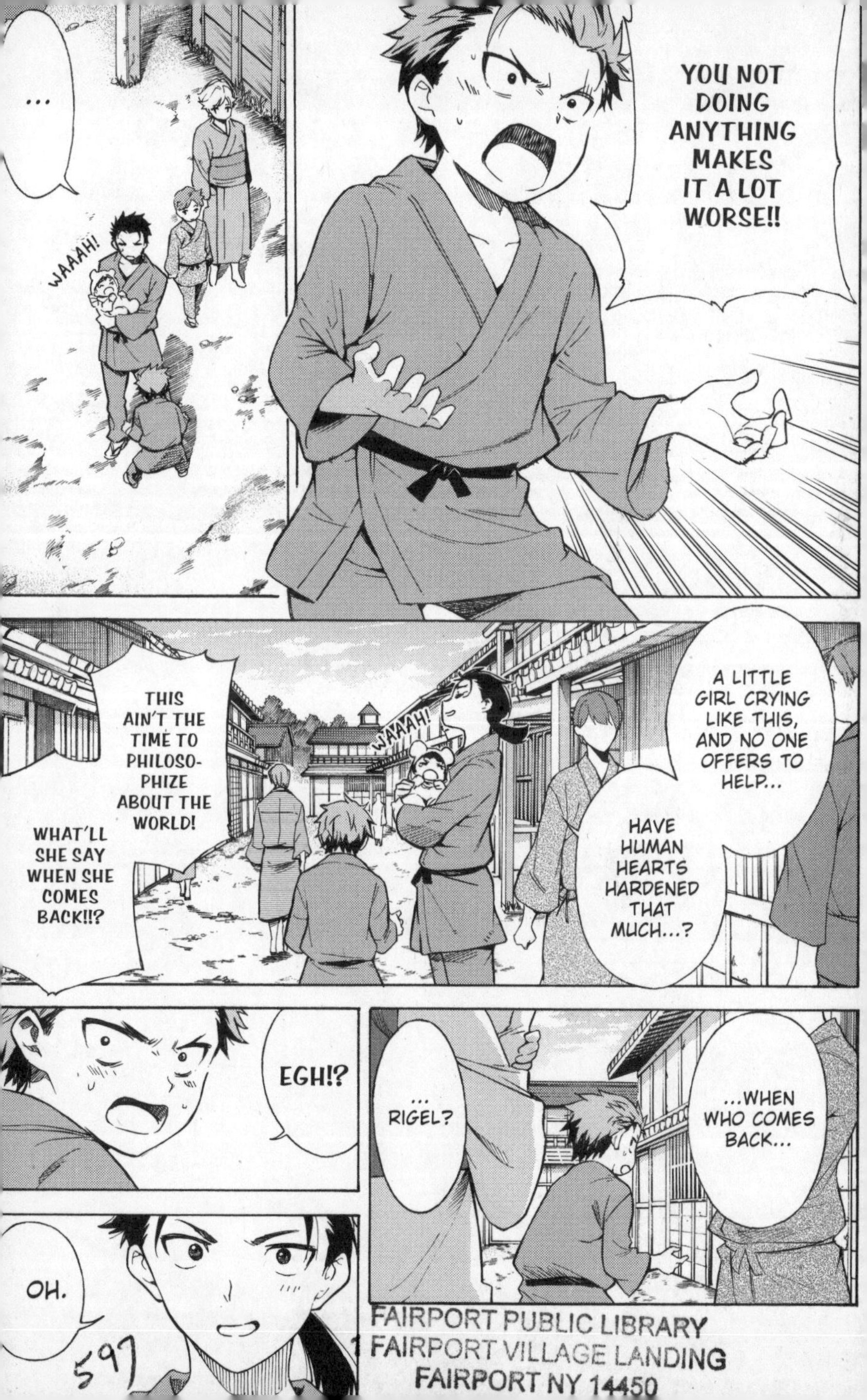
YOU NOT DOING ANYTHING MAKES IT A LOT WORSE!!
WAAAH!
...
A LITTLE GIRL CRYING LIKE THIS, AND NO ONE OFFERS TO HELP...
HAVE HUMAN HEARTS HARDENED THAT MUCH...?
WAAAH!
THIS AIN'T THE TIME TO PHILOSO-PHIZE ABOUT THE WORLD!
WHAT'LL SHE SAY WHEN SHE COMES BACK!!?
...WHEN WHO COMES BACK...
... RIGEL?
EGH!?
OH.

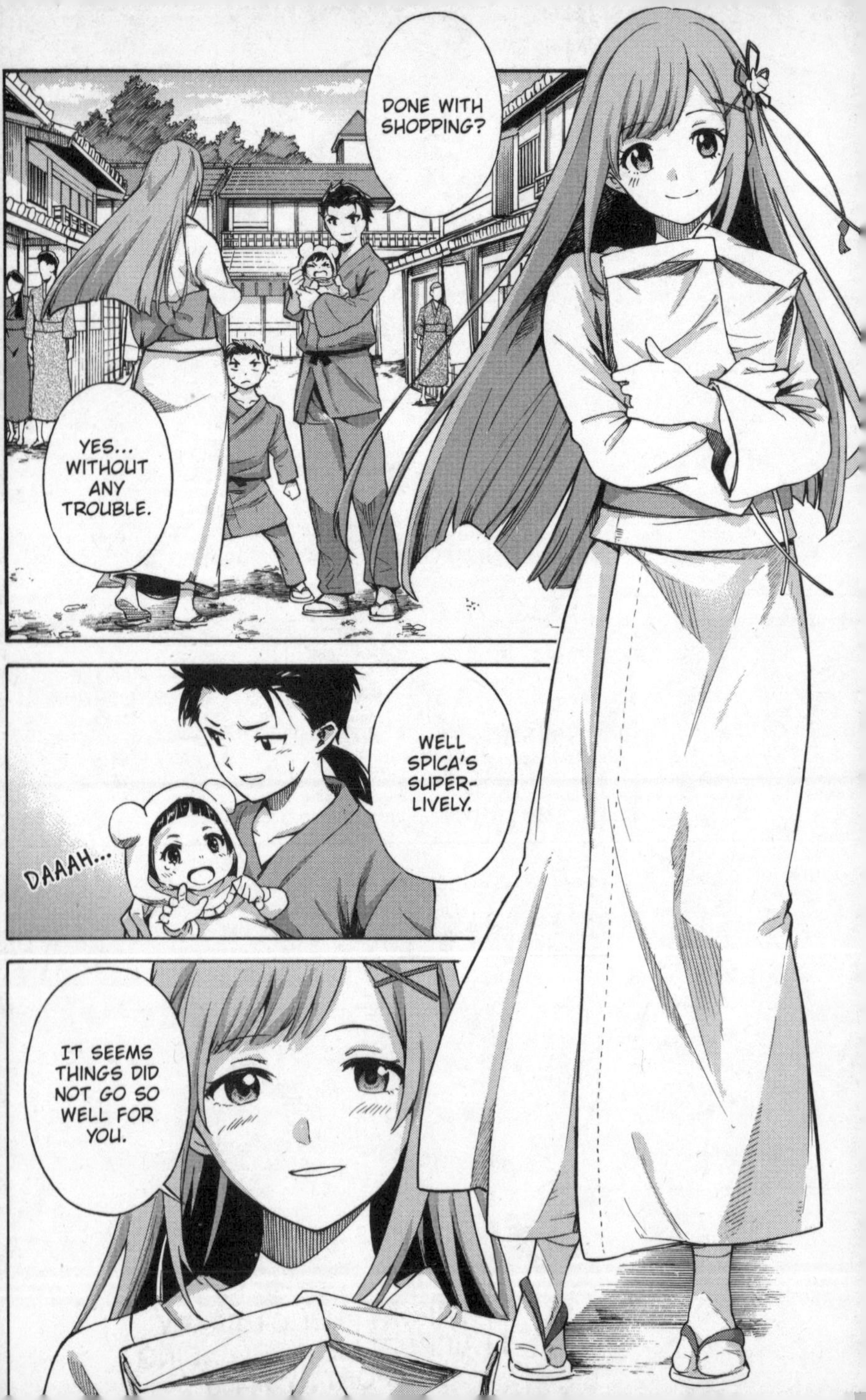
DONE WITH SHOPPING?
YES... WITHOUT ANY TROUBLE.
WELL SPICA'S SUPER-LIVELY.
DAAAH...
IT SEEMS THINGS DID NOT GO SO WELL FOR YOU.

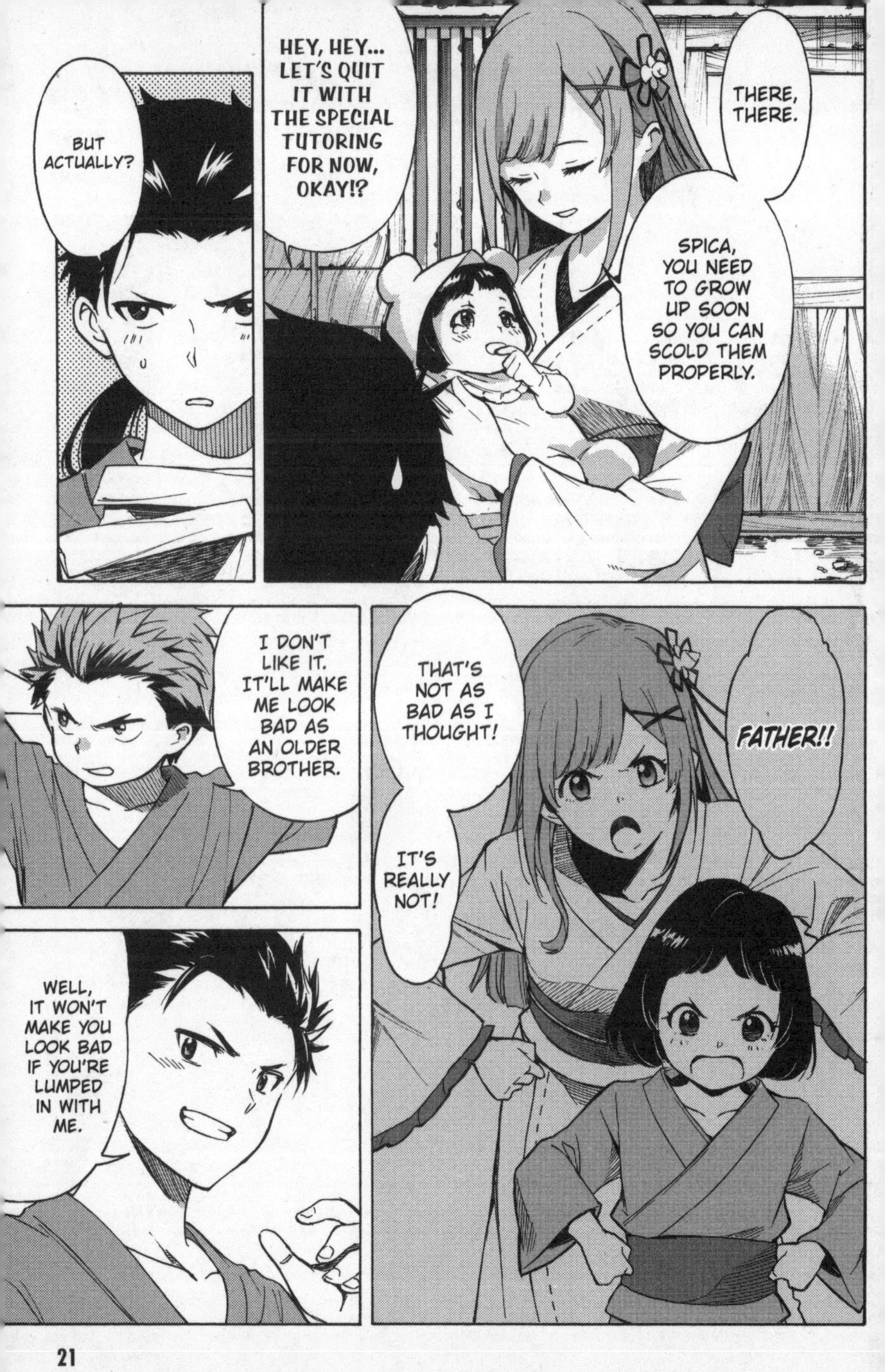
THERE, THERE.
SPICA, YOU NEED TO GROW UP SOON SO YOU CAN SCOLD THEM PROPERLY.
HEY, HEY... LET'S QUIT IT WITH THE SPECIAL TUTORING FOR NOW, OKAY!?
BUT ACTUALLY?
FATHER!!
THAT'S NOT AS BAD AS I THOUGHT!
IT'S REALLY NOT!
I DON'T LIKE IT. IT'LL MAKE ME LOOK BAD AS AN OLDER BROTHER.
WELL, IT WON'T MAKE YOU LOOK BAD IF YOU'RE LUMPED IN WITH ME.

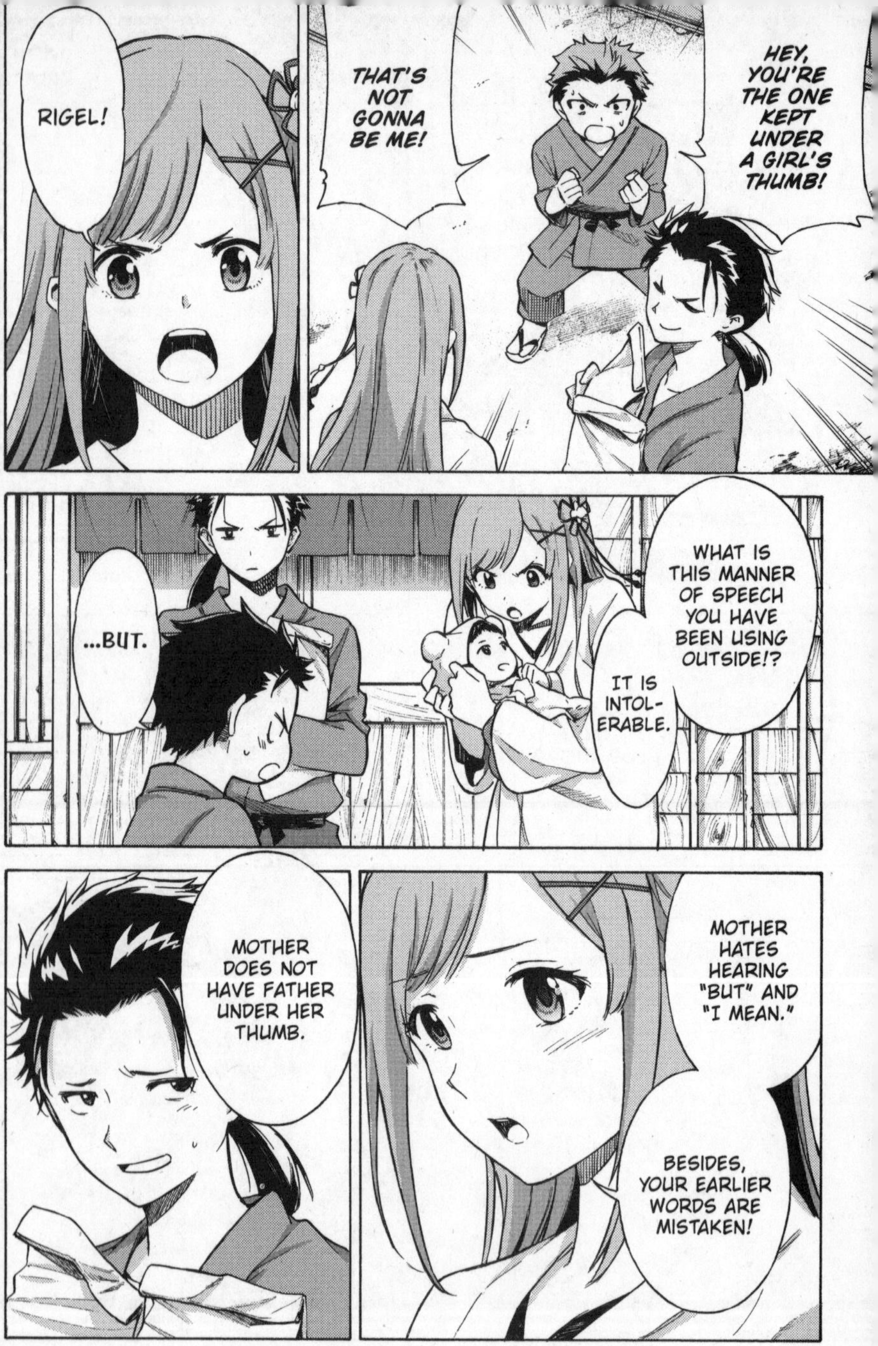
HEY, YOU'RE THE ONE KEPT UNDER A GIRL'S THUMB!
THAT'S NOT GONNA BE ME!
RIGEL!
WHAT IS THIS MANNER OF SPEECH YOU HAVE BEEN USING OUTSIDE!?
IT IS INTOL-ERABLE.
...BUT.
MOTHER HATES HEARING "BUT" AND "I MEAN."
BESIDES, YOUR EARLIER WORDS ARE MISTAKEN!
MOTHER DOES NOT HAVE FATHER UNDER HER THUMB.

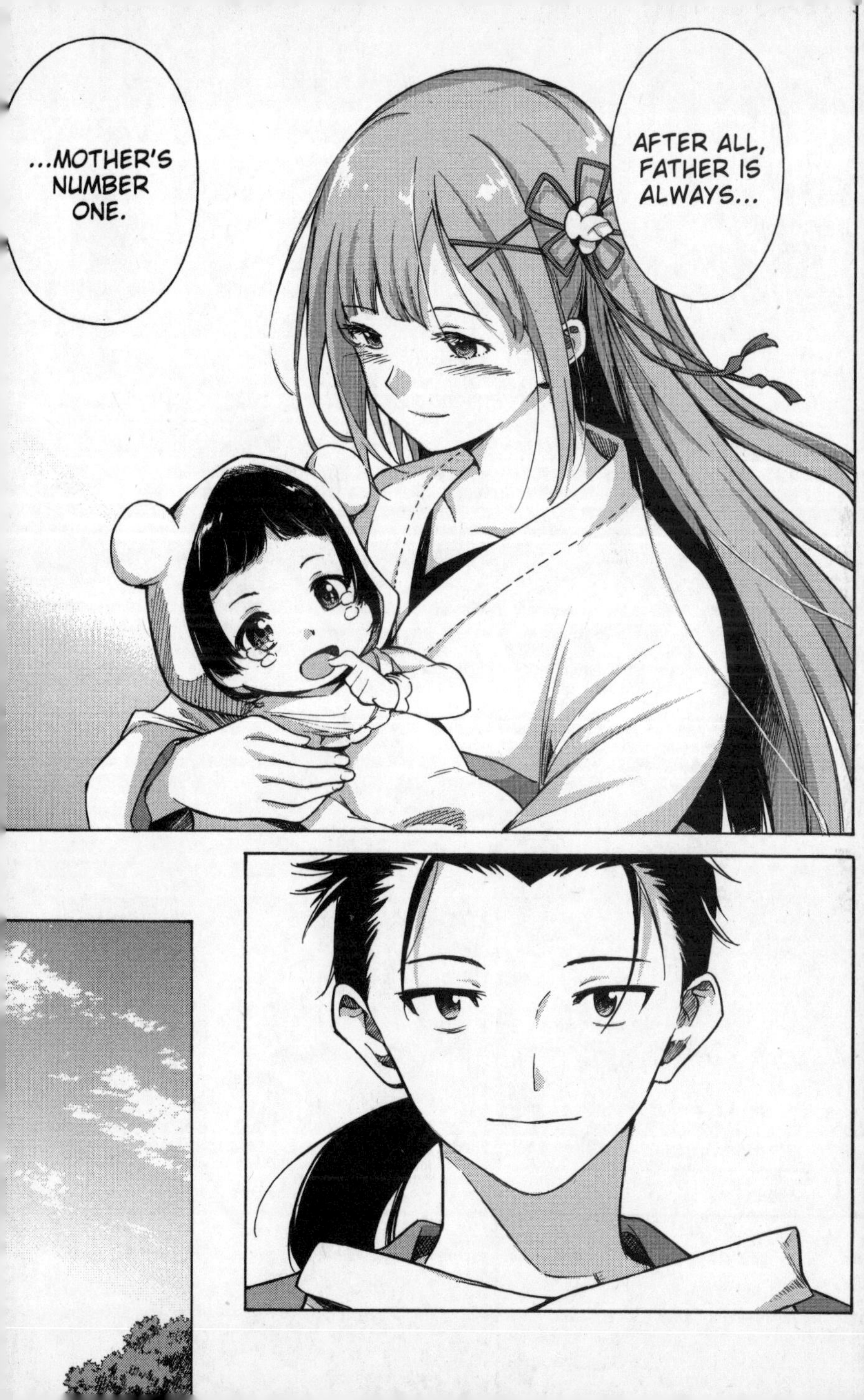
AFTER ALL, FATHER IS ALWAYS...
...MOTHER'S NUMBER ONE.

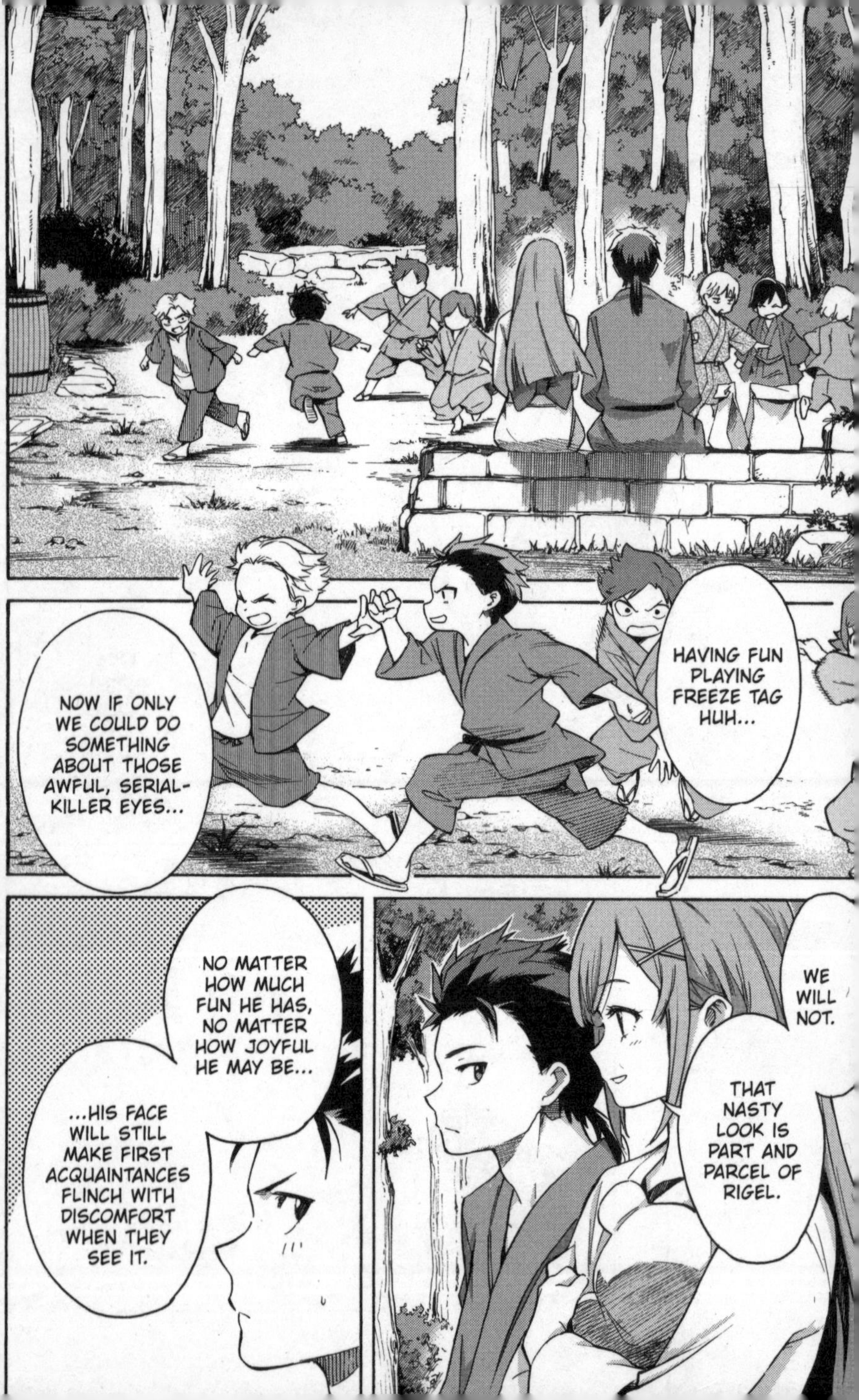
HAVING FUN PLAYING FREEZE TAG HUH...
NOW IF ONLY WE COULD DO SOMETHING ABOUT THOSE AWFUL, SERIAL-KILLER EYES...
WE WILL NOT.
THAT NASTY LOOK IS PART AND PARCEL OF RIGEL.
NO MATTER HOW MUCH FUN HE HAS, NO MATTER HOW JOYFUL HE MAY BE...
...HIS FACE WILL STILL MAKE FIRST ACQUAINTANCES FLINCH WITH DISCOMFORT WHEN THEY SEE IT.

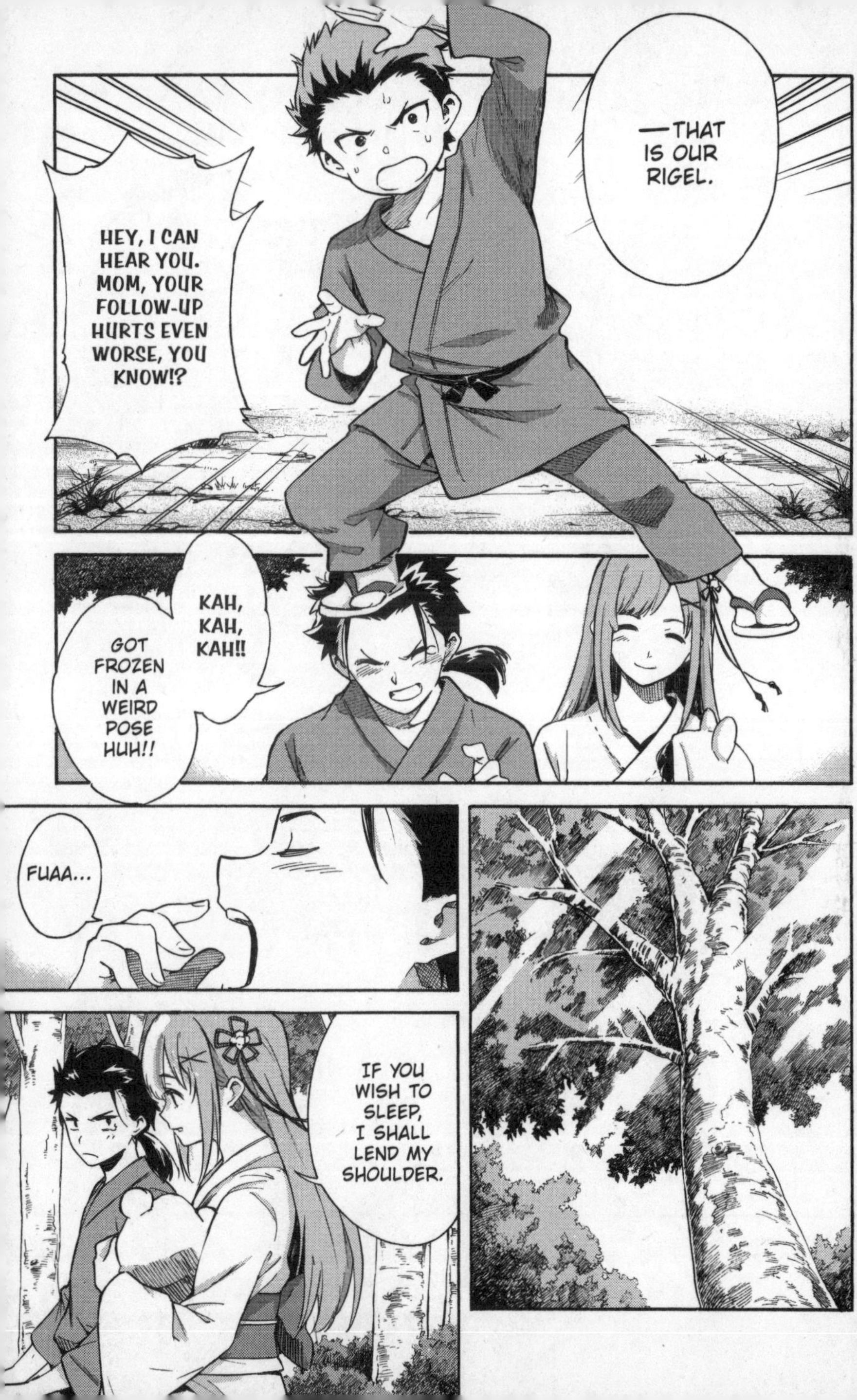
—THAT IS OUR RIGEL.
HEY, I CAN HEAR YOU. MOM, YOUR FOLLOW-UP HURTS EVEN WORSE, YOU KNOW!?
KAH, KAH, KAH!!
GOT FROZEN IN A WEIRD POSE HUH!!
FUAA...
IF YOU WISH TO SLEEP, I SHALL LEND MY SHOULDER.

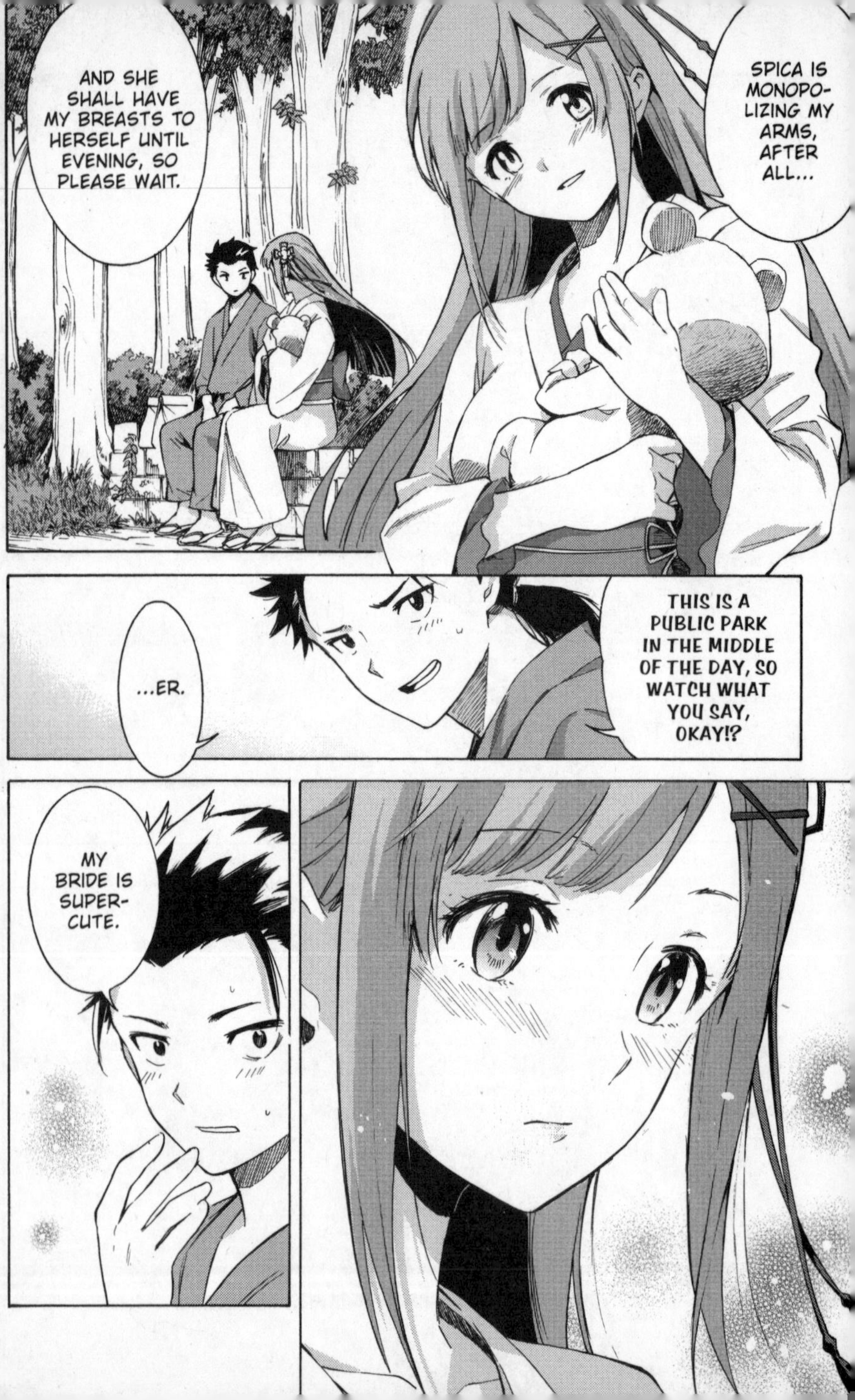
SPICA IS MONOPO-LIZING MY ARMS, AFTER ALL...
AND SHE SHALL HAVE MY BREASTS TO HERSELF UNTIL EVENING, SO PLEASE WAIT.
THIS IS A PUBLIC PARK IN THE MIDDLE OF THE DAY, SO WATCH WHAT YOU SAY, OKAY!?
...ER.
MY BRIDE IS SUPER-CUTE.

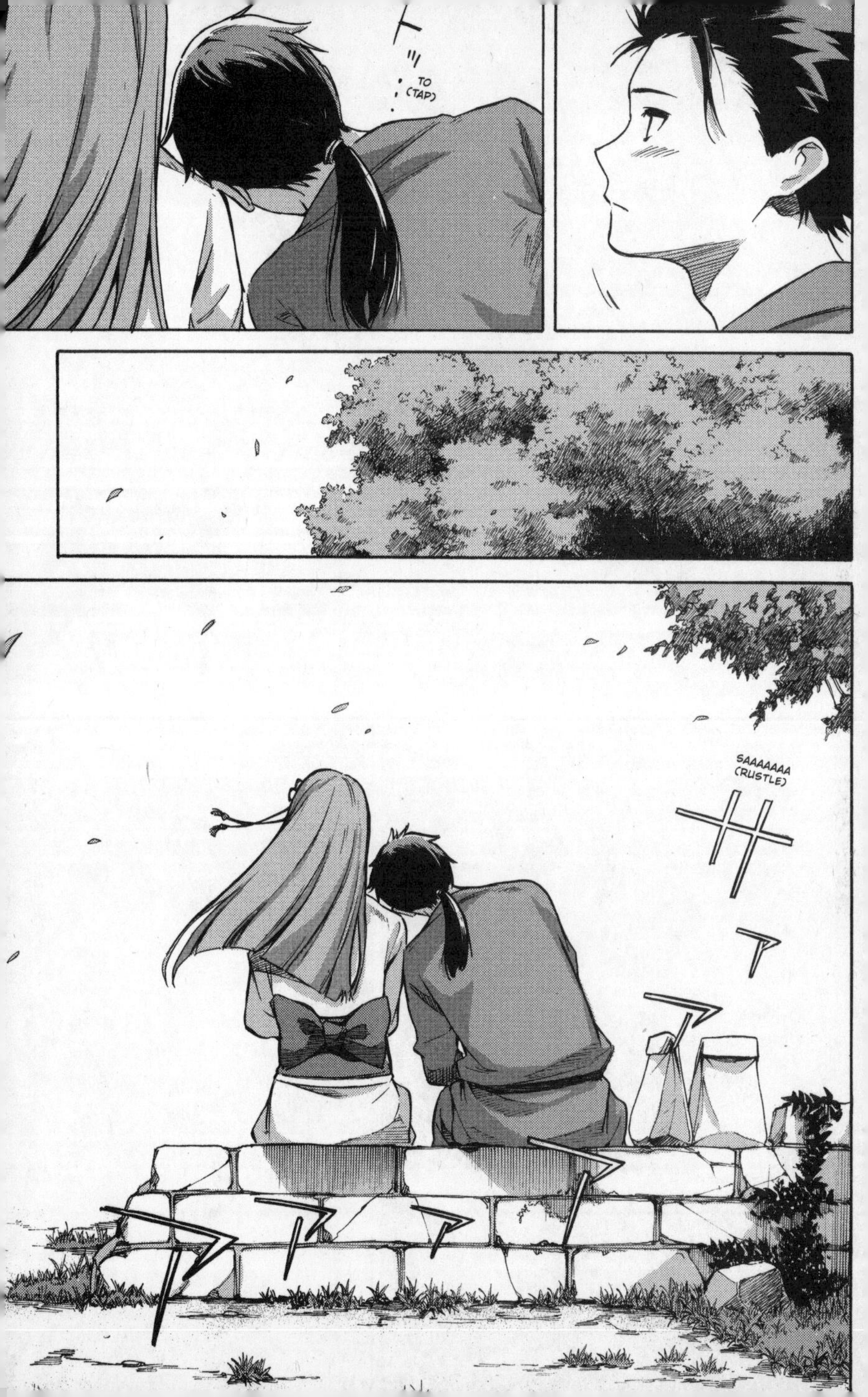
TO
(TAP)
SAAAAAAA
(RUSTLE)

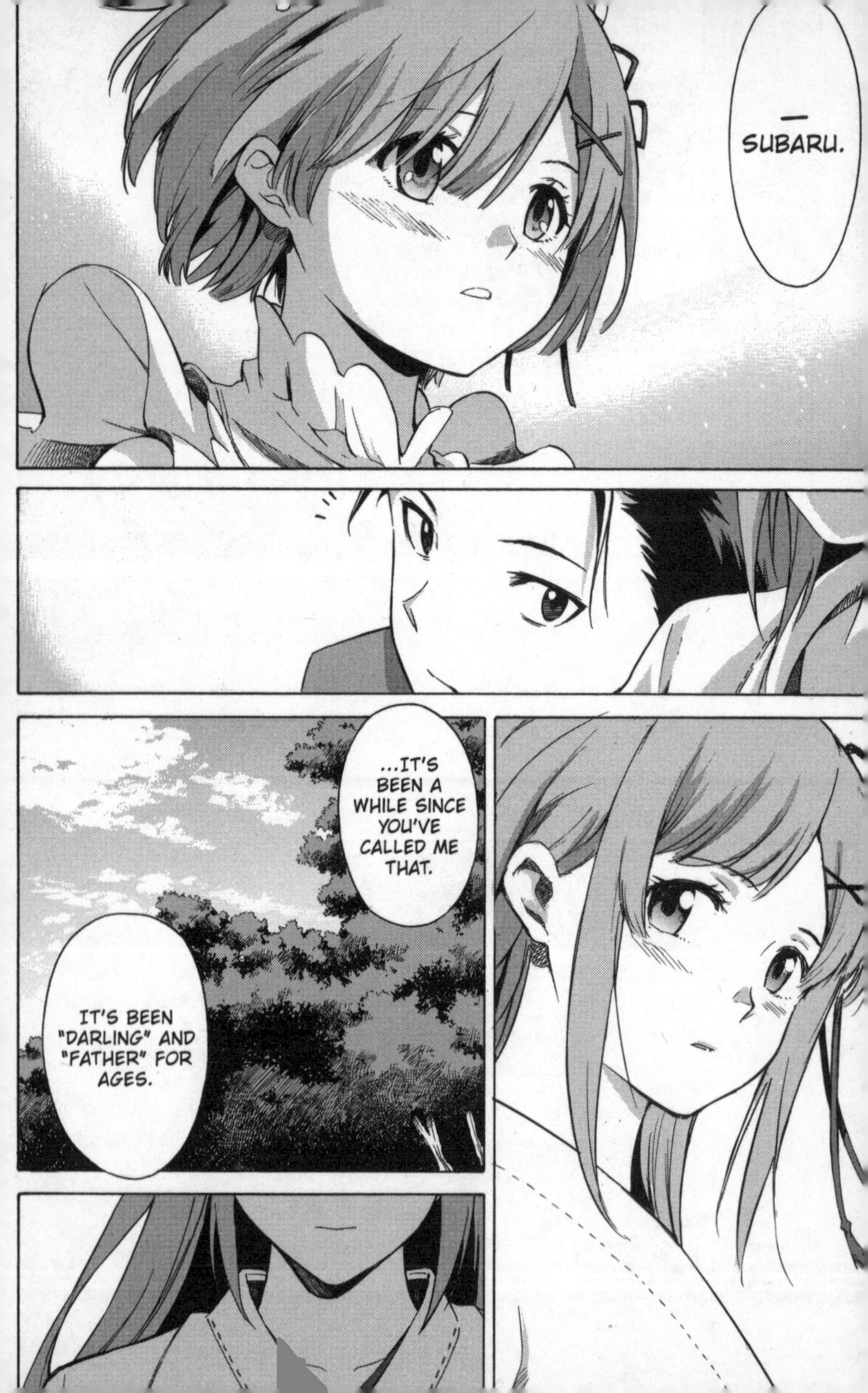
—SUBARU.
...IT'S BEEN A WHILE SINCE YOU'VE CALLED ME THAT.
IT'S BEEN "DARLING" AND "FATHER" FOR AGES.

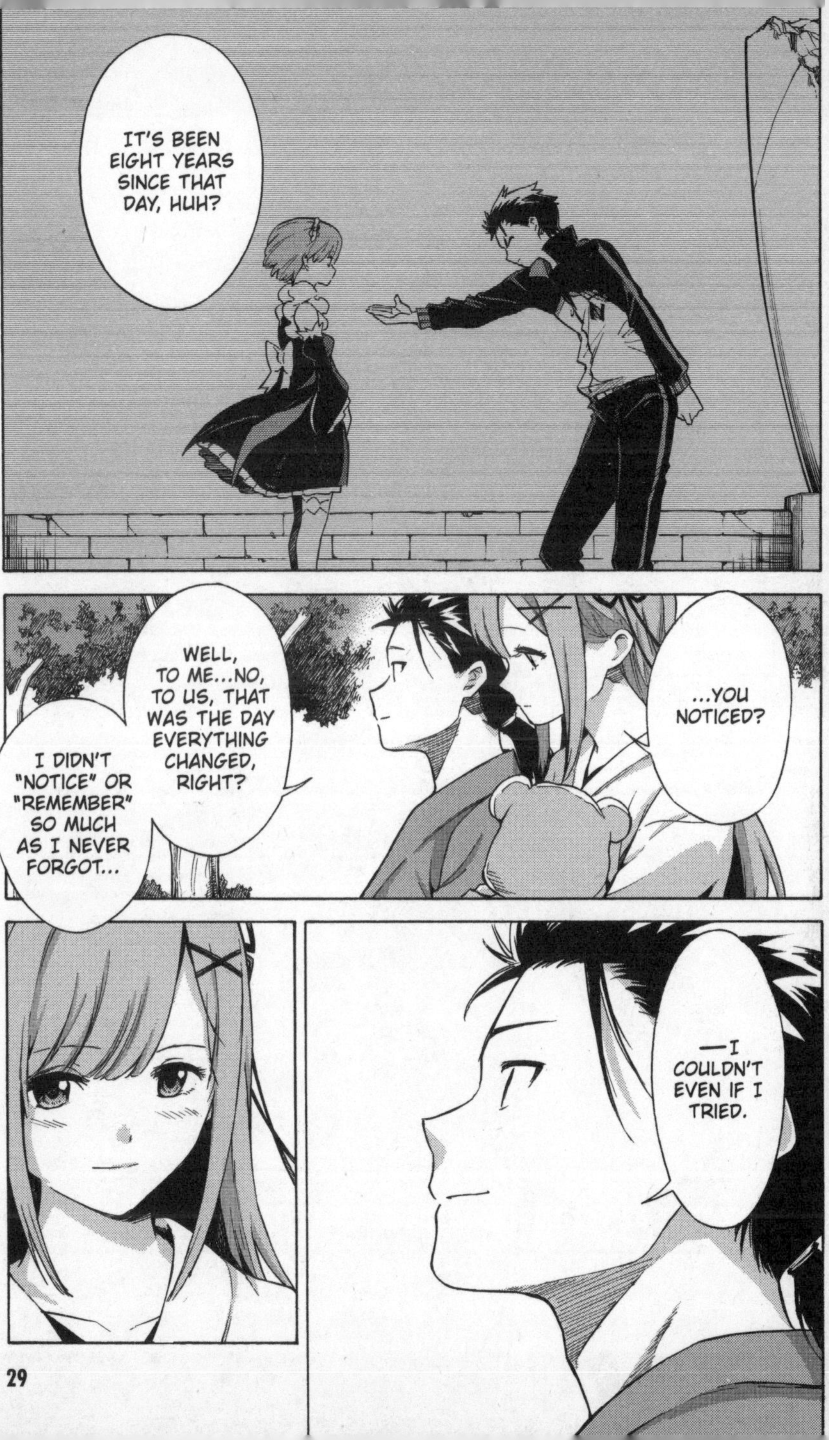
IT'S BEEN EIGHT YEARS SINCE THAT DAY, HUH?
...YOU NOTICED?
WELL, TO ME...NO, TO US, THAT WAS THE DAY EVERYTHING CHANGED, RIGHT?
I DIDN'T "NOTICE" OR "REMEMBER" SO MUCH AS I NEVER FORGOT...
—I COULDN'T EVEN IF I TRIED.

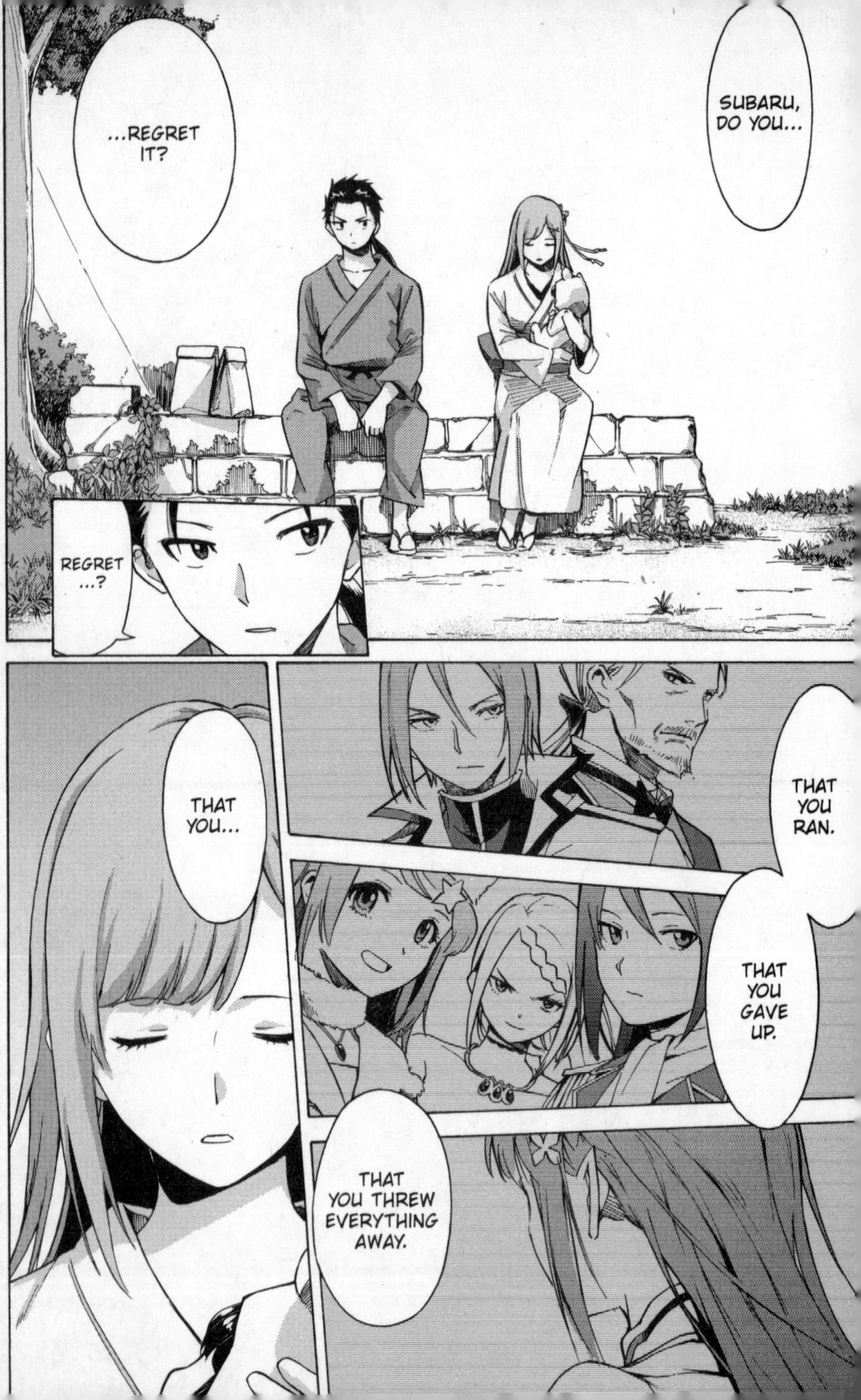
SUBARU, DO YOU...
...REGRET IT?
REGRET ...?
THAT YOU RAN.
THAT YOU GAVE UP.
THAT YOU THREW EVERYTHING AWAY.
THAT YOU...

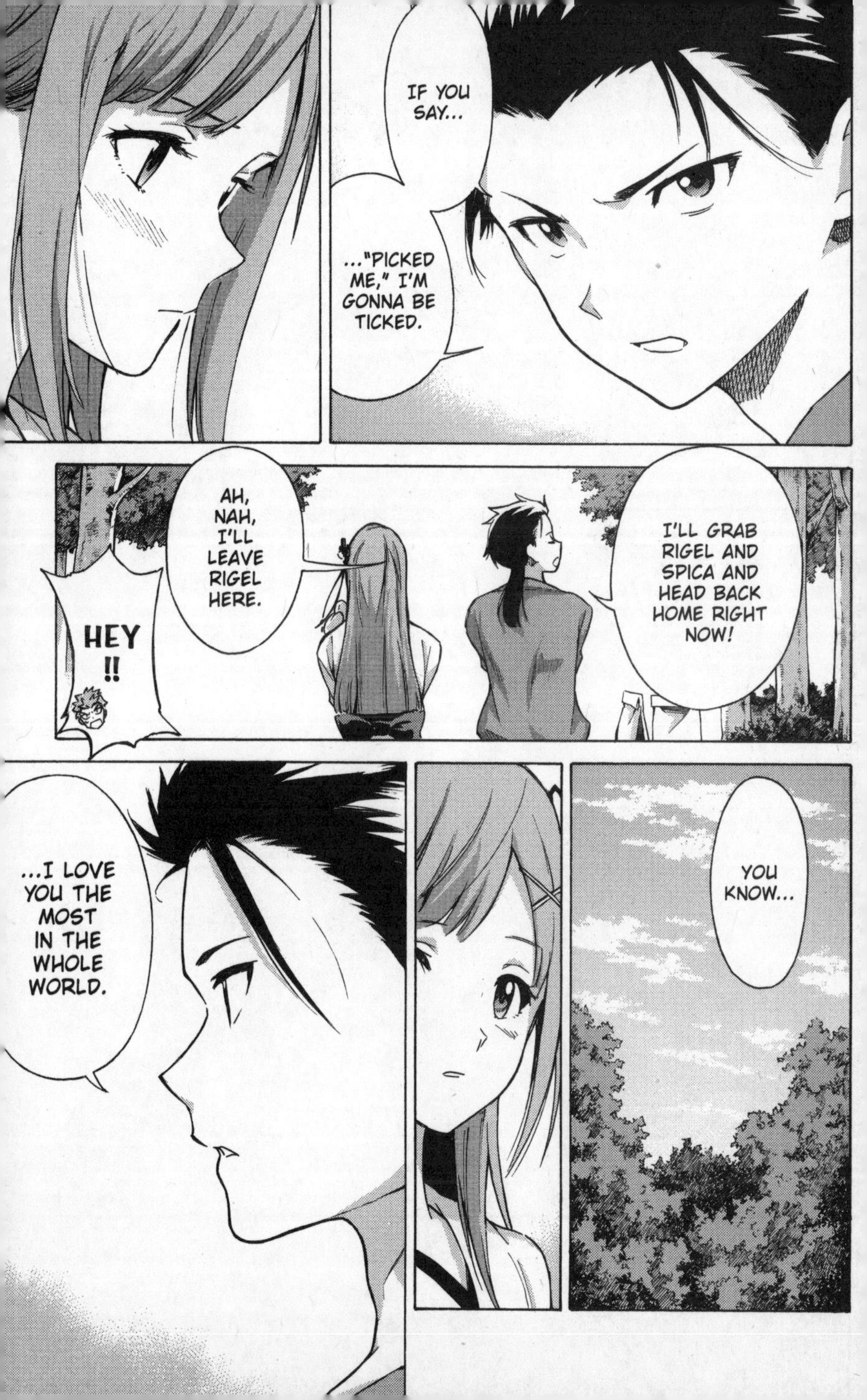
IF YOU SAY...
..."PICKED ME," I'M GONNA BE TICKED.
I'LL GRAB RIGEL AND SPICA AND HEAD BACK HOME RIGHT NOW!
AH, NAH, I'LL LEAVE RIGEL HERE.
HEY !!
YOU KNOW...
...I LOVE YOU THE MOST IN THE WHOLE WORLD.

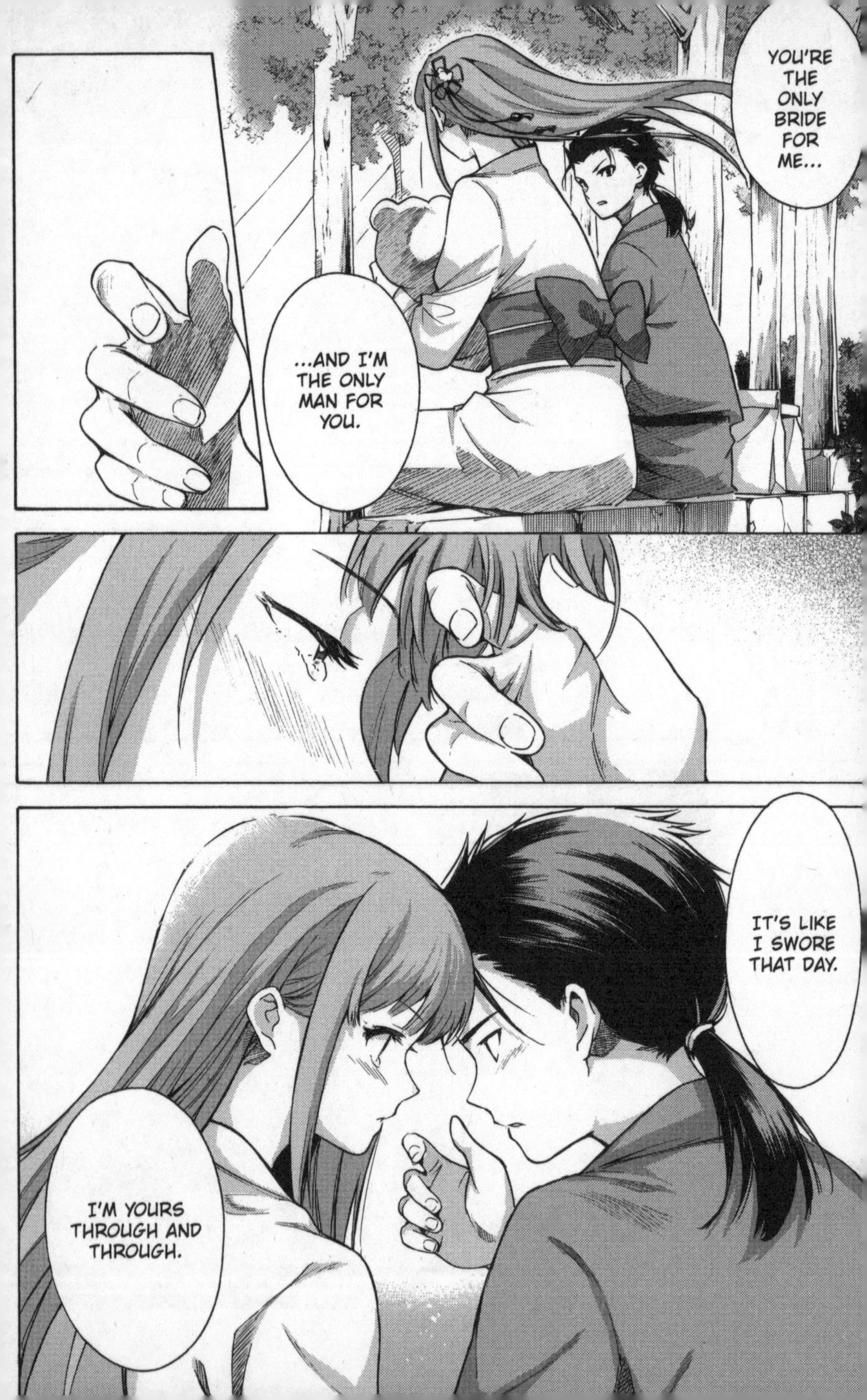
YOU'RE THE ONLY BRIDE FOR ME...
...AND I'M THE ONLY MAN FOR YOU.
IT'S LIKE I SWORE THAT DAY.
I'M YOURS THROUGH AND THROUGH.

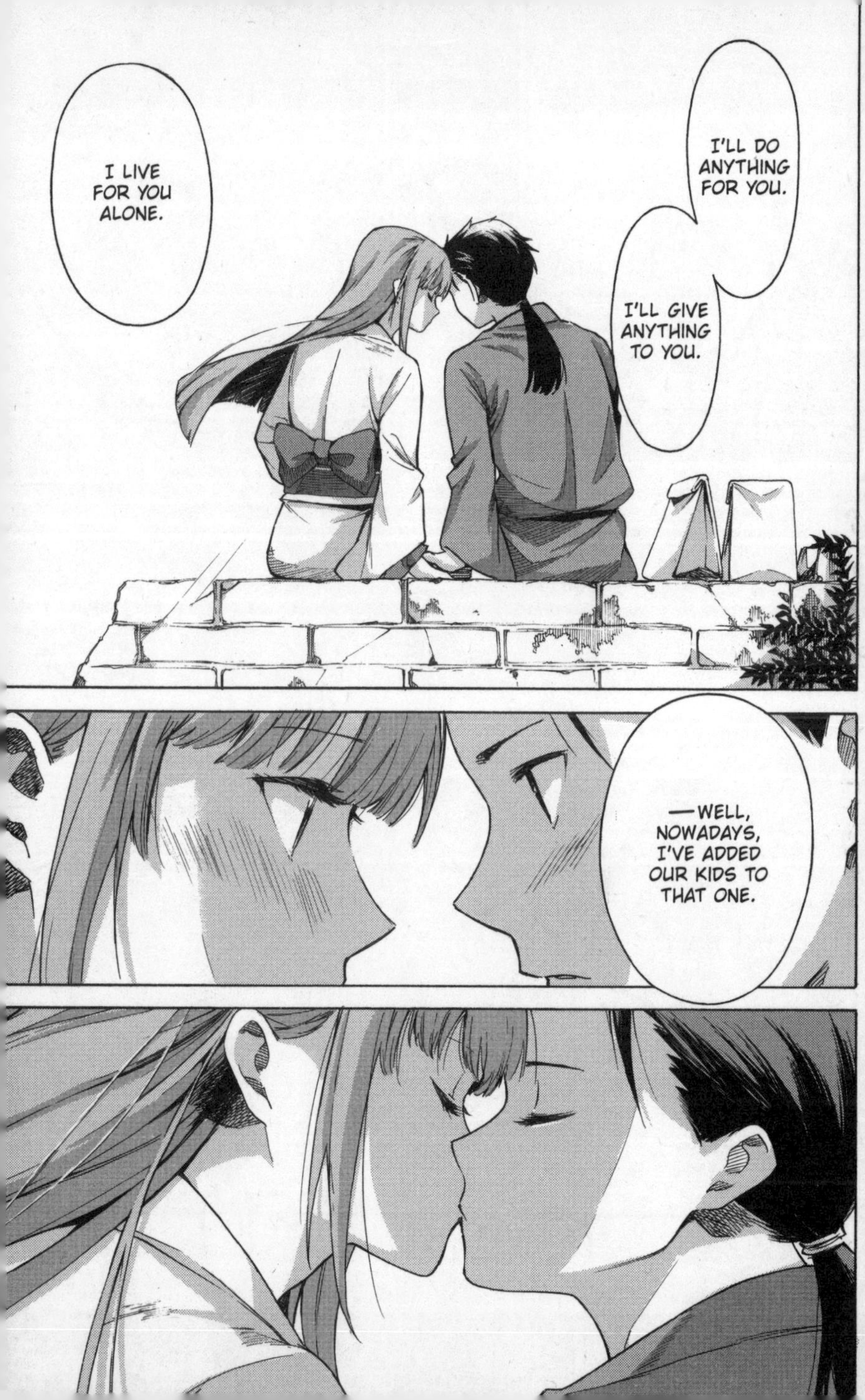
I'LL DO ANYTHING FOR YOU.
I'LL GIVE ANYTHING TO YOU.
I LIVE FOR YOU ALONE.
—WELL, NOWADAYS, I'VE ADDED OUR KIDS TO THAT ONE.

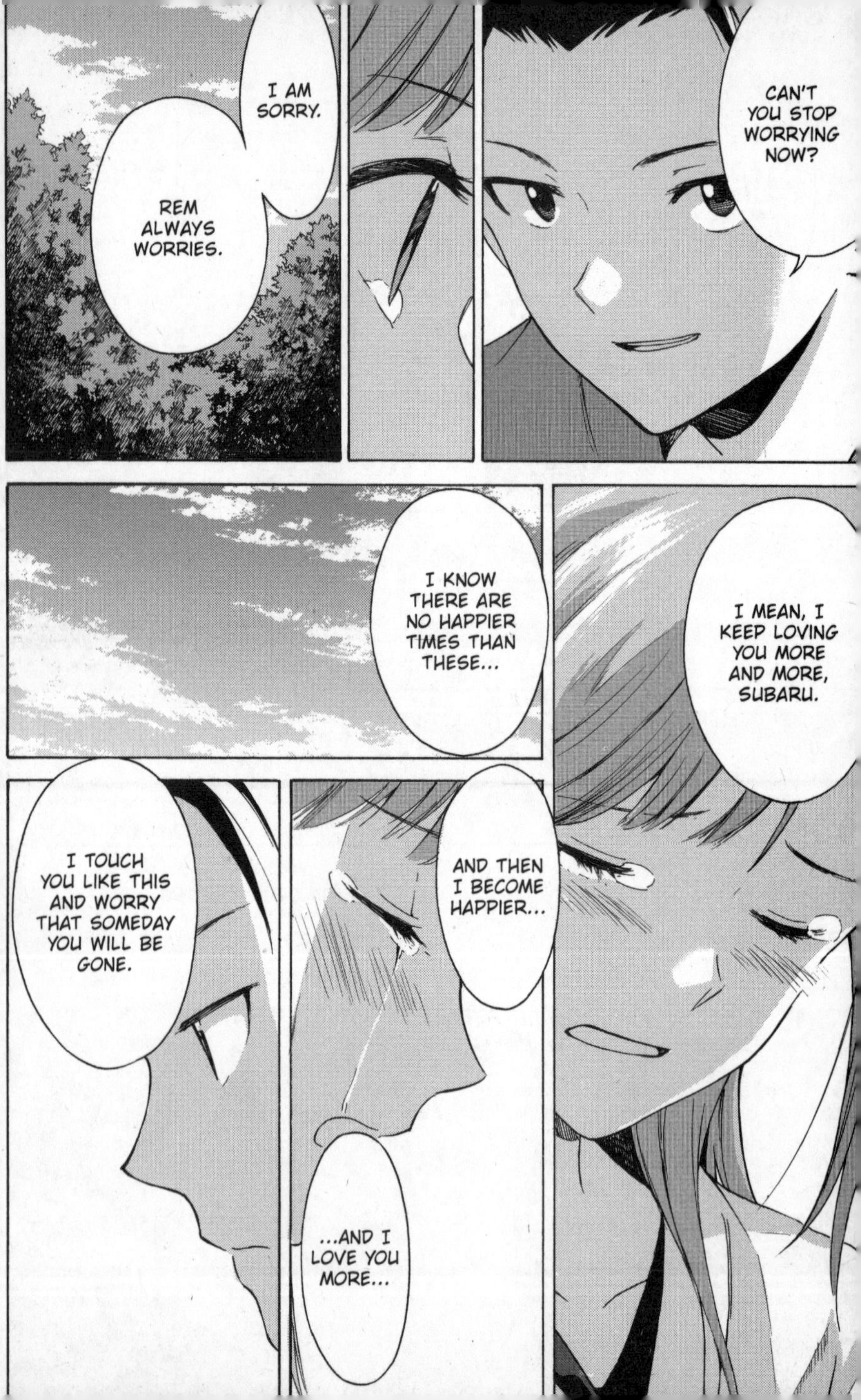
CAN'T YOU STOP WORRYING NOW?
I AM SORRY.
REM ALWAYS WORRIES.
I MEAN, I KEEP LOVING YOU MORE AND MORE, SUBARU.
I KNOW THERE ARE NO HAPPIER TIMES THAN THESE...
AND THEN I BECOME HAPPIER...
...AND I LOVE YOU MORE...
I TOUCH YOU LIKE THIS AND WORRY THAT SOMEDAY YOU WILL BE GONE.

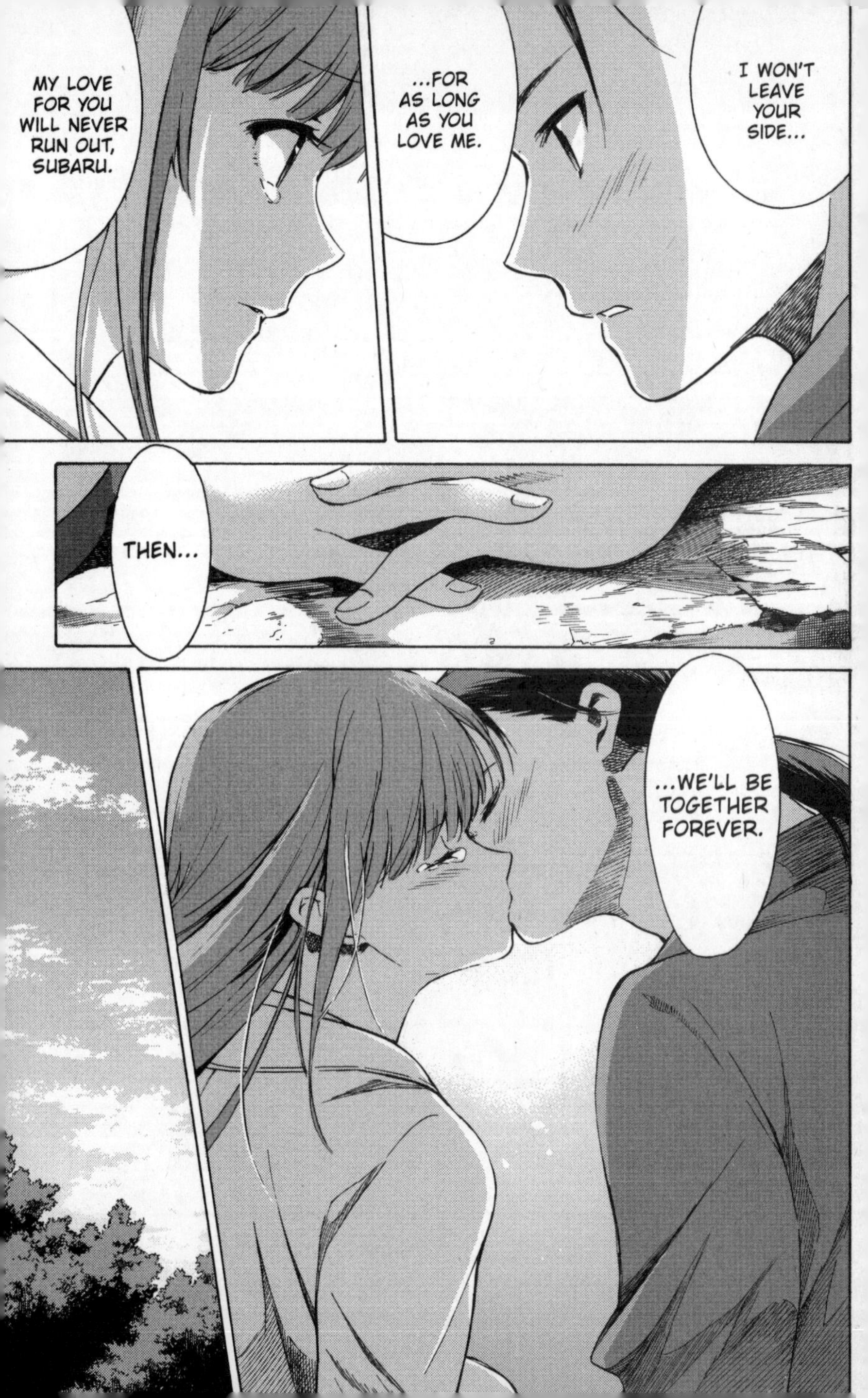
I WON'T LEAVE YOUR SIDE...
...FOR AS LONG AS YOU LOVE ME.
MY LOVE FOR YOU WILL NEVER RUN OUT, SUBARU.
THEN...
...WE'LL BE TOGETHER FOREVER.

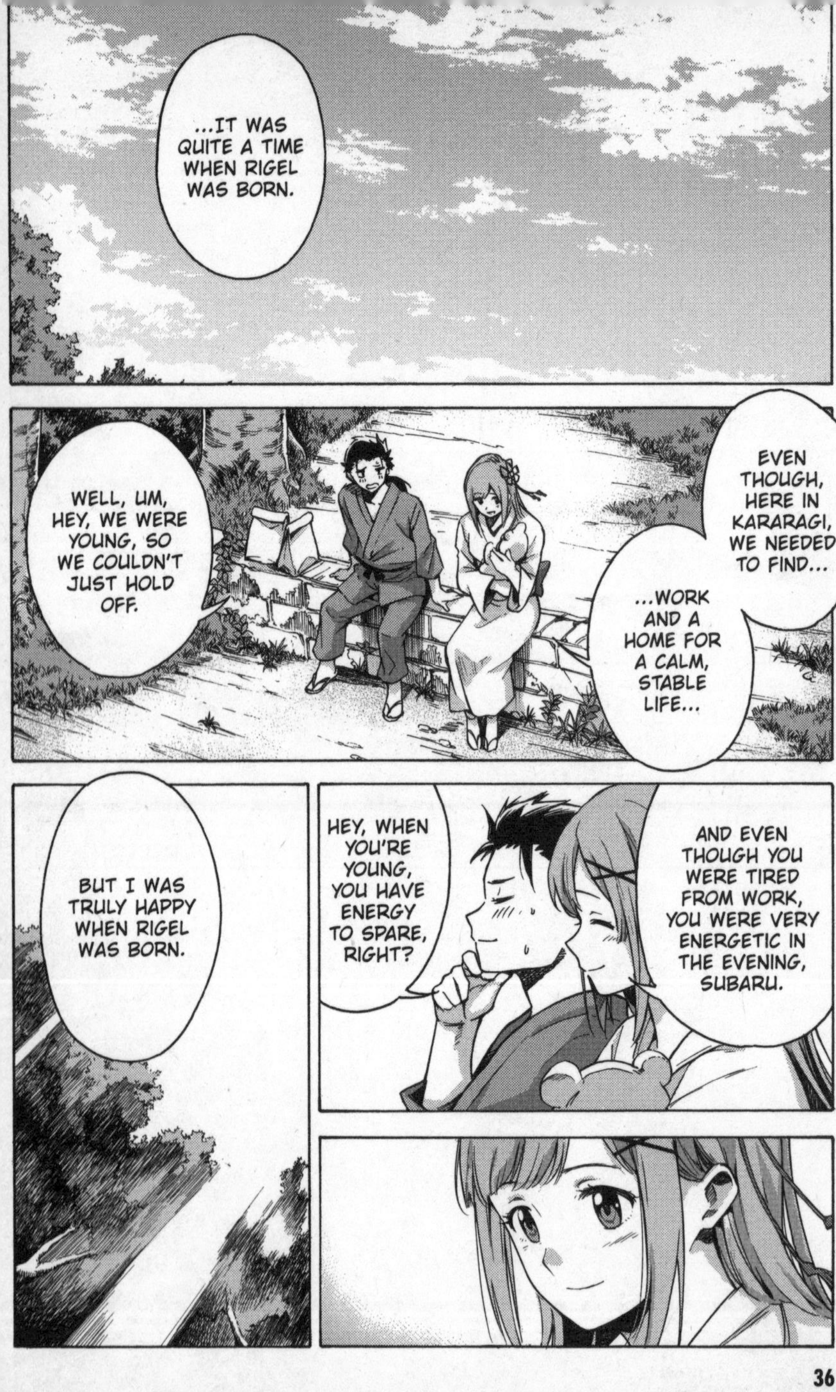
...IT WAS QUITE A TIME WHEN RIGEL WAS BORN.
EVEN THOUGH, HERE IN KARARAGI, WE NEEDED TO FIND...
...WORK AND A HOME FOR A CALM, STABLE LIFE...
WELL, UM, HEY, WE WERE YOUNG, SO WE COULDN'T JUST HOLD OFF.
AND EVEN THOUGH YOU WERE TIRED FROM WORK, YOU WERE VERY ENERGETIC IN THE EVENING, SUBARU.
HEY, WHEN YOU'RE YOUNG, YOU HAVE ENERGY TO SPARE, RIGHT?
BUT I WAS TRULY HAPPY WHEN RIGEL WAS BORN.

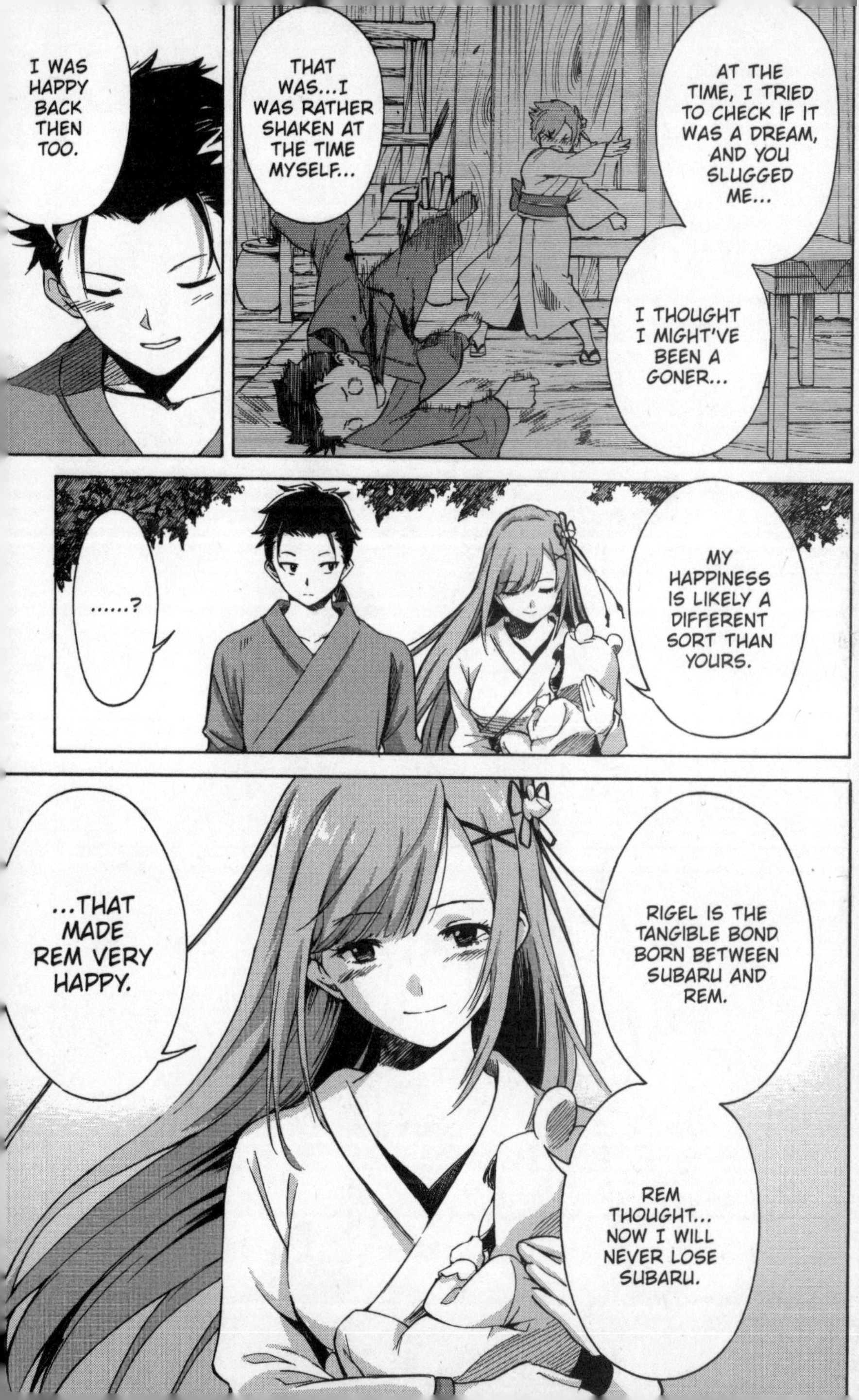
AT THE TIME, I TRIED TO CHECK IF IT WAS A DREAM, AND YOU SLUGGED ME...
I THOUGHT I MIGHT'VE BEEN A GONER...
THAT WAS...I WAS RATHER SHAKEN AT THE TIME MYSELF...
I WAS HAPPY BACK THEN TOO.
MY HAPPINESS IS LIKELY A DIFFERENT SORT THAN YOURS.
......?
RIGEL IS THE TANGIBLE BOND BORN BETWEEN SUBARU AND REM.
REM THOUGHT... NOW I WILL NEVER LOSE SUBARU.
...THAT MADE REM VERY HAPPY.

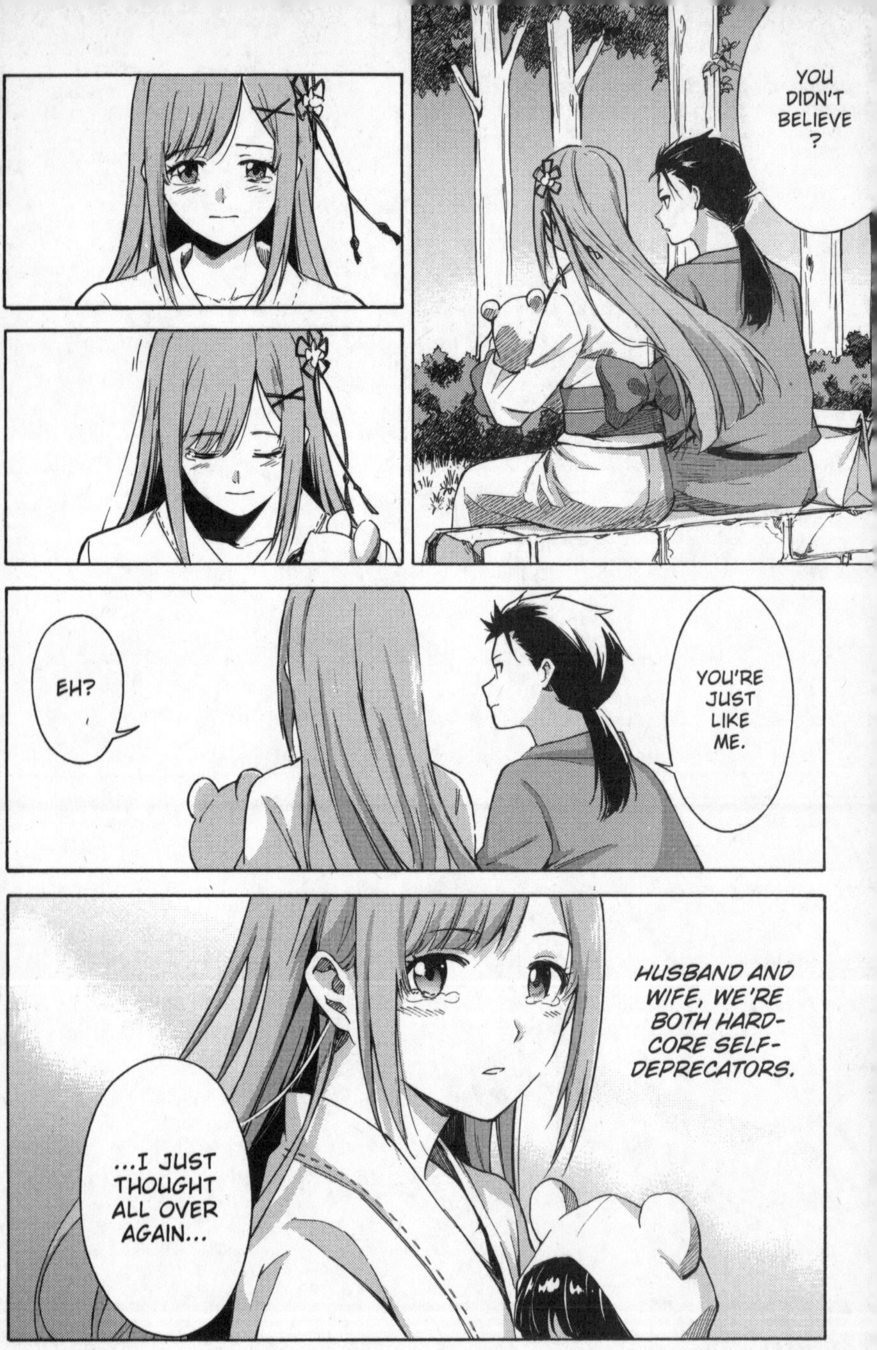
YOU DIDN'T BELIEVE ?
YOU'RE JUST LIKE ME.
EH?
HUSBAND AND WIFE, WE'RE BOTH HARD-CORE SELF-DEPRECATORS.
...I JUST THOUGHT ALL OVER AGAIN...

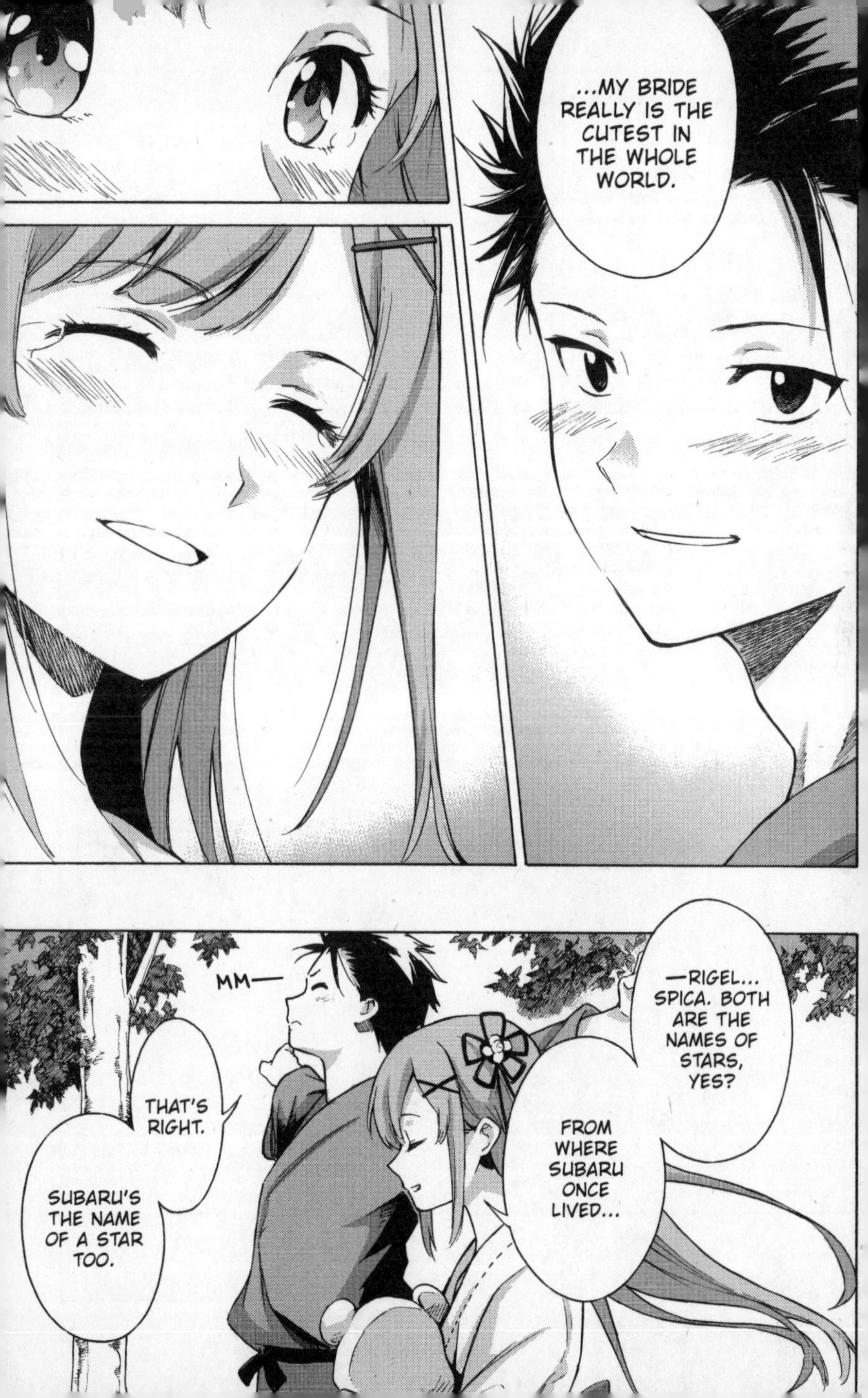
...MY BRIDE REALLY IS THE CUTEST IN THE WHOLE WORLD.
—RIGEL... SPICA. BOTH ARE THE NAMES OF STARS, YES?
FROM WHERE SUBARU ONCE LIVED...
MM—
THAT'S RIGHT.
SUBARU'S THE NAME OF A STAR TOO.

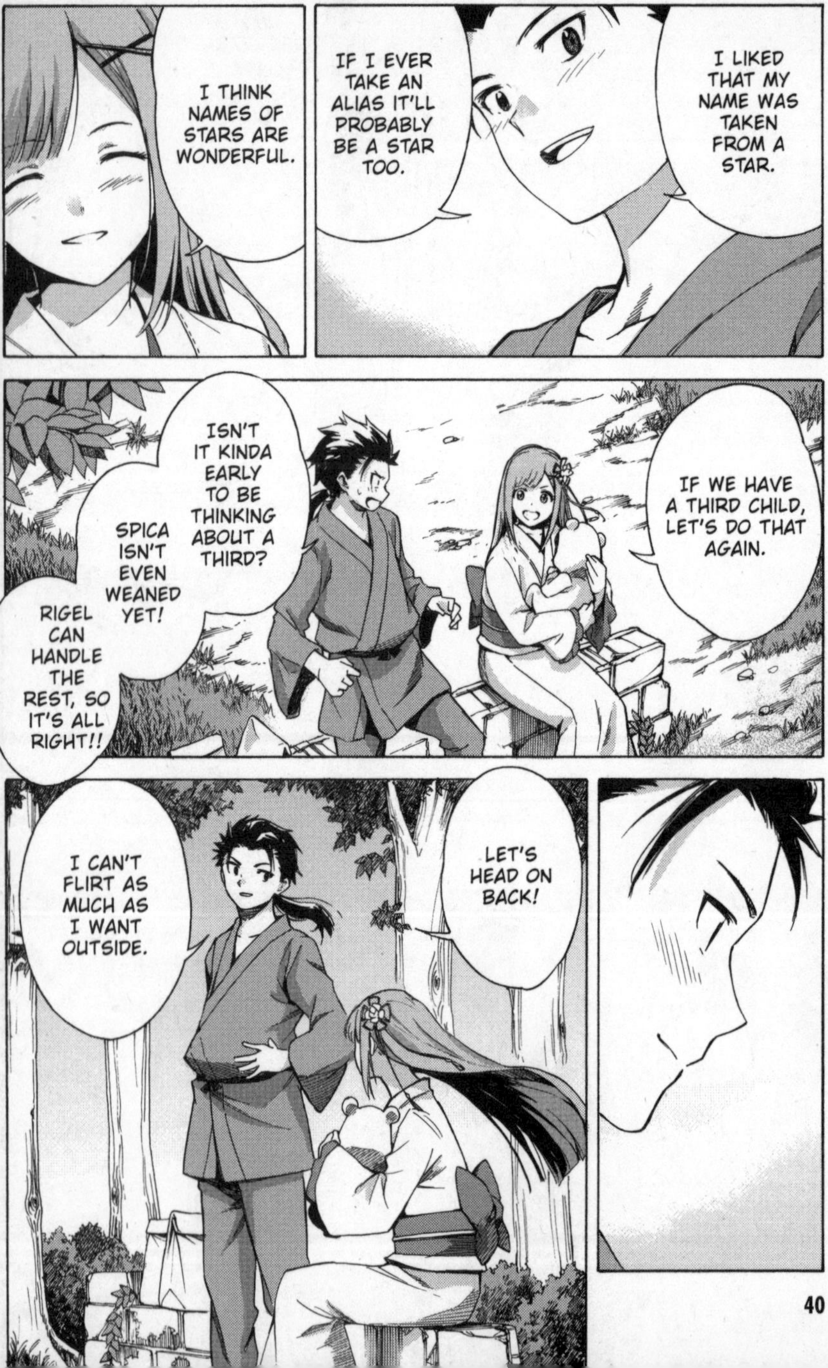
I LIKED THAT MY NAME WAS TAKEN FROM A STAR.
IF I EVER TAKE AN ALIAS IT'LL PROBABLY BE A STAR TOO.
I THINK NAMES OF STARS ARE WONDERFUL.
IF WE HAVE A THIRD CHILD, LET'S DO THAT AGAIN.
ISN'T IT KINDA EARLY TO BE THINKING ABOUT A THIRD?
SPICA ISN'T EVEN WEANED YET!
RIGEL CAN HANDLE THE REST, SO IT'S ALL RIGHT!!
LET'S HEAD ON BACK!
I CAN'T FLIRT AS MUCH AS I WANT OUTSIDE.

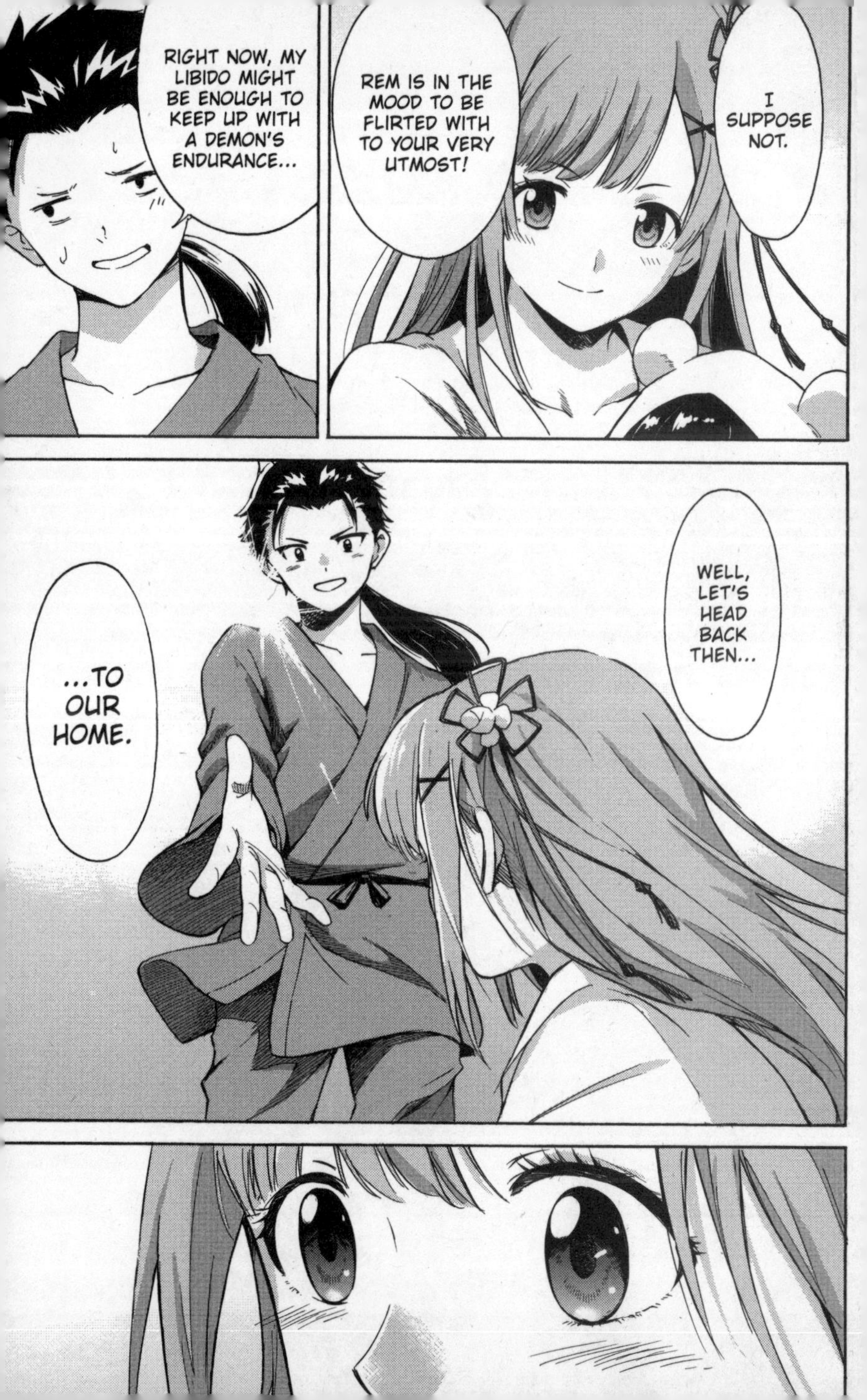
I SUPPOSE NOT.
REM IS IN THE MOOD TO BE FLIRTED WITH TO YOUR VERY UTMOST!
RIGHT NOW, MY LIBIDO MIGHT BE ENOUGH TO KEEP UP WITH A DEMON'S ENDURANCE...
WELL, LET'S HEAD BACK THEN...
...TO OUR HOME.

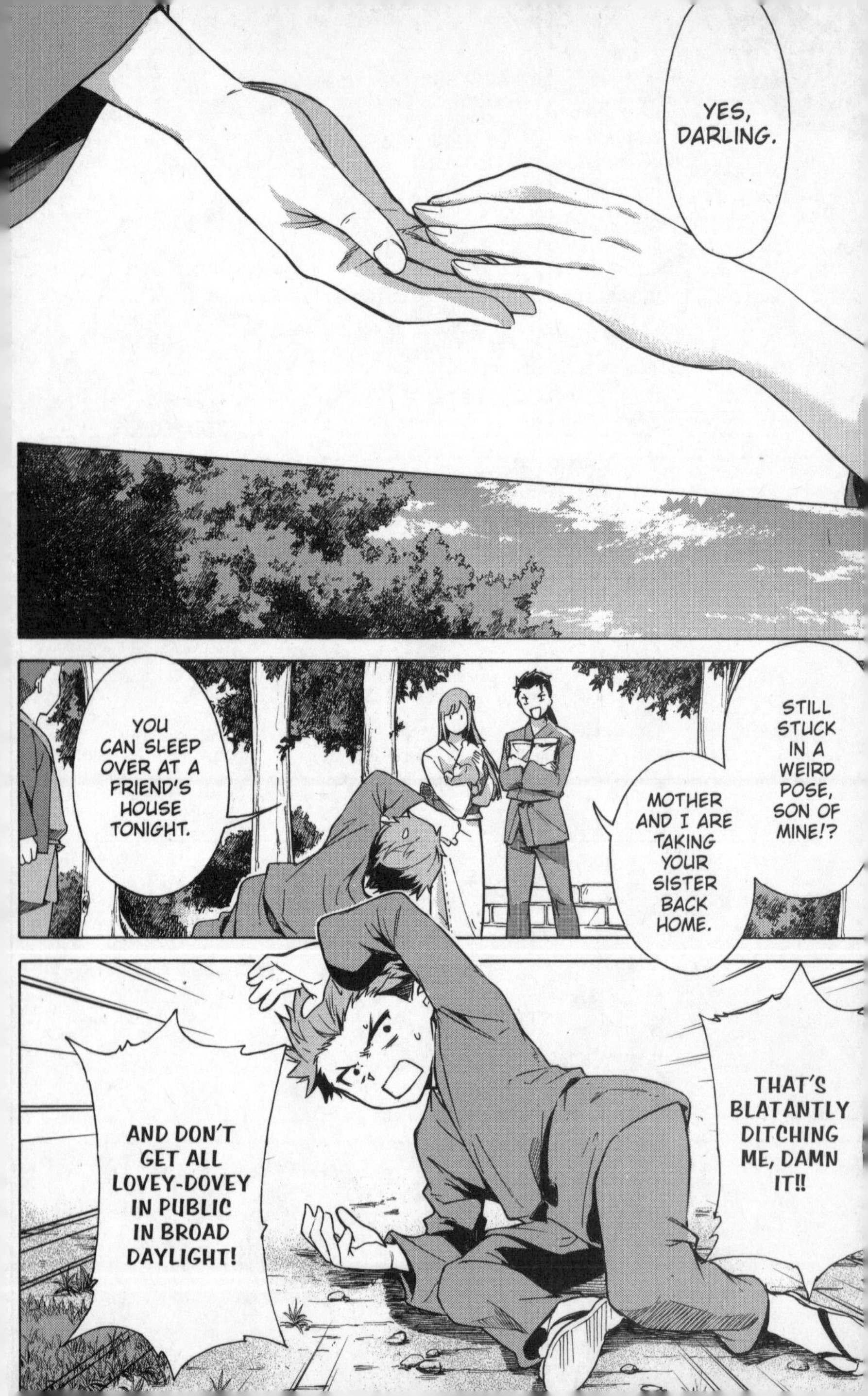
YES, DARLING.
STILL STUCK IN A WEIRD POSE, SON OF MINE!?
MOTHER AND I ARE TAKING YOUR SISTER BACK HOME.
YOU CAN SLEEP OVER AT A FRIEND'S HOUSE TONIGHT.
THAT'S BLATANTLY DITCHING ME, DAMN IT!!
AND DON'T GET ALL LOVEY-DOVEY IN PUBLIC IN BROAD DAYLIGHT!

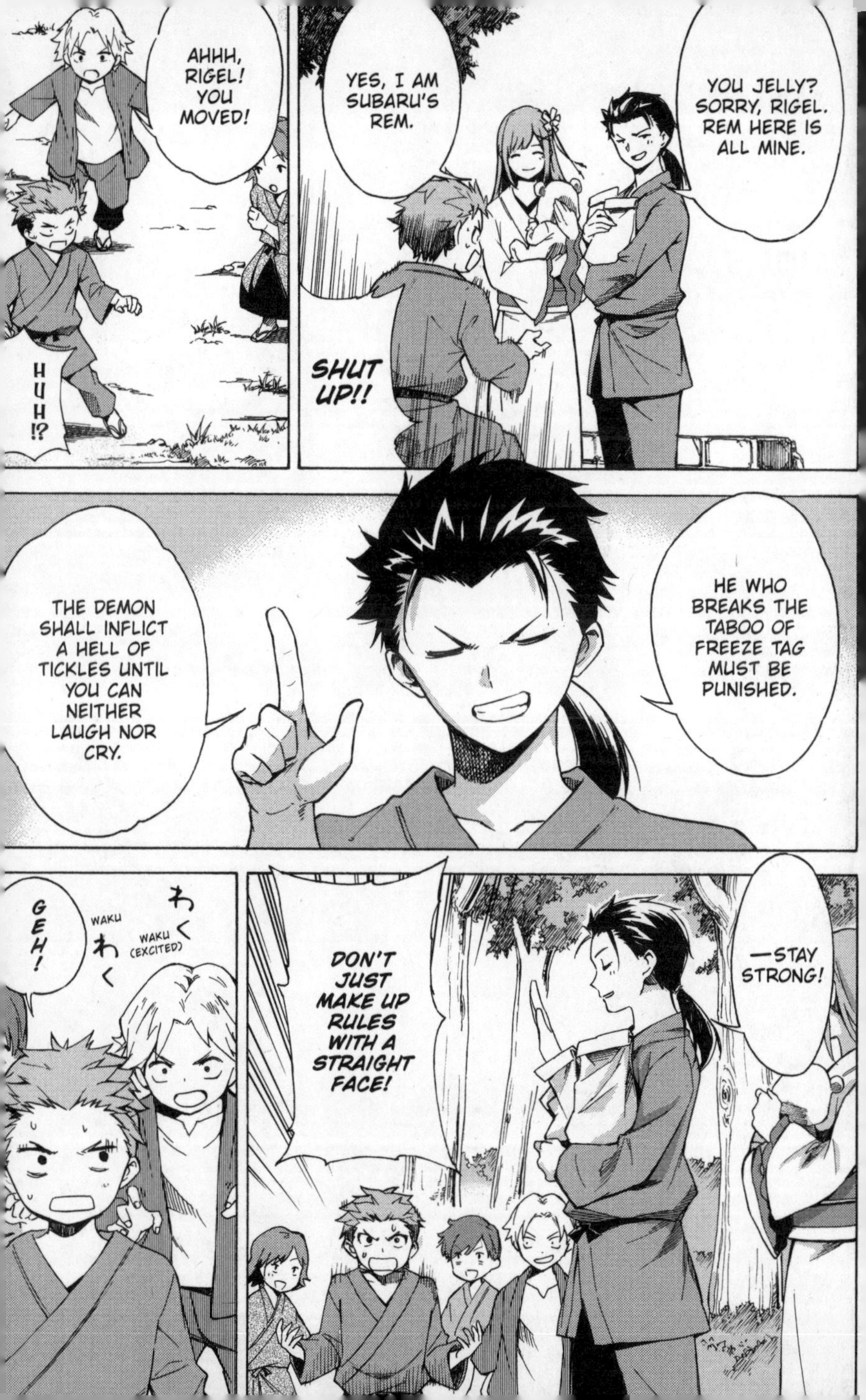
YOU JELLY? SORRY, RIGEL. REM HERE IS ALL MINE.
YES, I AM SUBARU'S REM.
SHUT UP!!
AHHH, RIGEL! YOU MOVED!
HUH!?
HE WHO BREAKS THE TABOO OF FREEZE TAG MUST BE PUNISHED.
THE DEMON SHALL INFLICT A HELL OF TICKLES UNTIL YOU CAN NEITHER LAUGH NOR CRY.
—STAY STRONG!
DON'T JUST MAKE UP RULES WITH A STRAIGHT FACE!
わく WAKU
わく WAKU (EXCITED)
GEH!

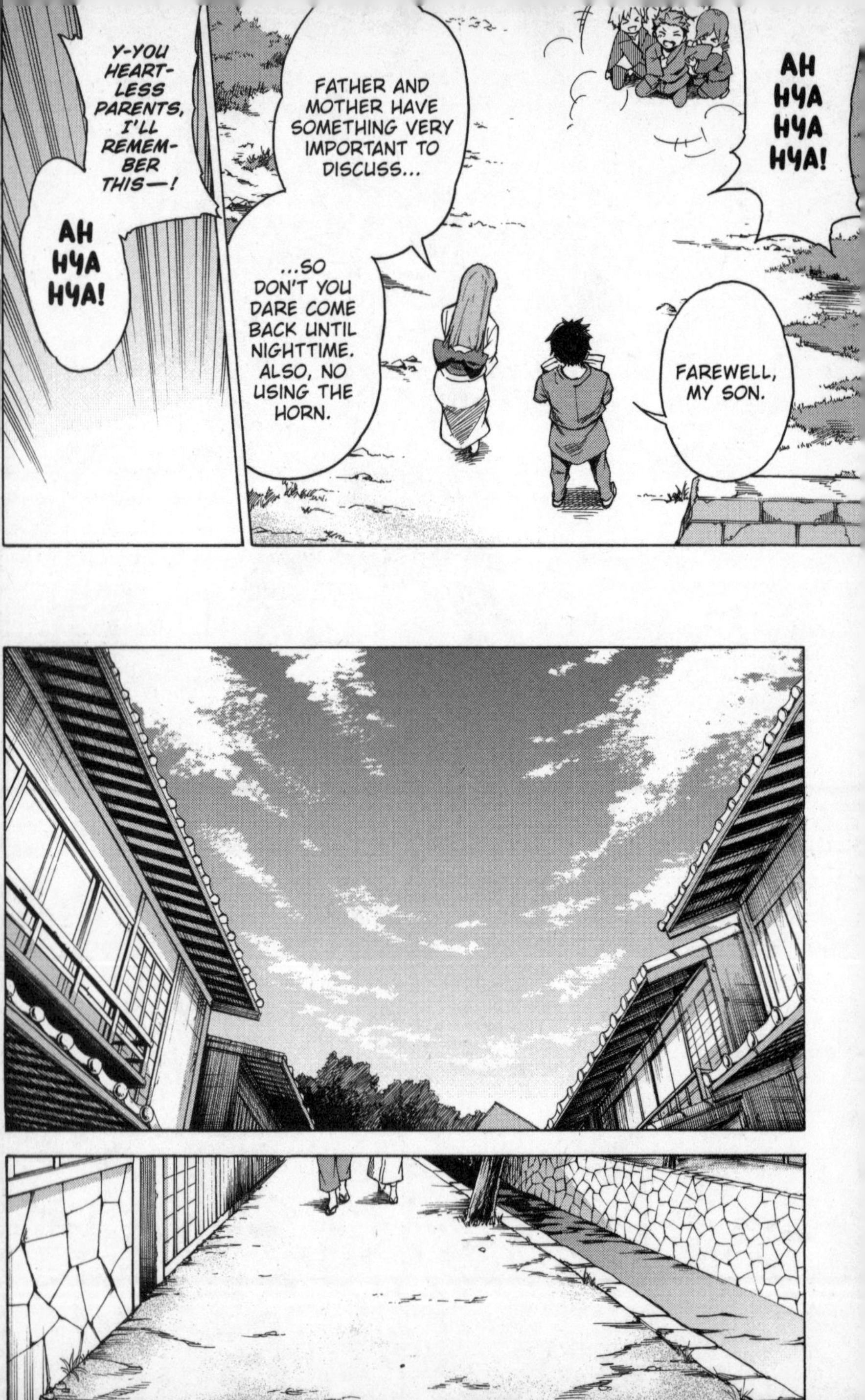
AH HYA HYA HYA!
FATHER AND MOTHER HAVE SOMETHING VERY IMPORTANT TO DISCUSS...
...SO DON'T YOU DARE COME BACK UNTIL NIGHTTIME. ALSO, NO USING THE HORN.
FAREWELL, MY SON.
Y-YOU HEARTLESS PARENTS, I'LL REMEMBER THIS—!
AH HYA HYA!

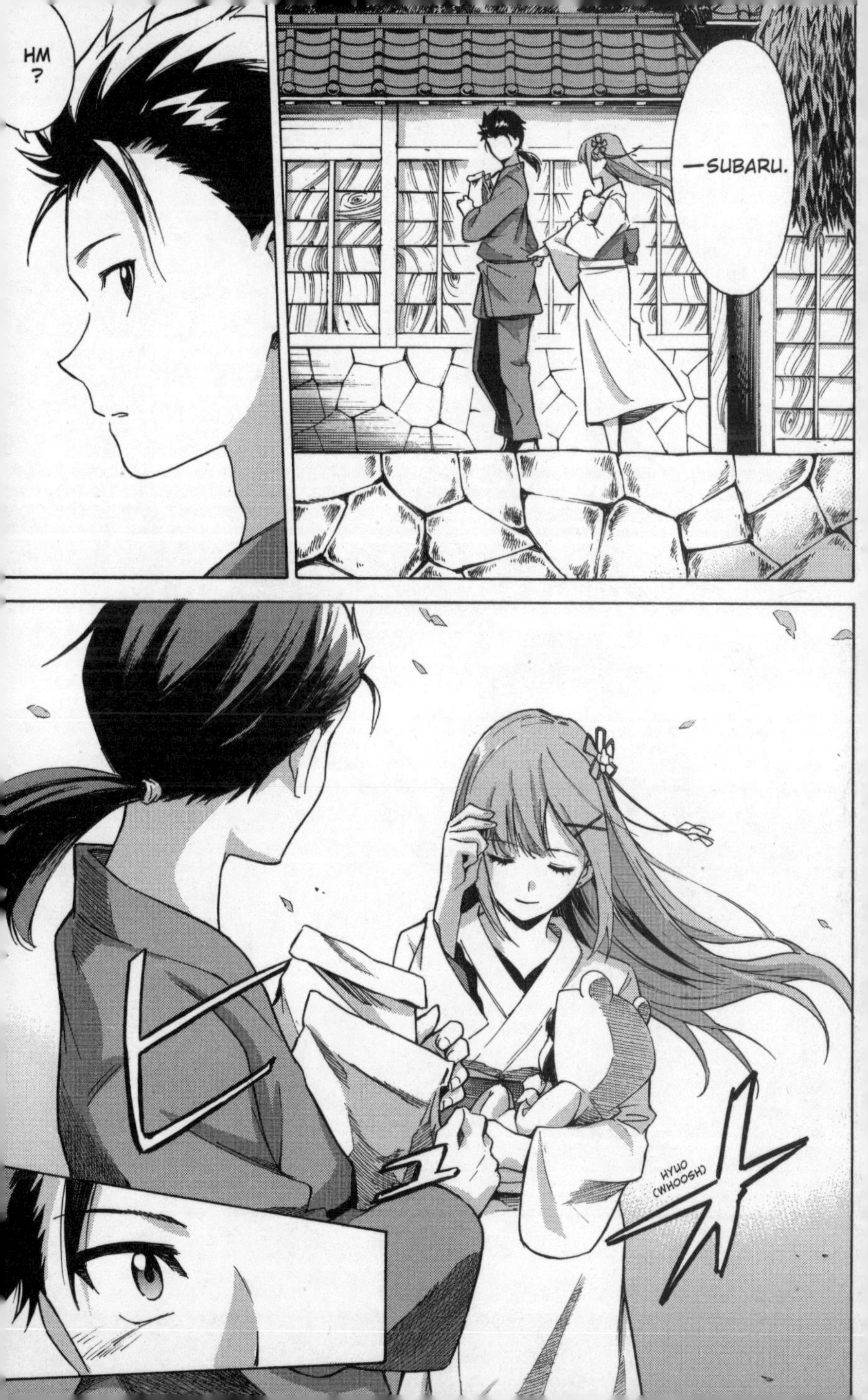
—SUBARU.
HM?
HYUO
(WHOOSH)

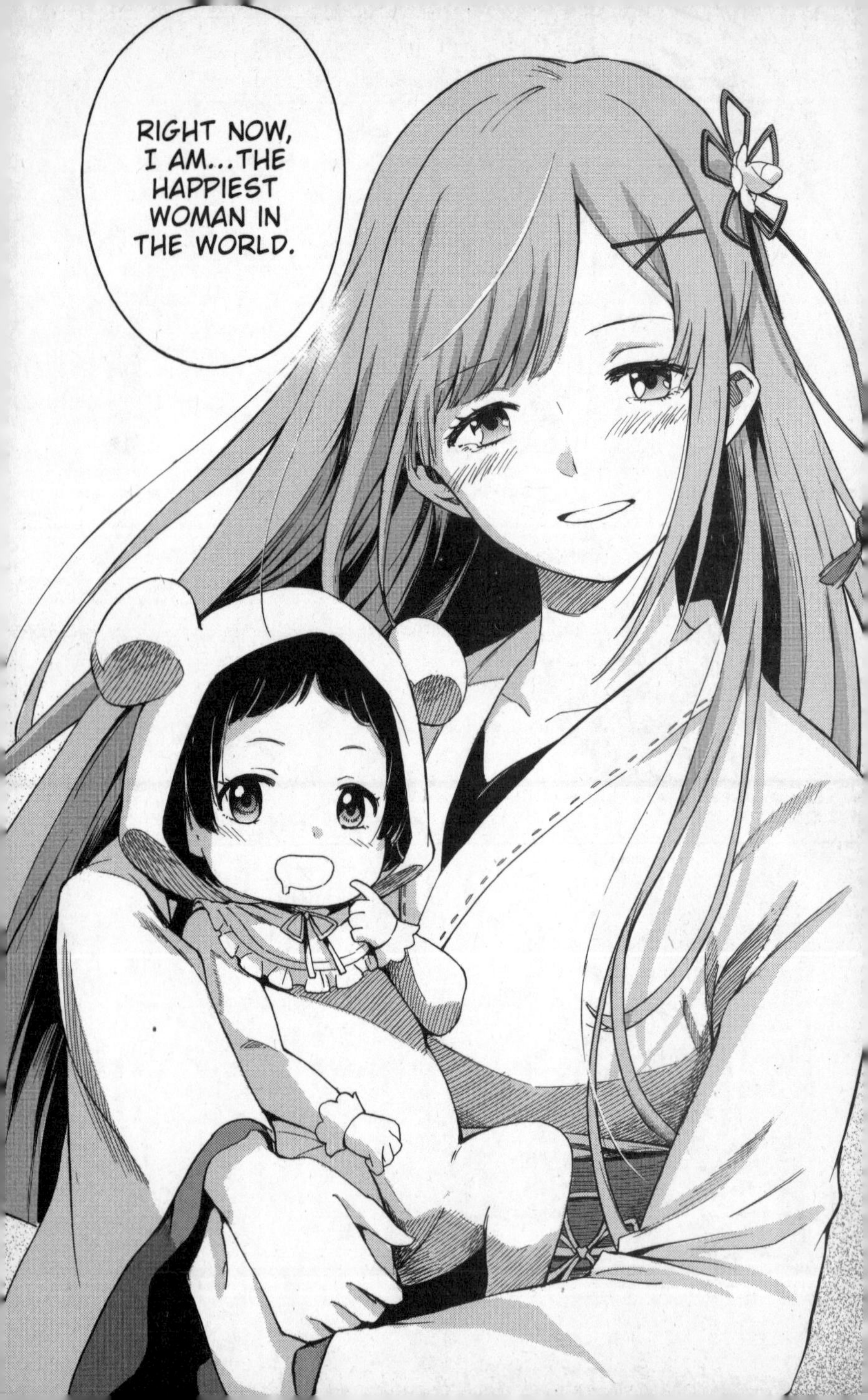
RIGHT NOW, I AM...THE HAPPIEST WOMAN IN THE WORLD.

Re:ZERO -Starting Life in Another World-

The only ability Subaru Natsuki gets when he's summoned to another world is
time travel via his own death. But to save her, he'll die as many times as it takes.

Truth of Zero

The only ability Subaru Natsuki gets when he's
summoned to another world is time travel via his own
death. But to save her, he'll die as many times as it takes.

Re:ZERO -Starting
Life in Another World-

Episode 52
Let Us Feast

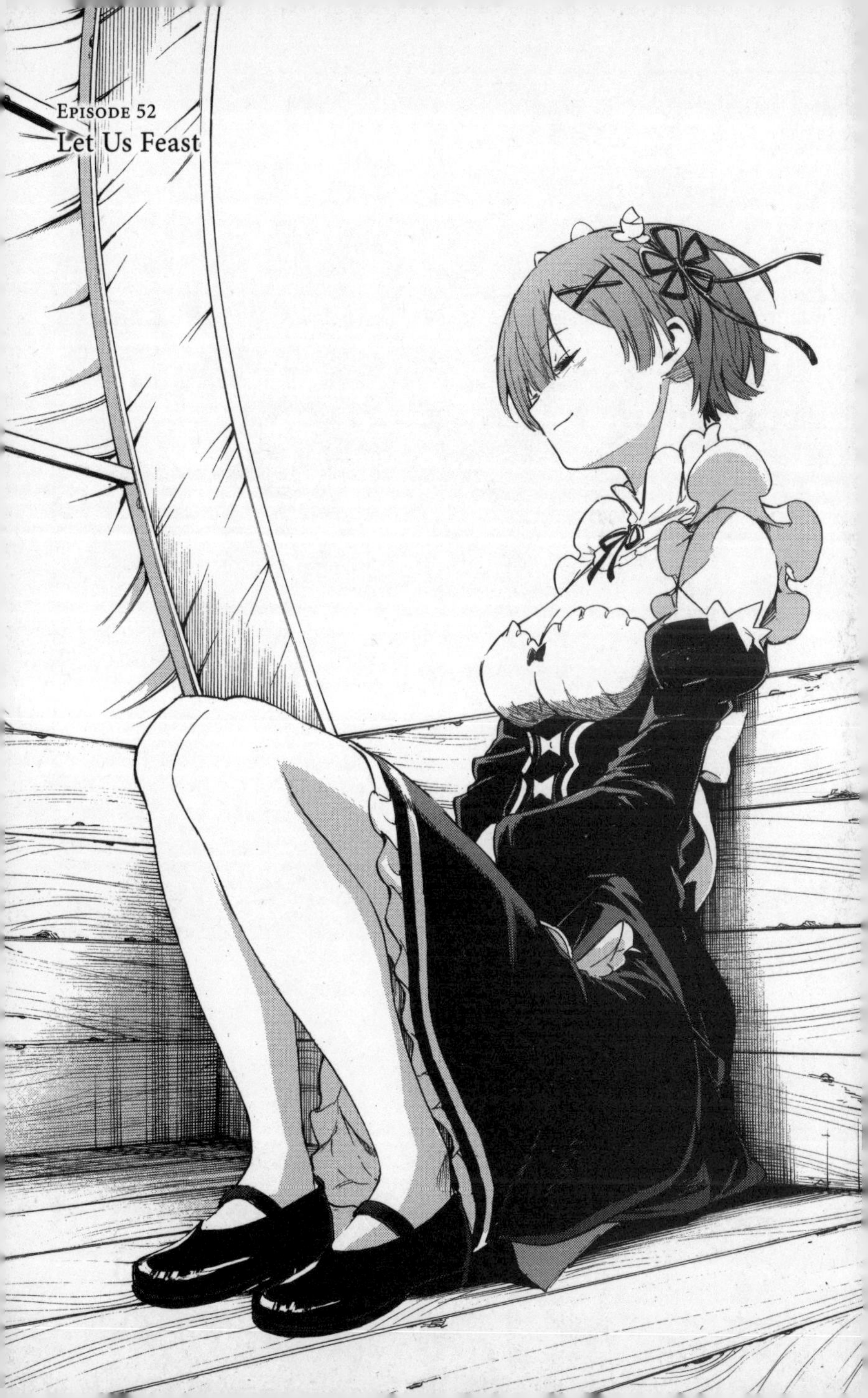

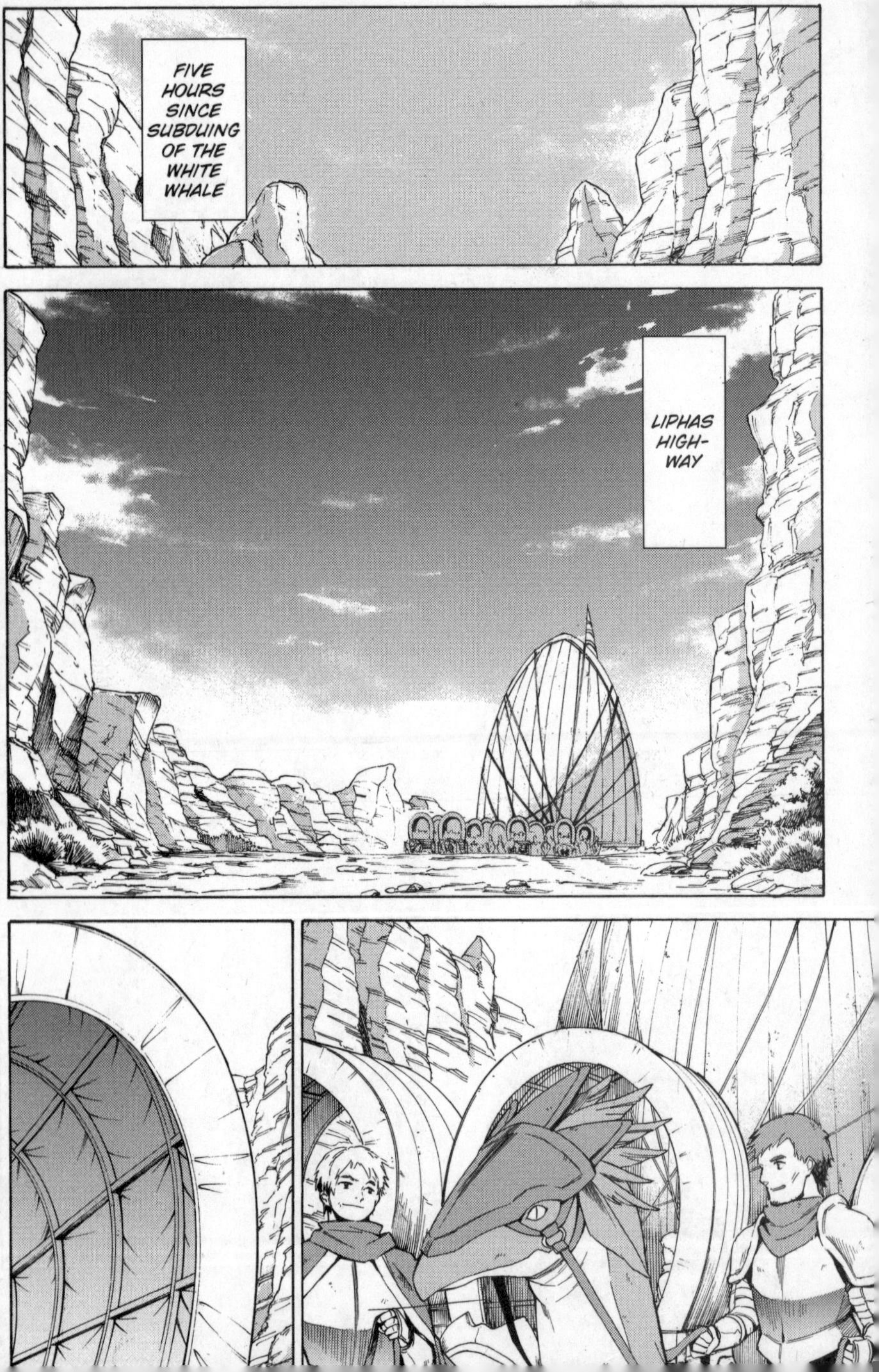
FIVE HOURS SINCE SUBDUING OF THE WHITE WHALE
LIPHAS HIGH-WAY

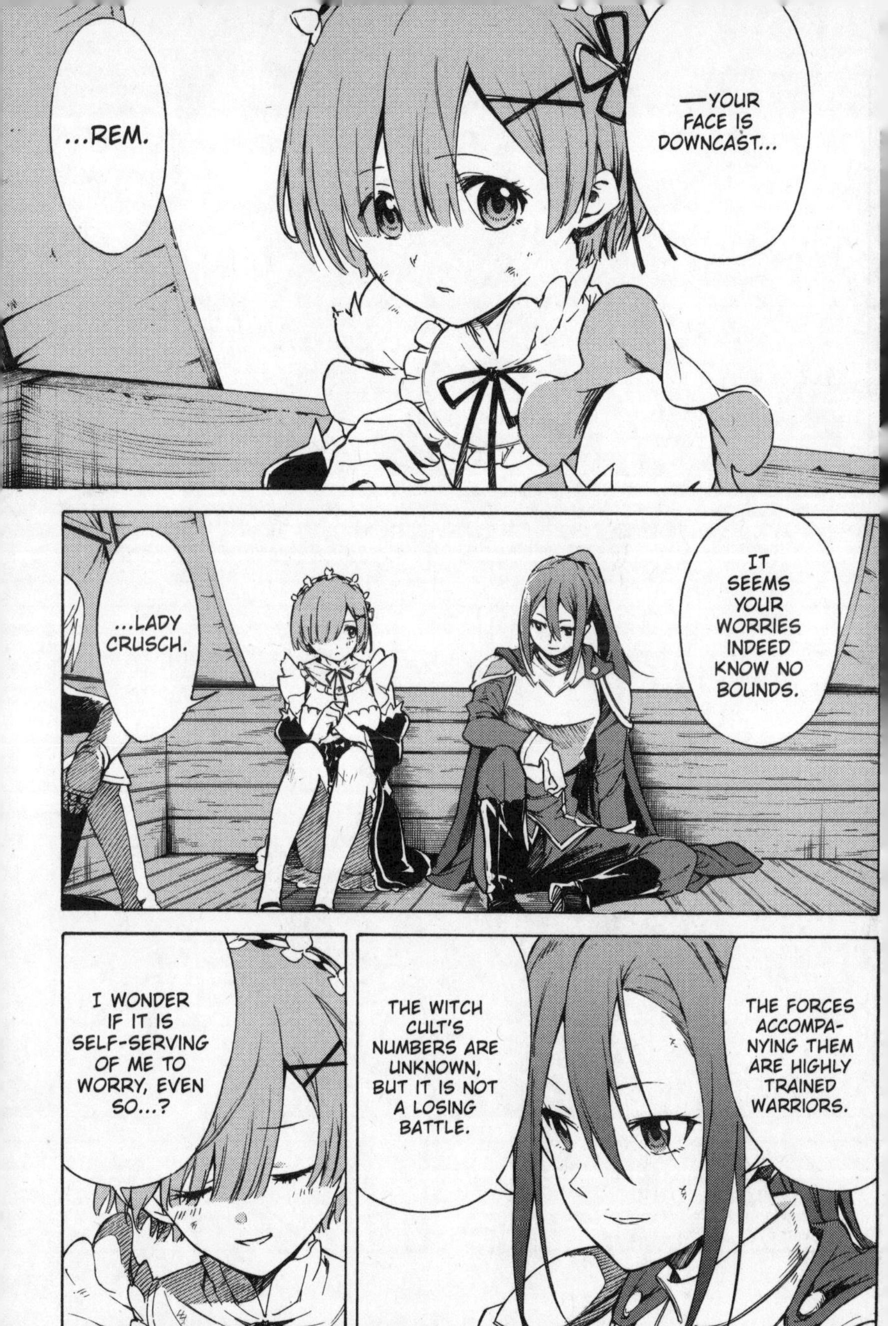
—YOUR FACE IS DOWNCAST...
...REM.
IT SEEMS YOUR WORRIES INDEED KNOW NO BOUNDS.
...LADY CRUSCH.
THE FORCES ACCOMPA-NYING THEM ARE HIGHLY TRAINED WARRIORS.
THE WITCH CULT'S NUMBERS ARE UNKNOWN, BUT IT IS NOT A LOSING BATTLE.
I WONDER IF IT IS SELF-SERVING OF ME TO WORRY, EVEN SO...?

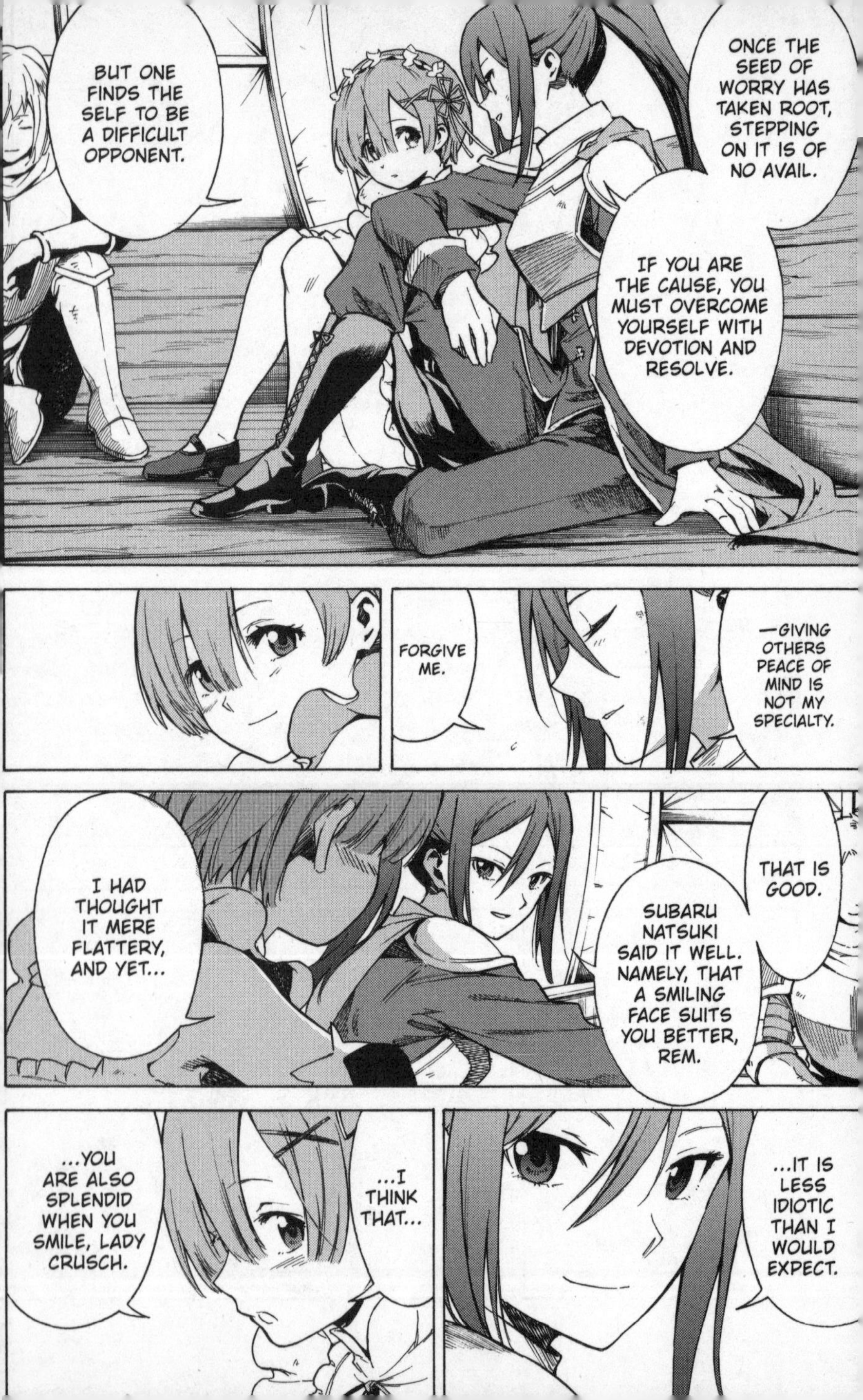
ONCE THE SEED OF WORRY HAS TAKEN ROOT, STEPPING ON IT IS OF NO AVAIL.
IF YOU ARE THE CAUSE, YOU MUST OVERCOME YOURSELF WITH DEVOTION AND RESOLVE.
BUT ONE FINDS THE SELF TO BE A DIFFICULT OPPONENT.
—GIVING OTHERS PEACE OF MIND IS NOT MY SPECIALTY.
FORGIVE ME.
THAT IS GOOD.
SUBARU NATSUKI SAID IT WELL. NAMELY, THAT A SMILING FACE SUITS YOU BETTER, REM.
I HAD THOUGHT IT MERE FLATTERY, AND YET...
...IT IS LESS IDIOTIC THAN I WOULD EXPECT.
...I THINK THAT...
...YOU ARE ALSO SPLENDID WHEN YOU SMILE, LADY CRUSCH.

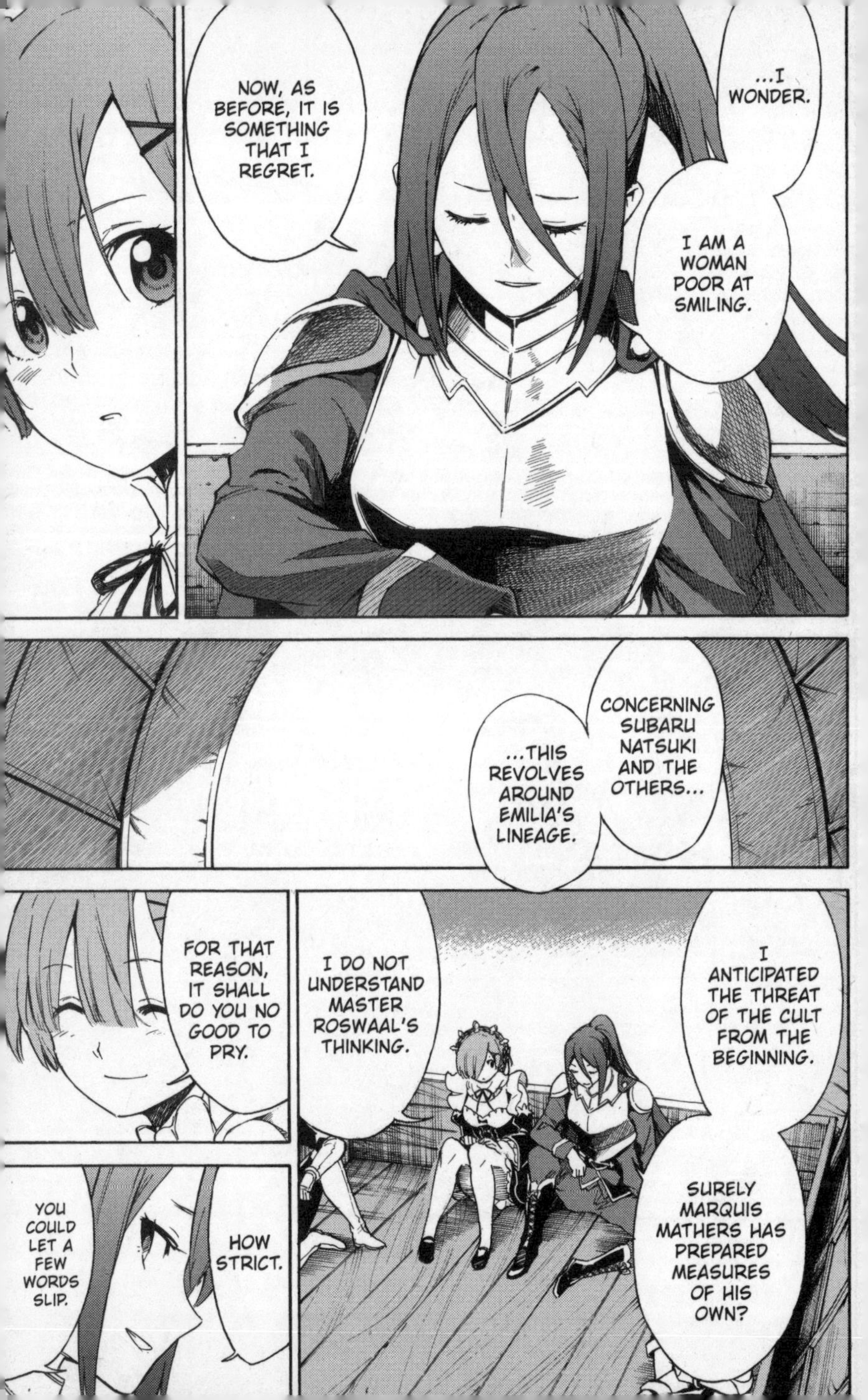
...I WONDER.
I AM A WOMAN POOR AT SMILING.
NOW, AS BEFORE, IT IS SOMETHING THAT I REGRET.
CONCERNING SUBARU NATSUKI AND THE OTHERS...
...THIS REVOLVES AROUND EMILIA'S LINEAGE.
I ANTICIPATED THE THREAT OF THE CULT FROM THE BEGINNING.
SURELY MARQUIS MATHERS HAS PREPARED MEASURES OF HIS OWN?
I DO NOT UNDERSTAND MASTER ROSWAAL'S THINKING.
FOR THAT REASON, IT SHALL DO YOU NO GOOD TO PRY.
HOW STRICT.
YOU COULD LET A FEW WORDS SLIP.

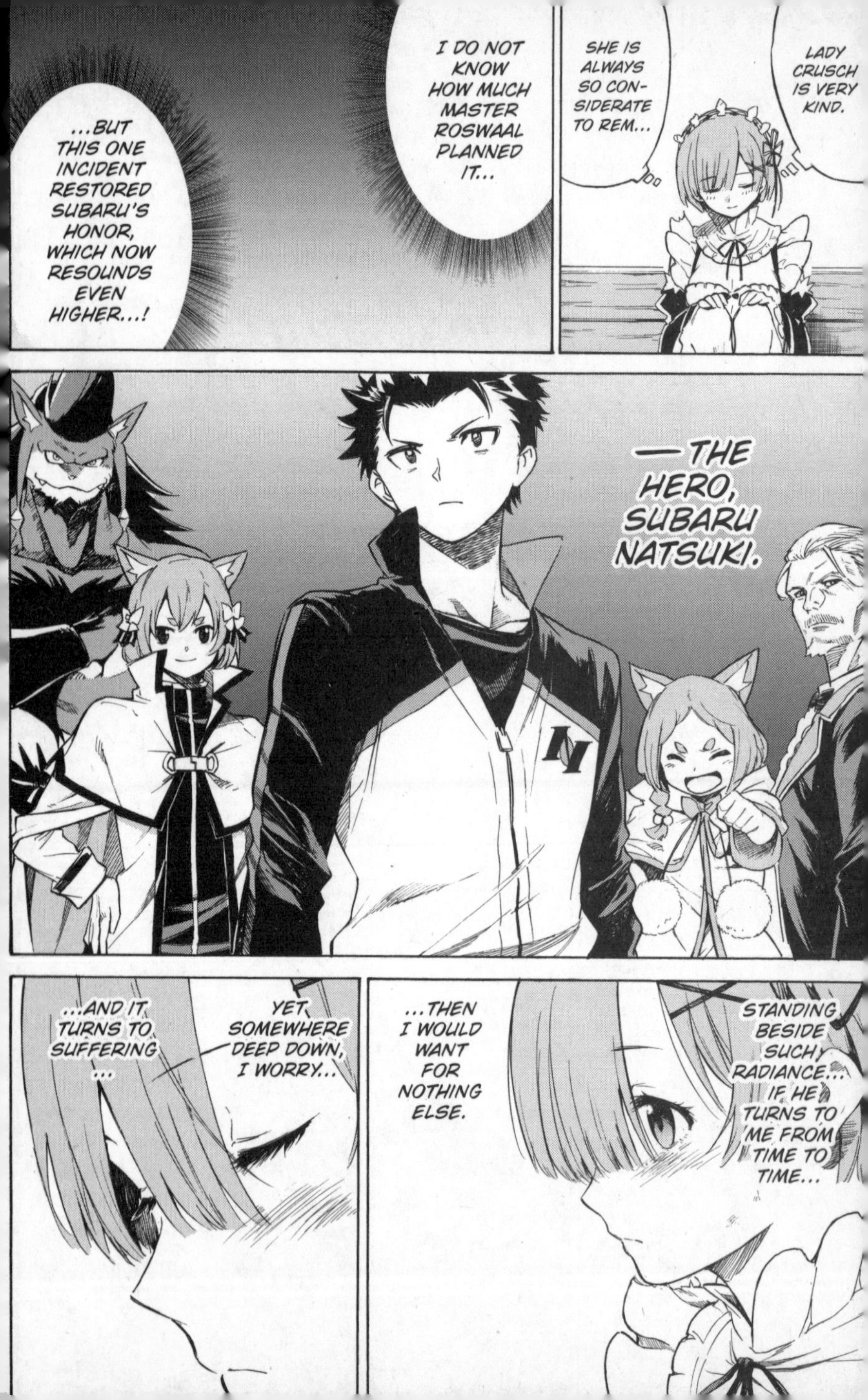
LADY CRUSCH IS VERY KIND.
SHE IS ALWAYS SO CONSIDERATE TO REM...
I DO NOT KNOW HOW MUCH MASTER ROSWAAL PLANNED IT...
...BUT THIS ONE INCIDENT RESTORED SUBARU'S HONOR, WHICH NOW RESOUNDS EVEN HIGHER...!
—THE HERO, SUBARU NATSUKI.
STANDING BESIDE SUCH RADIANCE... IF HE TURNS TO ME FROM TIME TO TIME...
...THEN I WOULD WANT FOR NOTHING ELSE.
YET SOMEWHERE DEEP DOWN, I WORRY...
...AND IT TURNS TO SUFFERING...

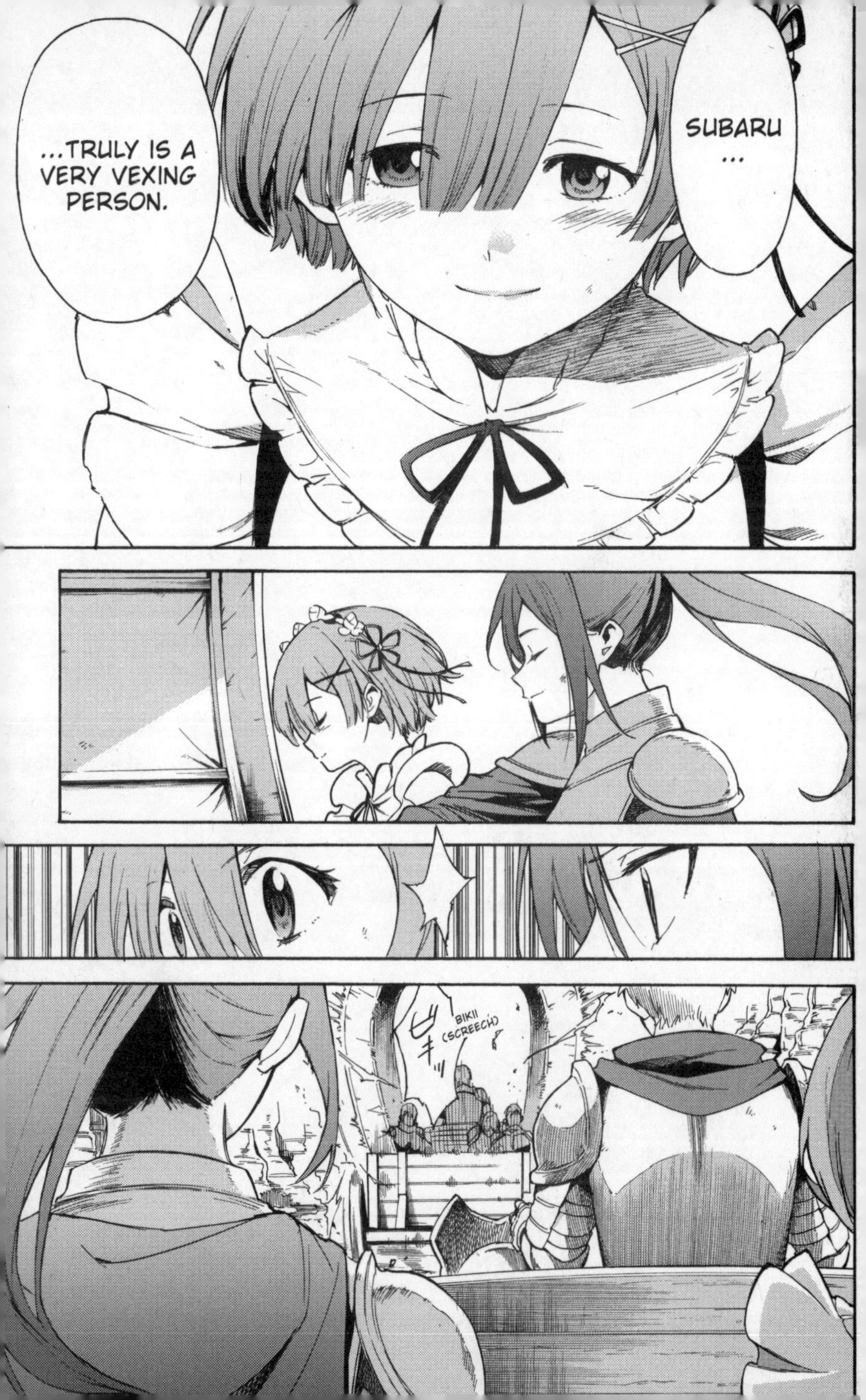
SUBARU ...
...TRULY IS A VERY VEXING PERSON.
BIKII (SCREECH)

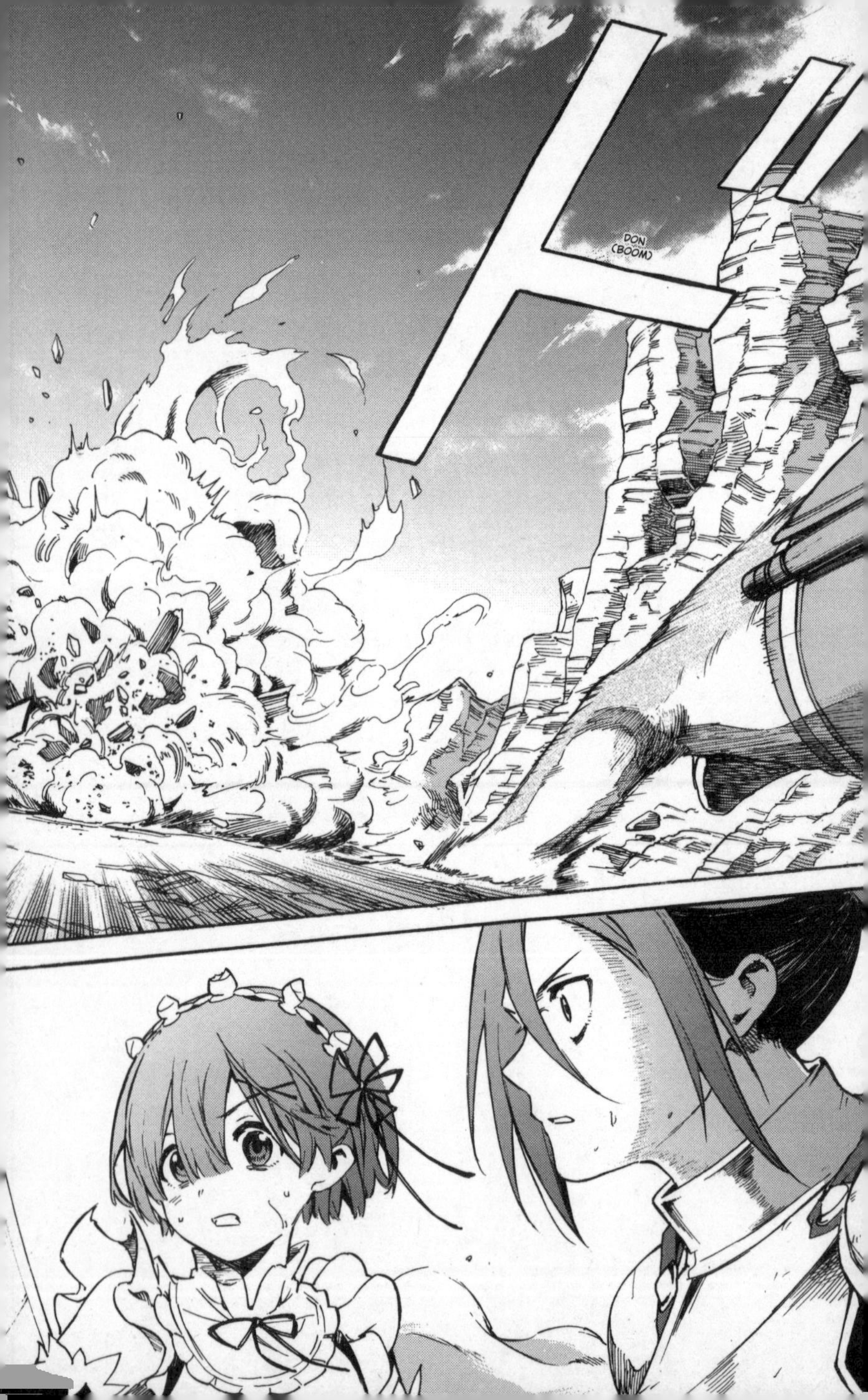
DON
(BOOM)

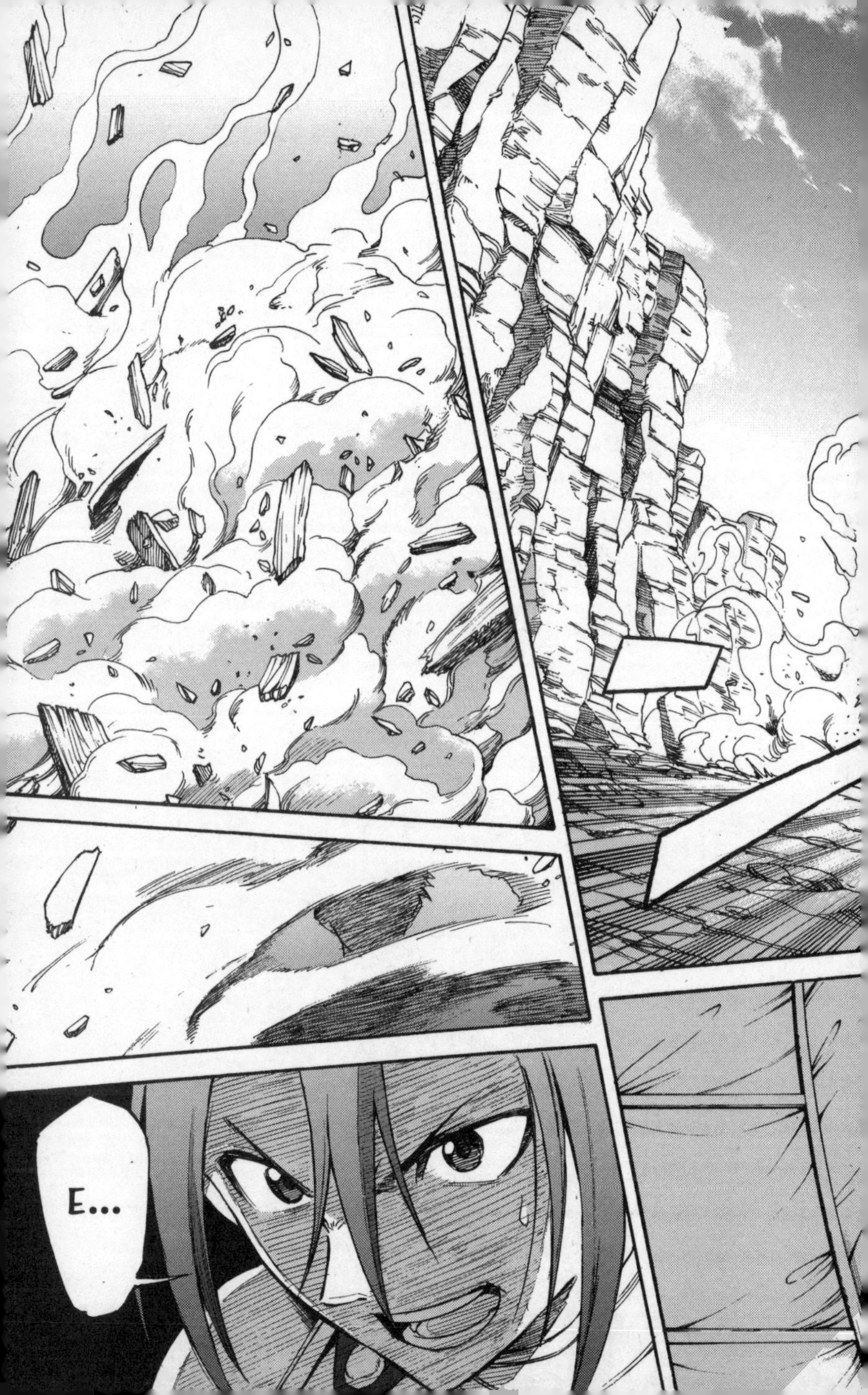
E...

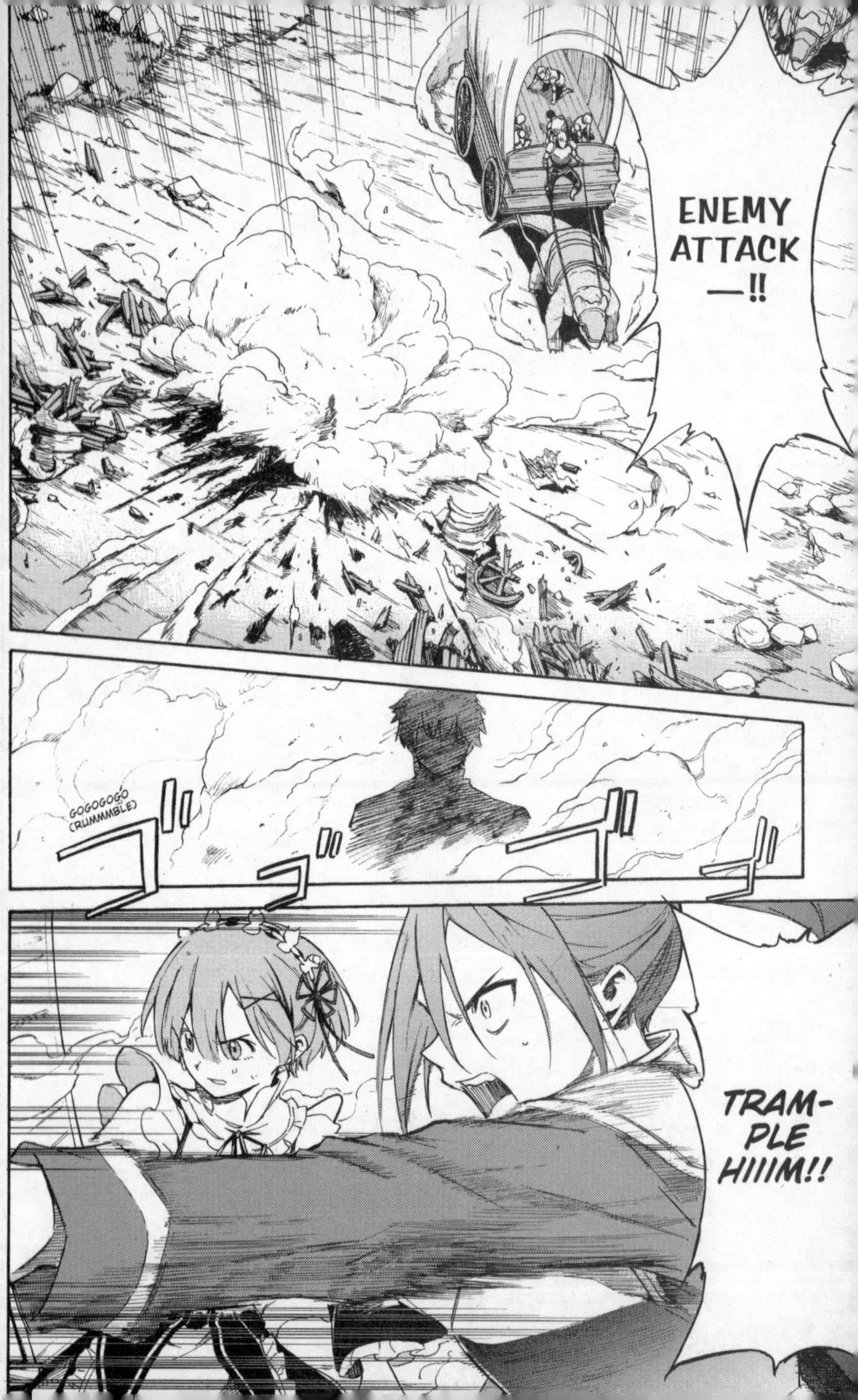
ENEMY ATTACK—!!
GOGOGOGO (RUMMMBLE)
TRAM-PLE HIIIM!!

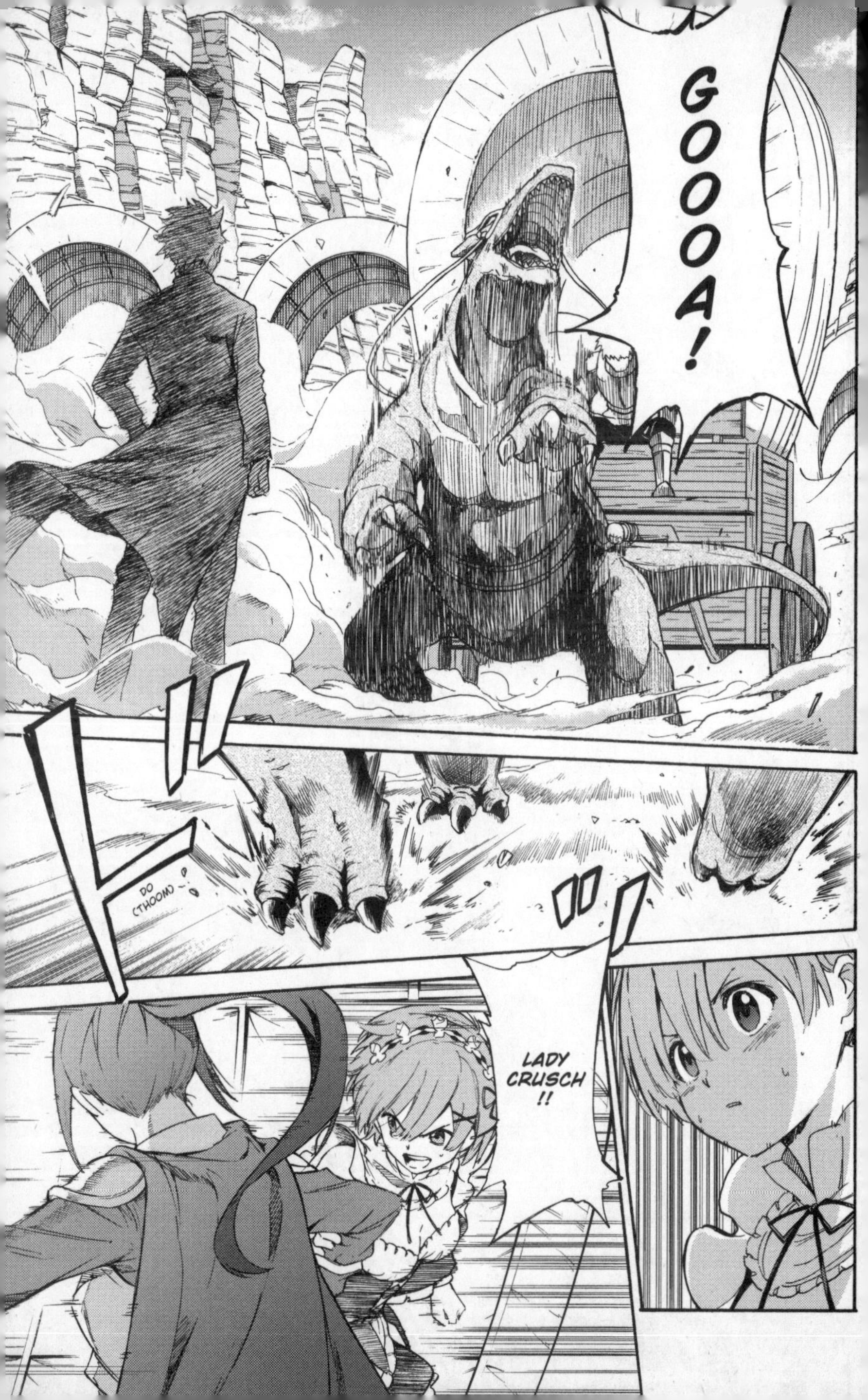
GOOOOA!
DO (THOOM)
LADY CRUSCH !!

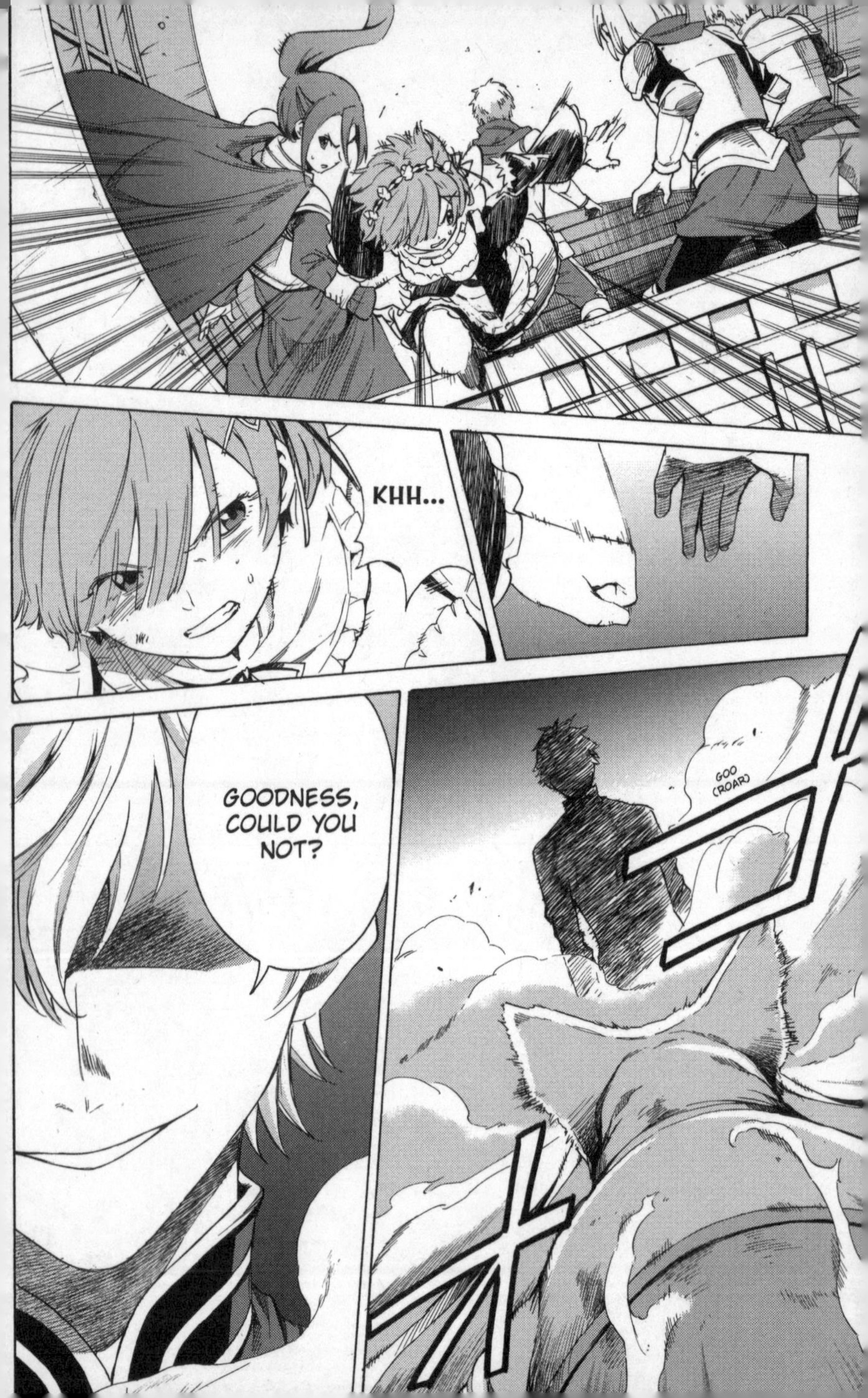
KHH...
GOO (ROAR)
GOODNESS, COULD YOU NOT?

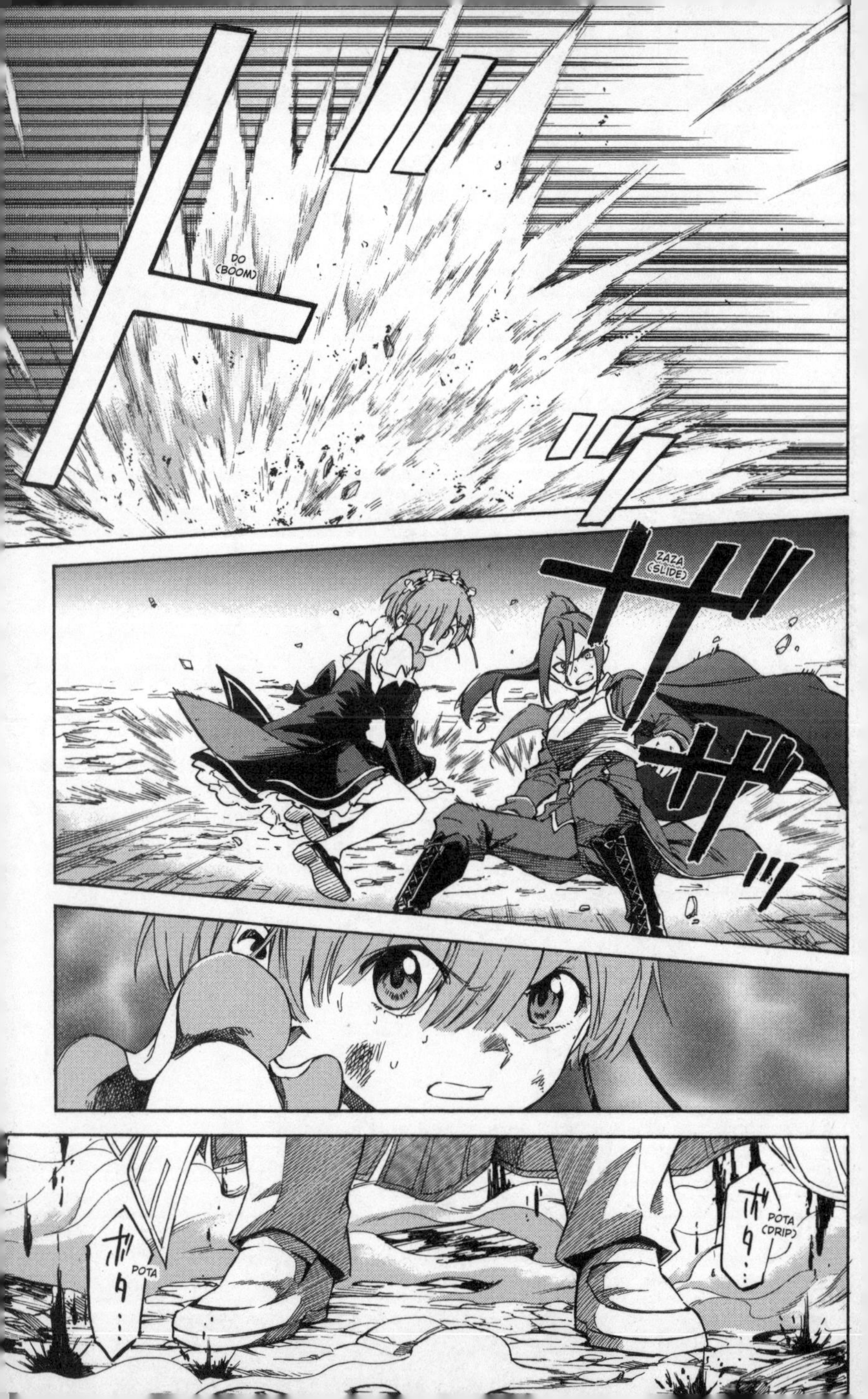
ドッ
DO
(BOOM)
ザザザッ
ZAZA
(SLIDE)
ボタ…
POTA
(DRIP)
ボタ…
POTA

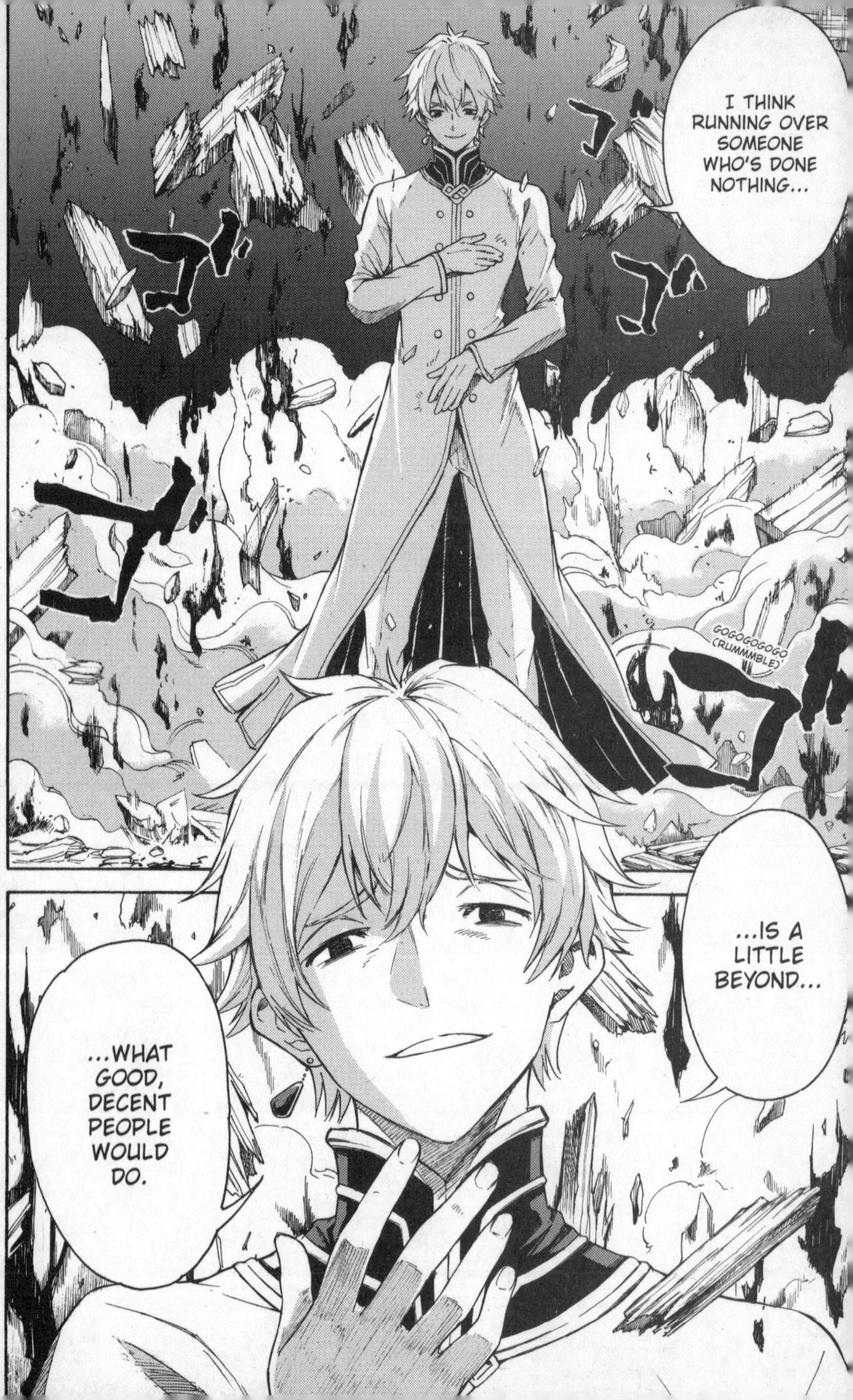
I THINK RUNNING OVER SOMEONE WHO'S DONE NOTHING...
GOGOGOGOGO (RUMMMBLE)
...IS A LITTLE BEYOND...
...WHAT GOOD, DECENT PEOPLE WOULD DO.

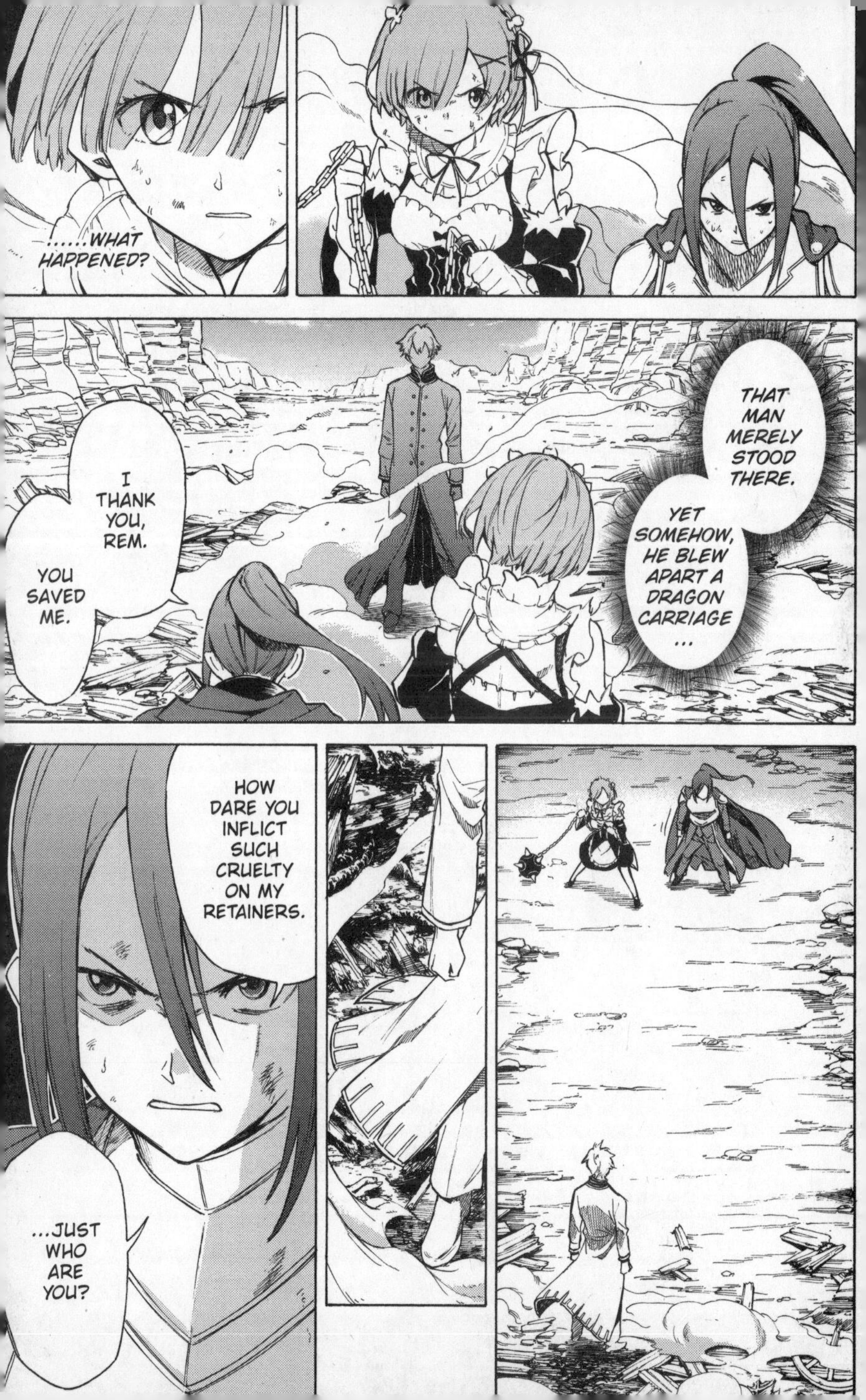
......WHAT HAPPENED?
THAT MAN MERELY STOOD THERE.
YET SOMEHOW, HE BLEW APART A DRAGON CARRIAGE ...
I THANK YOU, REM.
YOU SAVED ME.
HOW DARE YOU INFLICT SUCH CRUELTY ON MY RETAINERS.
...JUST WHO ARE YOU?

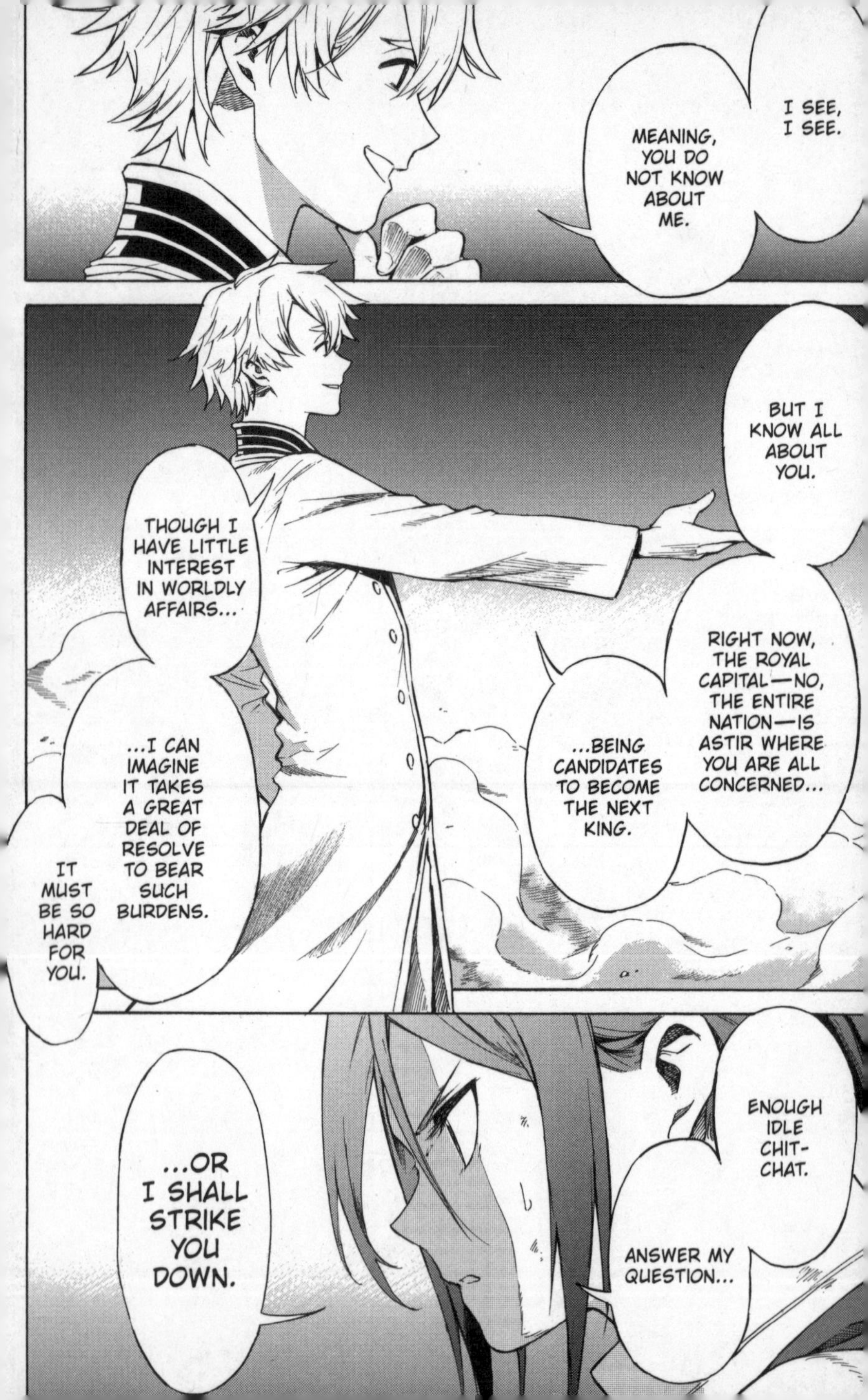
I SEE, I SEE.
MEANING, YOU DO NOT KNOW ABOUT ME.
BUT I KNOW ALL ABOUT YOU.
RIGHT NOW, THE ROYAL CAPITAL—NO, THE ENTIRE NATION—IS ASTIR WHERE YOU ARE ALL CONCERNED...
...BEING CANDIDATES TO BECOME THE NEXT KING.
THOUGH I HAVE LITTLE INTEREST IN WORLDLY AFFAIRS...
...I CAN IMAGINE IT TAKES A GREAT DEAL OF RESOLVE TO BEAR SUCH BURDENS.
IT MUST BE SO HARD FOR YOU.
ENOUGH IDLE CHIT-CHAT.
ANSWER MY QUESTION...
...OR I SHALL STRIKE YOU DOWN.

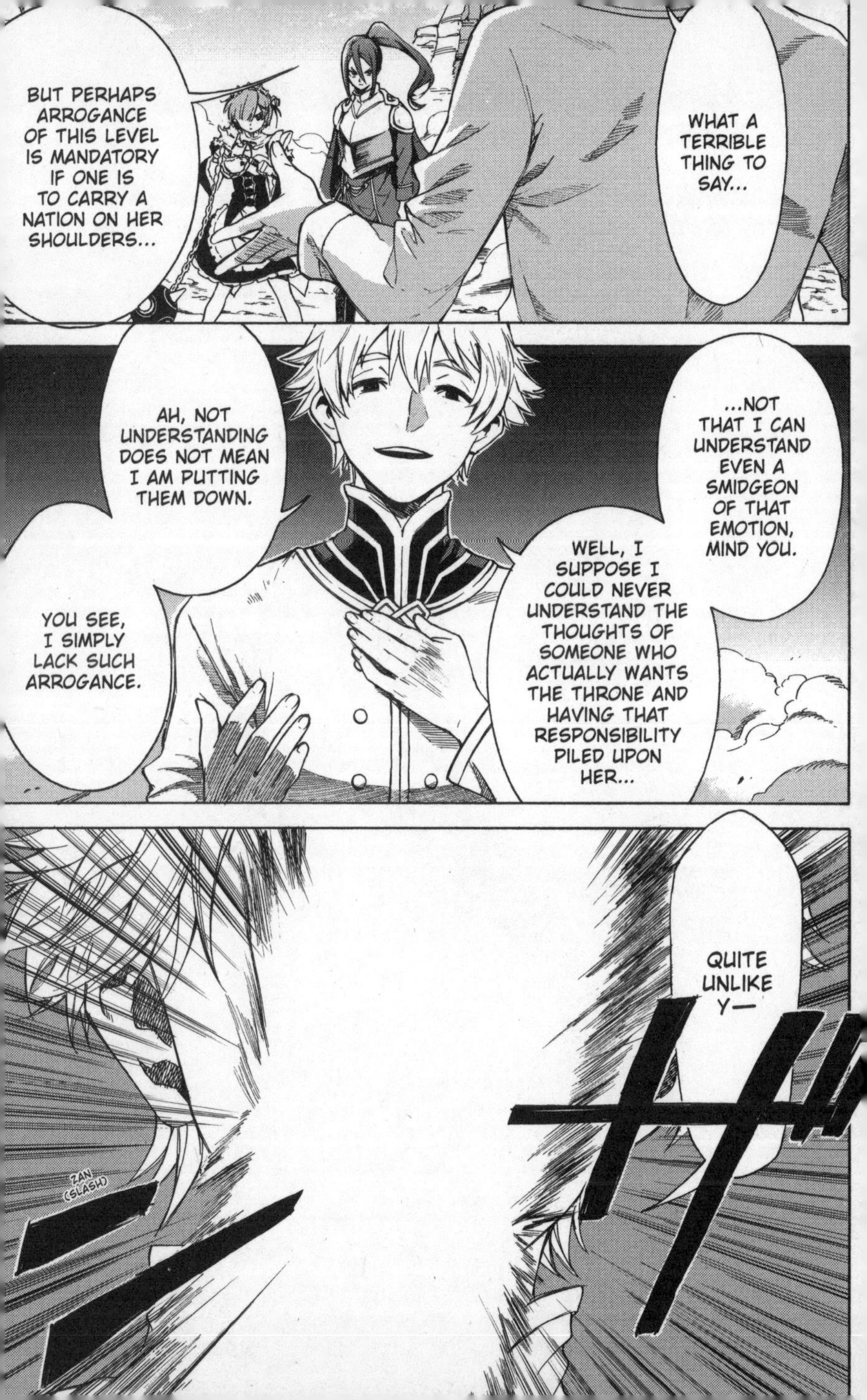
WHAT A TERRIBLE THING TO SAY...
BUT PERHAPS ARROGANCE OF THIS LEVEL IS MANDATORY IF ONE IS TO CARRY A NATION ON HER SHOULDERS...
...NOT THAT I CAN UNDERSTAND EVEN A SMIDGEON OF THAT EMOTION, MIND YOU.
WELL, I SUPPOSE I COULD NEVER UNDERSTAND THE THOUGHTS OF SOMEONE WHO ACTUALLY WANTS THE THRONE AND HAVING THAT RESPONSIBILITY PILED UPON HER...
AH, NOT UNDERSTANDING DOES NOT MEAN I AM PUTTING THEM DOWN.
YOU SEE, I SIMPLY LACK SUCH ARROGANCE.
QUITE UNLIKE Y—
ZAN (SLASH)

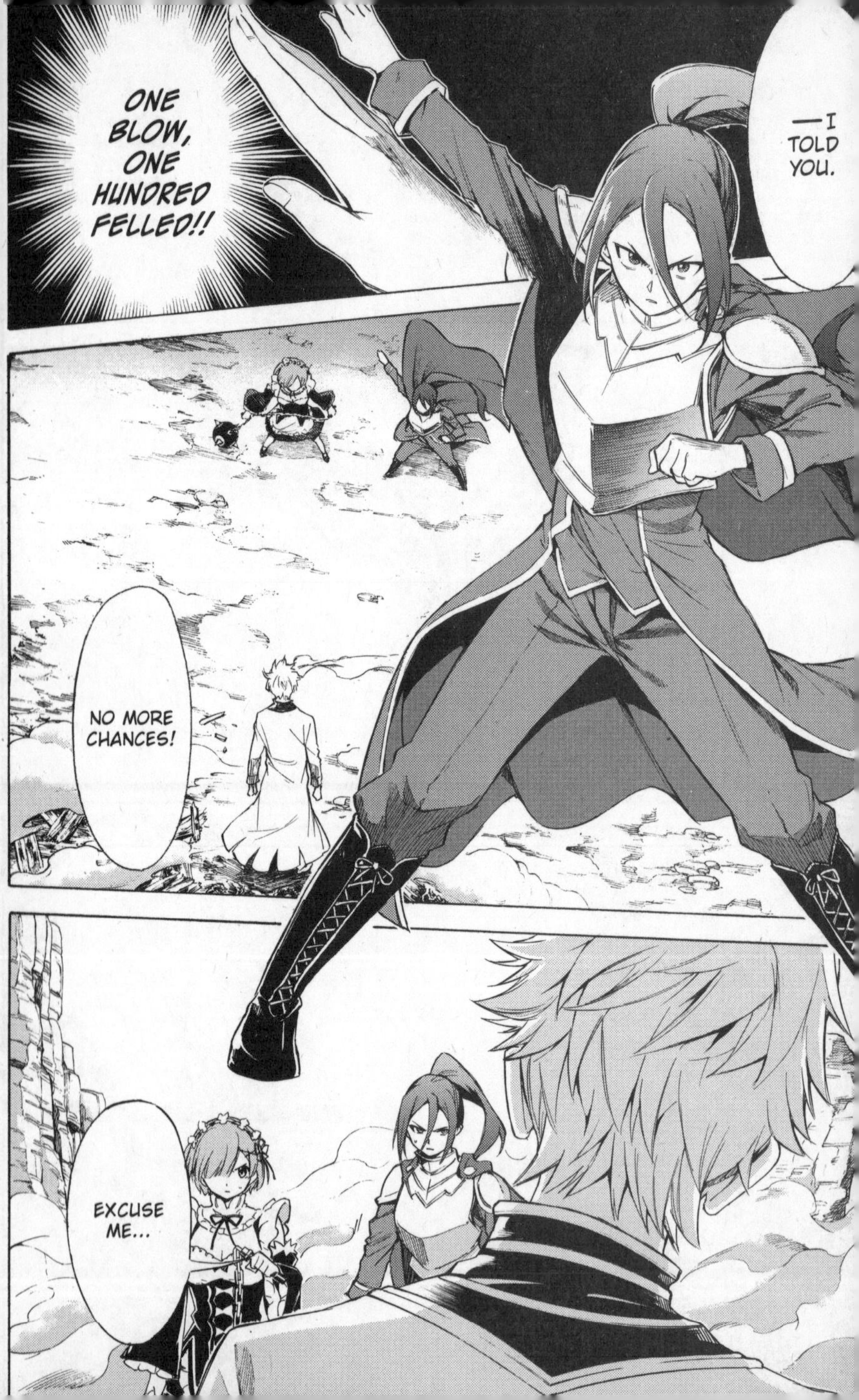
—I TOLD YOU.
ONE BLOW, ONE HUNDRED FELLED!!
NO MORE CHANCES!
EXCUSE ME...

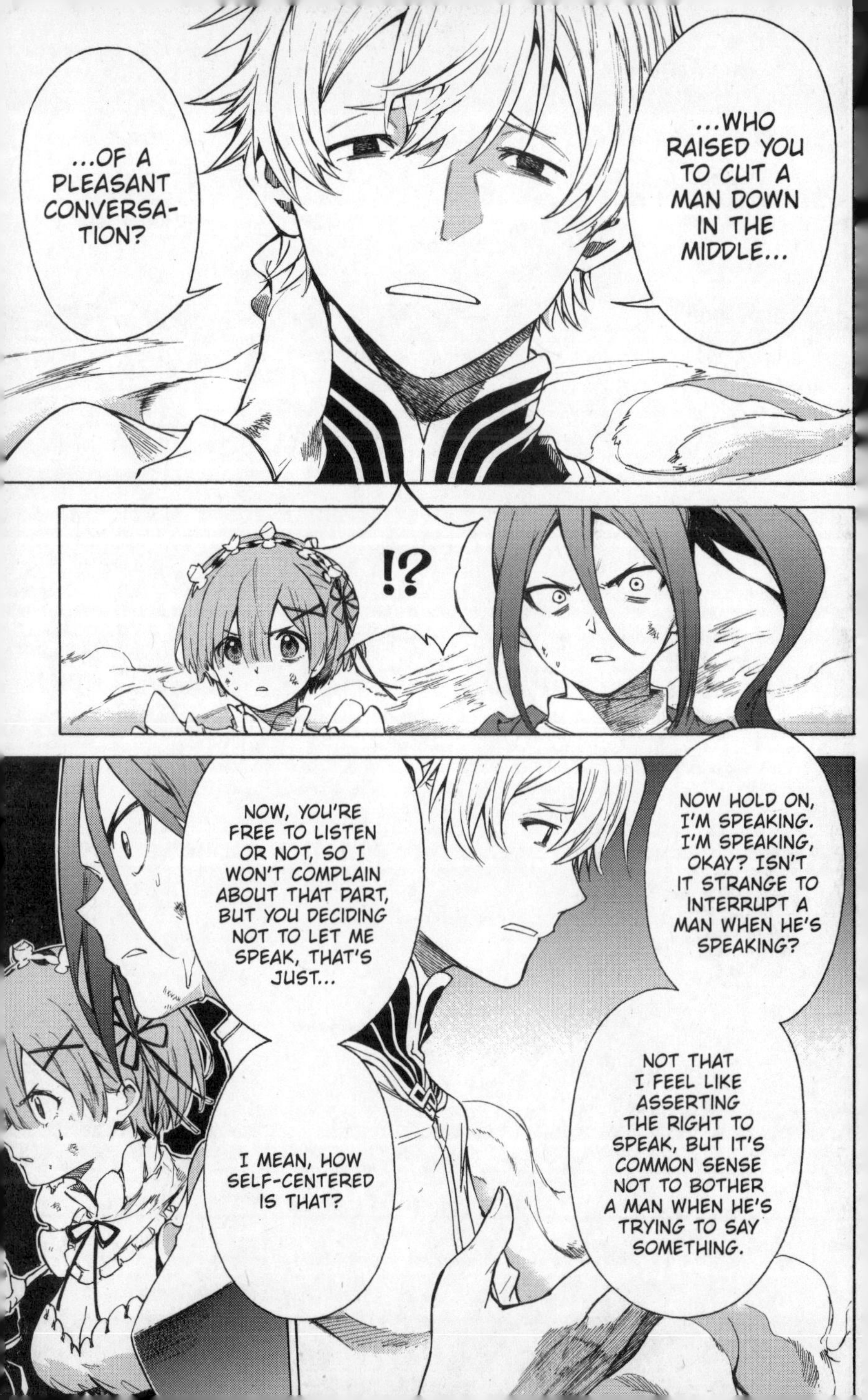
...WHO RAISED YOU TO CUT A MAN DOWN IN THE MIDDLE...
...OF A PLEASANT CONVERSA-TION?
!?
NOW HOLD ON, I'M SPEAKING. I'M SPEAKING, OKAY? ISN'T IT STRANGE TO INTERRUPT A MAN WHEN HE'S SPEAKING?
NOW, YOU'RE FREE TO LISTEN OR NOT, SO I WON'T COMPLAIN ABOUT THAT PART, BUT YOU DECIDING NOT TO LET ME SPEAK, THAT'S JUST...
NOT THAT I FEEL LIKE ASSERTING THE RIGHT TO SPEAK, BUT IT'S COMMON SENSE NOT TO BOTHER A MAN WHEN HE'S TRYING TO SAY SOMETHING.
I MEAN, HOW SELF-CENTERED IS THAT?

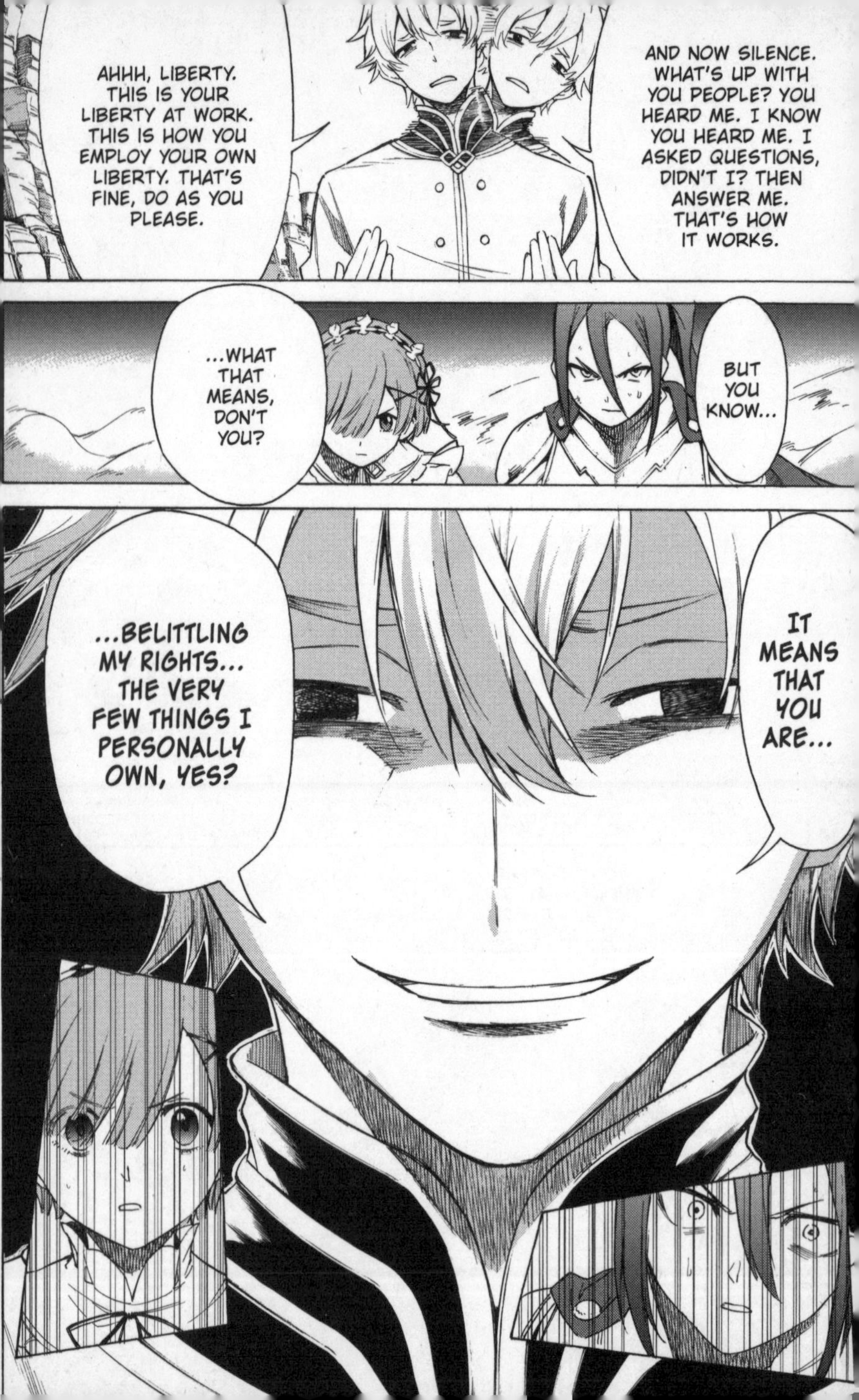
AND NOW SILENCE. WHAT'S UP WITH YOU PEOPLE? YOU HEARD ME. I KNOW YOU HEARD ME. I ASKED QUESTIONS, DIDN'T I? THEN ANSWER ME. THAT'S HOW IT WORKS.
AHHH, LIBERTY. THIS IS YOUR LIBERTY AT WORK. THIS IS HOW YOU EMPLOY YOUR OWN LIBERTY. THAT'S FINE, DO AS YOU PLEASE.
BUT YOU KNOW...
...WHAT THAT MEANS, DON'T YOU?
IT MEANS THAT YOU ARE...
...BELITTLING MY RIGHTS... THE VERY FEW THINGS I PERSONALLY OWN, YES?

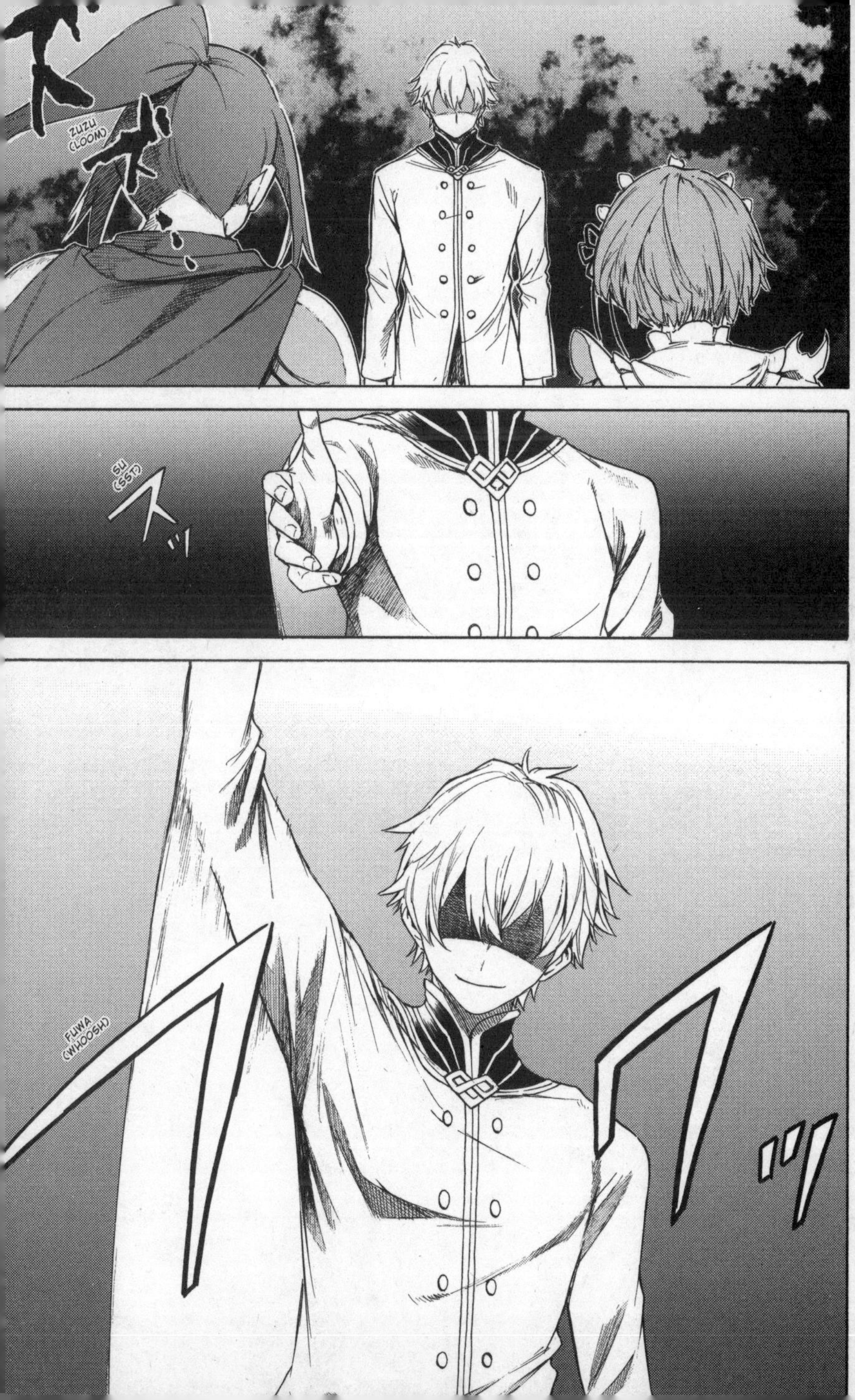
ZUZU (LOOM)
SU (SST)
FUWA (WHOOSH)

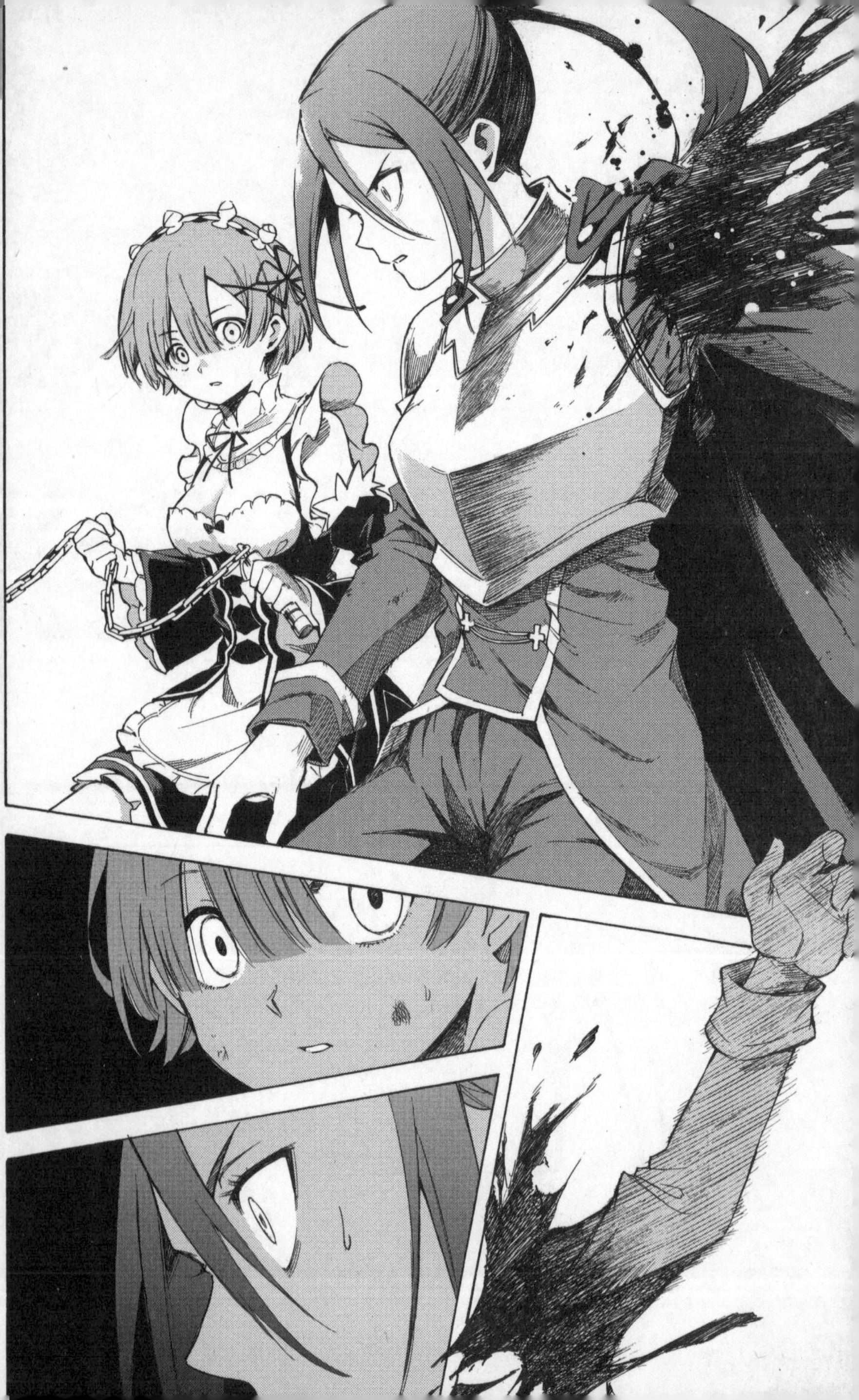

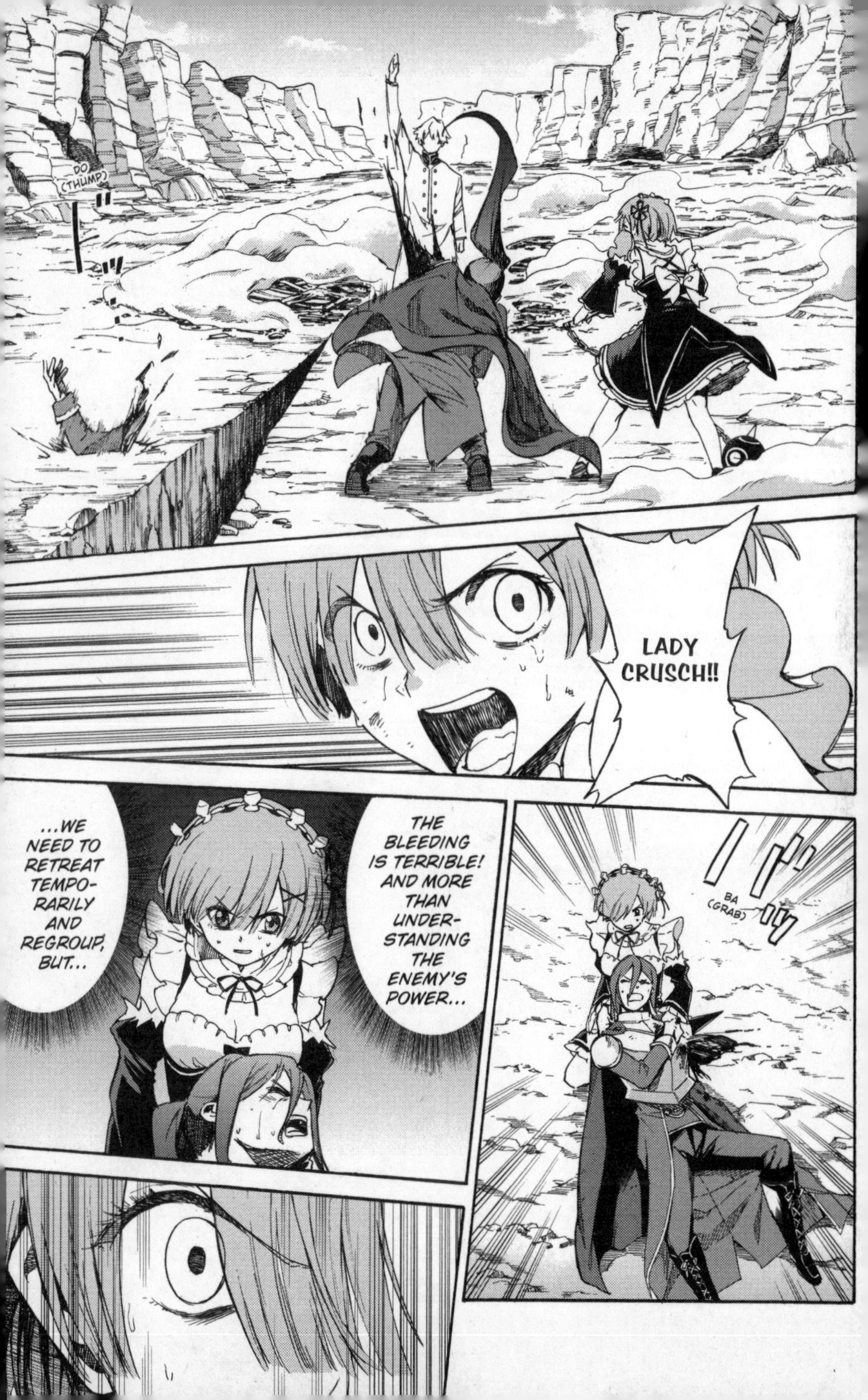
DO (THUMP)
LADY CRUSCH!!
BA (GRAB)
THE BLEEDING IS TERRIBLE! AND MORE THAN UNDER-STANDING THE ENEMY'S POWER...
...WE NEED TO RETREAT TEMPO-RARILY AND REGROUP, BUT...

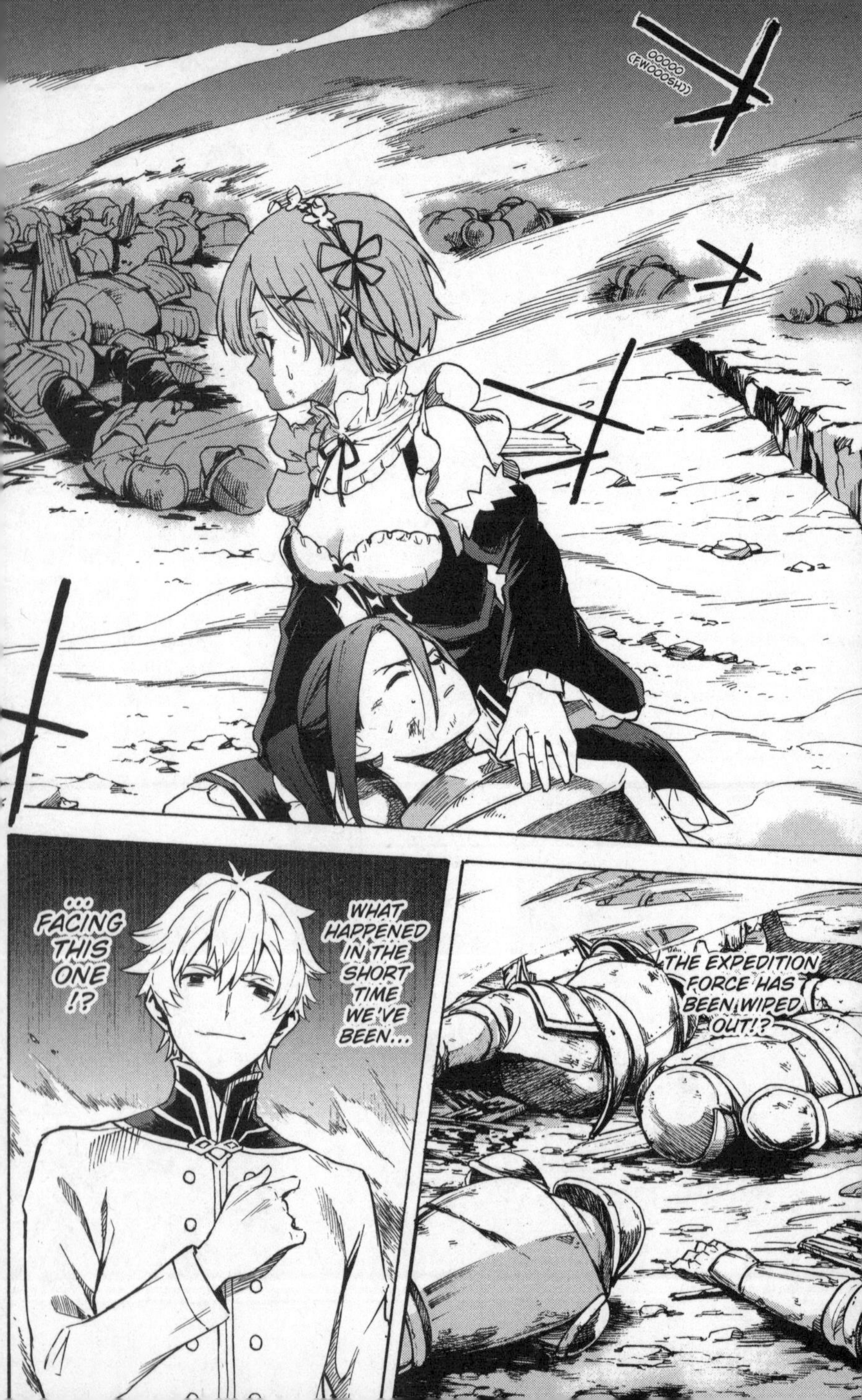
OOOOO
(FWOOOSH)
THE EXPEDITION FORCE HAS BEEN WIPED OUT!?
WHAT HAPPENED IN THE SHORT TIME WE'VE BEEN...
...FACING THIS ONE!?

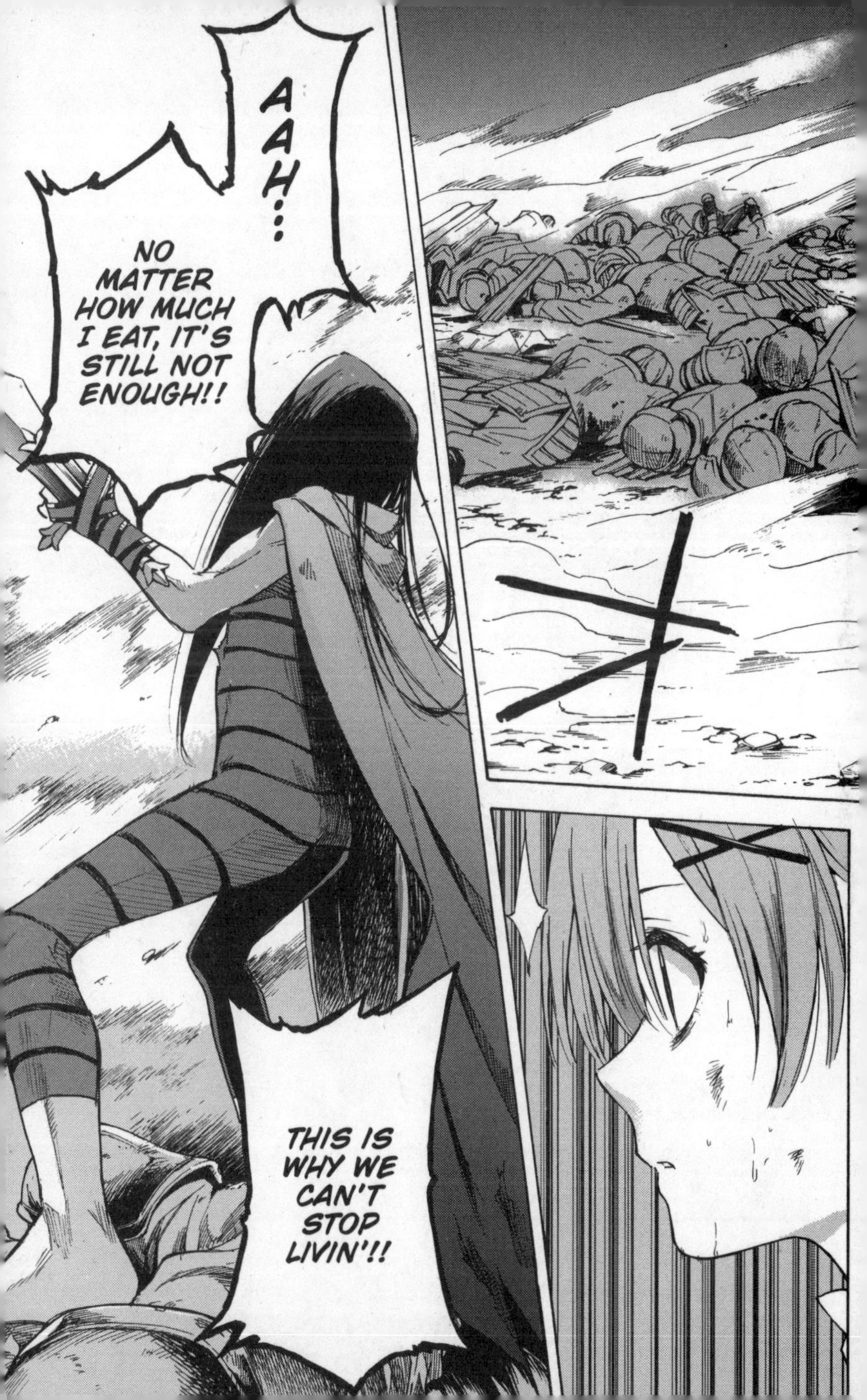
AAH...
NO MATTER HOW MUCH I EAT, IT'S STILL NOT ENOUGH!!
THIS IS WHY WE CAN'T STOP LIVIN'!!

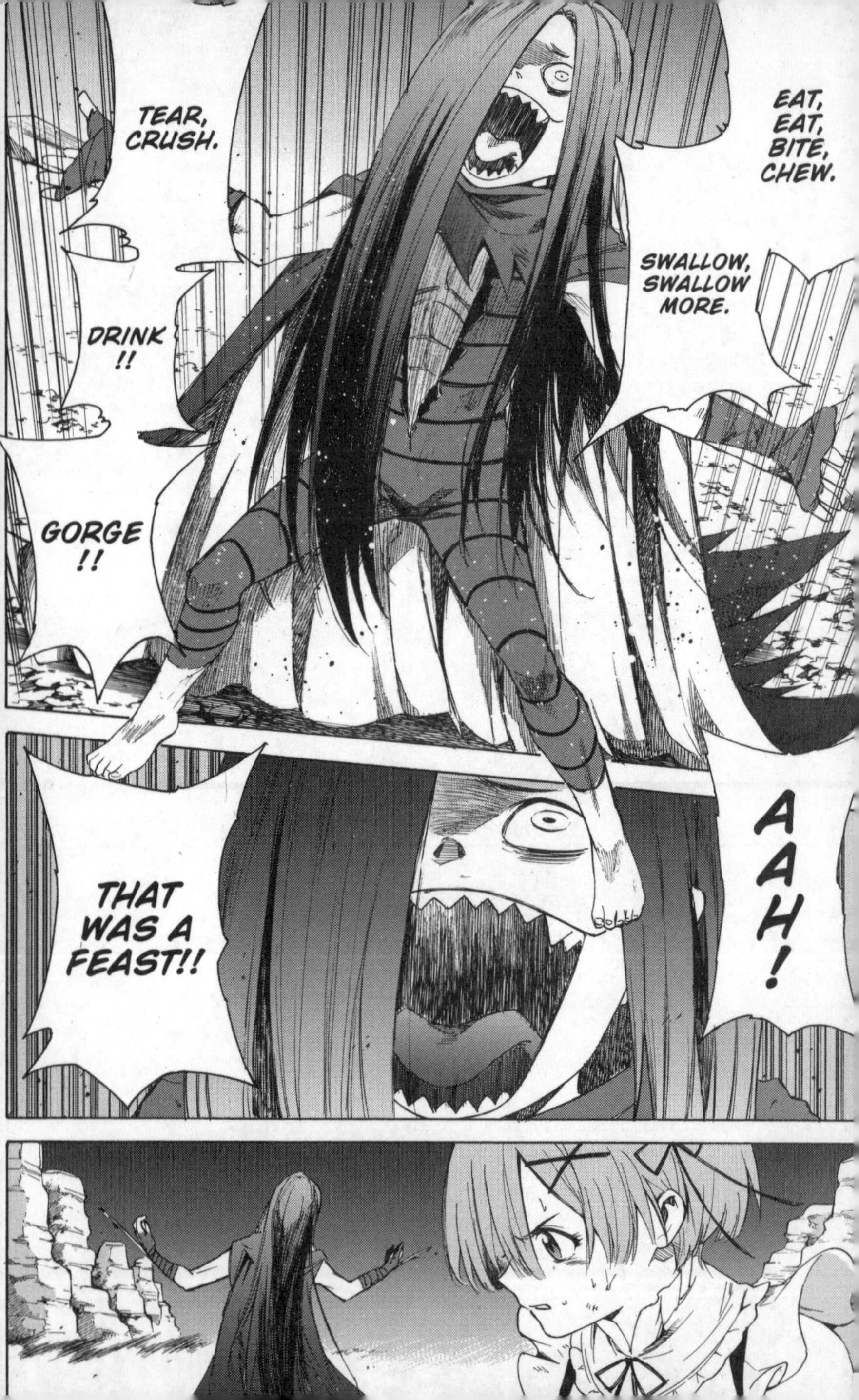
EAT, EAT, BITE, CHEW.
SWALLOW, SWALLOW MORE.
TEAR, CRUSH.
DRINK!!
GORGE!!
AAAH!
THAT WAS A FEAST!!

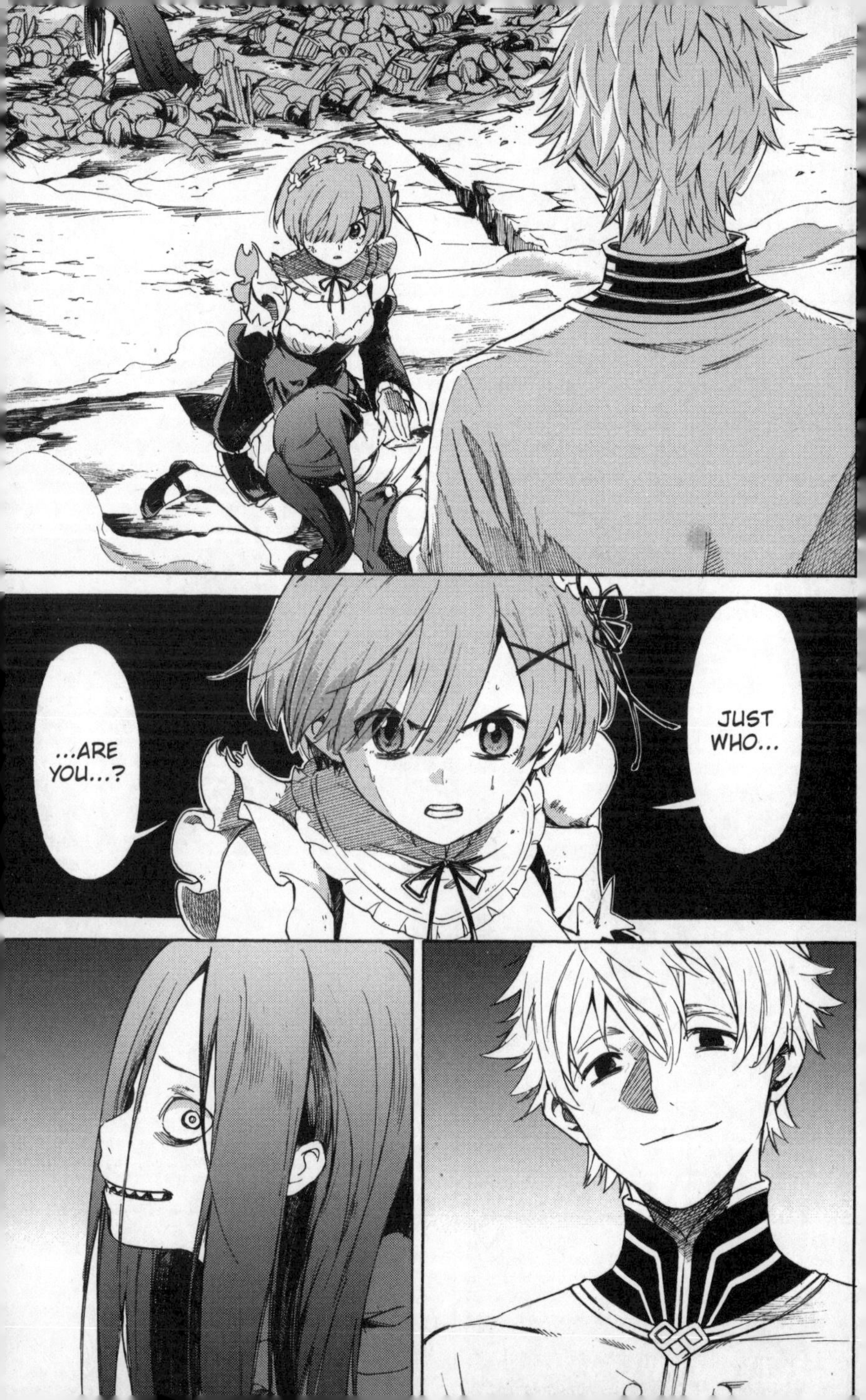
JUST WHO...
...ARE YOU...?

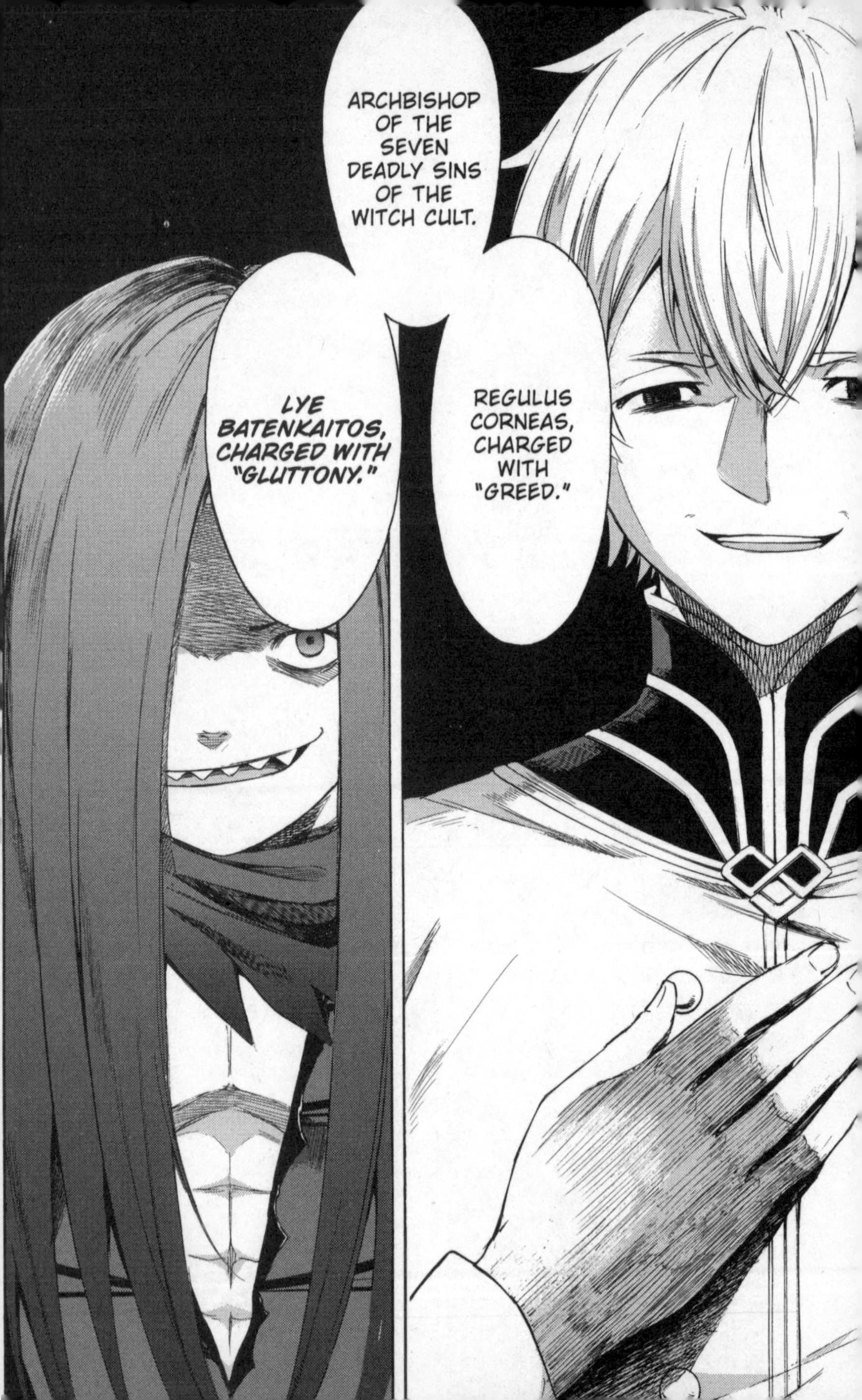
ARCHBISHOP OF THE SEVEN DEADLY SINS OF THE WITCH CULT.
REGULUS CORNEAS, CHARGED WITH "GREED."
LYE BATENKAITOS, CHARGED WITH "GLUTTONY."

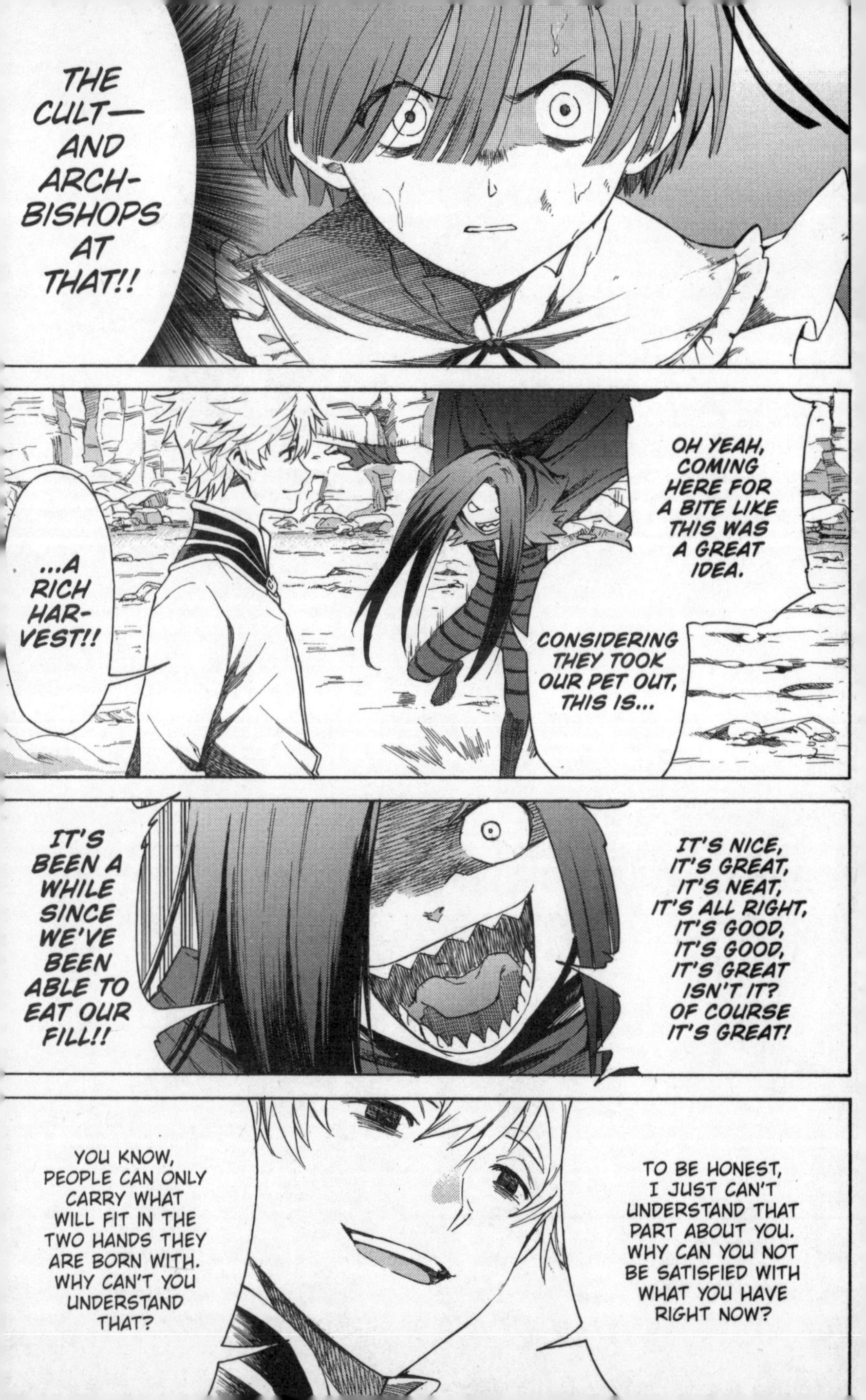
THE CULT— AND ARCH-BISHOPS AT THAT!!
OH YEAH, COMING HERE FOR A BITE LIKE THIS WAS A GREAT IDEA.
CONSIDERING THEY TOOK OUR PET OUT, THIS IS...
...A RICH HAR-VEST!!
IT'S NICE, IT'S GREAT, IT'S NEAT, IT'S ALL RIGHT, IT'S GOOD, IT'S GOOD, IT'S GREAT ISN'T IT? OF COURSE IT'S GREAT!
IT'S BEEN A WHILE SINCE WE'VE BEEN ABLE TO EAT OUR FILL!!
TO BE HONEST, I JUST CAN'T UNDERSTAND THAT PART ABOUT YOU. WHY CAN YOU NOT BE SATISFIED WITH WHAT YOU HAVE RIGHT NOW?
YOU KNOW, PEOPLE CAN ONLY CARRY WHAT WILL FIT IN THE TWO HANDS THEY ARE BORN WITH. WHY CAN'T YOU UNDERSTAND THAT?

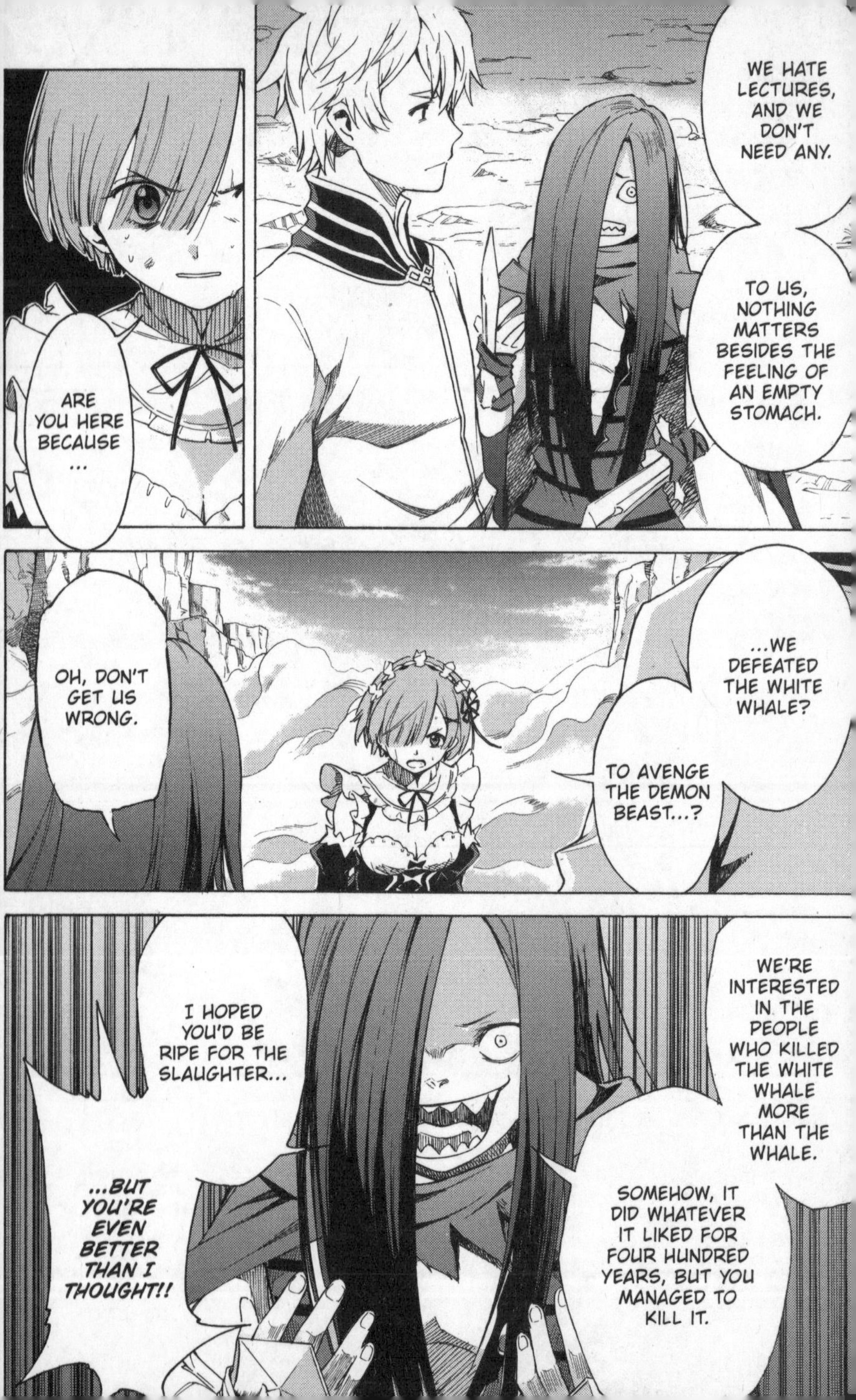
WE HATE LECTURES, AND WE DON'T NEED ANY.
TO US, NOTHING MATTERS BESIDES THE FEELING OF AN EMPTY STOMACH.
ARE YOU HERE BECAUSE ...
...WE DEFEATED THE WHITE WHALE?
TO AVENGE THE DEMON BEAST...?
OH, DON'T GET US WRONG.
WE'RE INTERESTED IN THE PEOPLE WHO KILLED THE WHITE WHALE MORE THAN THE WHALE.
SOMEHOW, IT DID WHATEVER IT LIKED FOR FOUR HUNDRED YEARS, BUT YOU MANAGED TO KILL IT.
I HOPED YOU'D BE RIPE FOR THE SLAUGHTER...
...BUT YOU'RE EVEN BETTER THAN I THOUGHT!!

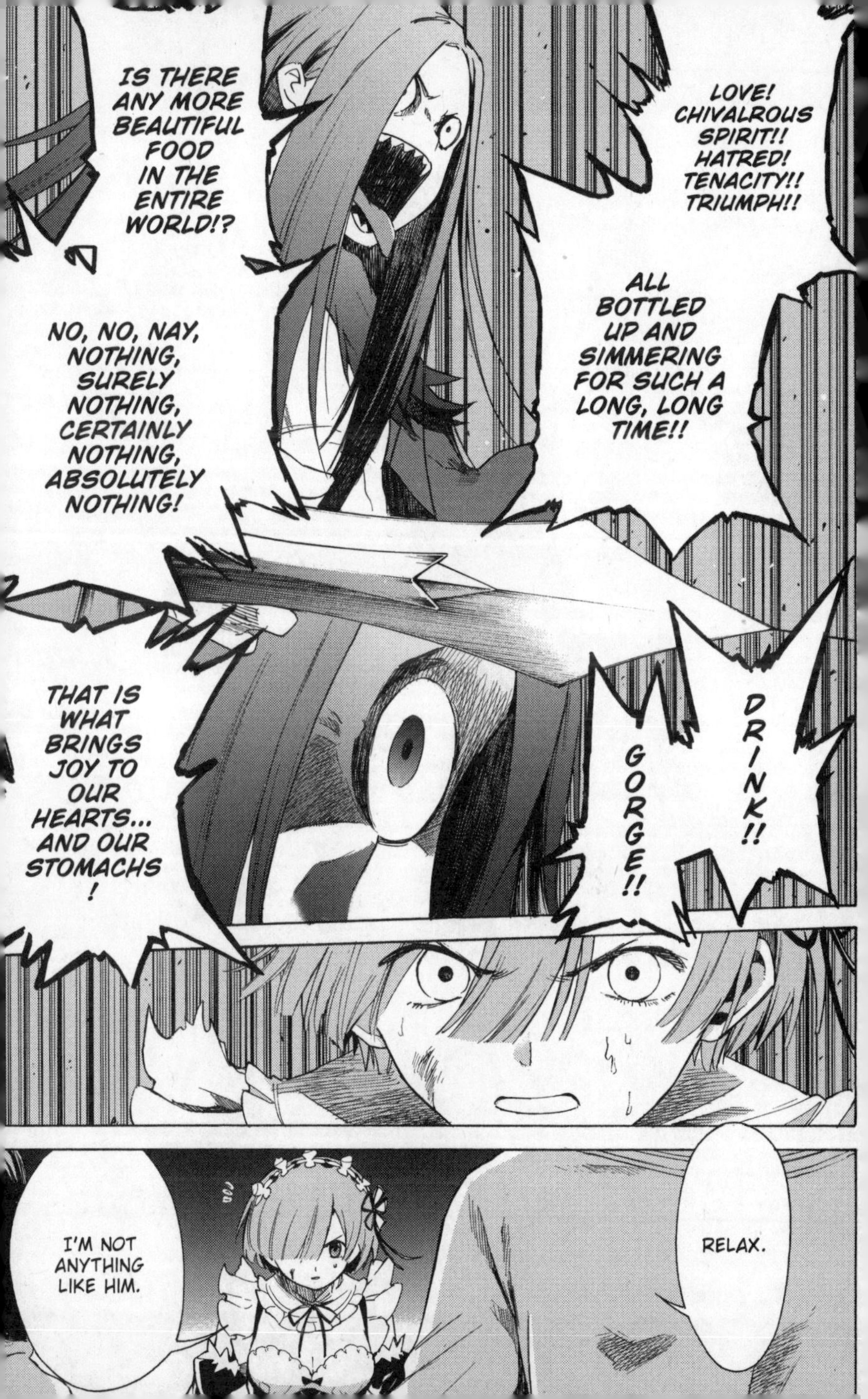
LOVE! CHIVALROUS SPIRIT!! HATRED! TENACITY!! TRIUMPH!!
ALL BOTTLED UP AND SIMMERING FOR SUCH A LONG, LONG TIME!!
IS THERE ANY MORE BEAUTIFUL FOOD IN THE ENTIRE WORLD!?
NO, NO, NAY, NOTHING, SURELY NOTHING, CERTAINLY NOTHING, ABSOLUTELY NOTHING!
DRINK!!
GORGE!!
THAT IS WHAT BRINGS JOY TO OUR HEARTS... AND OUR STOMACHS!
RELAX.
I'M NOT ANYTHING LIKE HIM.

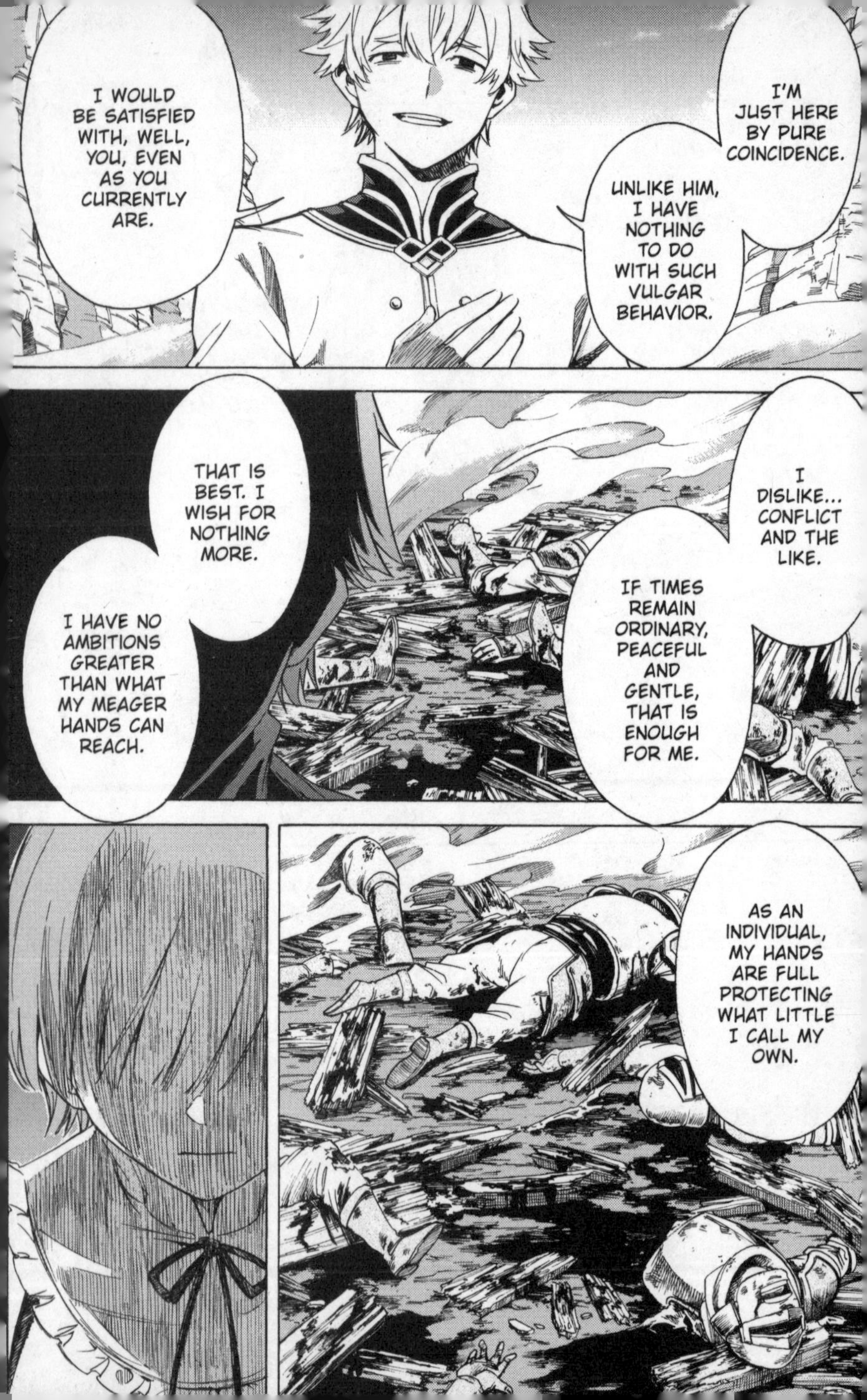
I'M JUST HERE BY PURE COINCIDENCE.
UNLIKE HIM, I HAVE NOTHING TO DO WITH SUCH VULGAR BEHAVIOR.
I WOULD BE SATISFIED WITH, WELL, YOU, EVEN AS YOU CURRENTLY ARE.
I DISLIKE... CONFLICT AND THE LIKE.
IF TIMES REMAIN ORDINARY, PEACEFUL AND GENTLE, THAT IS ENOUGH FOR ME.
THAT IS BEST. I WISH FOR NOTHING MORE.
I HAVE NO AMBITIONS GREATER THAN WHAT MY MEAGER HANDS CAN REACH.
AS AN INDIVIDUAL, MY HANDS ARE FULL PROTECTING WHAT LITTLE I CALL MY OWN.

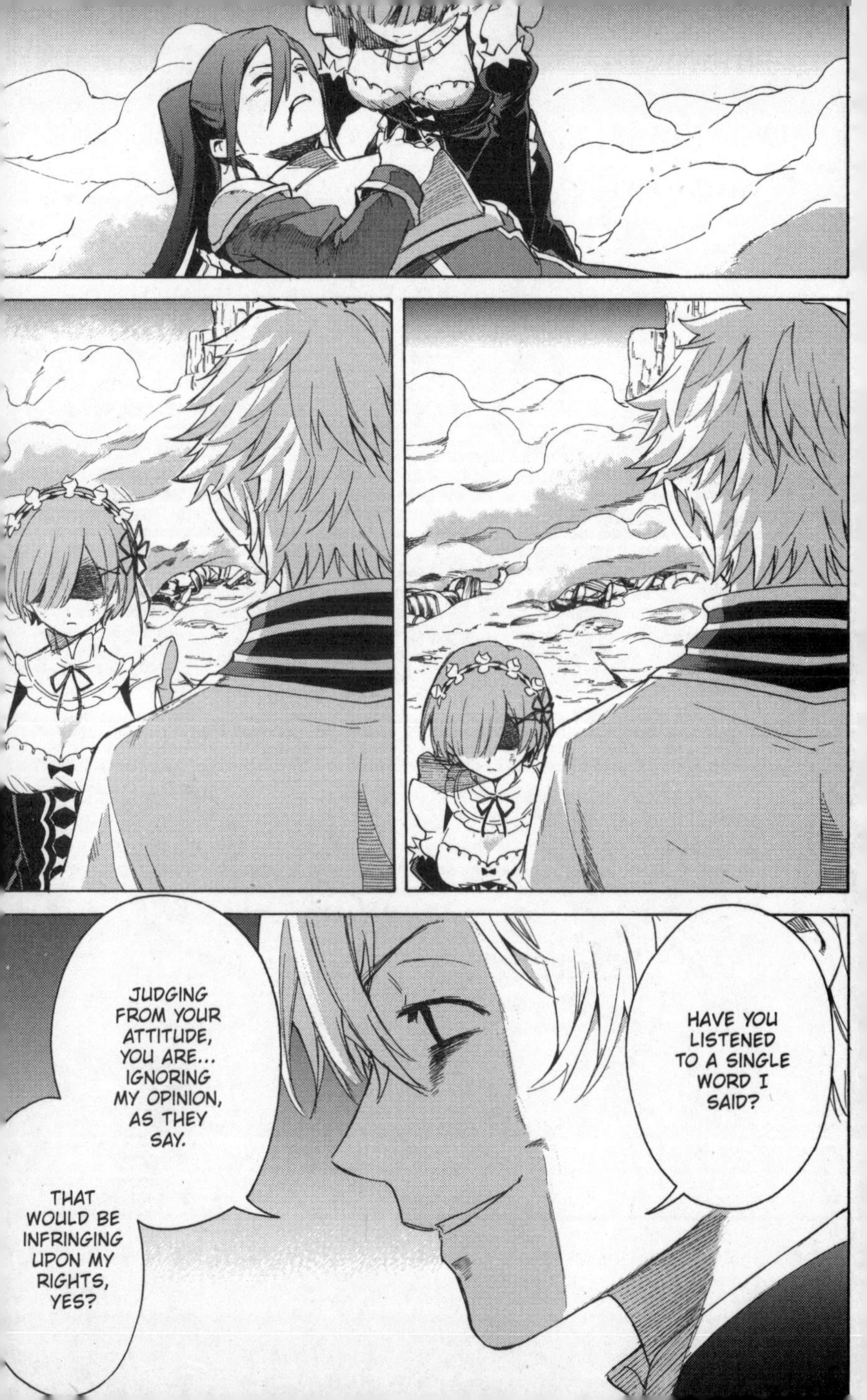
HAVE YOU LISTENED TO A SINGLE WORD I SAID?
JUDGING FROM YOUR ATTITUDE, YOU ARE... IGNORING MY OPINION, AS THEY SAY.
THAT WOULD BE INFRINGING UPON MY RIGHTS, YES?

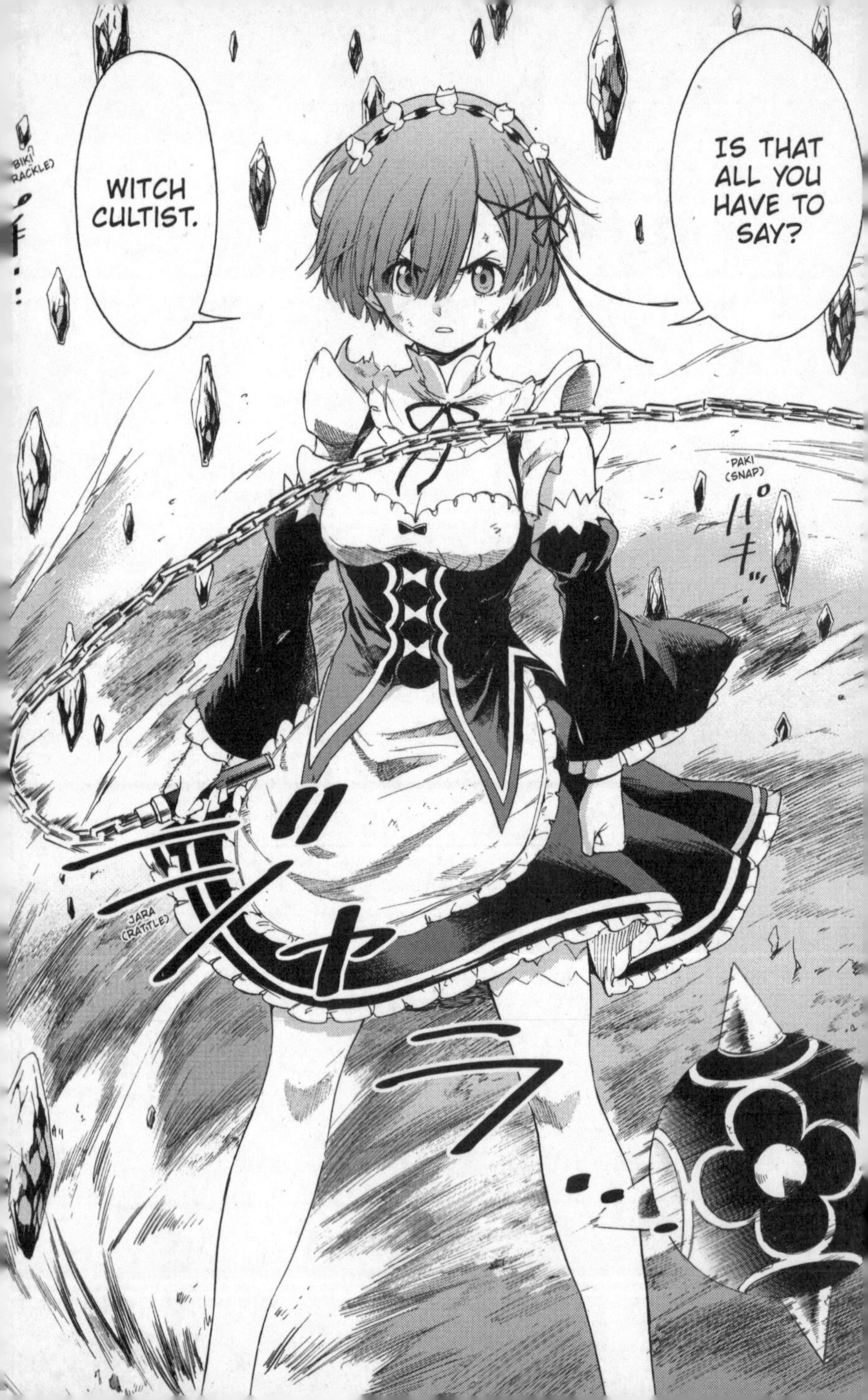
IS THAT ALL YOU HAVE TO SAY?
WITCH CULTIST.
BIKI
RACKLE)
PAKI (SNAP)
JARA (RATTLE)

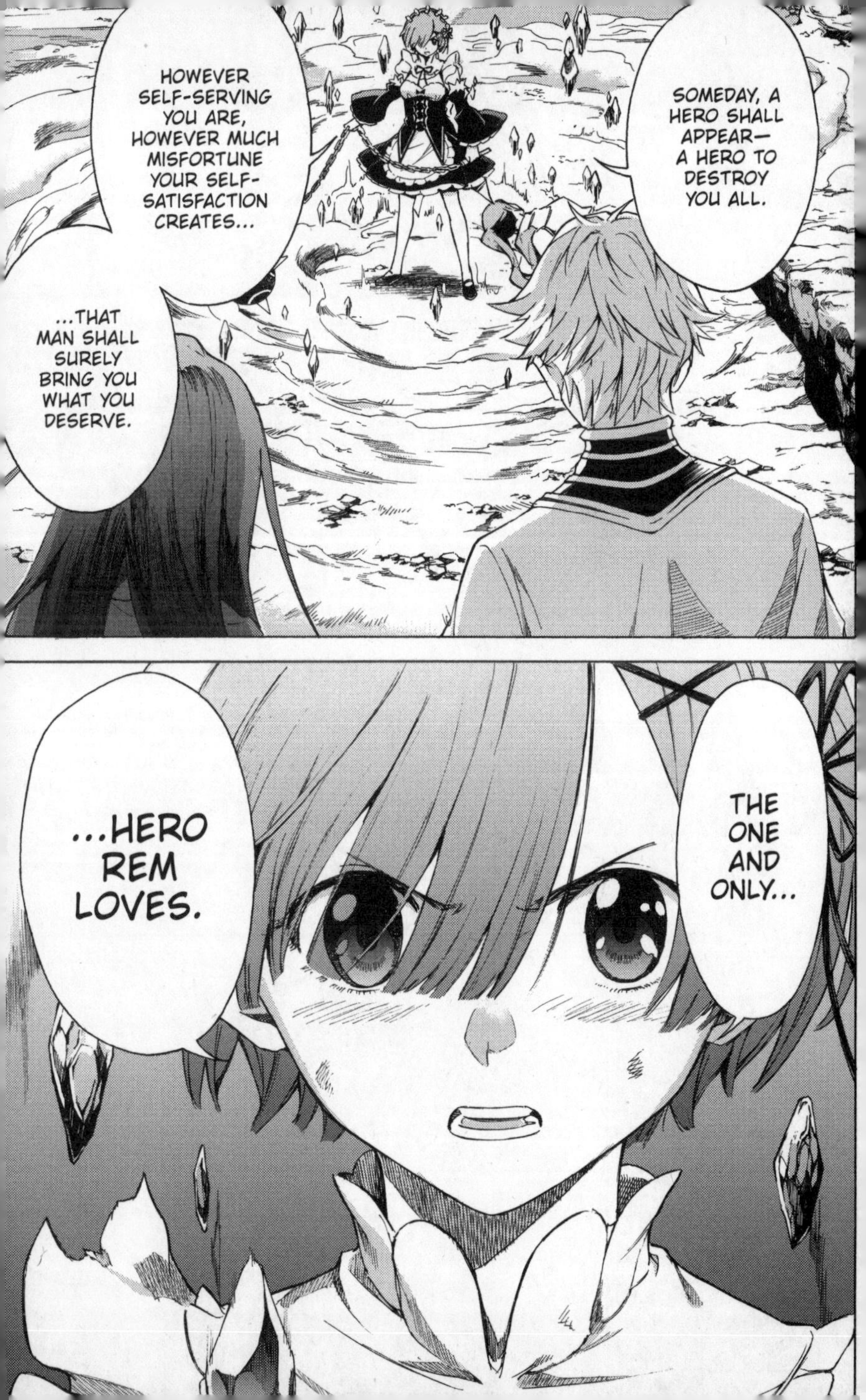
SOMEDAY, A HERO SHALL APPEAR— A HERO TO DESTROY YOU ALL.
HOWEVER SELF-SERVING YOU ARE, HOWEVER MUCH MISFORTUNE YOUR SELF-SATISFACTION CREATES...
...THAT MAN SHALL SURELY BRING YOU WHAT YOU DESERVE.
THE ONE AND ONLY...
...HERO REM LOVES.

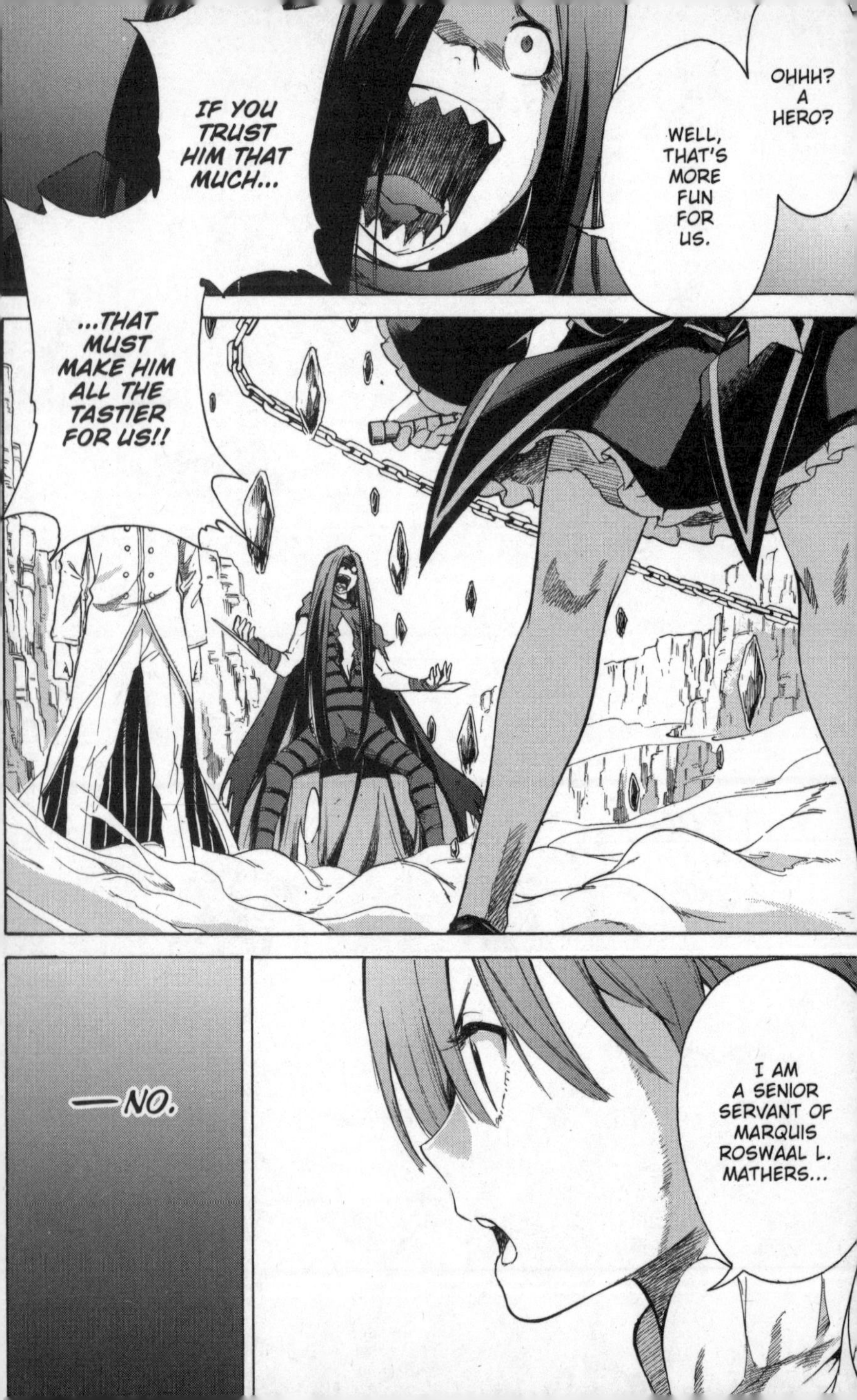
OHHH? A HERO?
WELL, THAT'S MORE FUN FOR US.
IF YOU TRUST HIM THAT MUCH...
...THAT MUST MAKE HIM ALL THE TASTIER FOR US!!
I AM A SENIOR SERVANT OF MARQUIS ROSWAAL L. MATHERS...
—NO.

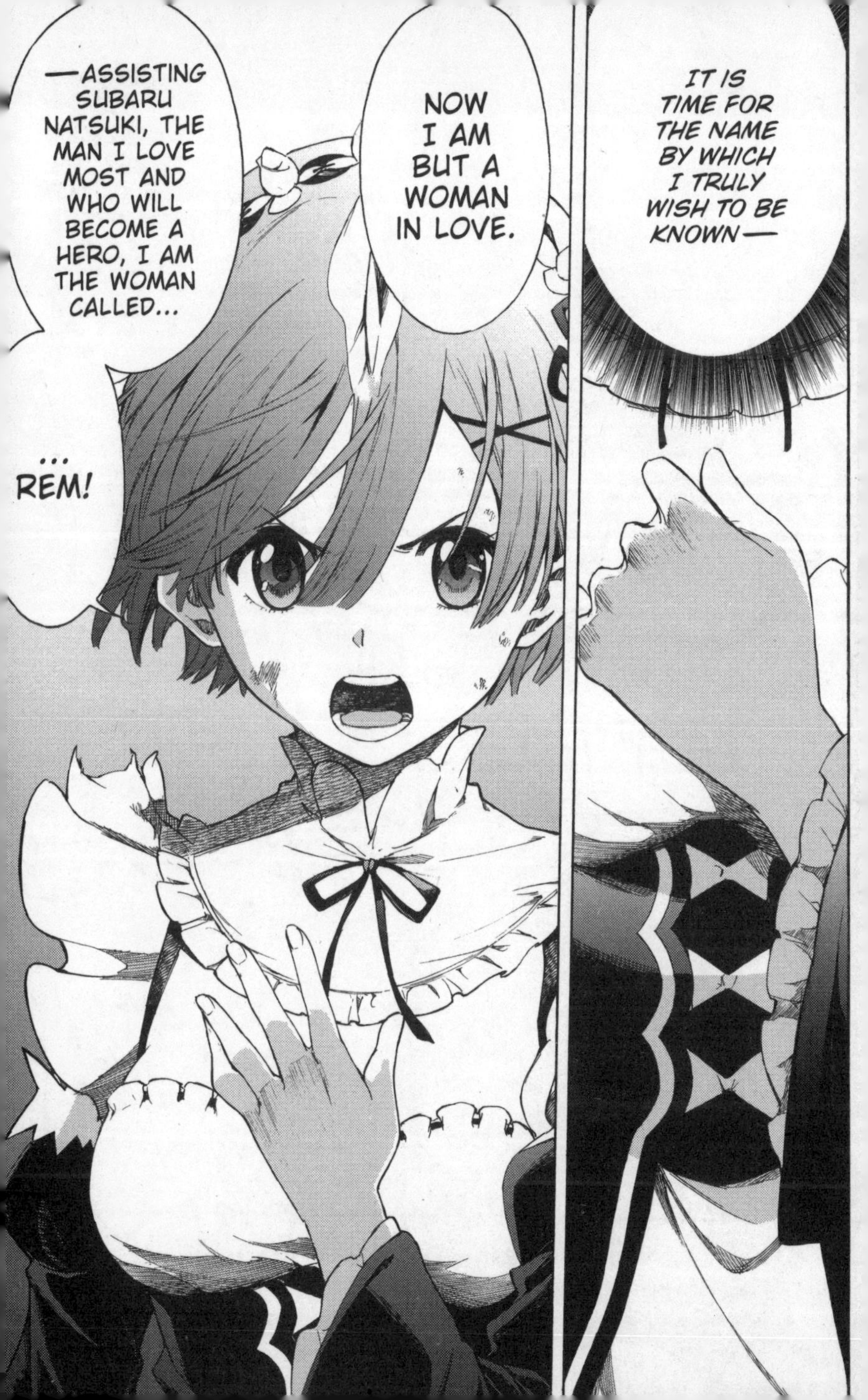
IT IS TIME FOR THE NAME BY WHICH I TRULY WISH TO BE KNOWN—
NOW I AM BUT A WOMAN IN LOVE.
—ASSISTING SUBARU NATSUKI, THE MAN I LOVE MOST AND WHO WILL BECOME A HERO, I AM THE WOMAN CALLED...
...REM!

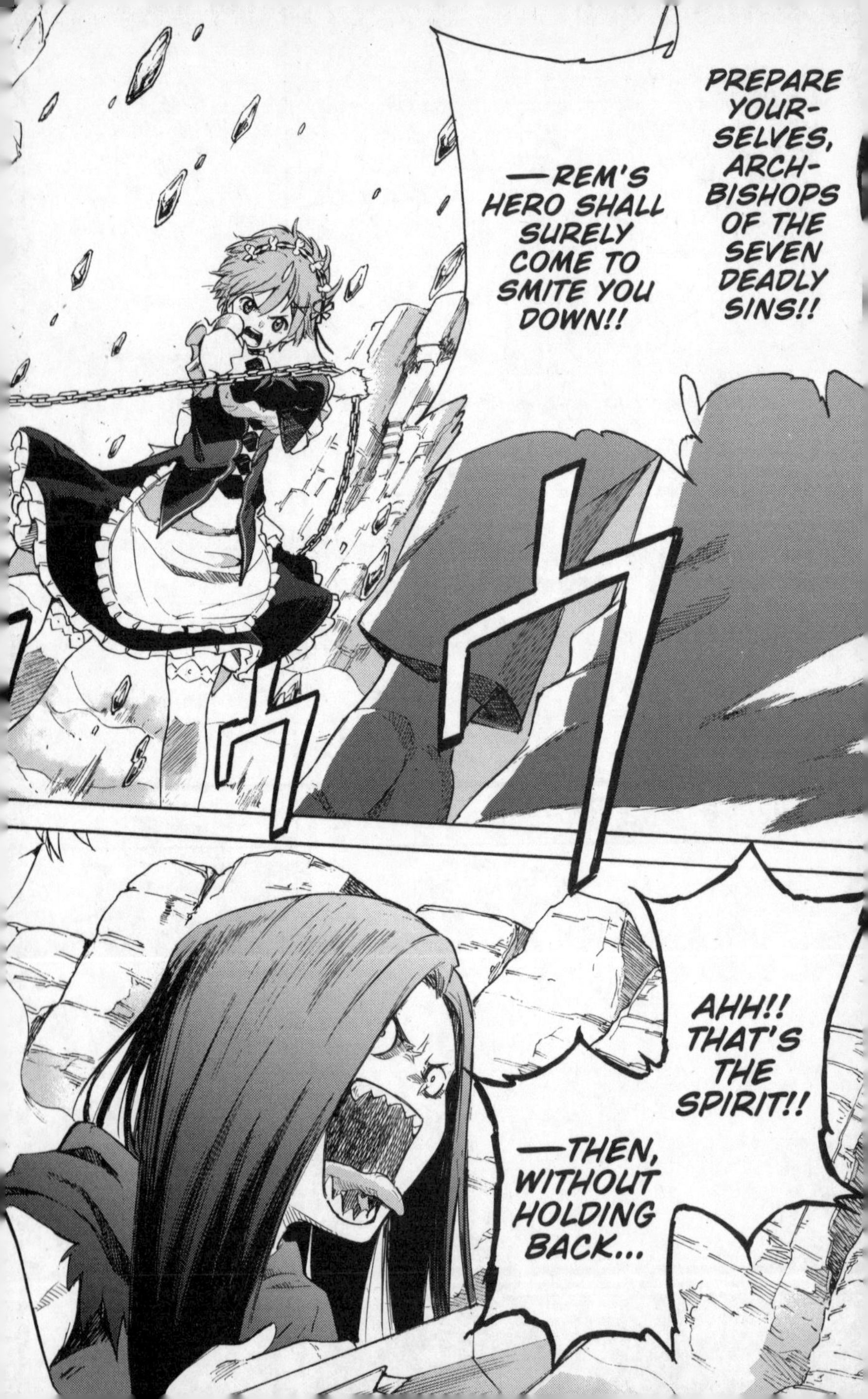
PREPARE YOURSELVES, ARCHBISHOPS OF THE SEVEN DEADLY SINS!!
—REM'S HERO SHALL SURELY COME TO SMITE YOU DOWN!!
AHH!! THAT'S THE SPIRIT!!
—THEN, WITHOUT HOLDING BACK...

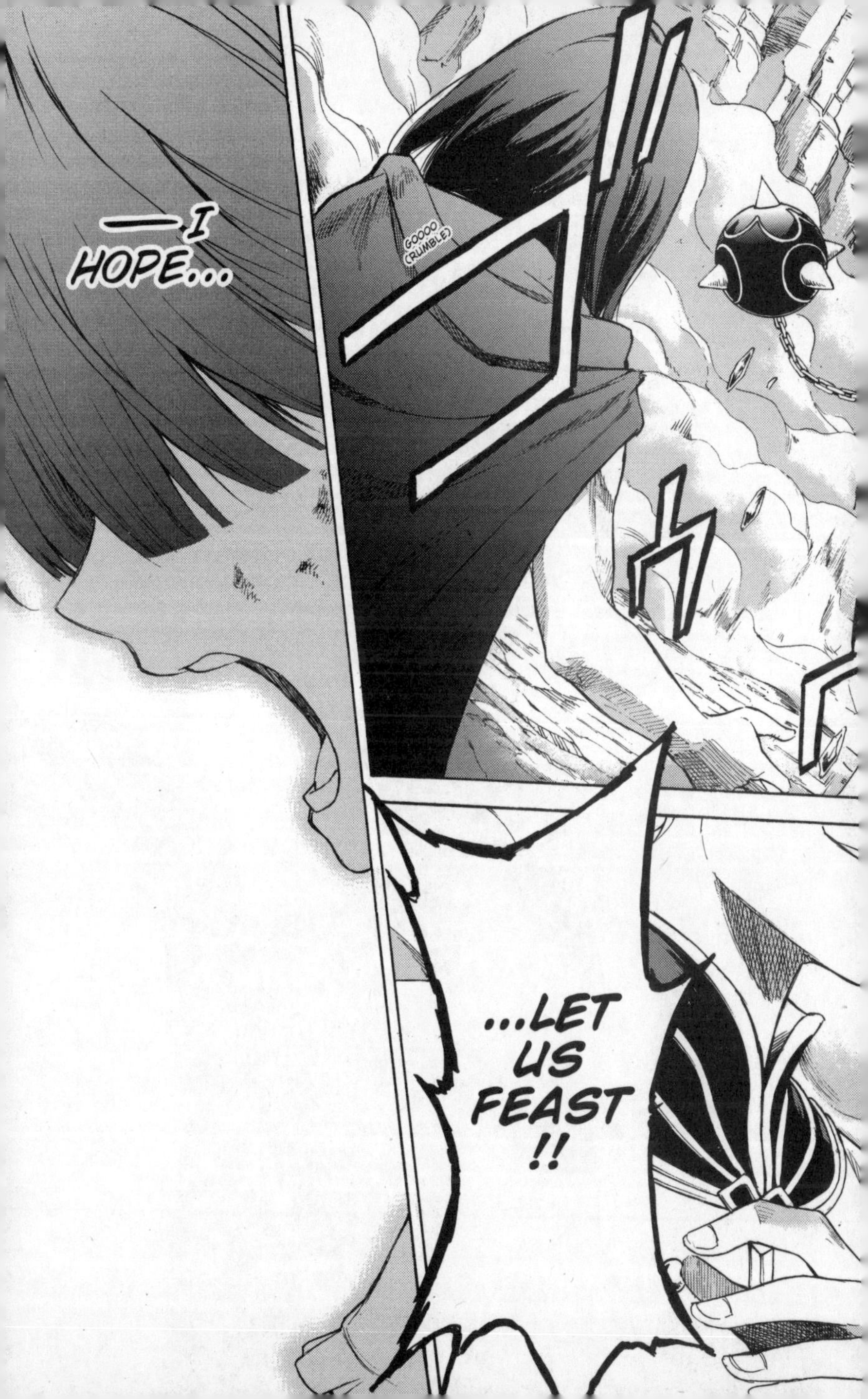
GOOOO (RUMBLE)
...LET US FEAST!!
—I HOPE...

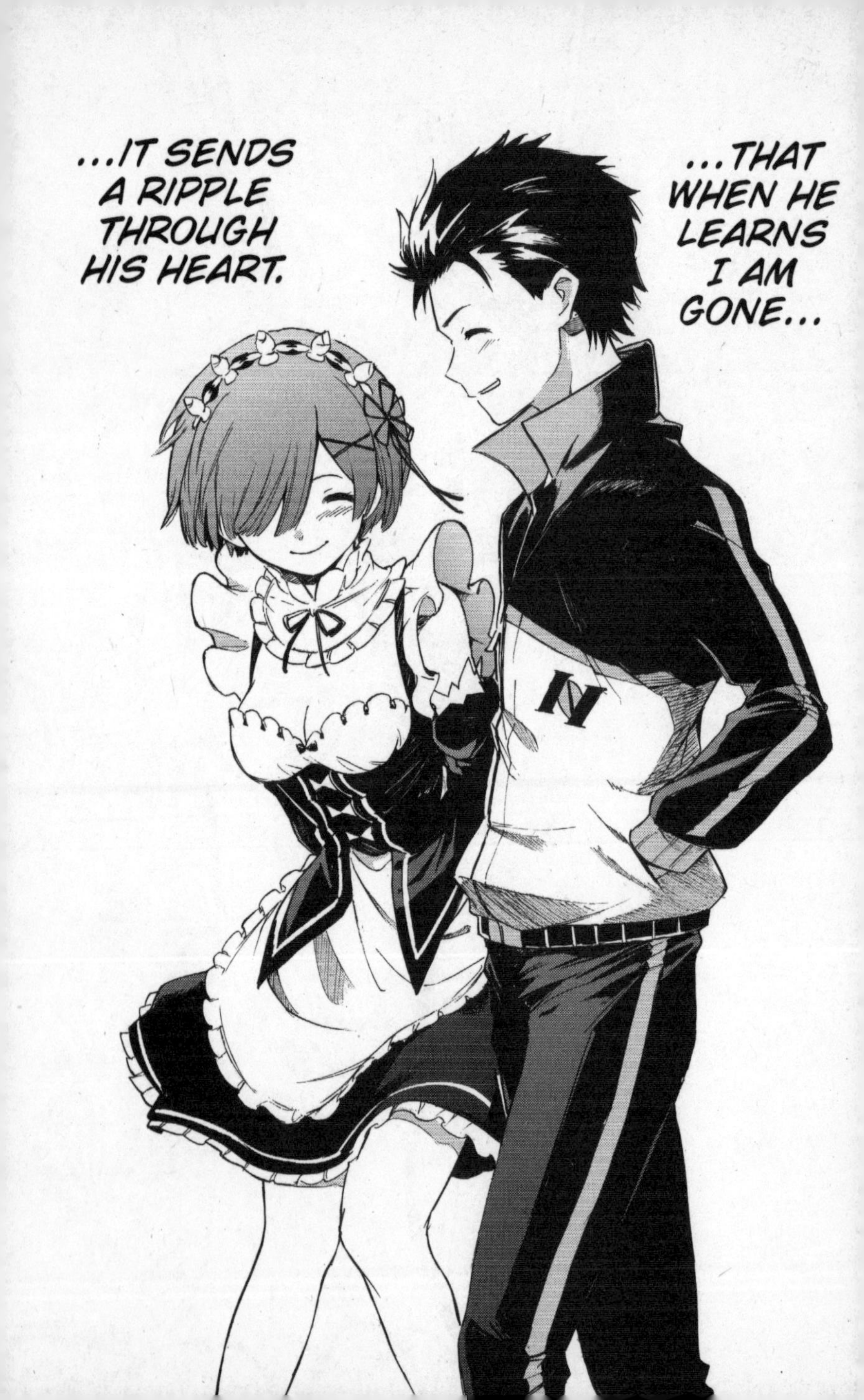
...THAT WHEN HE LEARNS I AM GONE...
...IT SENDS A RIPPLE THROUGH HIS HEART.

Truth of Zero
The only ability Subaru Natsuki gets when he's summoned to another world is
time travel via his own death. But to save her, he'll die as many times as it takes.

Re:ZERO
-Starting Life in
Another World-

Re:ZERO
-Starting Life in Another World-

Truth of Zero

The only ability Subaru Natsuki gets when he's summoned to another world is time
travel via his own death. But to save her, he'll die as many times as it takes.

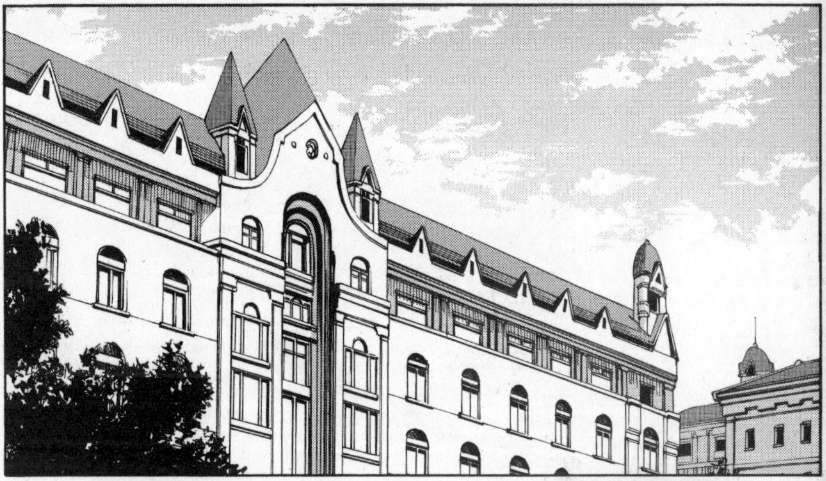
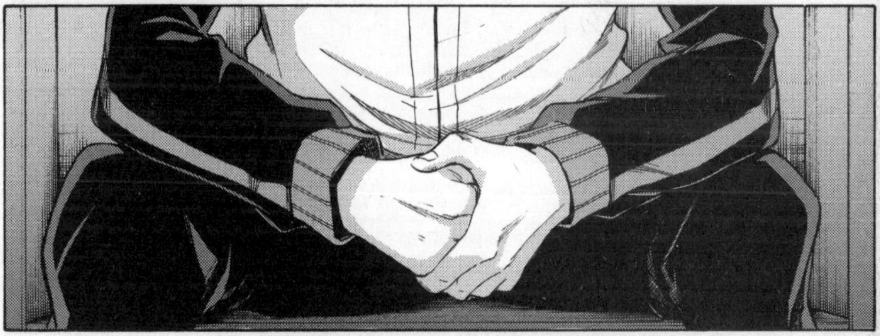
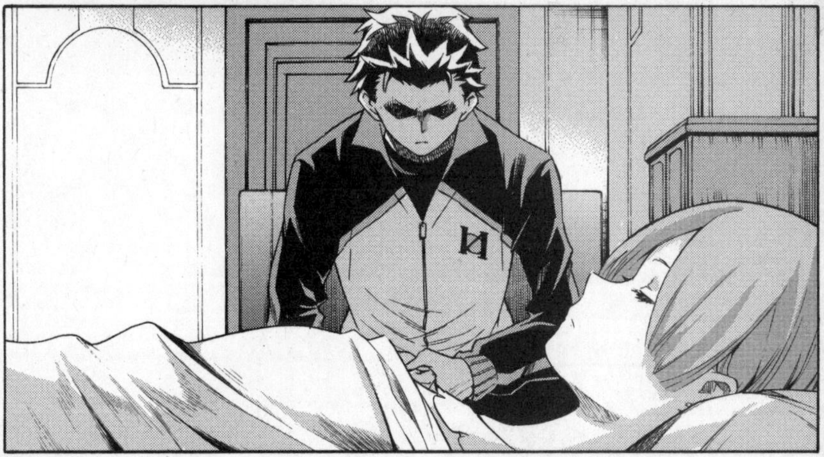

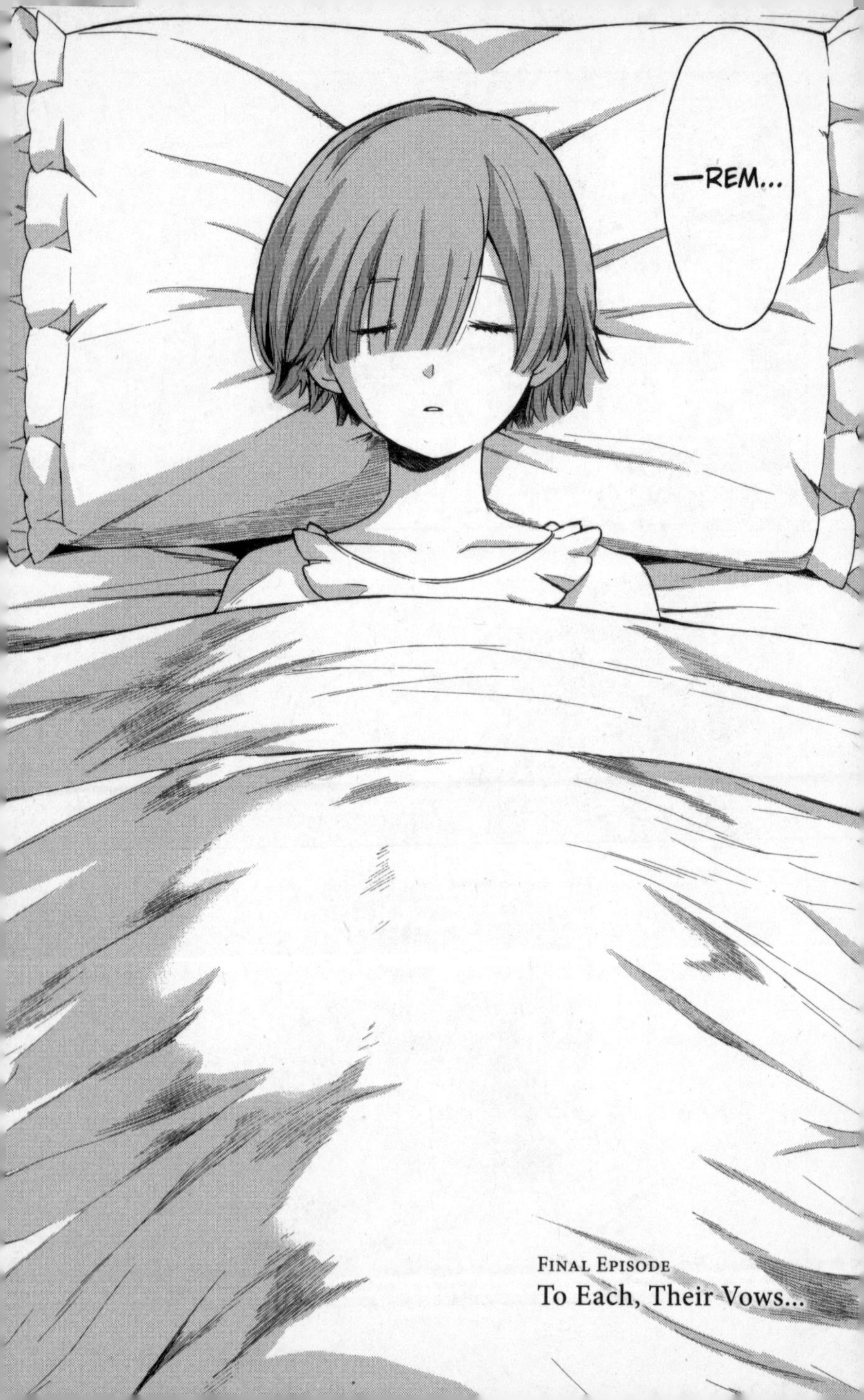
—REM...

Final Episode
To Each, Their Vows...

—WHO IS REM?

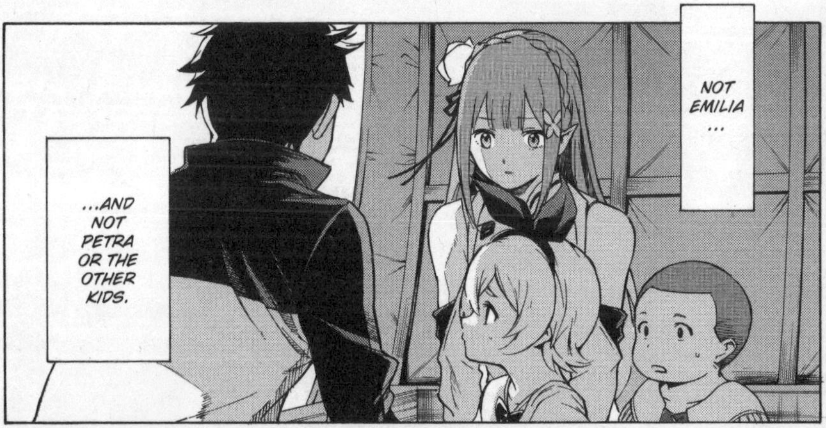
NOT EMILIA ...
...AND NOT PETRA OR THE OTHER KIDS.

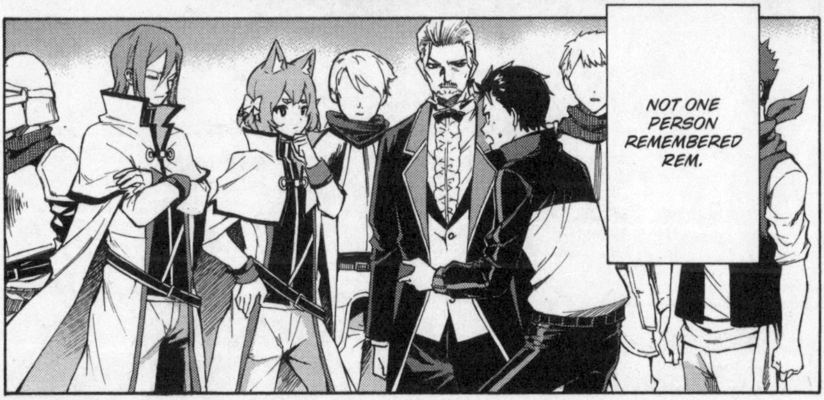
NOT ONE PERSON REMEMBERED REM.

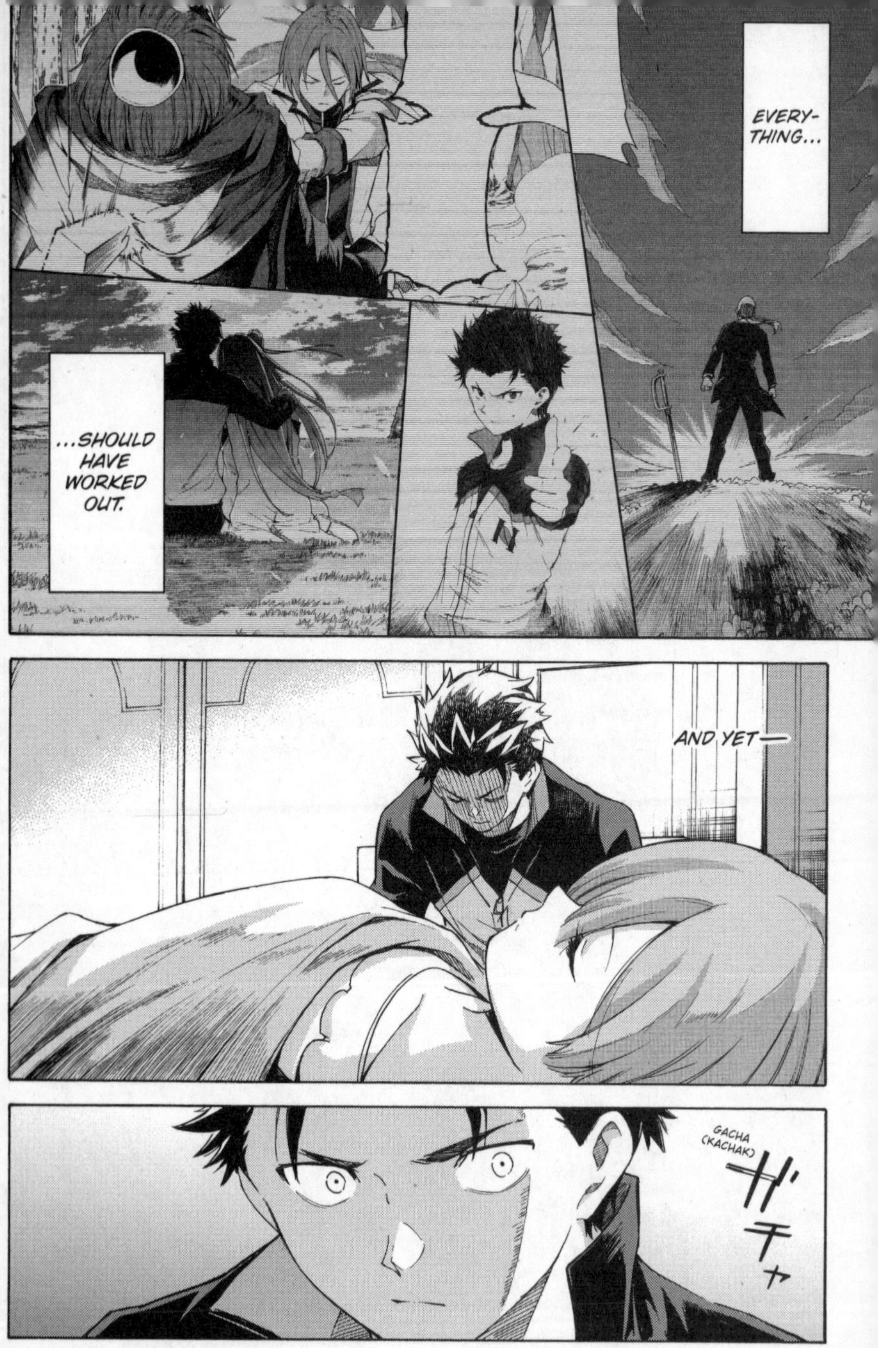
EVERY-
THING...
...SHOULD
HAVE
WORKED
OUT.
AND YET—
GACHA
(KACHAK)
ガチャ

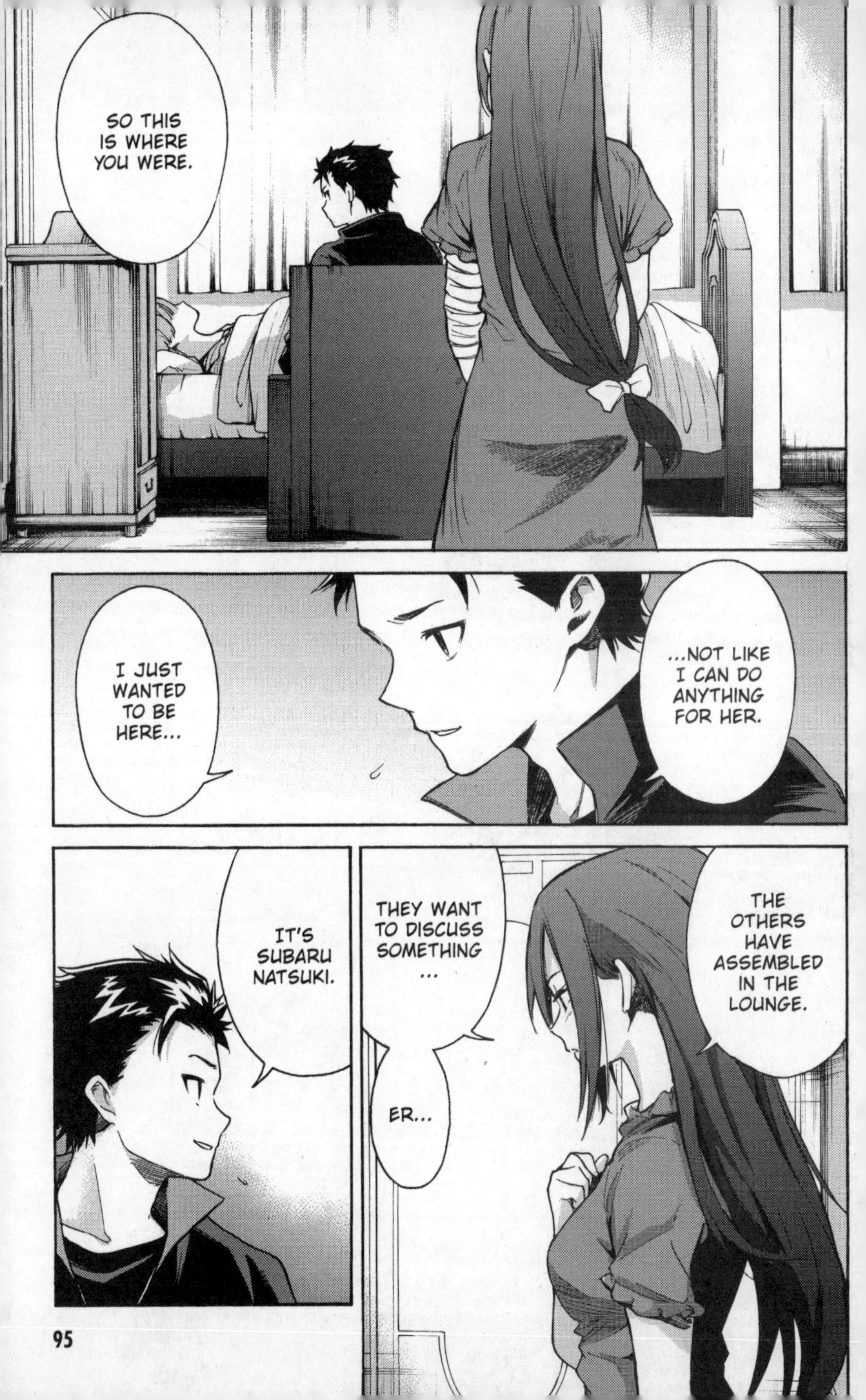
SO THIS IS WHERE YOU WERE.
...NOT LIKE I CAN DO ANYTHING FOR HER.
I JUST WANTED TO BE HERE...
THE OTHERS HAVE ASSEMBLED IN THE LOUNGE.
THEY WANT TO DISCUSS SOMETHING ...
ER...
IT'S SUBARU NATSUKI.

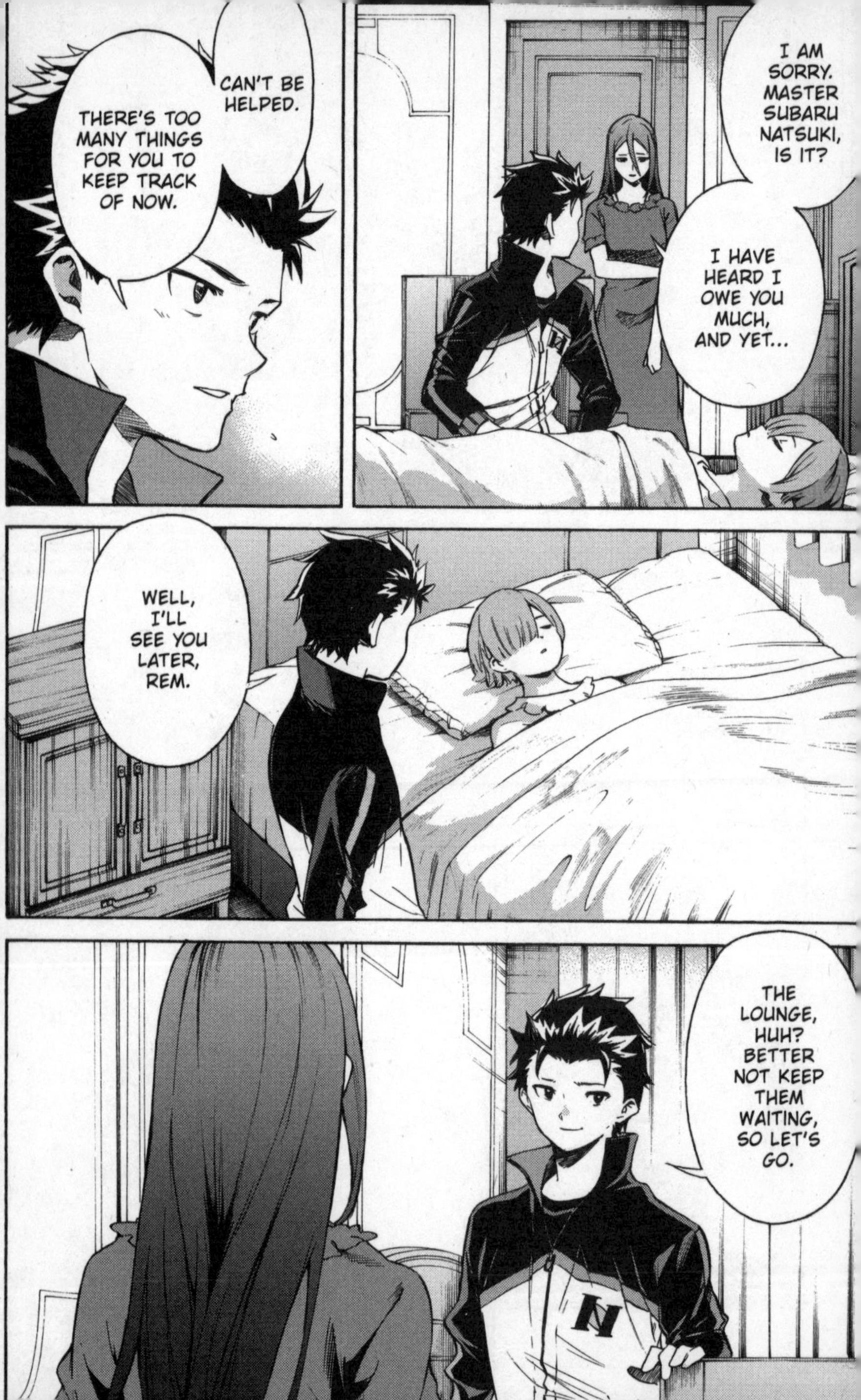
I AM SORRY. MASTER SUBARU NATSUKI, IS IT?
I HAVE HEARD I OWE YOU MUCH, AND YET...
CAN'T BE HELPED.
THERE'S TOO MANY THINGS FOR YOU TO KEEP TRACK OF NOW.
WELL, I'LL SEE YOU LATER, REM.
THE LOUNGE, HUH? BETTER NOT KEEP THEM WAITING, SO LET'S GO.

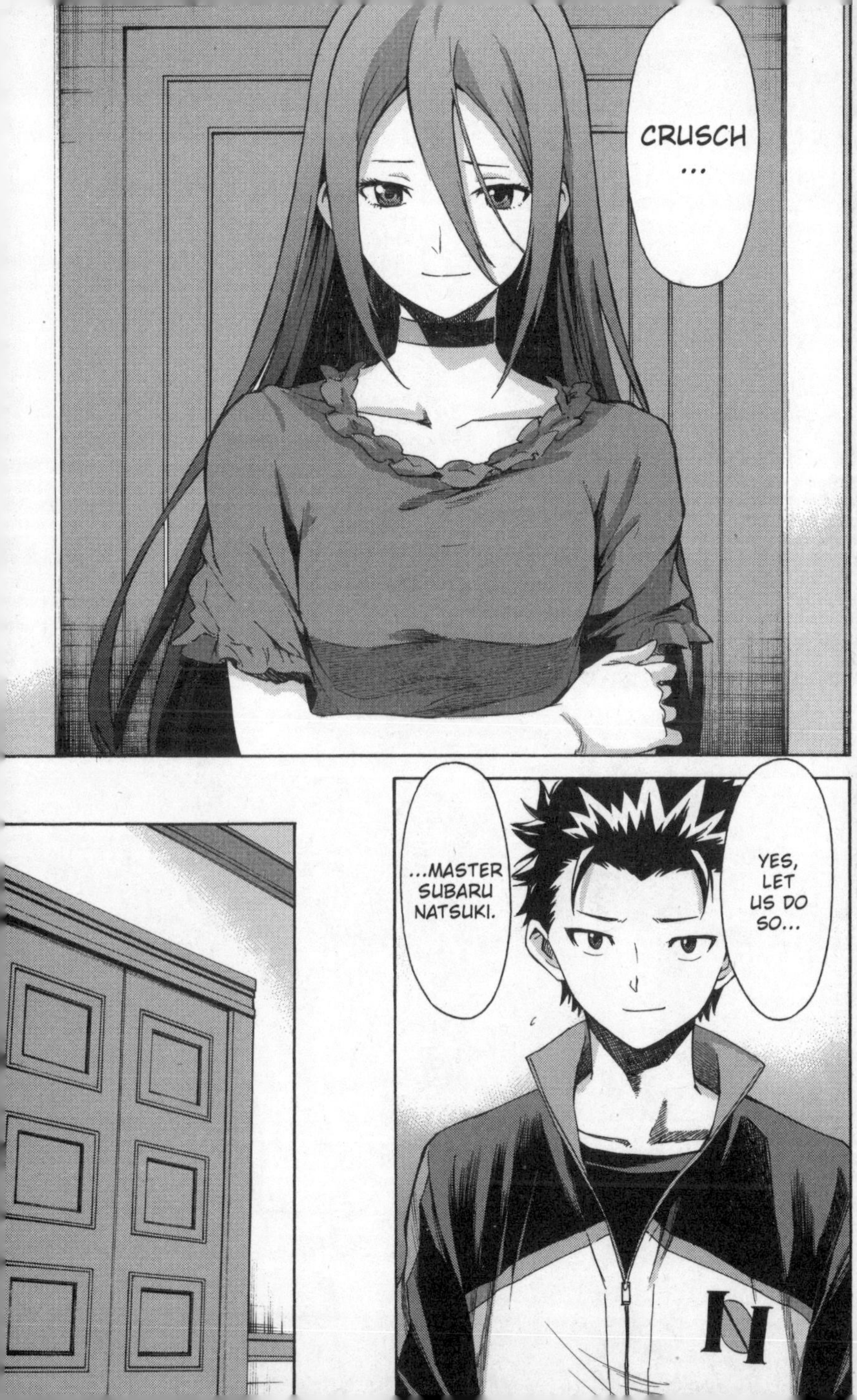
CRUSCH ...
YES, LET US DO SO...
...MASTER SUBARU NATSUKI.

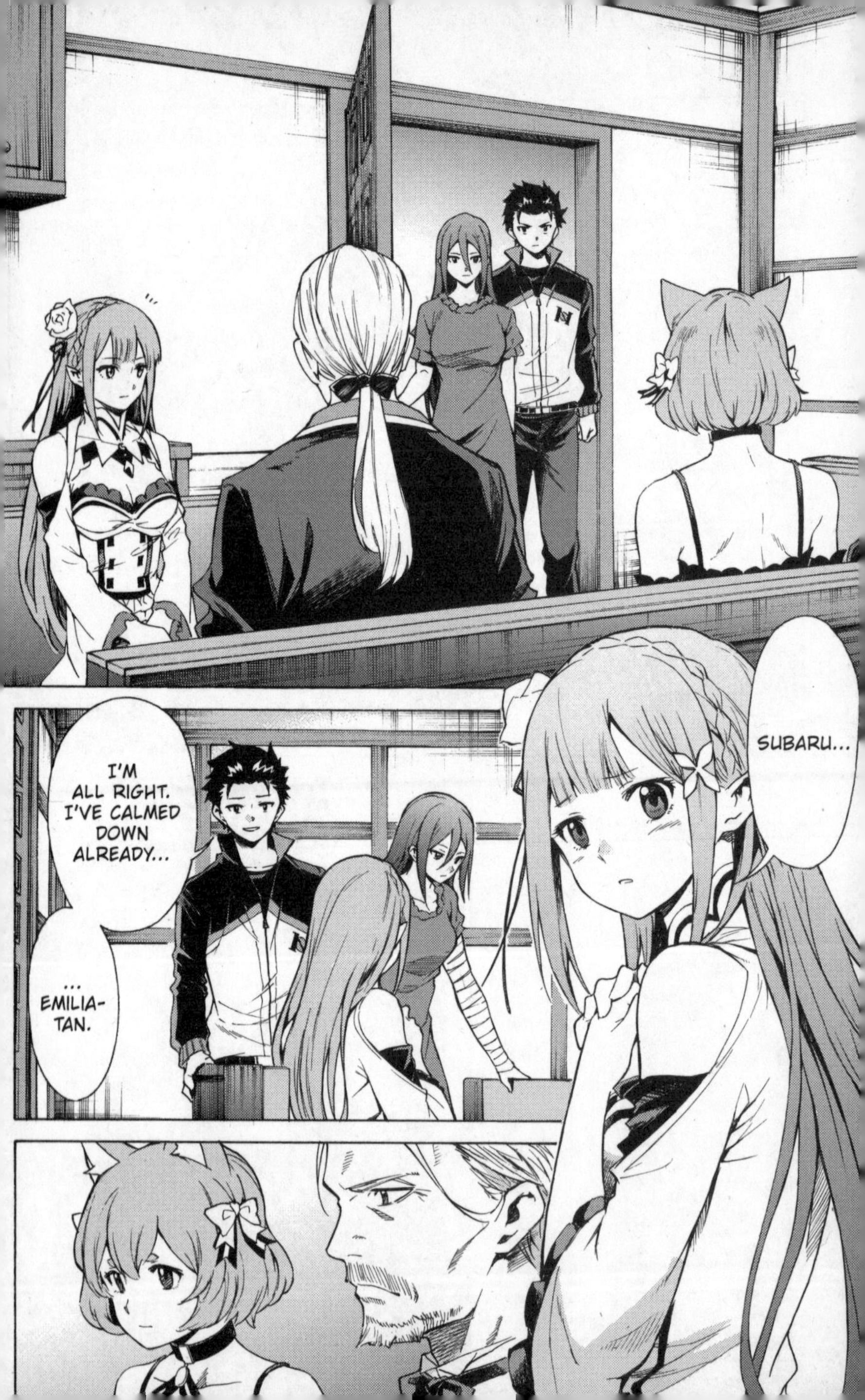
SUBARU...
I'M ALL RIGHT. I'VE CALMED DOWN ALREADY...
... EMILIA-TAN.

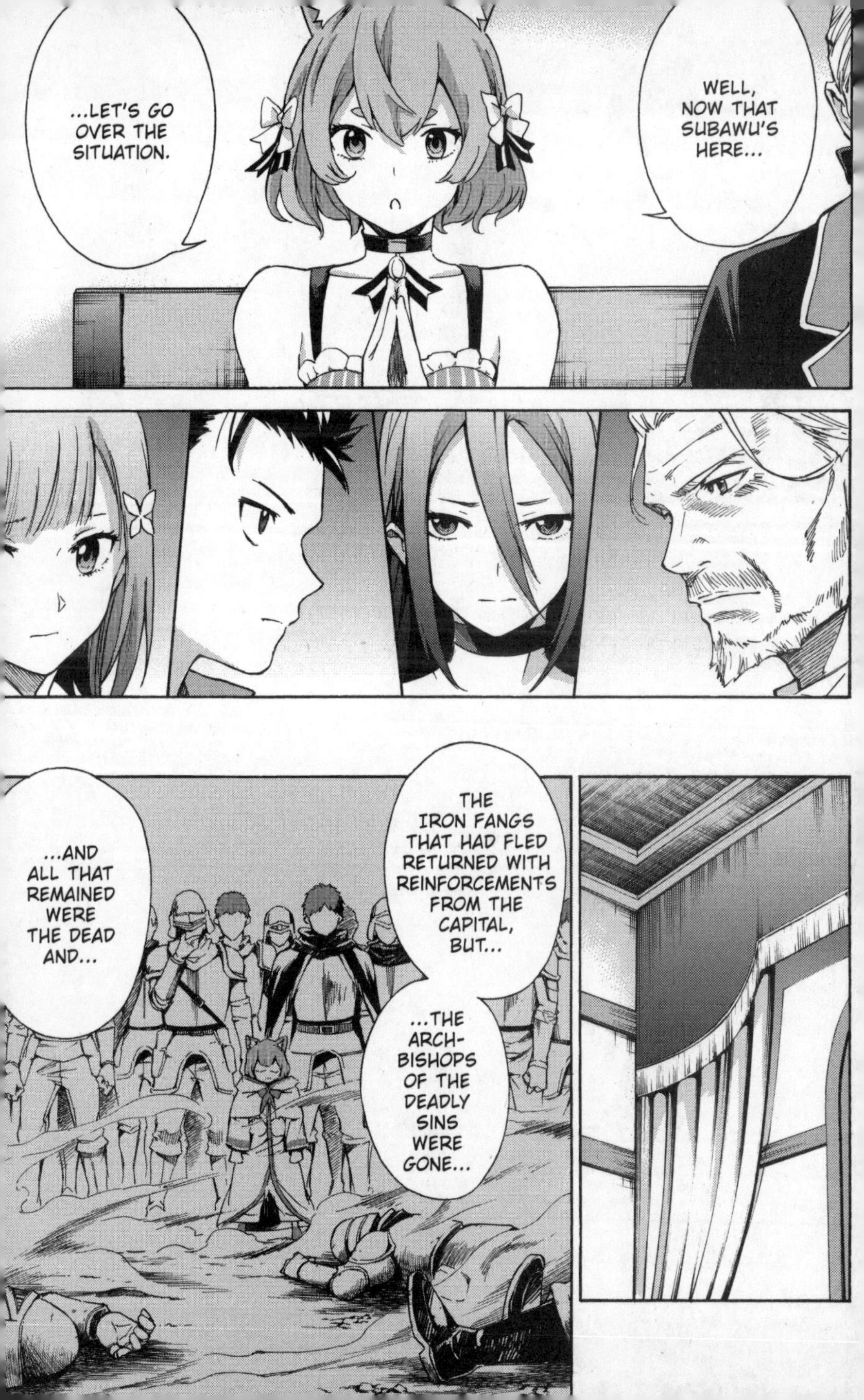
WELL, NOW THAT SUBAWU'S HERE...
...LET'S GO OVER THE SITUATION.
THE IRON FANGS THAT HAD FLED RETURNED WITH REINFORCEMENTS FROM THE CAPITAL, BUT...
...THE ARCH-BISHOPS OF THE DEADLY SINS WERE GONE...
...AND ALL THAT REMAINED WERE THE DEAD AND...

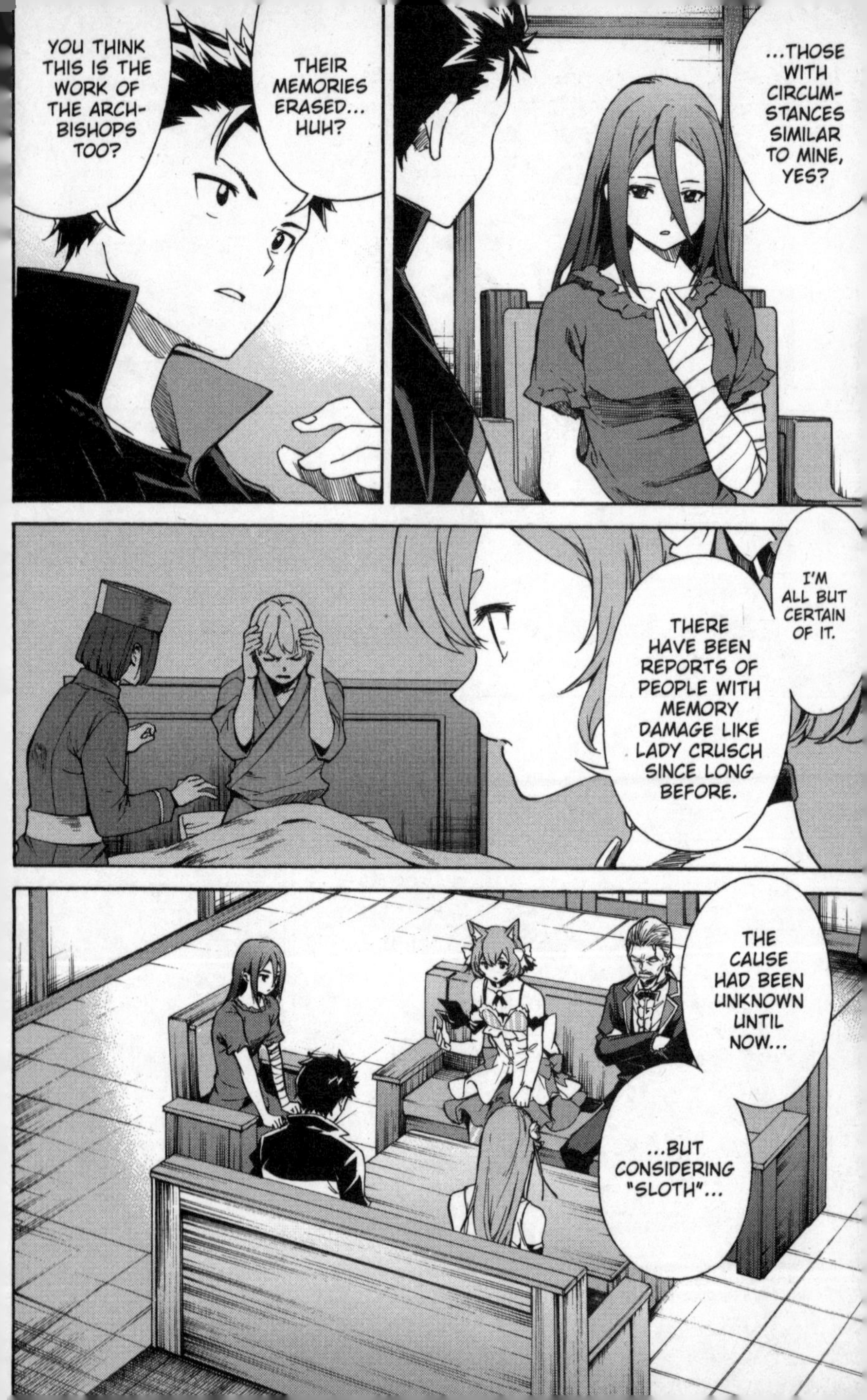
...THOSE WITH CIRCUMSTANCES SIMILAR TO MINE, YES?
THEIR MEMORIES ERASED... HUH?
YOU THINK THIS IS THE WORK OF THE ARCHBISHOPS TOO?
I'M ALL BUT CERTAIN OF IT.
THERE HAVE BEEN REPORTS OF PEOPLE WITH MEMORY DAMAGE LIKE LADY CRUSCH SINCE LONG BEFORE.
THE CAUSE HAD BEEN UNKNOWN UNTIL NOW...
...BUT CONSIDERING "SLOTH"...

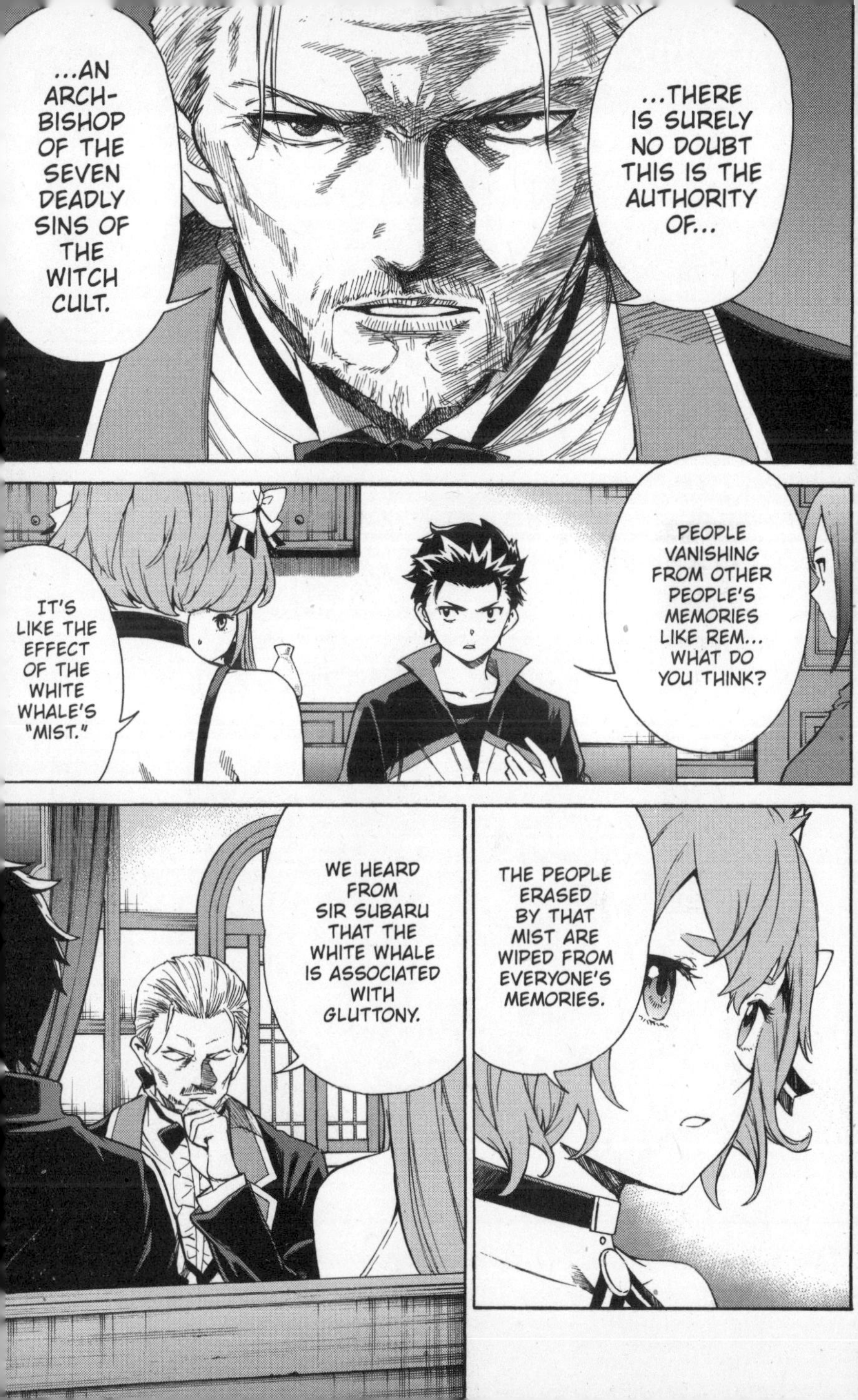
...THERE IS SURELY NO DOUBT THIS IS THE AUTHORITY OF...
...AN ARCH-BISHOP OF THE SEVEN DEADLY SINS OF THE WITCH CULT.
PEOPLE VANISHING FROM OTHER PEOPLE'S MEMORIES LIKE REM... WHAT DO YOU THINK?
IT'S LIKE THE EFFECT OF THE WHITE WHALE'S "MIST."
THE PEOPLE ERASED BY THAT MIST ARE WIPED FROM EVERYONE'S MEMORIES.
WE HEARD FROM SIR SUBARU THAT THE WHITE WHALE IS ASSOCIATED WITH GLUTTONY.

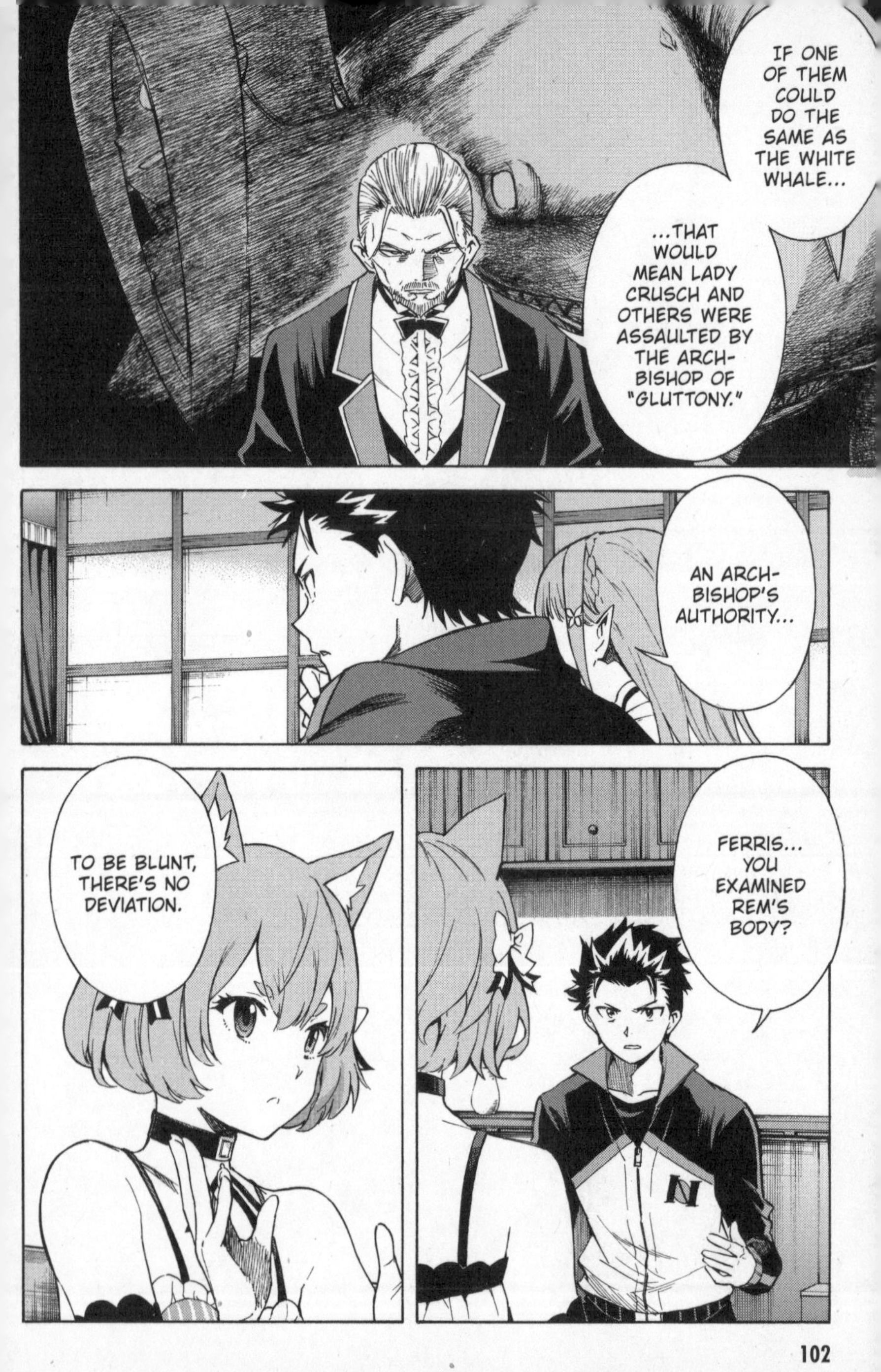
IF ONE OF THEM COULD DO THE SAME AS THE WHITE WHALE...
...THAT WOULD MEAN LADY CRUSCH AND OTHERS WERE ASSAULTED BY THE ARCH-BISHOP OF "GLUTTONY."
AN ARCH-BISHOP'S AUTHORITY...
FERRIS... YOU EXAMINED REM'S BODY?
TO BE BLUNT, THERE'S NO DEVIATION.

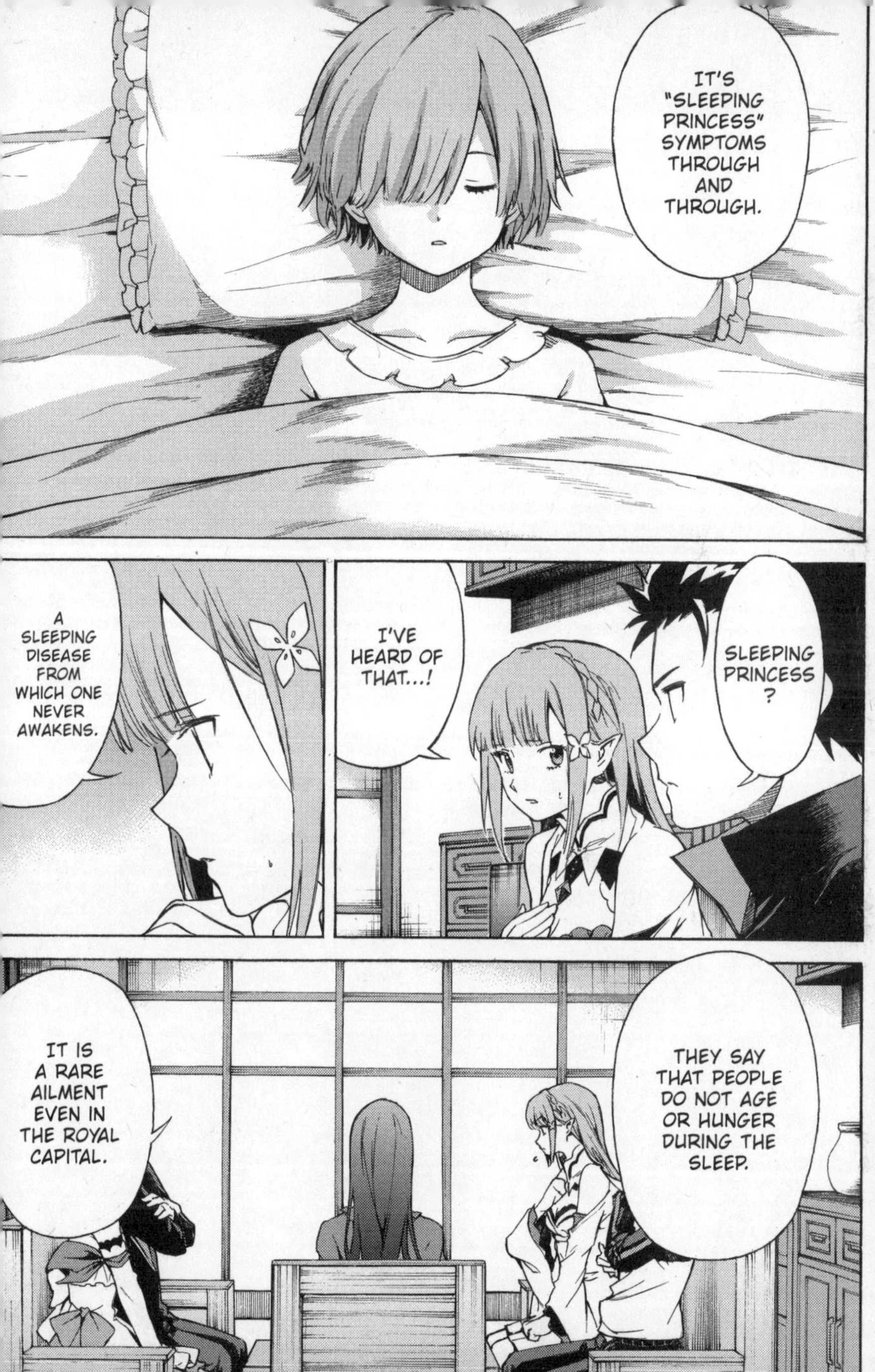
IT'S "SLEEPING PRINCESS" SYMPTOMS THROUGH AND THROUGH.
SLEEPING PRINCESS?
I'VE HEARD OF THAT...!
A SLEEPING DISEASE FROM WHICH ONE NEVER AWAKENS.
THEY SAY THAT PEOPLE DO NOT AGE OR HUNGER DURING THE SLEEP.
IT IS A RARE AILMENT EVEN IN THE ROYAL CAPITAL.

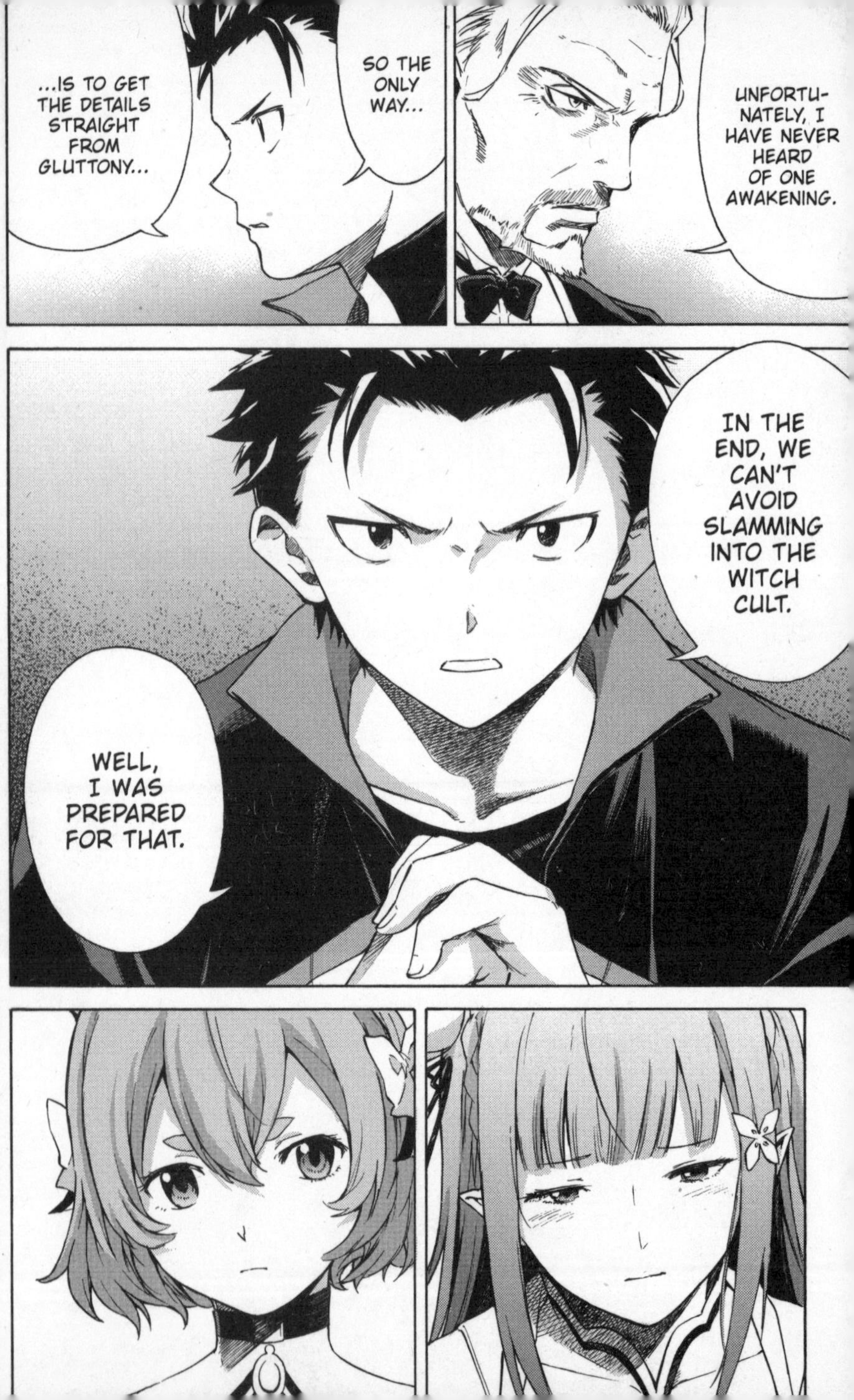
UNFORTUNATELY, I HAVE NEVER HEARD OF ONE AWAKENING.
SO THE ONLY WAY...
...IS TO GET THE DETAILS STRAIGHT FROM GLUTTONY...
IN THE END, WE CAN'T AVOID SLAMMING INTO THE WITCH CULT.
WELL, I WAS PREPARED FOR THAT.

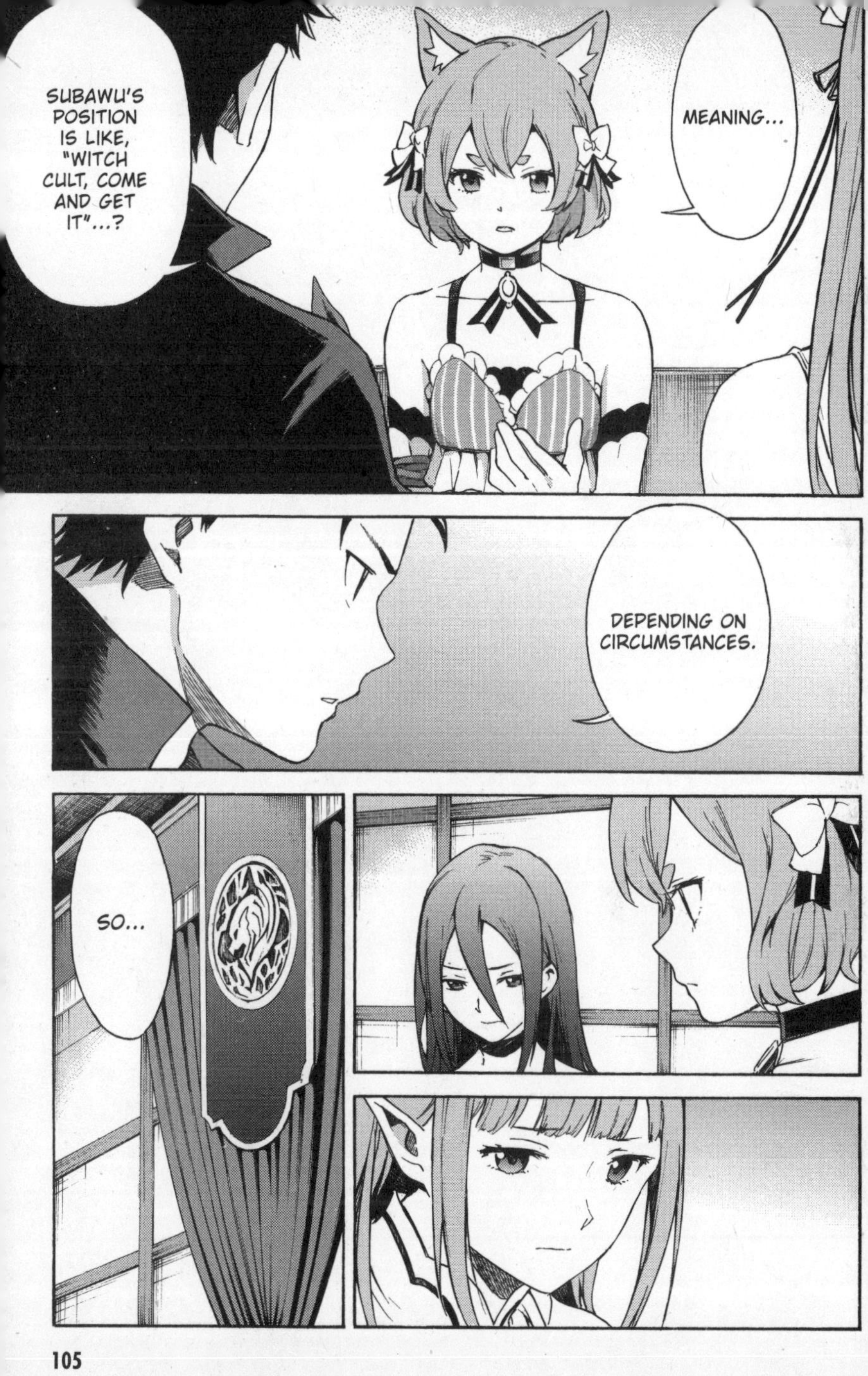
MEANING...
SUBAWU'S POSITION IS LIKE, "WITCH CULT, COME AND GET IT"...?
DEPENDING ON CIRCUMSTANCES.
SO...

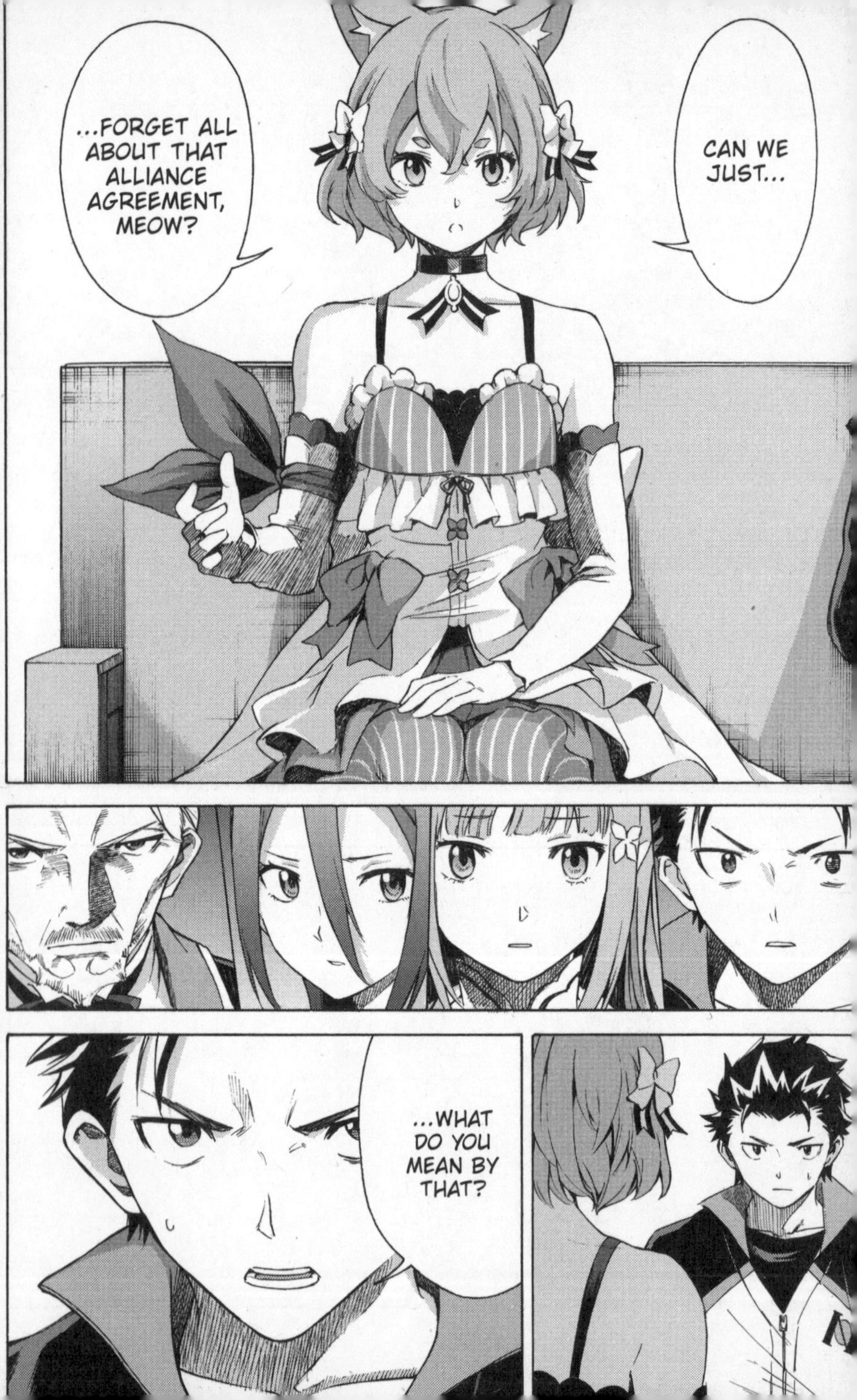
CAN WE JUST...
...FORGET ALL ABOUT THAT ALLIANCE AGREEMENT, MEOW?
...WHAT DO YOU MEAN BY THAT?

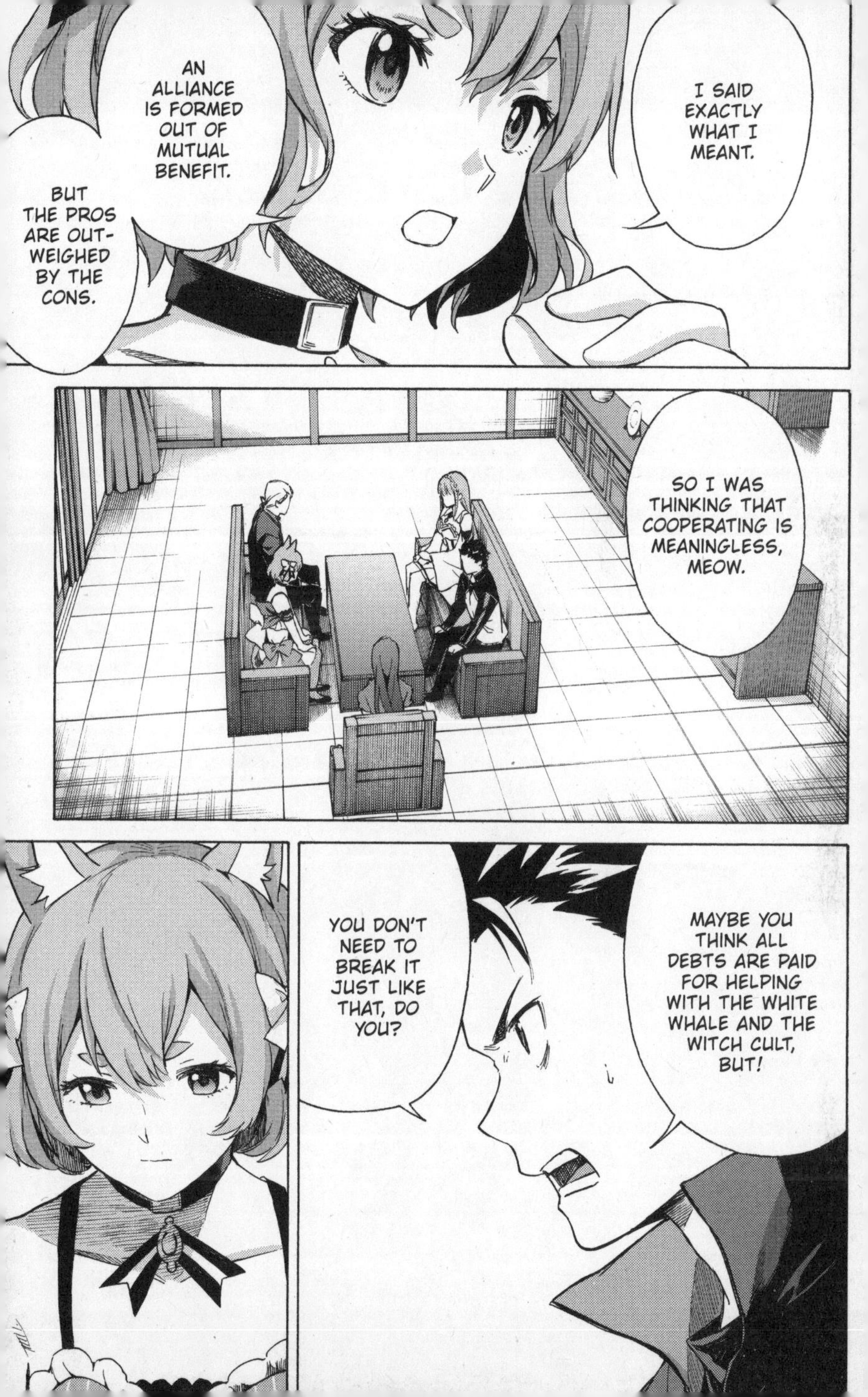
I SAID EXACTLY WHAT I MEANT.
AN ALLIANCE IS FORMED OUT OF MUTUAL BENEFIT.
BUT THE PROS ARE OUT-WEIGHED BY THE CONS.
SO I WAS THINKING THAT COOPERATING IS MEANINGLESS, MEOW.
MAYBE YOU THINK ALL DEBTS ARE PAID FOR HELPING WITH THE WHITE WHALE AND THE WITCH CULT, BUT!
YOU DON'T NEED TO BREAK IT JUST LIKE THAT, DO YOU?

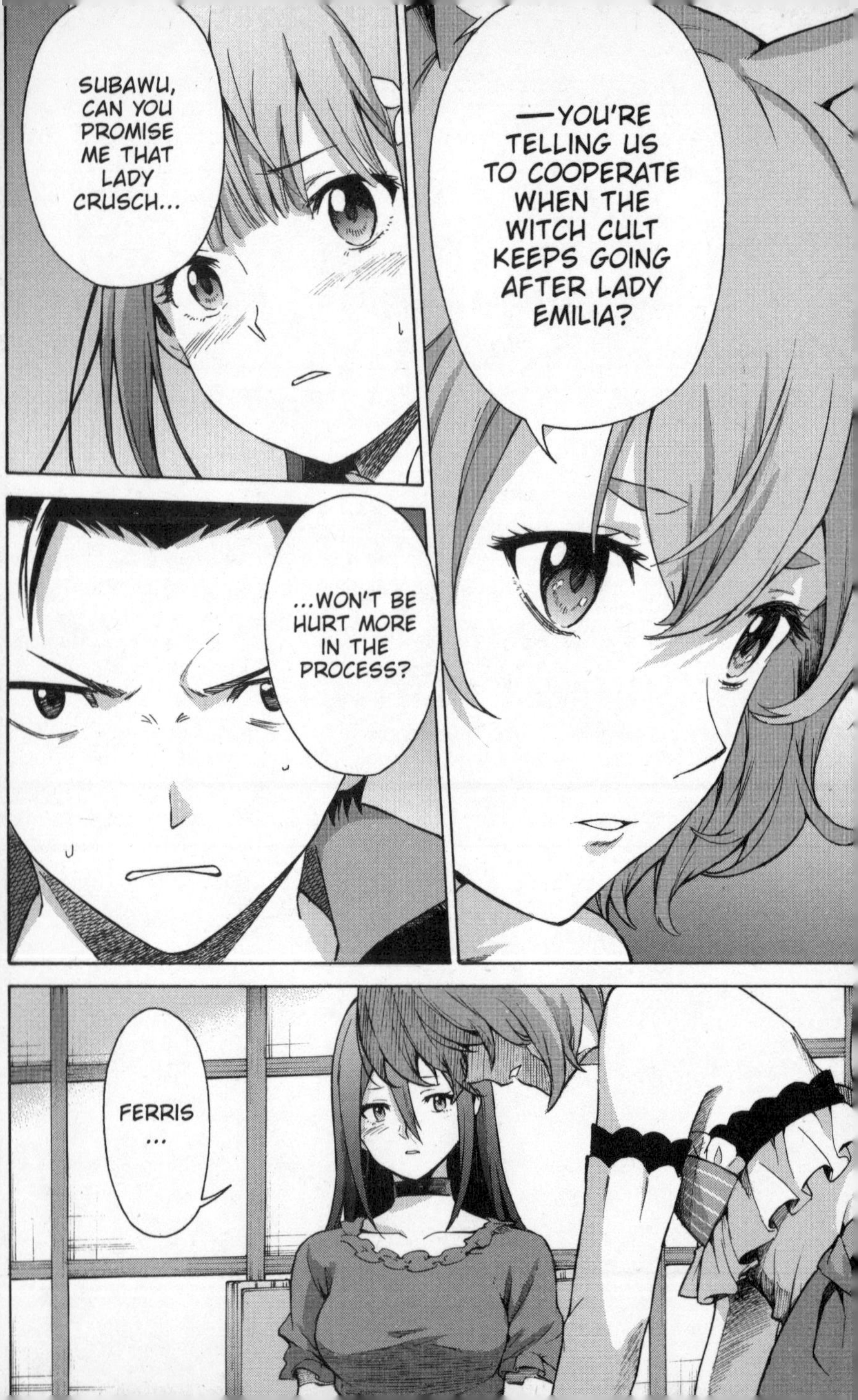
—YOU'RE TELLING US TO COOPERATE WHEN THE WITCH CULT KEEPS GOING AFTER LADY EMILIA?
SUBAWU, CAN YOU PROMISE ME THAT LADY CRUSCH...
...WON'T BE HURT MORE IN THE PROCESS?
FERRIS ...

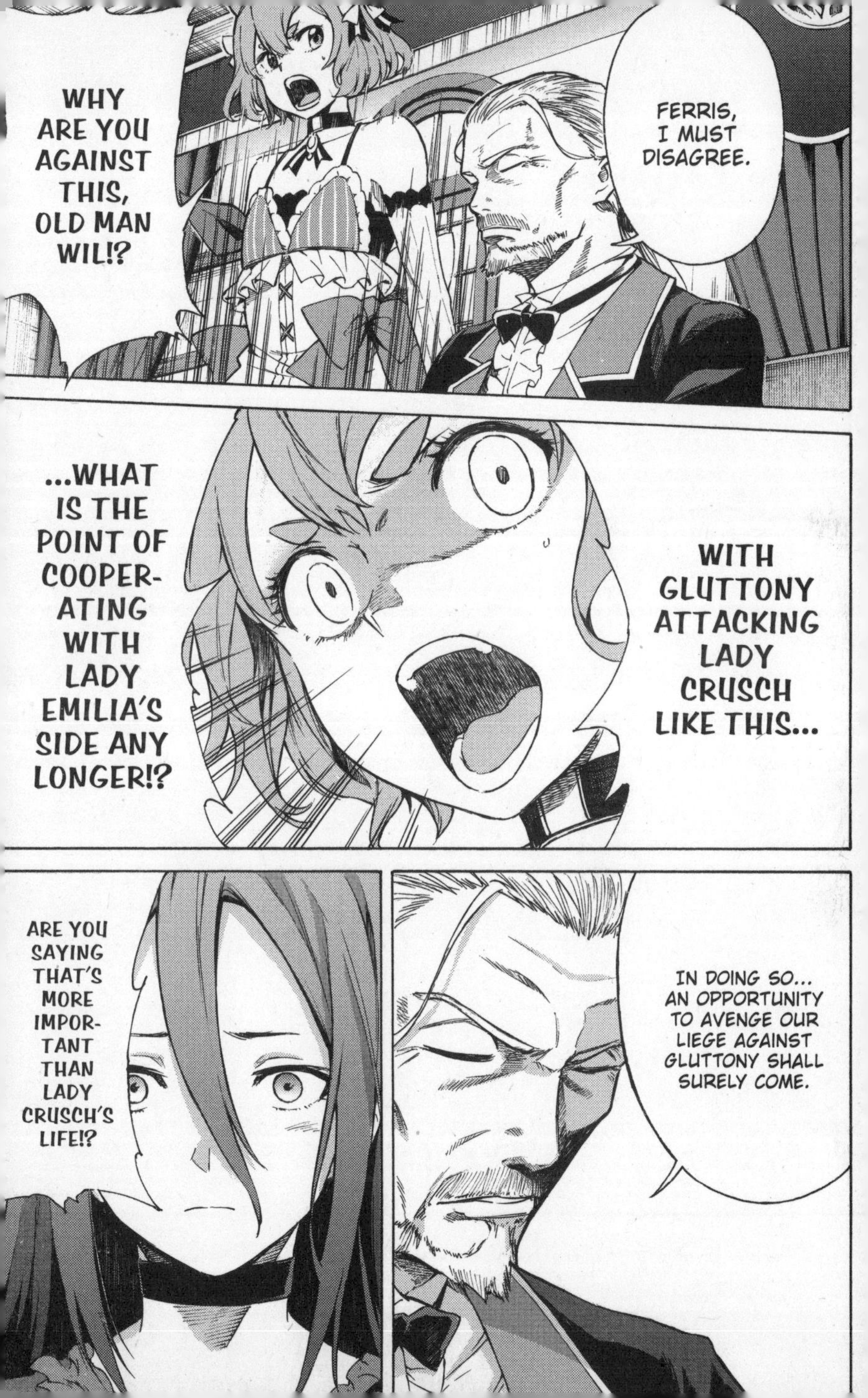
FERRIS, I MUST DISAGREE.
WHY ARE YOU AGAINST THIS, OLD MAN WIL!?
WITH GLUTTONY ATTACKING LADY CRUSCH LIKE THIS...
...WHAT IS THE POINT OF COOPER-ATING WITH LADY EMILIA'S SIDE ANY LONGER!?
IN DOING SO... AN OPPORTUNITY TO AVENGE OUR LIEGE AGAINST GLUTTONY SHALL SURELY COME.
ARE YOU SAYING THAT'S MORE IMPOR-TANT THAN LADY CRUSCH'S LIFE!?

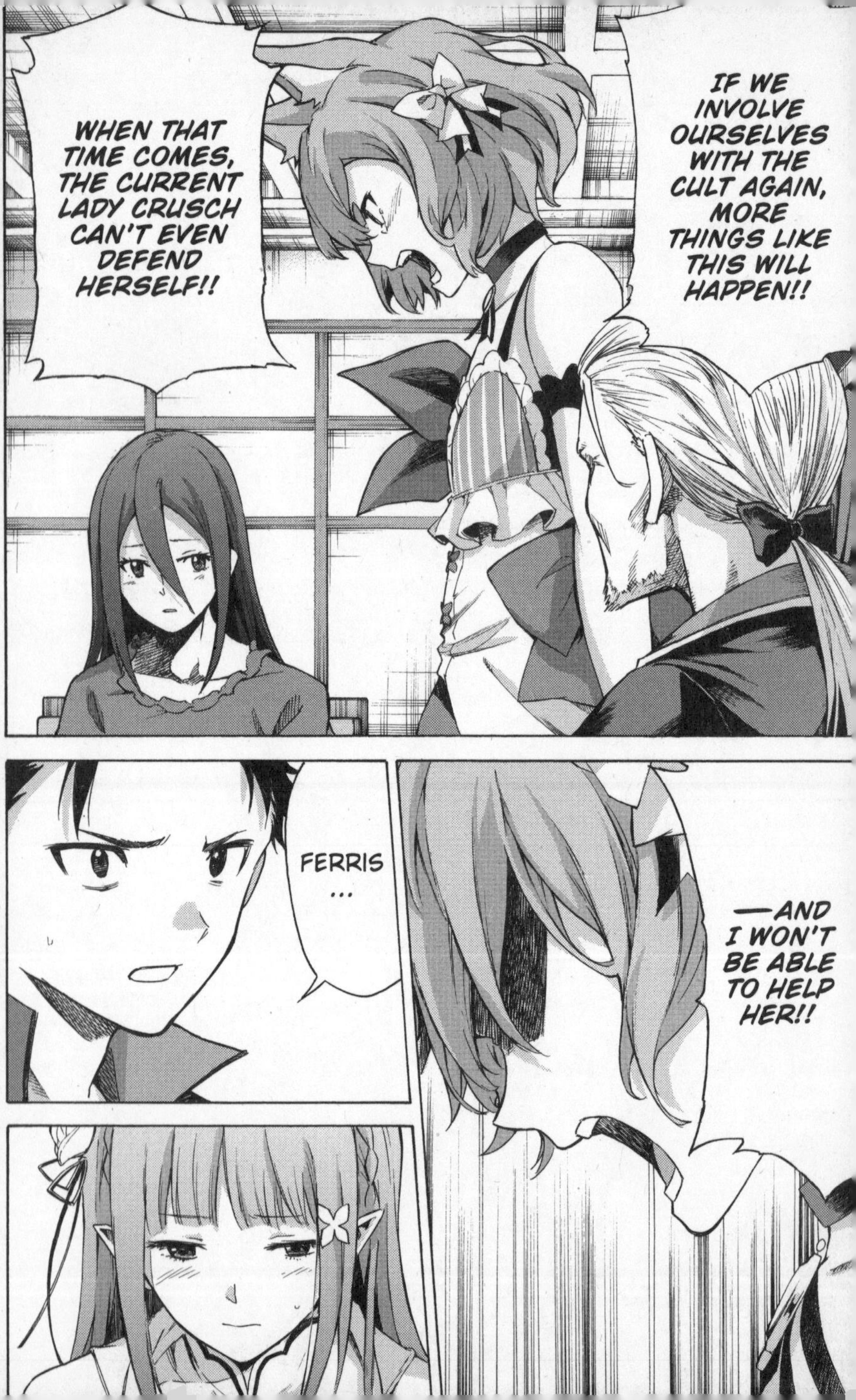
IF WE INVOLVE OURSELVES WITH THE CULT AGAIN, MORE THINGS LIKE THIS WILL HAPPEN!!
WHEN THAT TIME COMES, THE CURRENT LADY CRUSCH CAN'T EVEN DEFEND HERSELF!!
—AND I WON'T BE ABLE TO HELP HER!!
FERRIS...

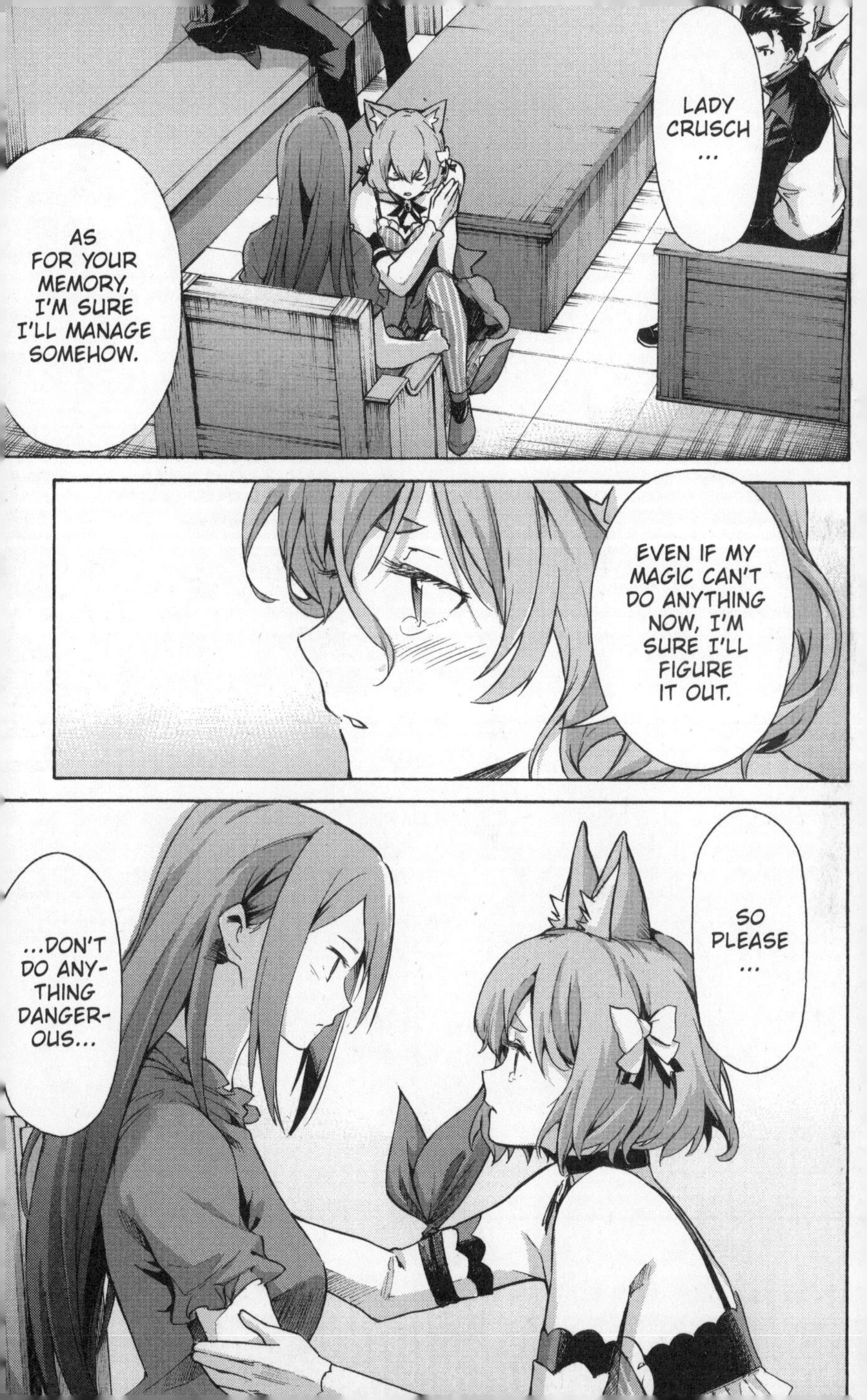
LADY CRUSCH ...
AS FOR YOUR MEMORY, I'M SURE I'LL MANAGE SOMEHOW.
EVEN IF MY MAGIC CAN'T DO ANYTHING NOW, I'M SURE I'LL FIGURE IT OUT.
SO PLEASE ...
...DON'T DO ANY-THING DANGER-OUS...

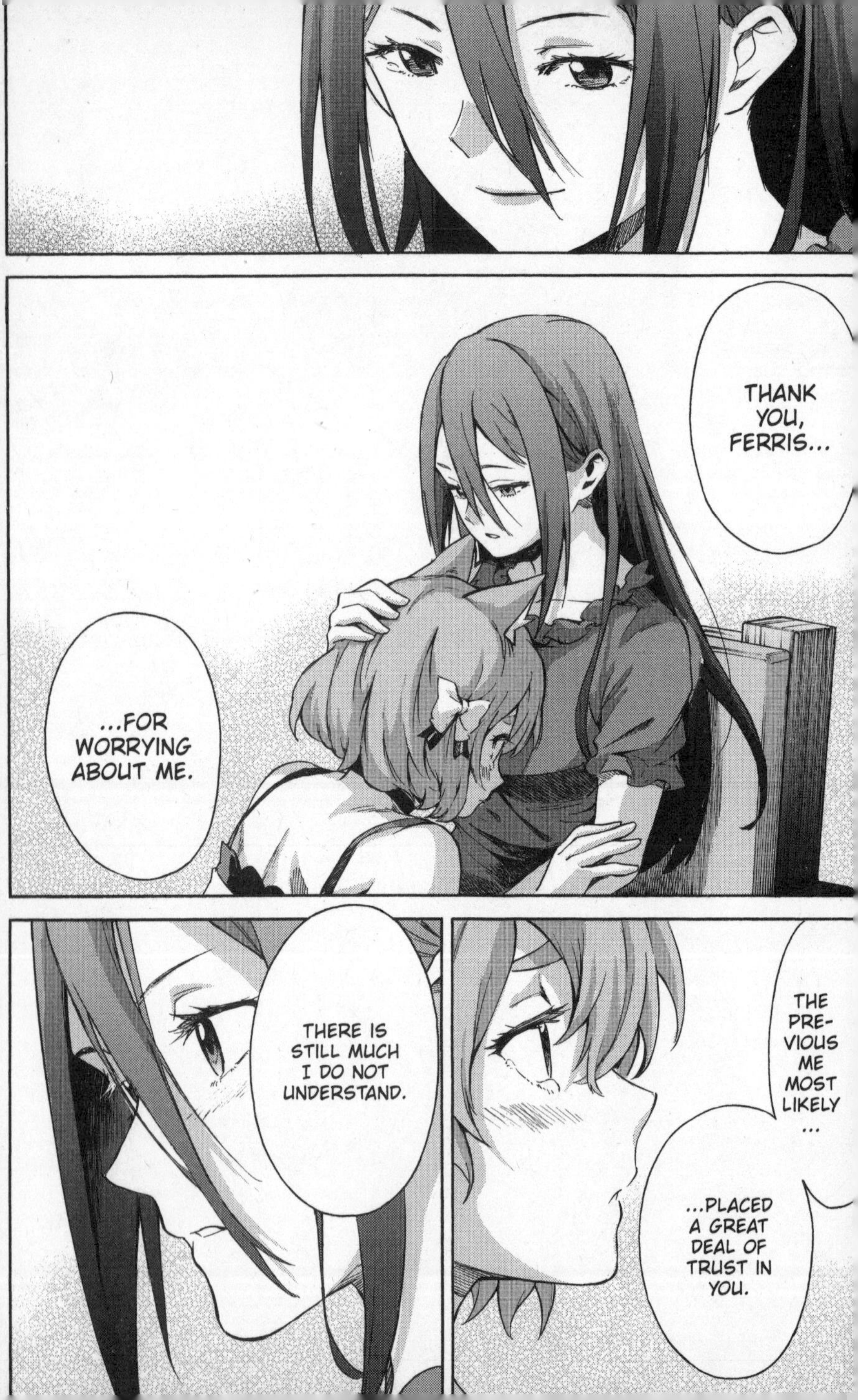
THANK YOU, FERRIS...
...FOR WORRYING ABOUT ME.
THE PRE-VIOUS ME MOST LIKELY...
...PLACED A GREAT DEAL OF TRUST IN YOU.
THERE IS STILL MUCH I DO NOT UNDERSTAND.

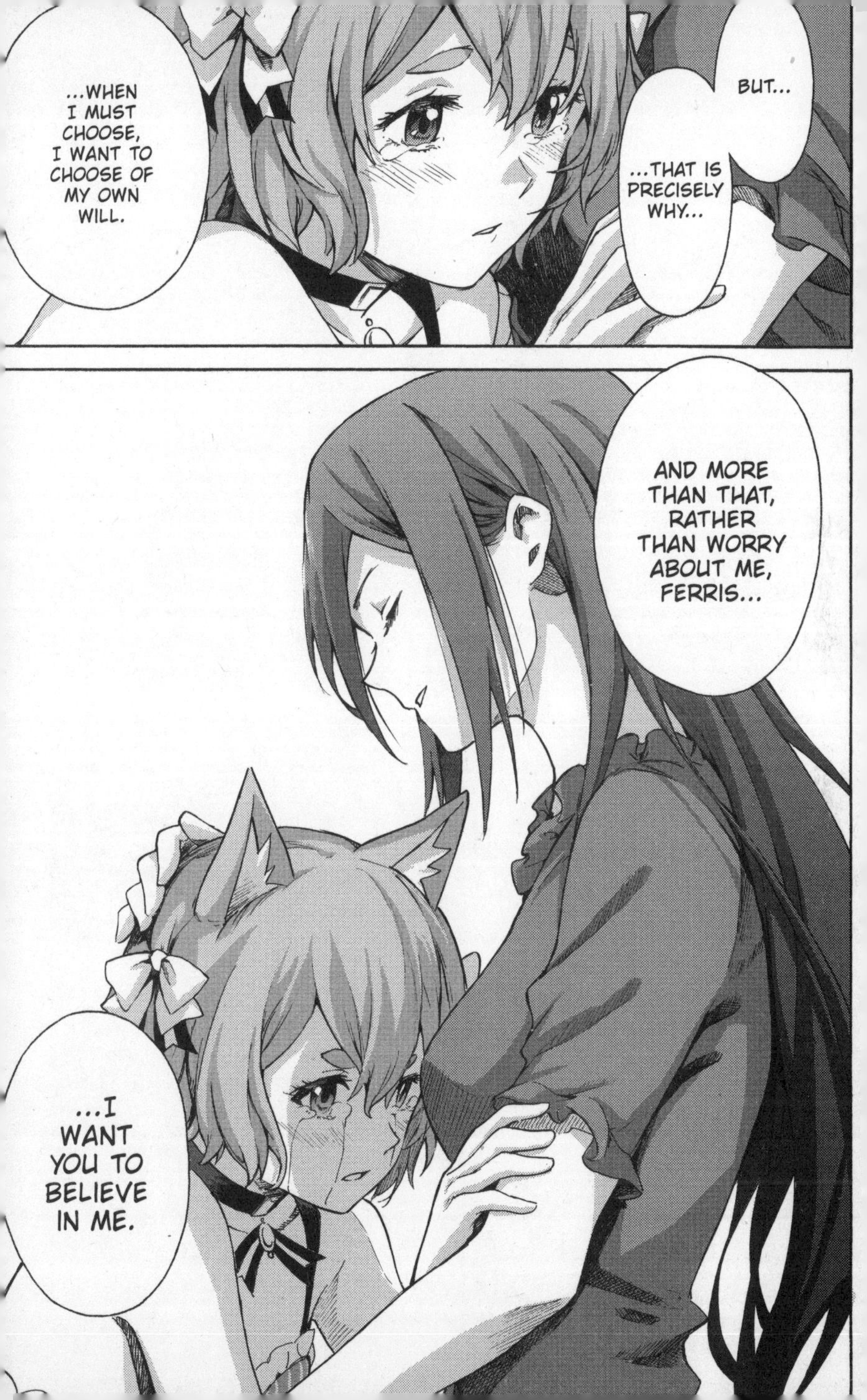
BUT...
...THAT IS PRECISELY WHY...
...WHEN I MUST CHOOSE, I WANT TO CHOOSE OF MY OWN WILL.
AND MORE THAN THAT, RATHER THAN WORRY ABOUT ME, FERRIS...
...I WANT YOU TO BELIEVE IN ME.

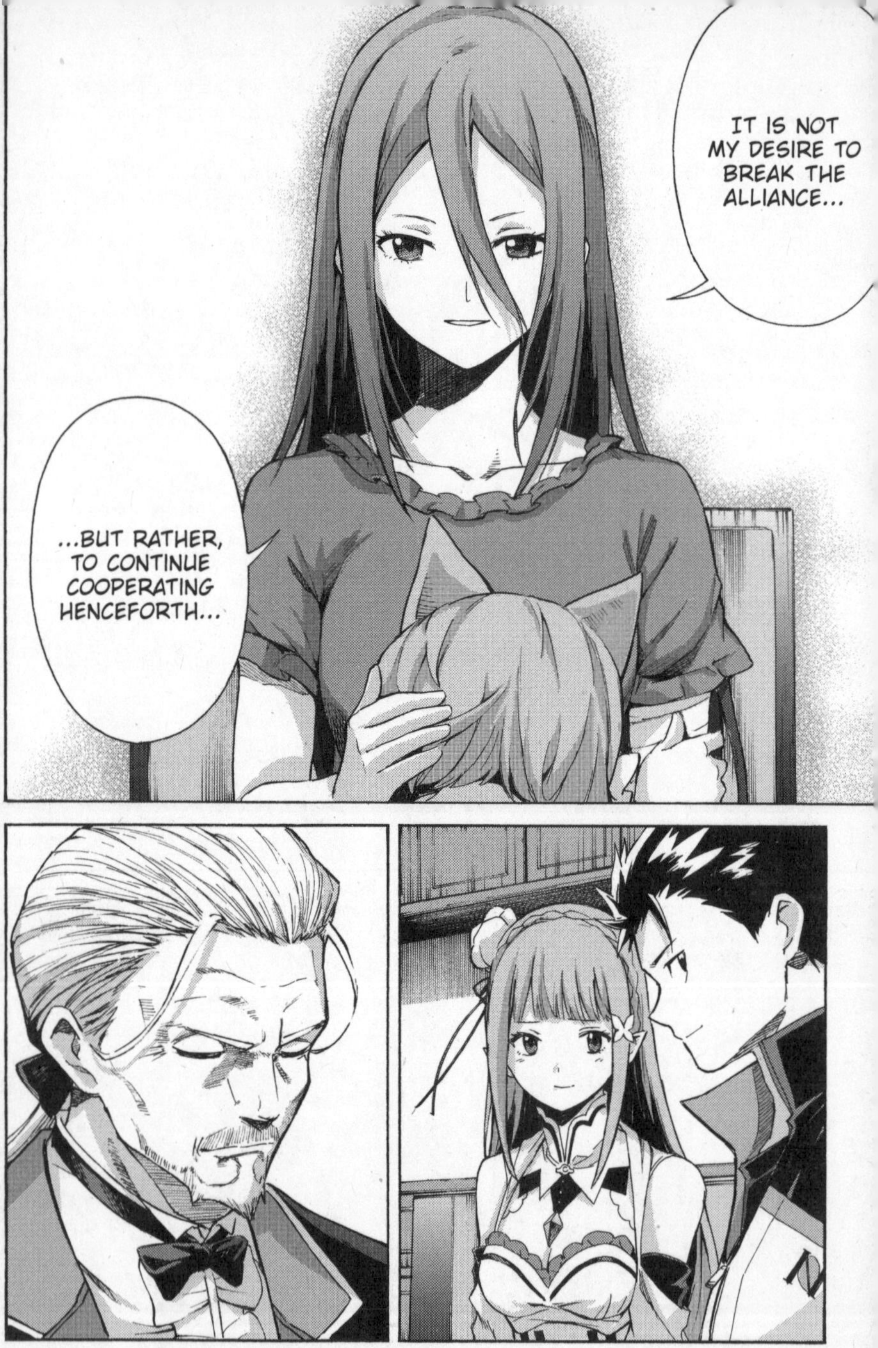
IT IS NOT MY DESIRE TO BREAK THE ALLIANCE...
...BUT RATHER, TO CONTINUE COOPERATING HENCEFORTH...

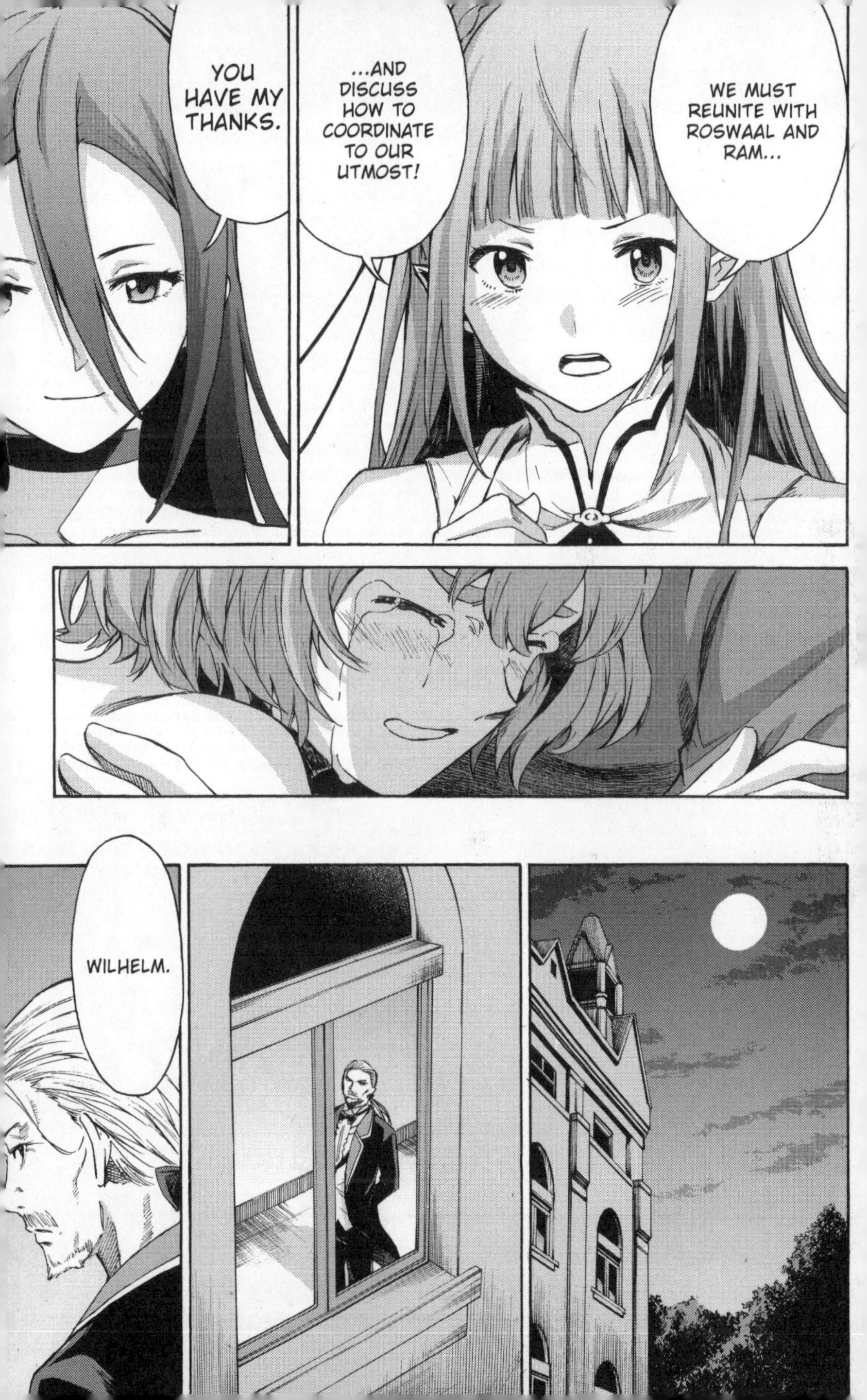
WE MUST REUNITE WITH ROSWAAL AND RAM...
...AND DISCUSS HOW TO COORDINATE TO OUR UTMOST!
YOU HAVE MY THANKS.
WILHELM.

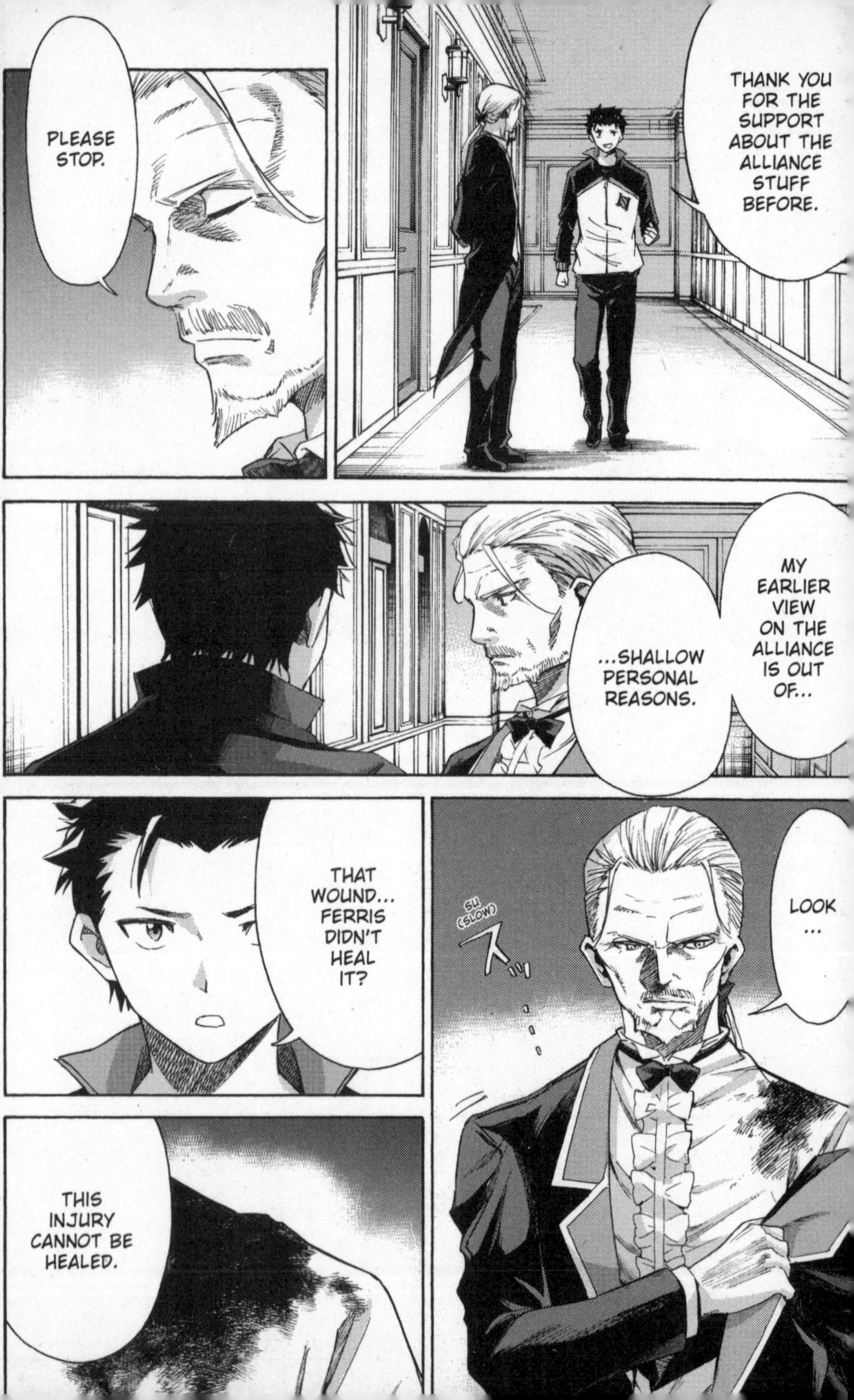
THANK YOU FOR THE SUPPORT ABOUT THE ALLIANCE STUFF BEFORE.
PLEASE STOP.
MY EARLIER VIEW ON THE ALLIANCE IS OUT OF...
...SHALLOW PERSONAL REASONS.
LOOK ...
SU (SLOW)
THAT WOUND... FERRIS DIDN'T HEAL IT?
THIS INJURY CANNOT BE HEALED.

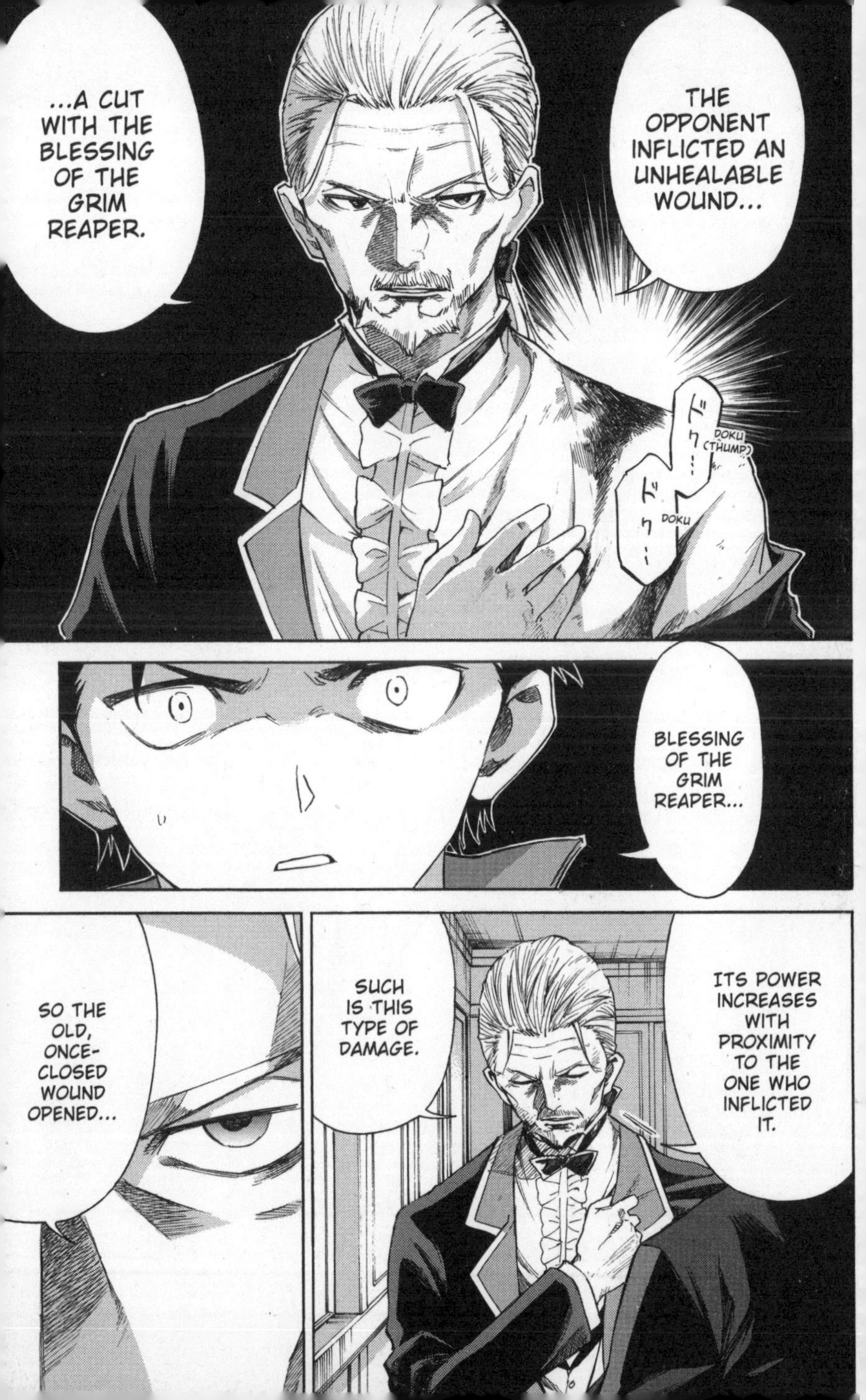
THE OPPONENT INFLICTED AN UNHEALABLE WOUND...
...A CUT WITH THE BLESSING OF THE GRIM REAPER.
ドク…
DOKU (THUMP)
ドク…
DOKU
BLESSING OF THE GRIM REAPER...
ITS POWER INCREASES WITH PROXIMITY TO THE ONE WHO INFLICTED IT.
SUCH IS THIS TYPE OF DAMAGE.
SO THE OLD, ONCE-CLOSED WOUND OPENED...

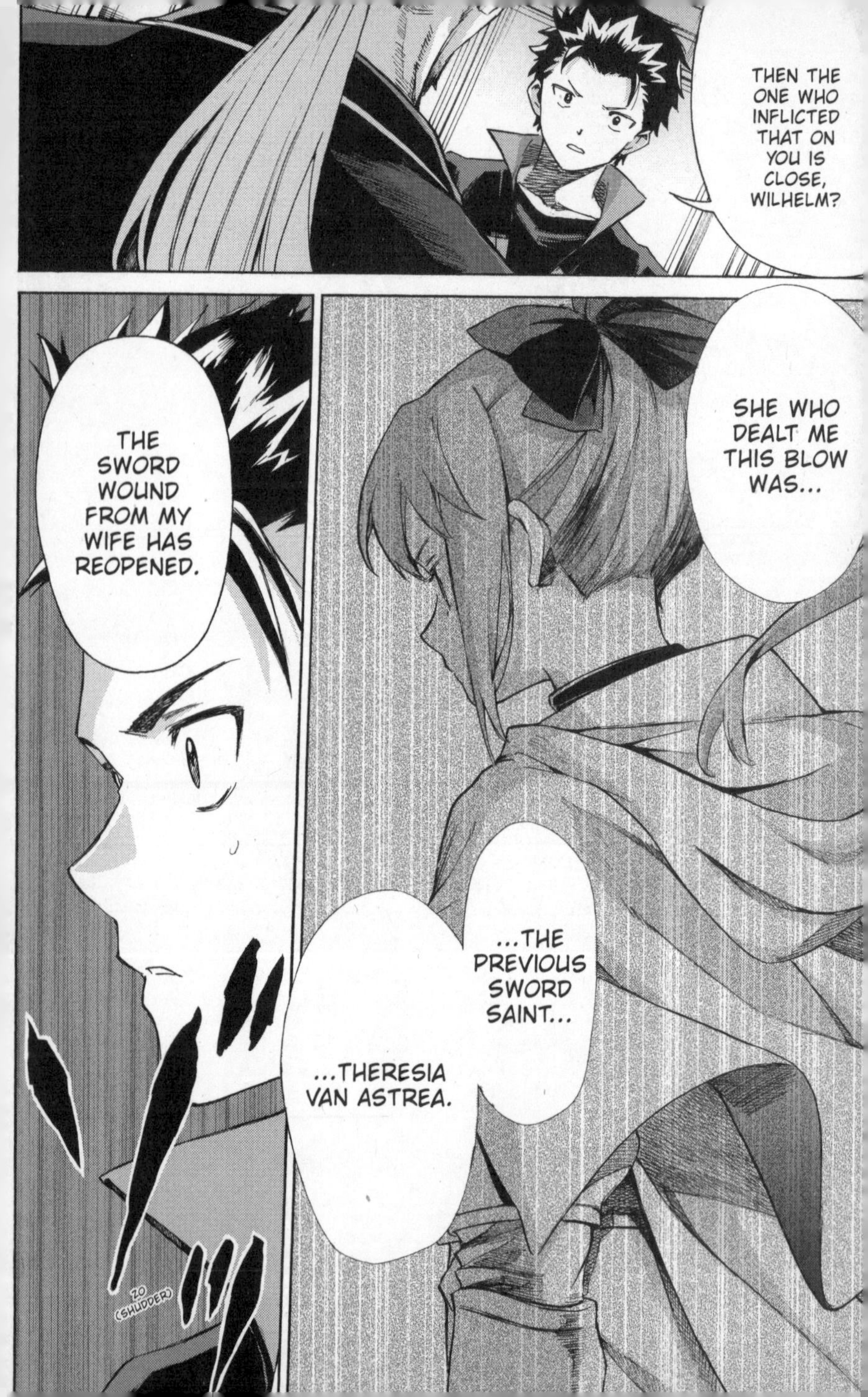
THEN THE ONE WHO INFLICTED THAT ON YOU IS CLOSE, WILHELM?
SHE WHO DEALT ME THIS BLOW WAS...
THE SWORD WOUND FROM MY WIFE HAS REOPENED.
...THE PREVIOUS SWORD SAINT...
...THERESIA VAN ASTREA.
ZO (SHUDDER)

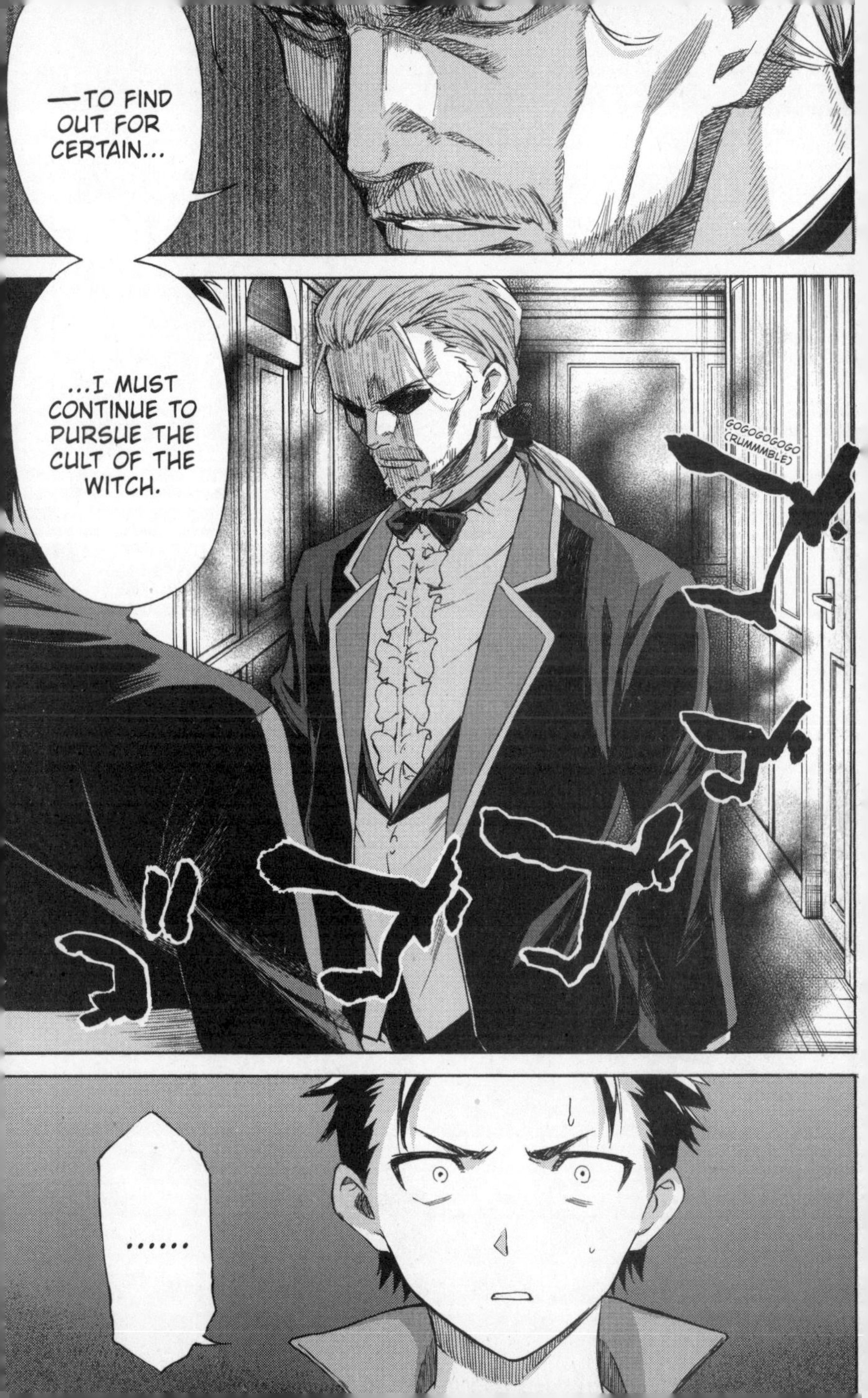
—TO FIND OUT FOR CERTAIN...
...I MUST CONTINUE TO PURSUE THE CULT OF THE WITCH.
GOGOGOGOGO (RUMMMBLE)
......

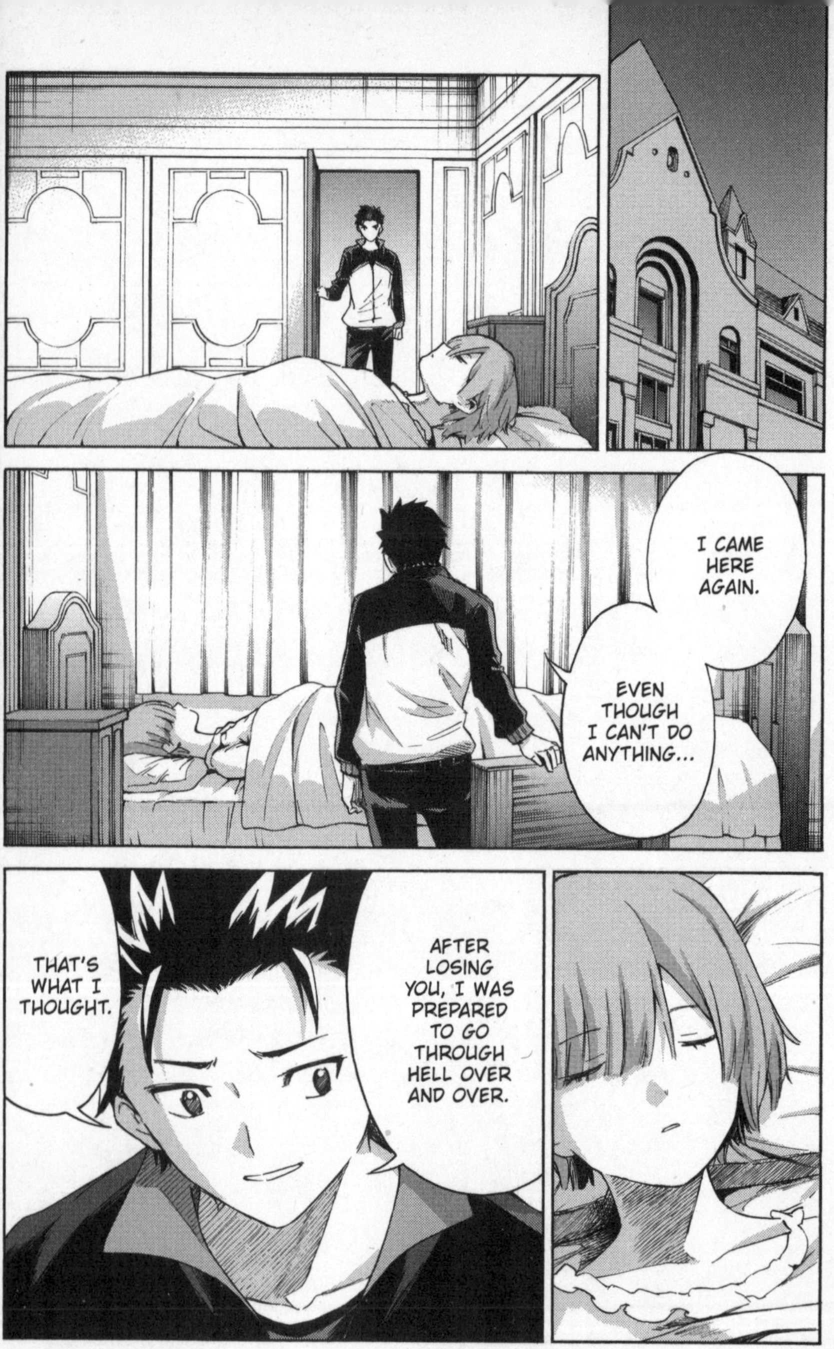
I CAME HERE AGAIN.
EVEN THOUGH I CAN'T DO ANYTHING...
AFTER LOSING YOU, I WAS PREPARED TO GO THROUGH HELL OVER AND OVER.
THAT'S WHAT I THOUGHT.

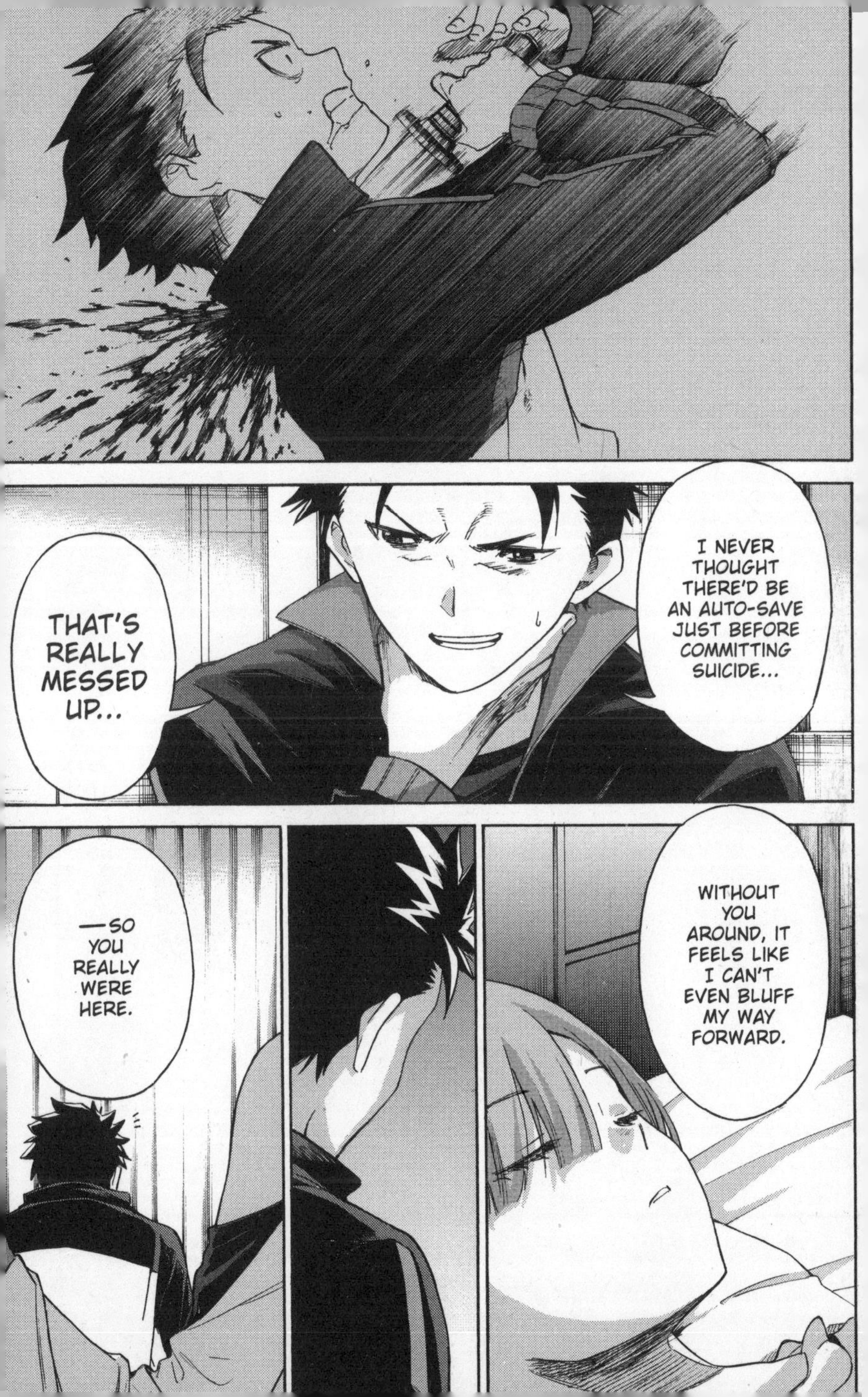
I NEVER THOUGHT THERE'D BE AN AUTO-SAVE JUST BEFORE COMMITTING SUICIDE...
THAT'S REALLY MESSED UP...
WITHOUT YOU AROUND, IT FEELS LIKE I CAN'T EVEN BLUFF MY WAY FORWARD.
—SO YOU REALLY WERE HERE.

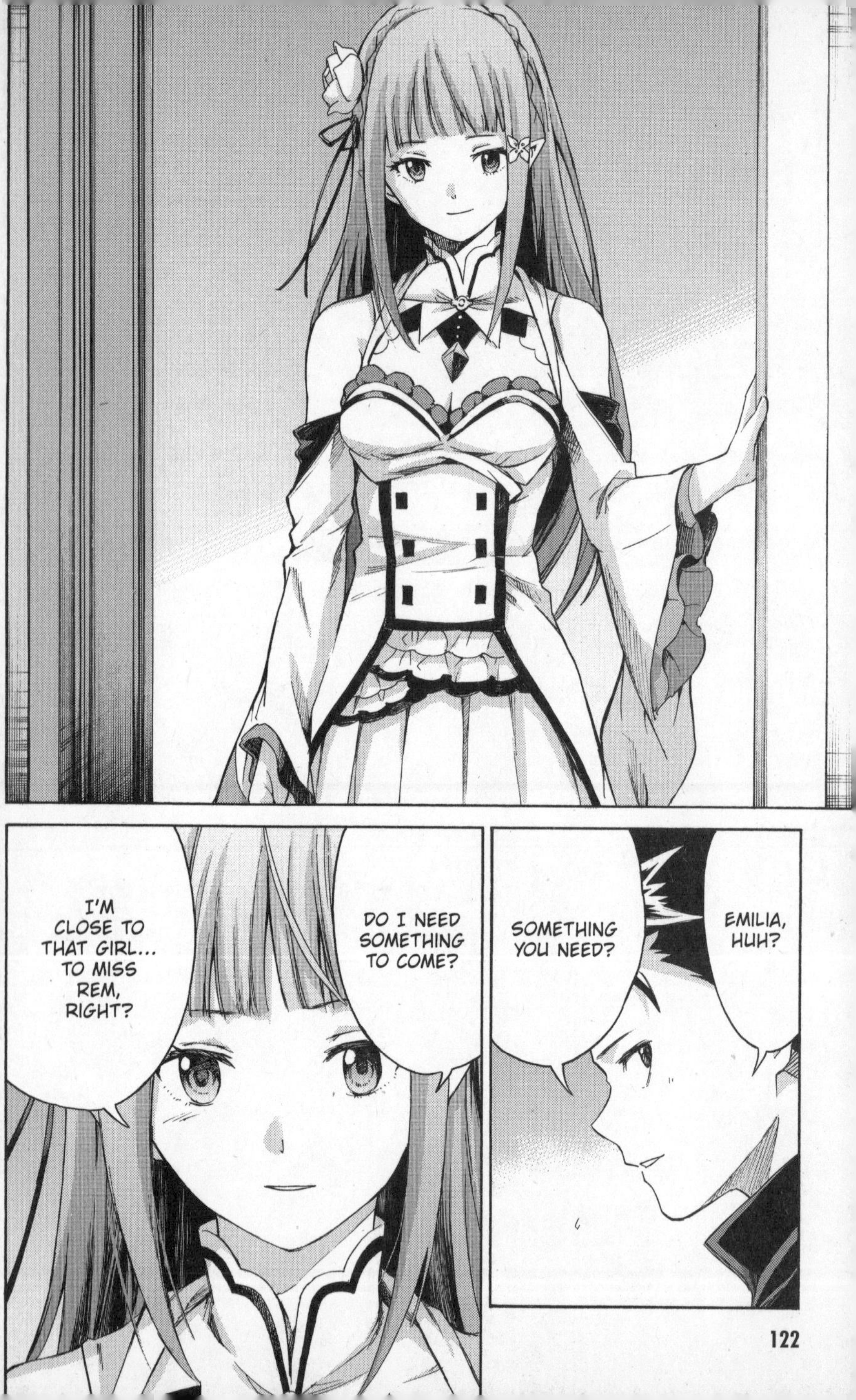
EMILIA, HUH?
SOMETHING YOU NEED?
DO I NEED SOMETHING TO COME?
I'M CLOSE TO THAT GIRL... TO MISS REM, RIGHT?

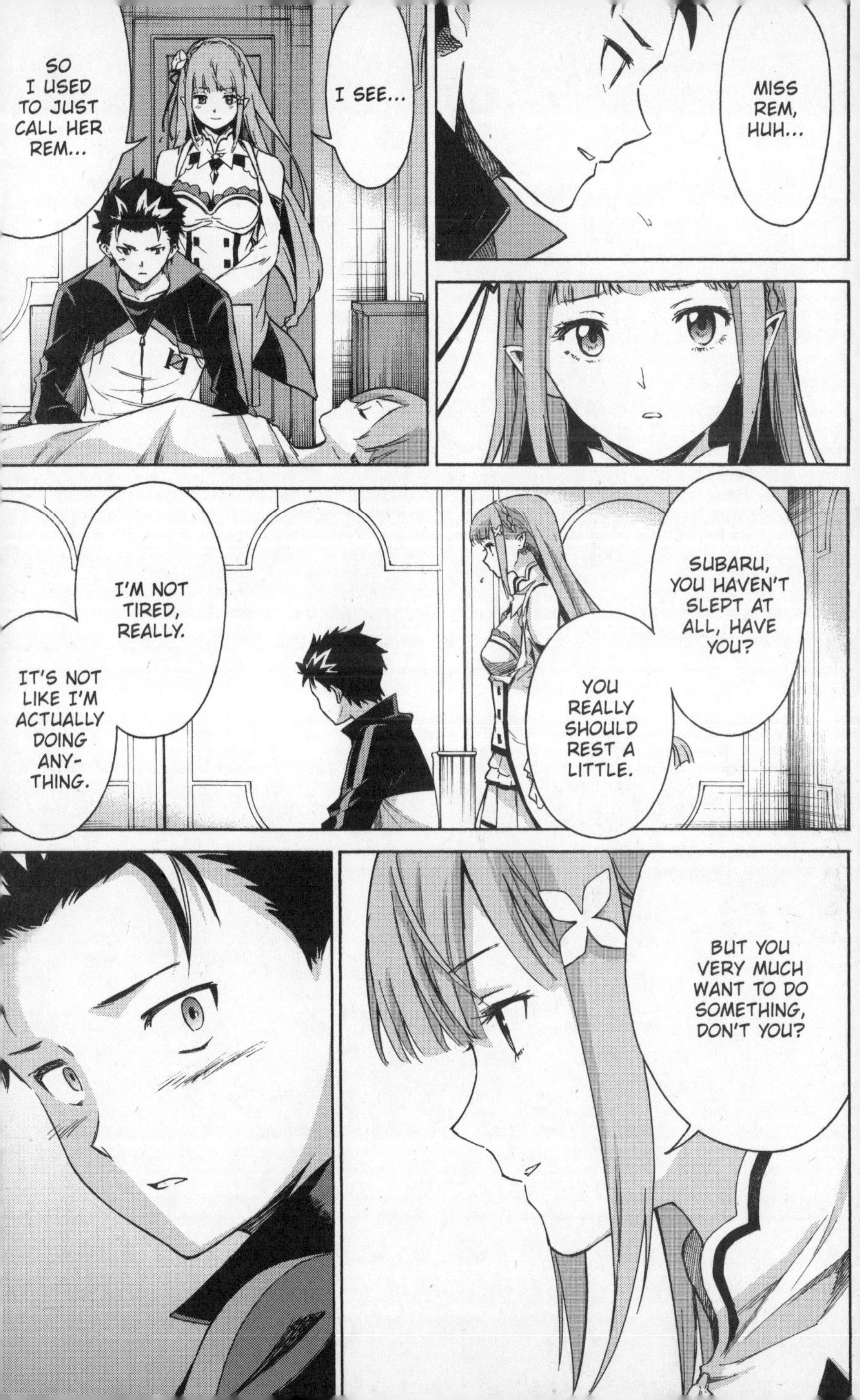
MISS REM, HUH...
I SEE...
SO I USED TO JUST CALL HER REM...
SUBARU, YOU HAVEN'T SLEPT AT ALL, HAVE YOU?
YOU REALLY SHOULD REST A LITTLE.
I'M NOT TIRED, REALLY.
IT'S NOT LIKE I'M ACTUALLY DOING ANY-THING.
BUT YOU VERY MUCH WANT TO DO SOMETHING, DON'T YOU?

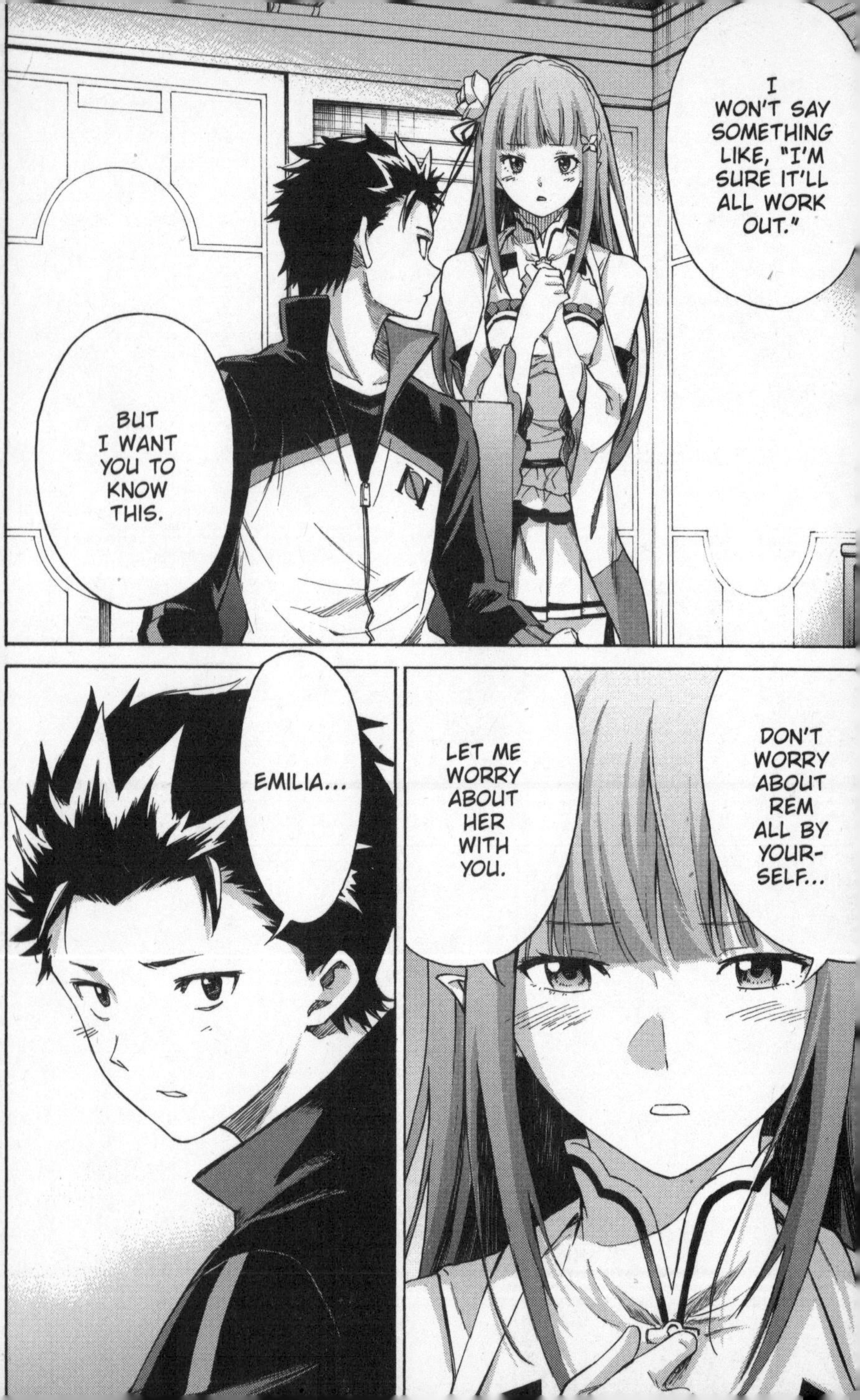
I WON'T SAY SOMETHING LIKE, "I'M SURE IT'LL ALL WORK OUT."
BUT I WANT YOU TO KNOW THIS.
DON'T WORRY ABOUT REM ALL BY YOURSELF...
LET ME WORRY ABOUT HER WITH YOU.
EMILIA...

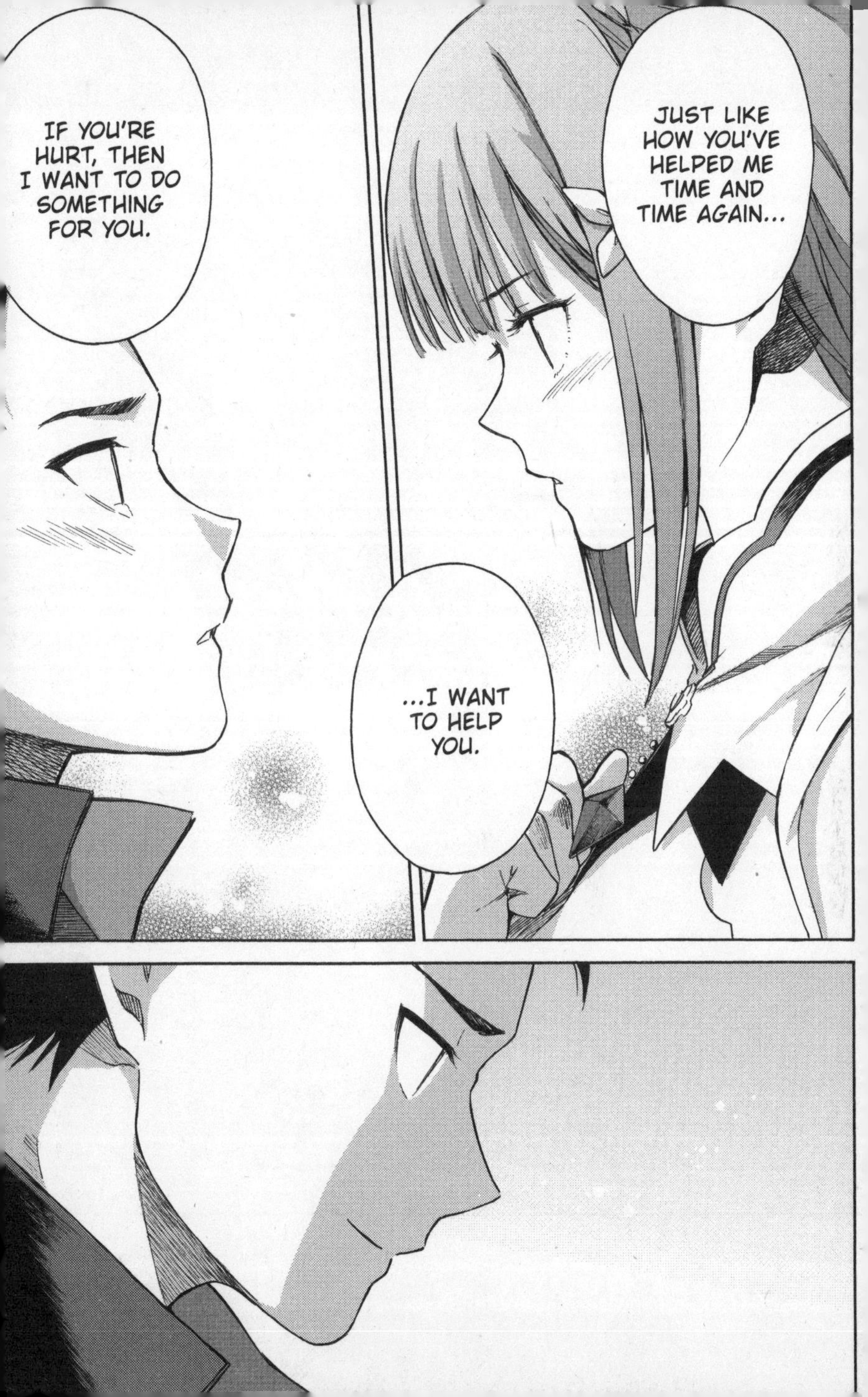
JUST LIKE HOW YOU'VE HELPED ME TIME AND TIME AGAIN...
...I WANT TO HELP YOU.
IF YOU'RE HURT, THEN I WANT TO DO SOMETHING FOR YOU.

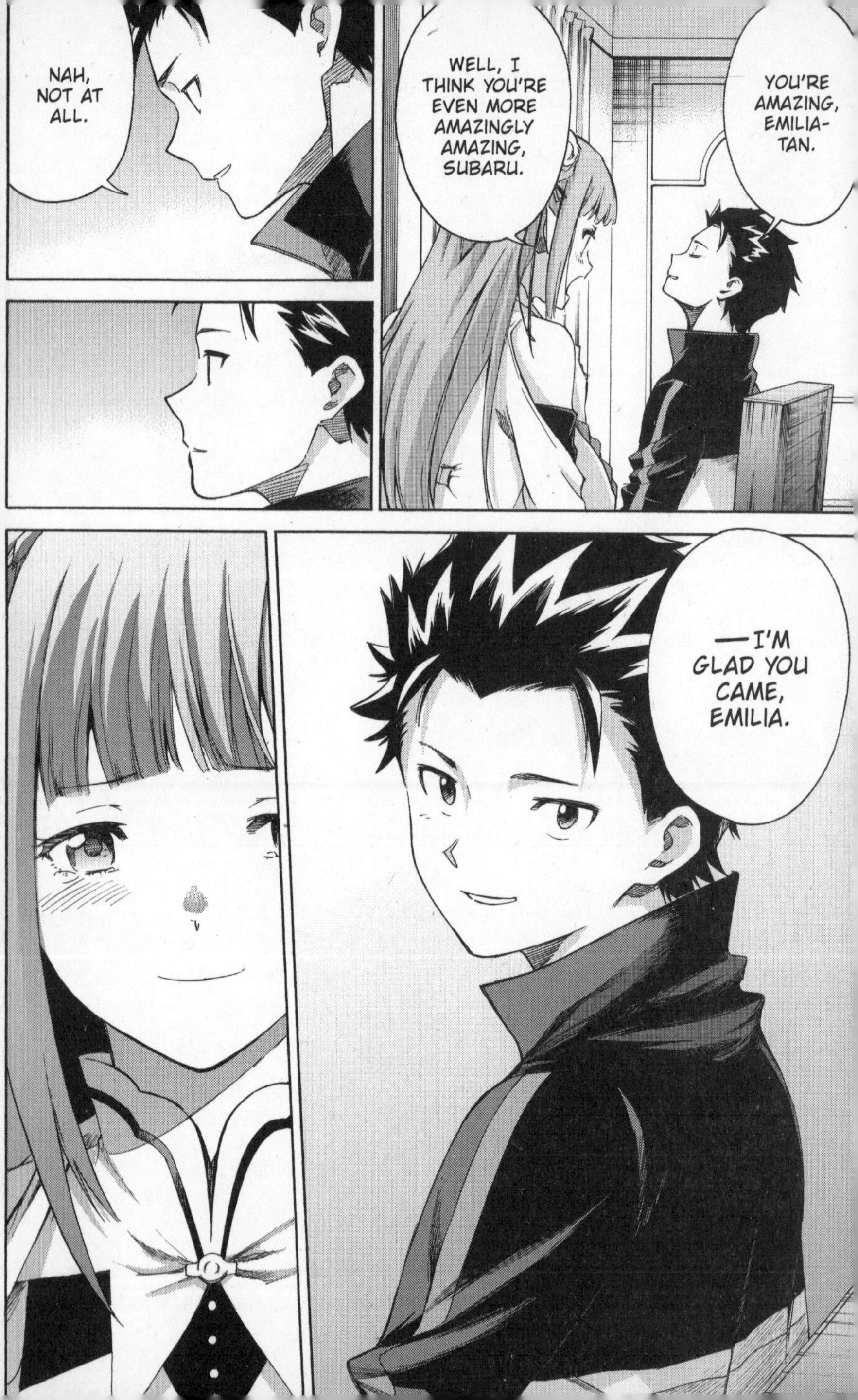
YOU'RE AMAZING, EMILIA-TAN.
WELL, I THINK YOU'RE EVEN MORE AMAZINGLY AMAZING, SUBARU.
NAH, NOT AT ALL.
—I'M GLAD YOU CAME, EMILIA.

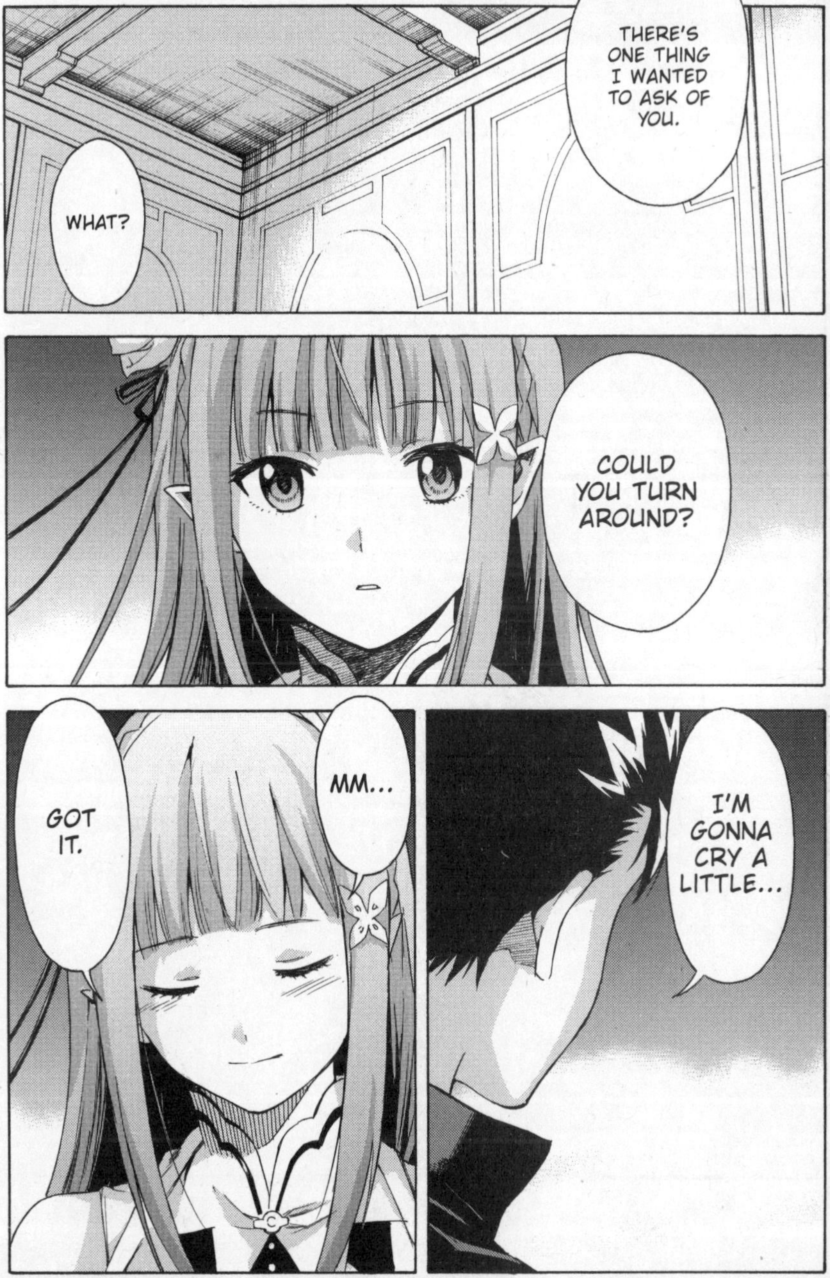
THERE'S ONE THING I WANTED TO ASK OF YOU.
WHAT?
COULD YOU TURN AROUND?
I'M GONNA CRY A LITTLE...
MM...
GOT IT.

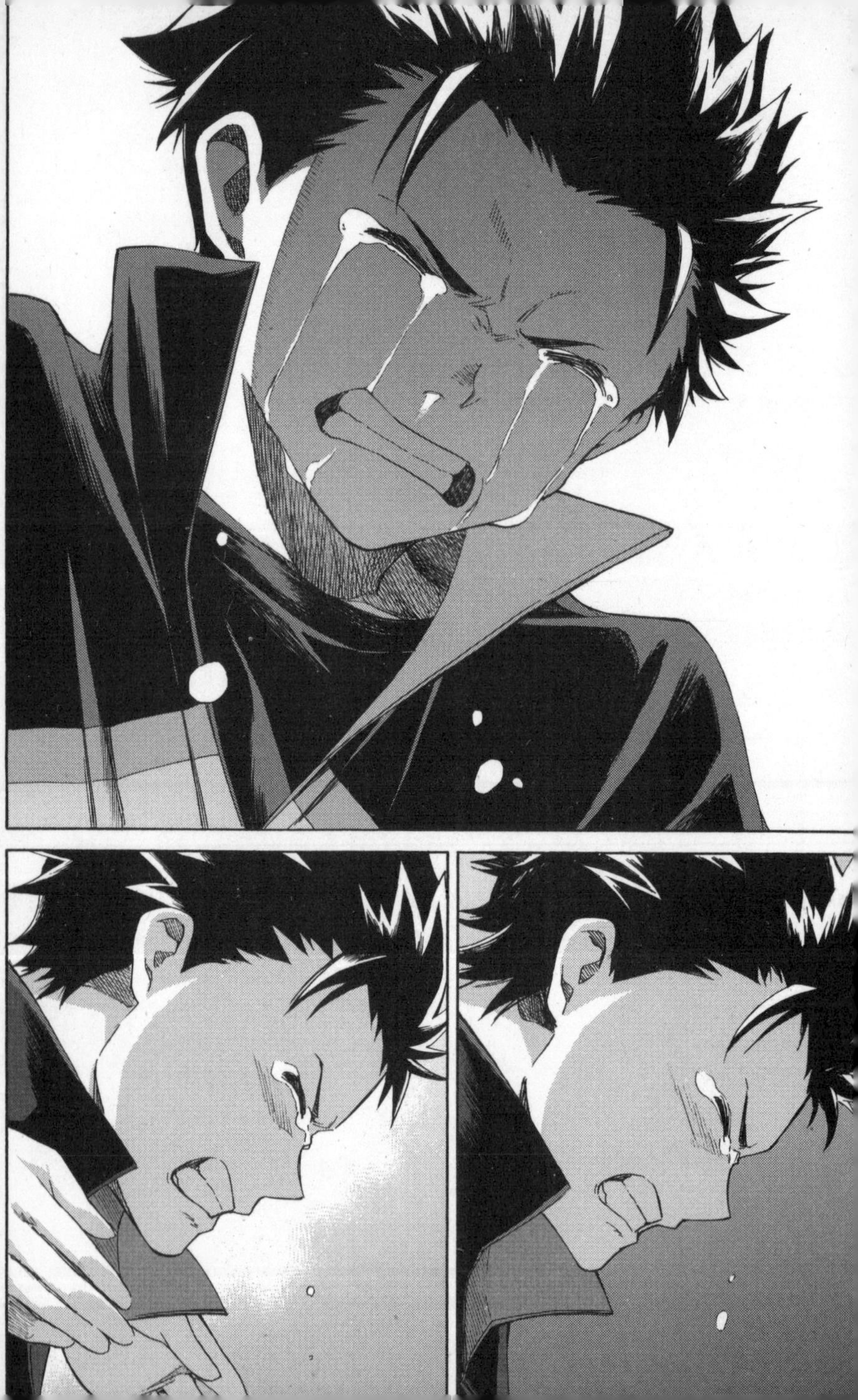

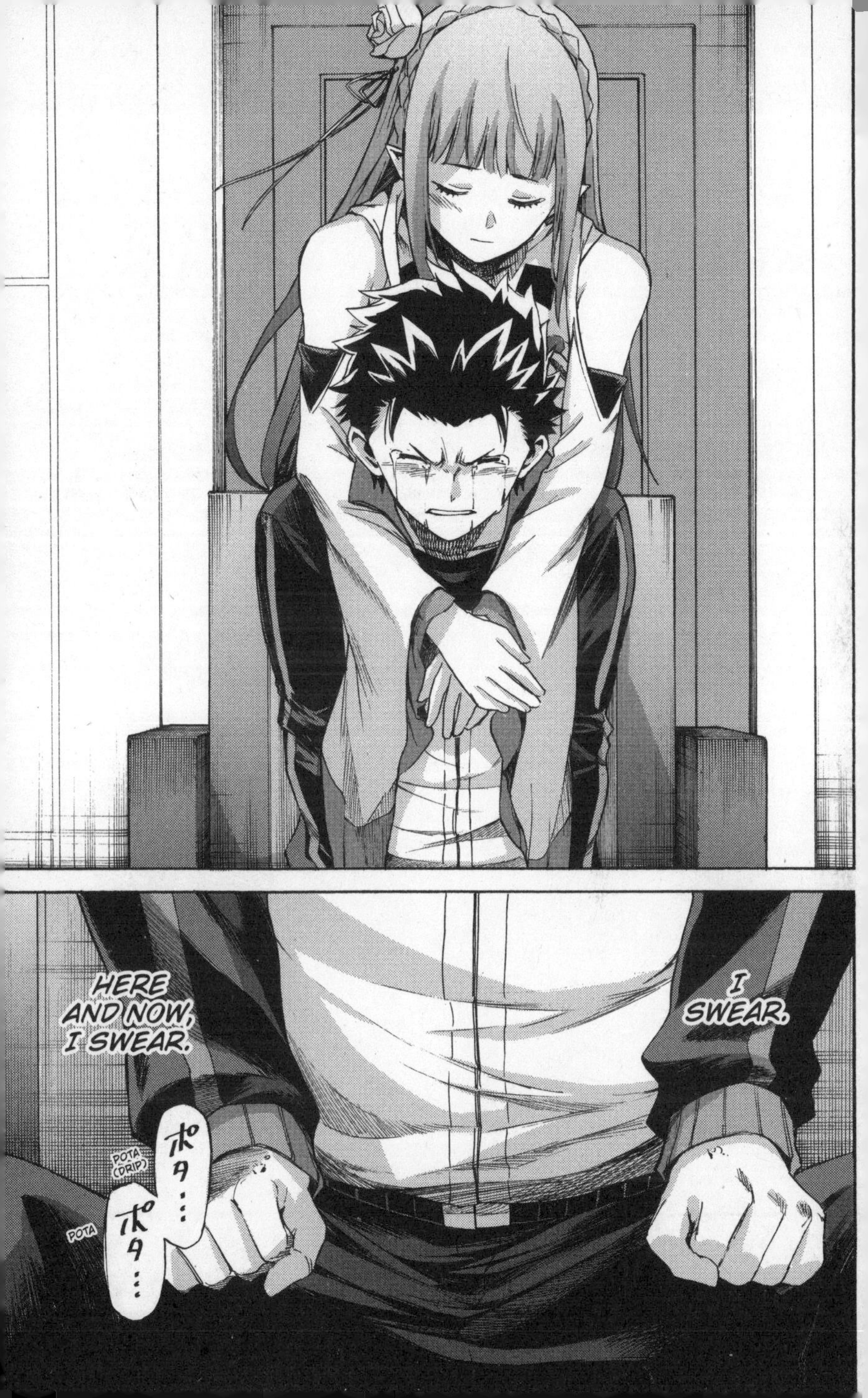
I SWEAR.
HERE AND NOW, I SWEAR.
ポタ…
POTA (DRIP)
ポタ…
POTA

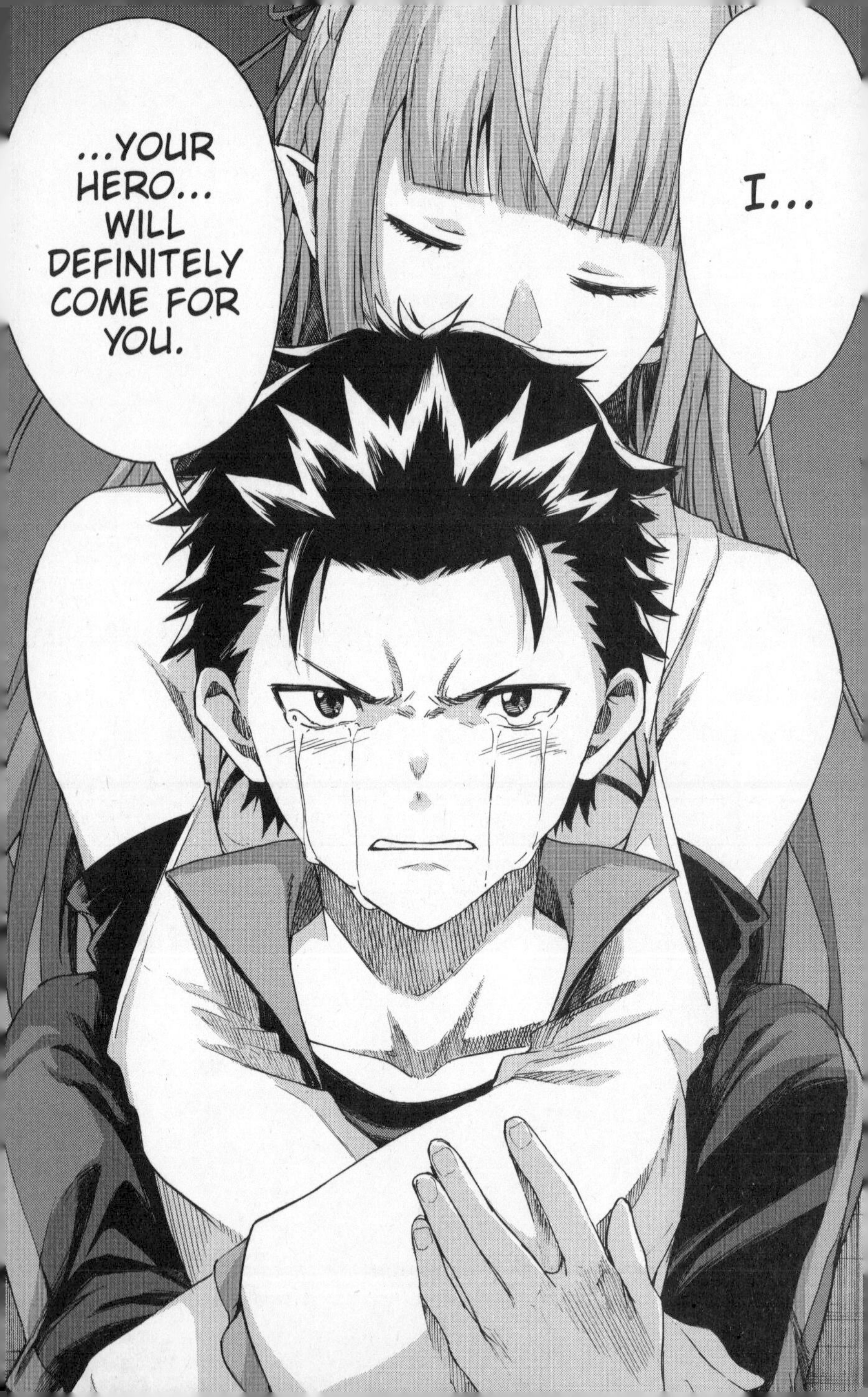
I...
...YOUR HERO... WILL DEFINITELY COME FOR YOU.

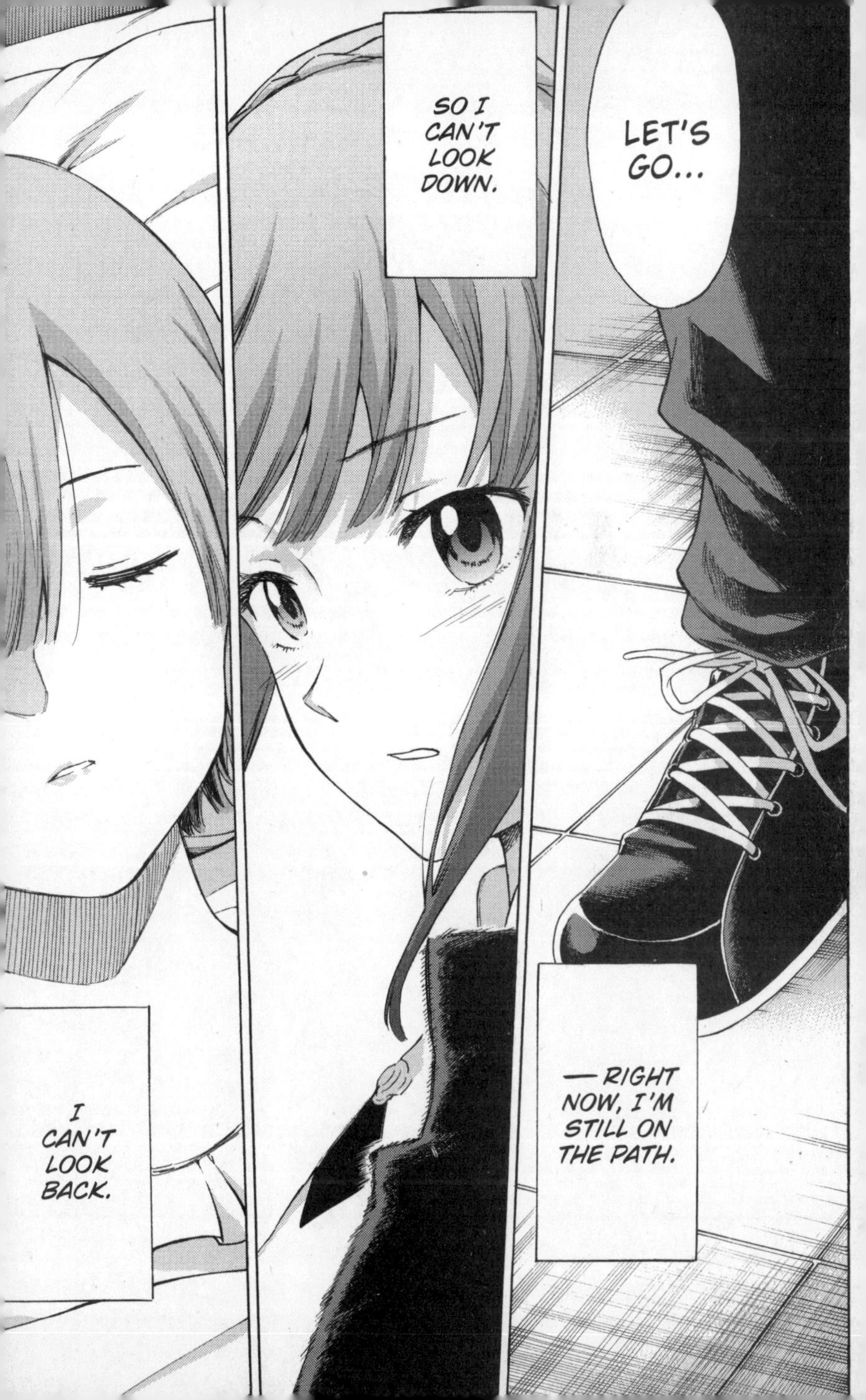
LET'S GO...
—RIGHT NOW, I'M STILL ON THE PATH.
SO I CAN'T LOOK DOWN.
I CAN'T LOOK BACK.

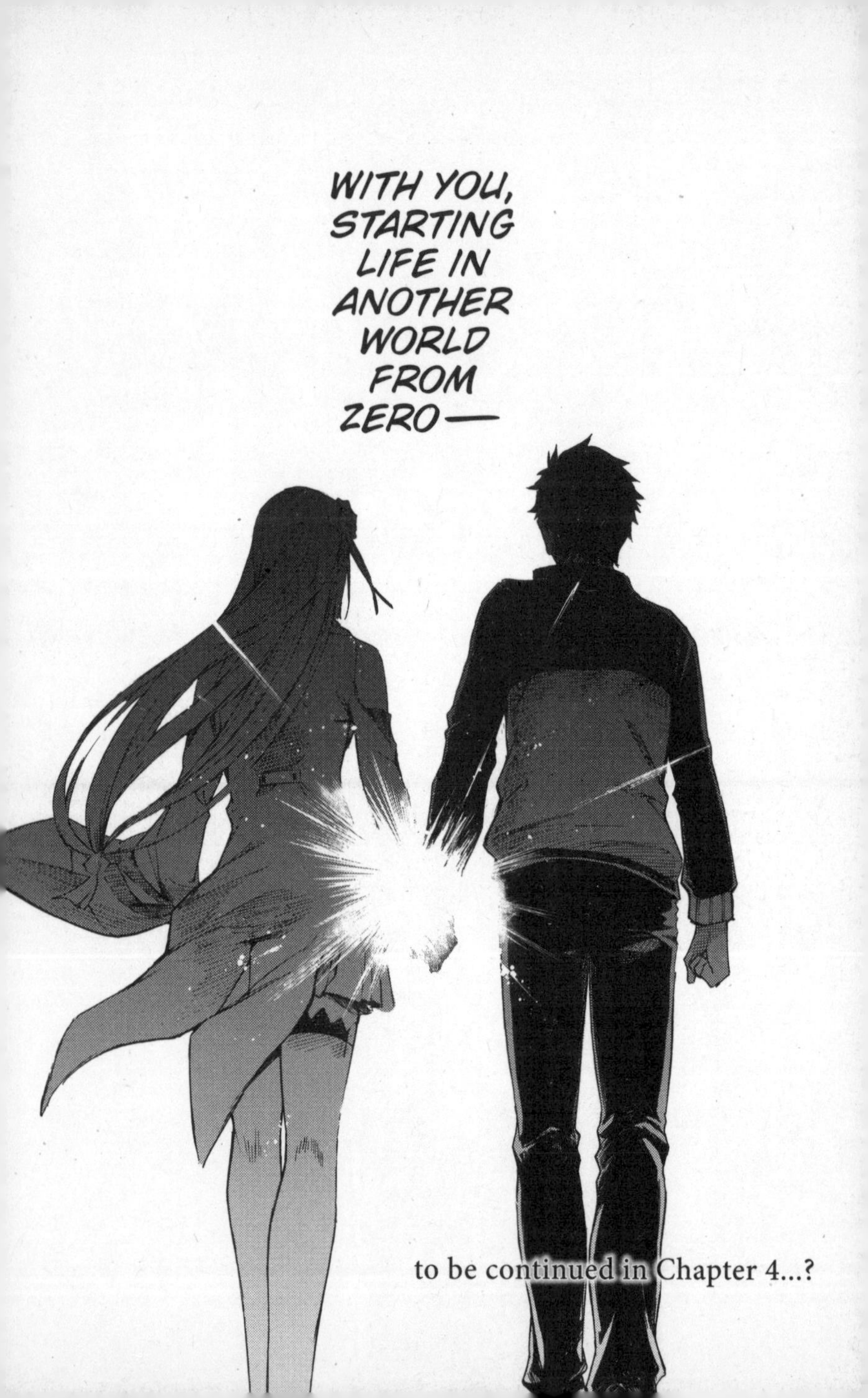
WITH YOU, STARTING LIFE IN ANOTHER WORLD FROM ZERO—
to be continued in Chapter 4...?

Re:ZERO -Starting Life in Another World-

The only ability Subaru Natsuki gets when he's summoned to another world is
time travel via his own death. But to save her, he'll die as many times as it takes.

Re:ZERO
-Starting Life in Another World-

Truth of Zero
The only ability Subaru Natsuki gets when he's summoned
to another world is time travel via his own death.
But to save her, he'll die as many times as it takes.

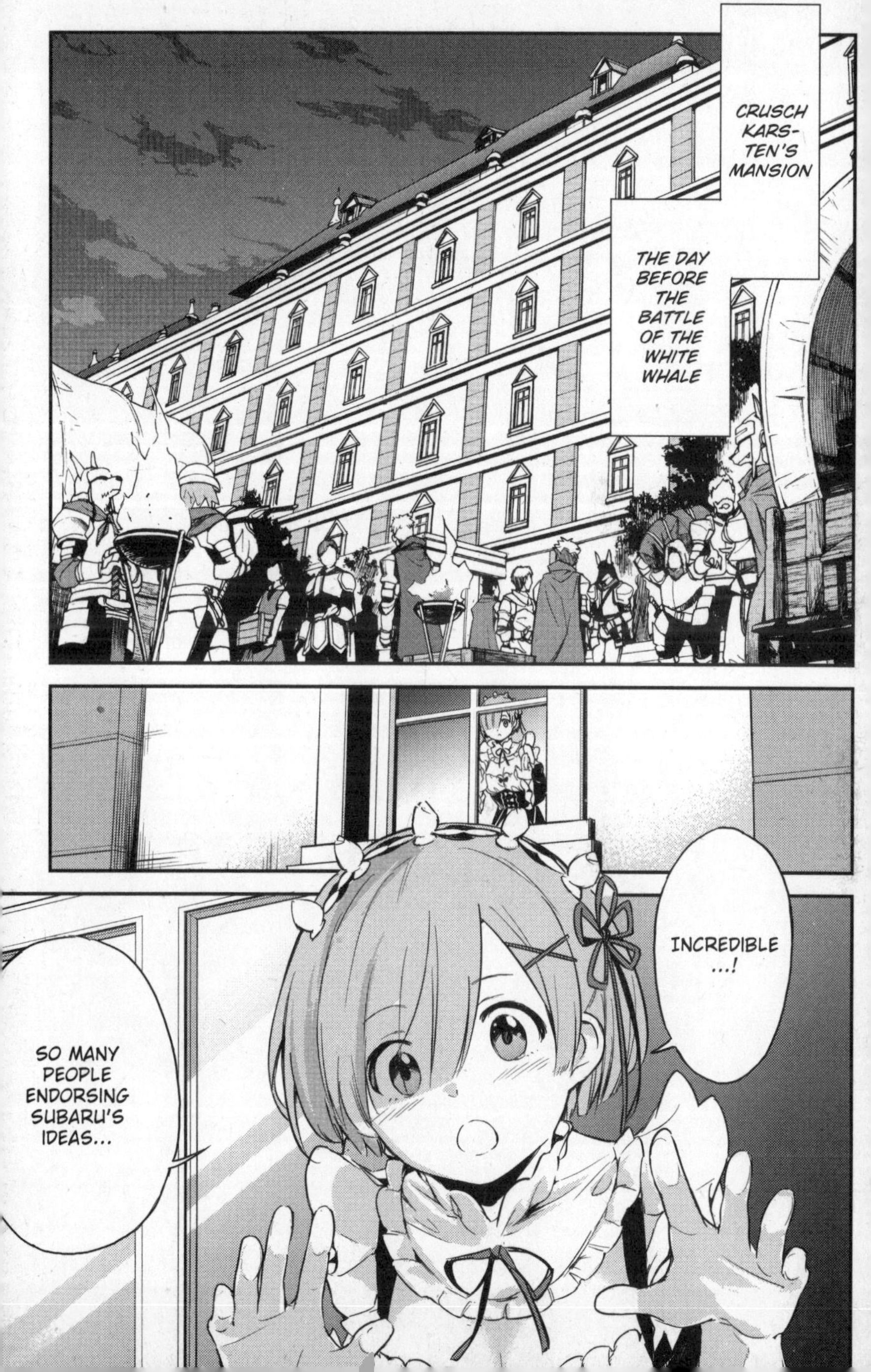
CRUSCH KARS-TEN'S MANSION
THE DAY BEFORE THE BATTLE OF THE WHITE WHALE
INCREDIBLE ...!
SO MANY PEOPLE ENDORSING SUBARU'S IDEAS...

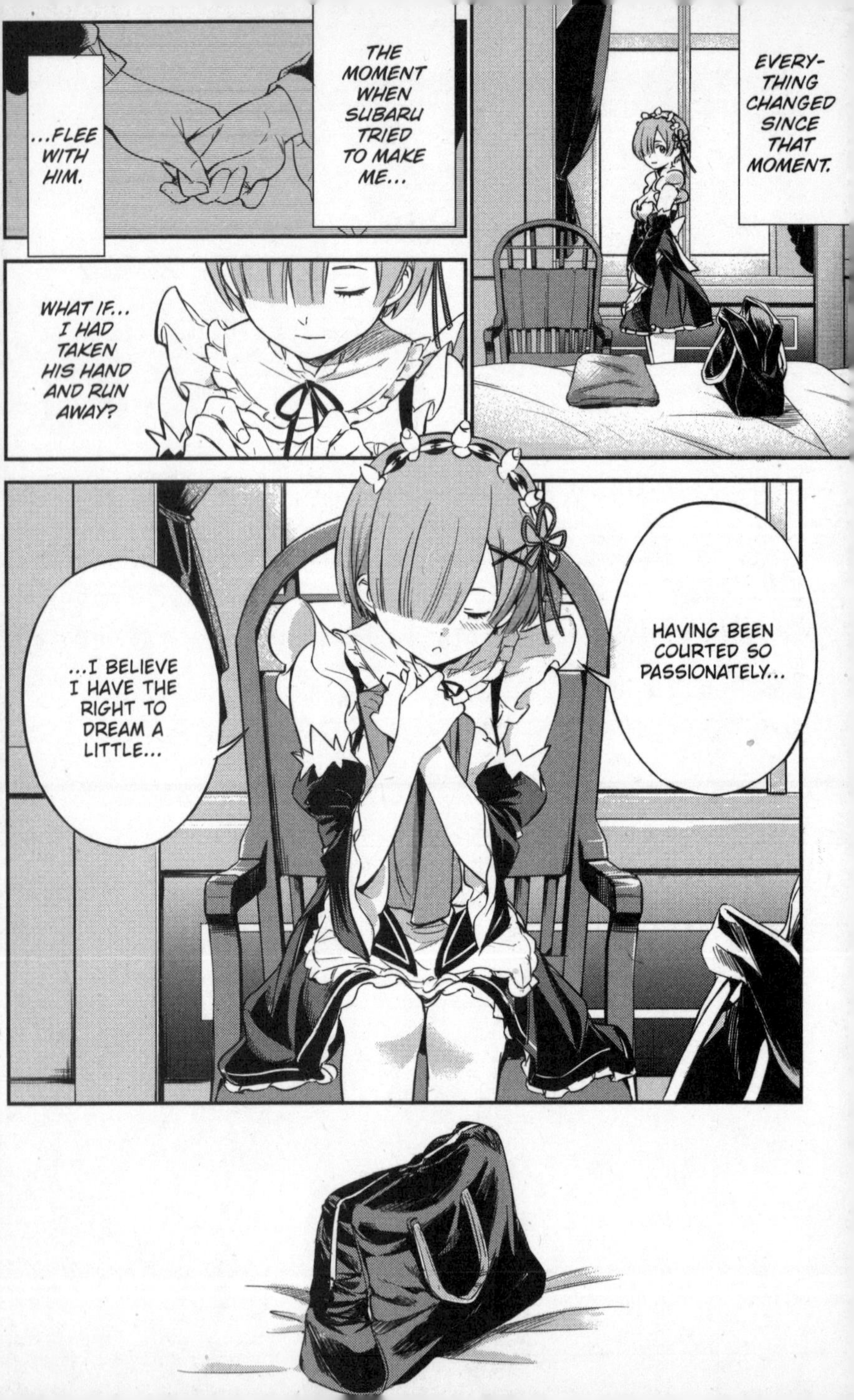
EVERYTHING CHANGED SINCE THAT MOMENT.
THE MOMENT WHEN SUBARU TRIED TO MAKE ME...
...FLEE WITH HIM.
WHAT IF... I HAD TAKEN HIS HAND AND RUN AWAY?
HAVING BEEN COURTED SO PASSIONATELY...
...I BELIEVE I HAVE THE RIGHT TO DREAM A LITTLE...

Special Story

On the Eve of Battle, Thinking of You

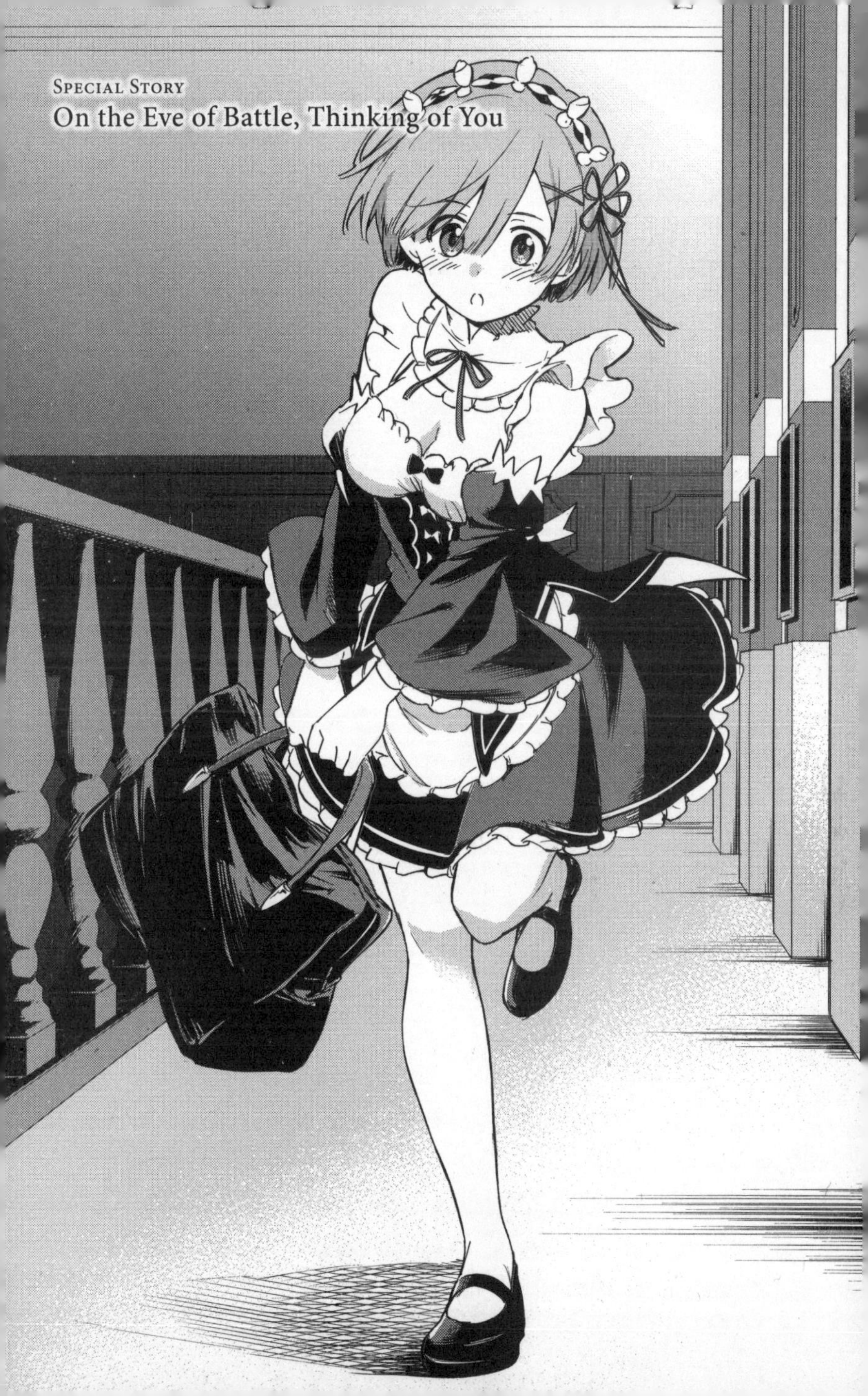

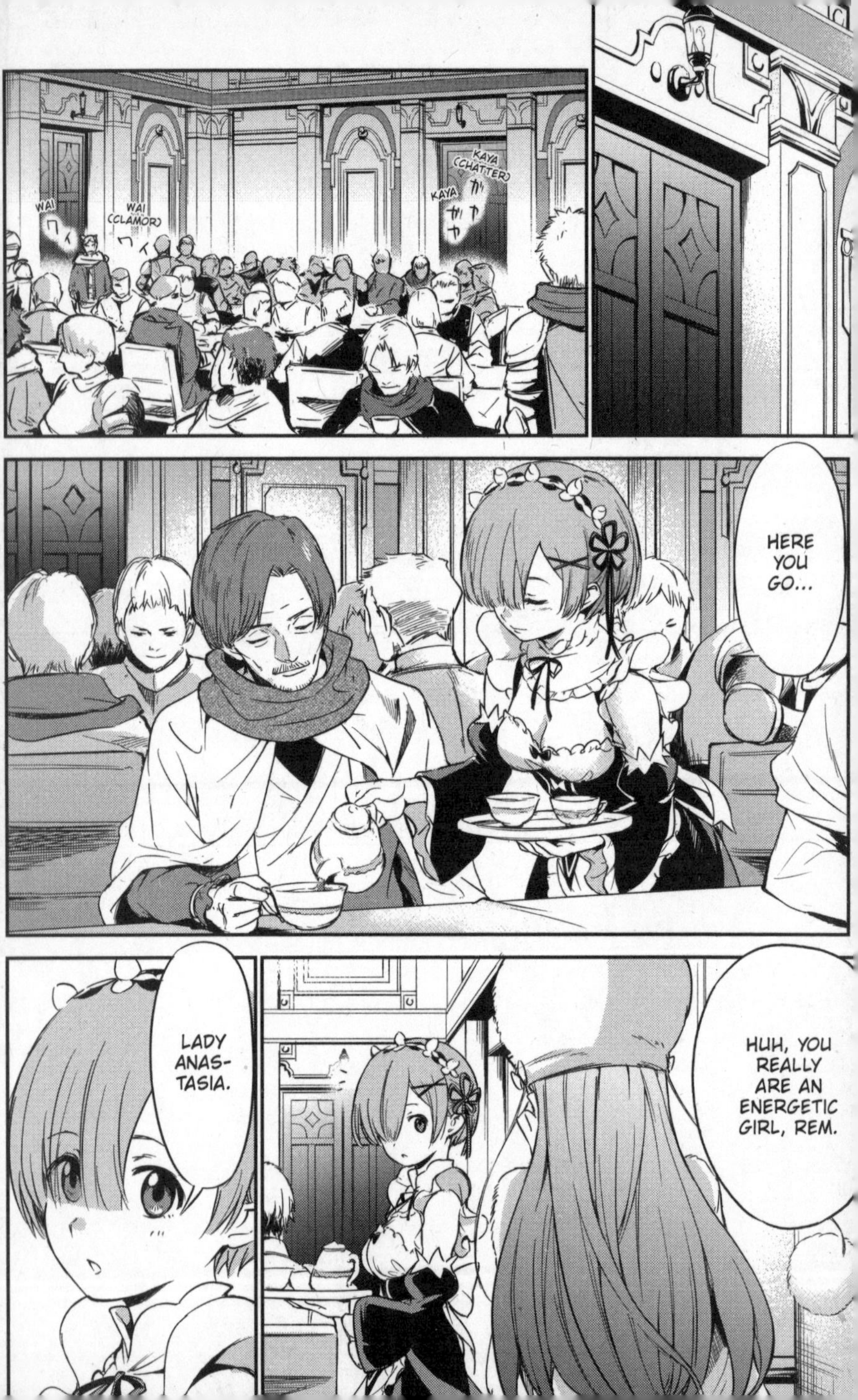
KAYA (CHATTER)
ガヤ
KAYA
ガヤ
WAI (CLAMOR)
ワイ
WAI
ワイ
HERE YOU GO...
HUH, YOU REALLY ARE AN ENERGETIC GIRL, REM.
LADY ANAS-TASIA.

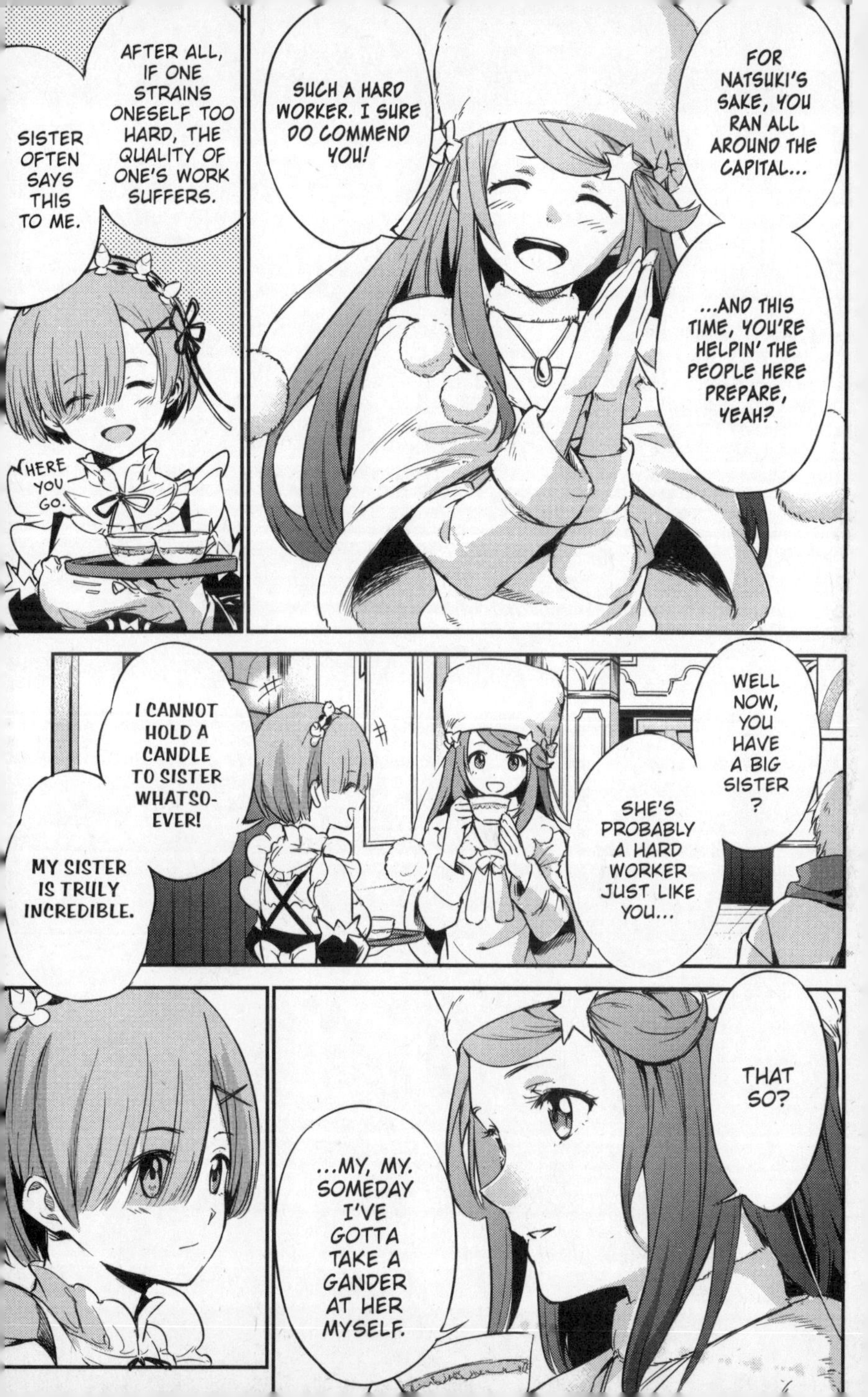
FOR NATSUKI'S SAKE, YOU RAN ALL AROUND THE CAPITAL...
...AND THIS TIME, YOU'RE HELPIN' THE PEOPLE HERE PREPARE, YEAH?
SUCH A HARD WORKER. I SURE DO COMMEND YOU!
AFTER ALL, IF ONE STRAINS ONESELF TOO HARD, THE QUALITY OF ONE'S WORK SUFFERS.
SISTER OFTEN SAYS THIS TO ME.
HERE YOU GO.
WELL NOW, YOU HAVE A BIG SISTER?
SHE'S PROBABLY A HARD WORKER JUST LIKE YOU...
I CANNOT HOLD A CANDLE TO SISTER WHATSOEVER!
MY SISTER IS TRULY INCREDIBLE.
THAT SO?
...MY, MY. SOMEDAY I'VE GOTTA TAKE A GANDER AT HER MYSELF.

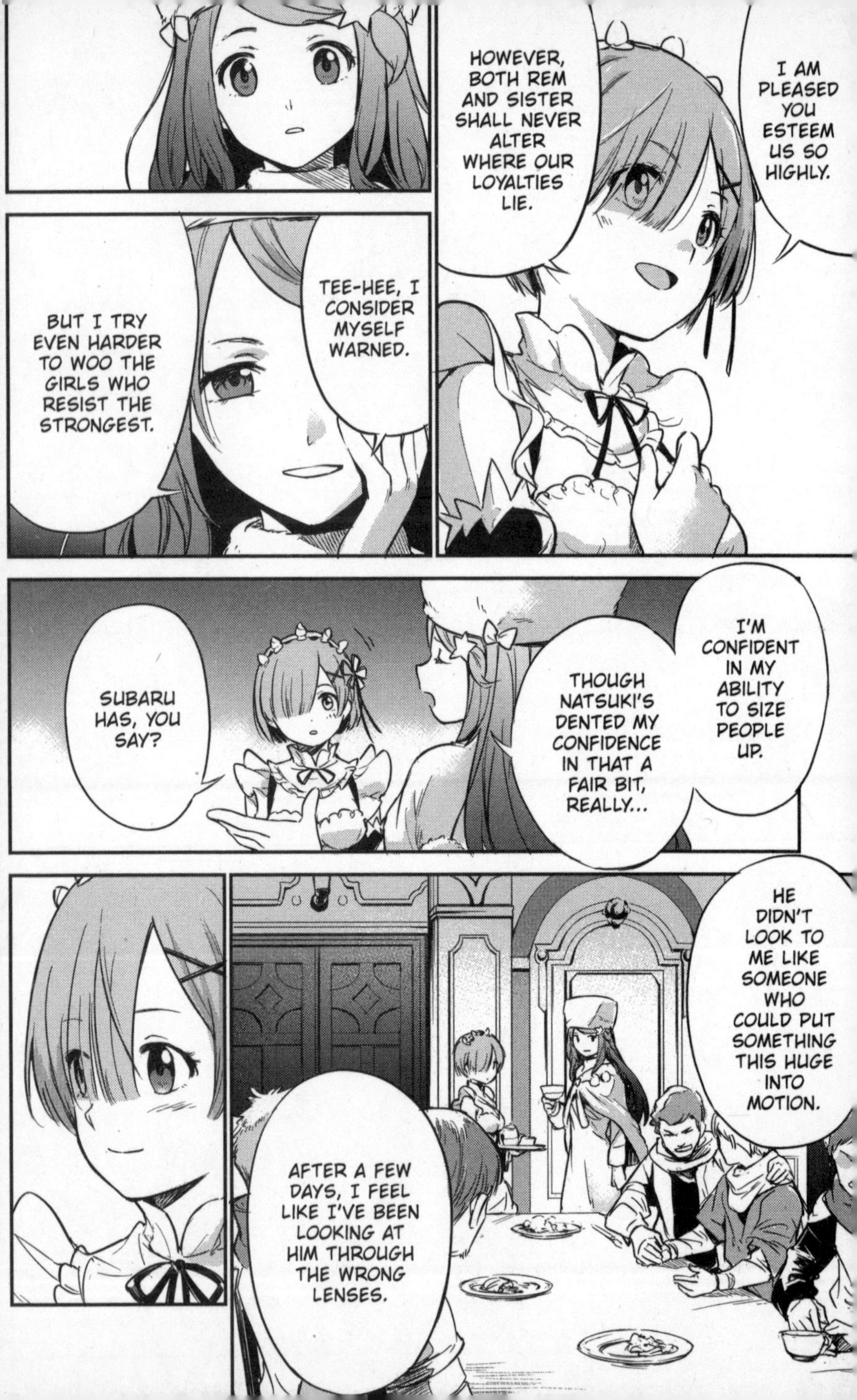
I AM PLEASED YOU ESTEEM US SO HIGHLY.
HOWEVER, BOTH REM AND SISTER SHALL NEVER ALTER WHERE OUR LOYALTIES LIE.
TEE-HEE, I CONSIDER MYSELF WARNED.
BUT I TRY EVEN HARDER TO WOO THE GIRLS WHO RESIST THE STRONGEST.
I'M CONFIDENT IN MY ABILITY TO SIZE PEOPLE UP.
THOUGH NATSUKI'S DENTED MY CONFIDENCE IN THAT A FAIR BIT, REALLY...
SUBARU HAS, YOU SAY?
HE DIDN'T LOOK TO ME LIKE SOMEONE WHO COULD PUT SOMETHING THIS HUGE INTO MOTION.
AFTER A FEW DAYS, I FEEL LIKE I'VE BEEN LOOKING AT HIM THROUGH THE WRONG LENSES.

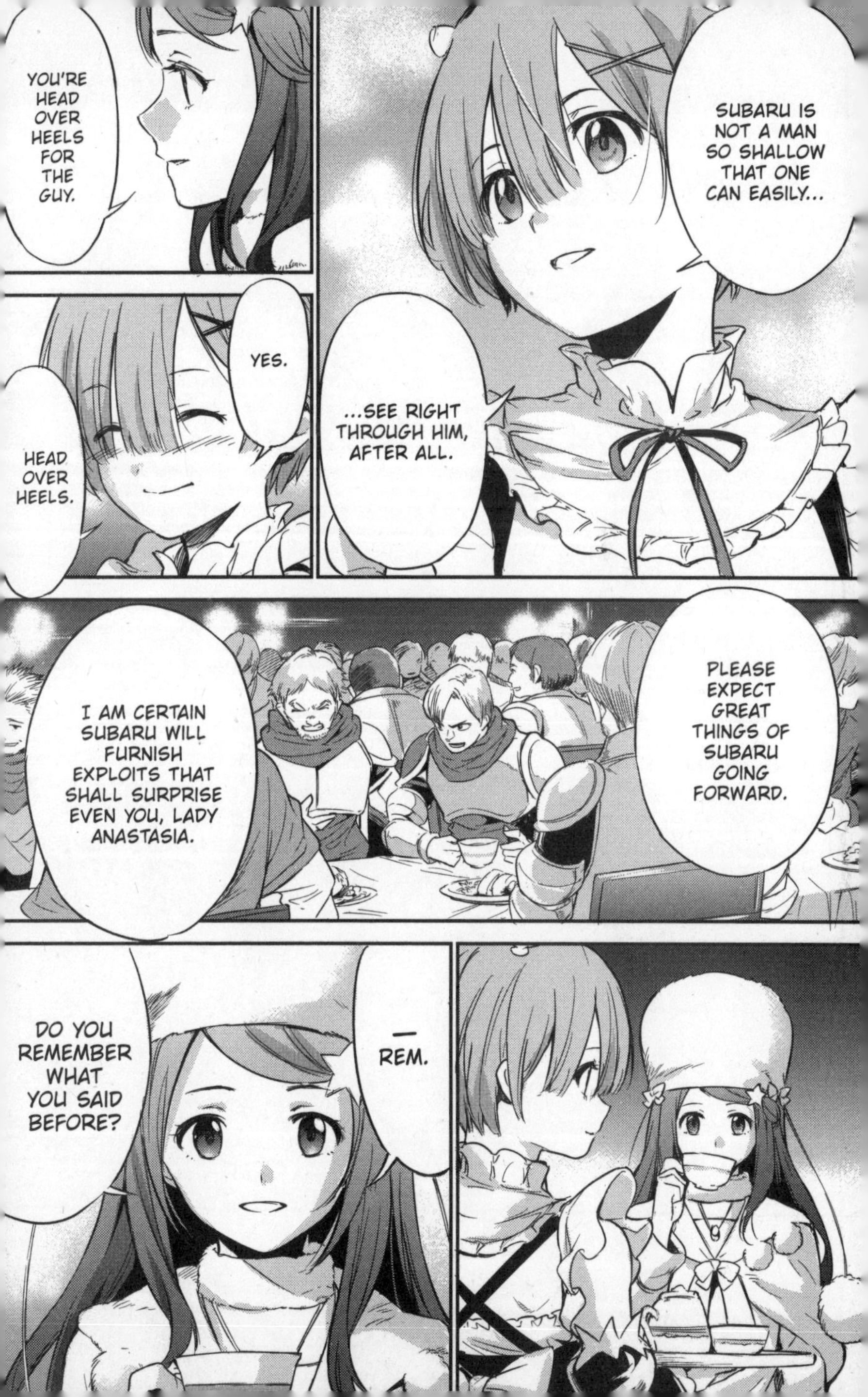
SUBARU IS NOT A MAN SO SHALLOW THAT ONE CAN EASILY...
...SEE RIGHT THROUGH HIM, AFTER ALL.
YOU'RE HEAD OVER HEELS FOR THE GUY.
YES.
HEAD OVER HEELS.
PLEASE EXPECT GREAT THINGS OF SUBARU GOING FORWARD.
I AM CERTAIN SUBARU WILL FURNISH EXPLOITS THAT SHALL SURPRISE EVEN YOU, LADY ANASTASIA.
— REM.
DO YOU REMEMBER WHAT YOU SAID BEFORE?

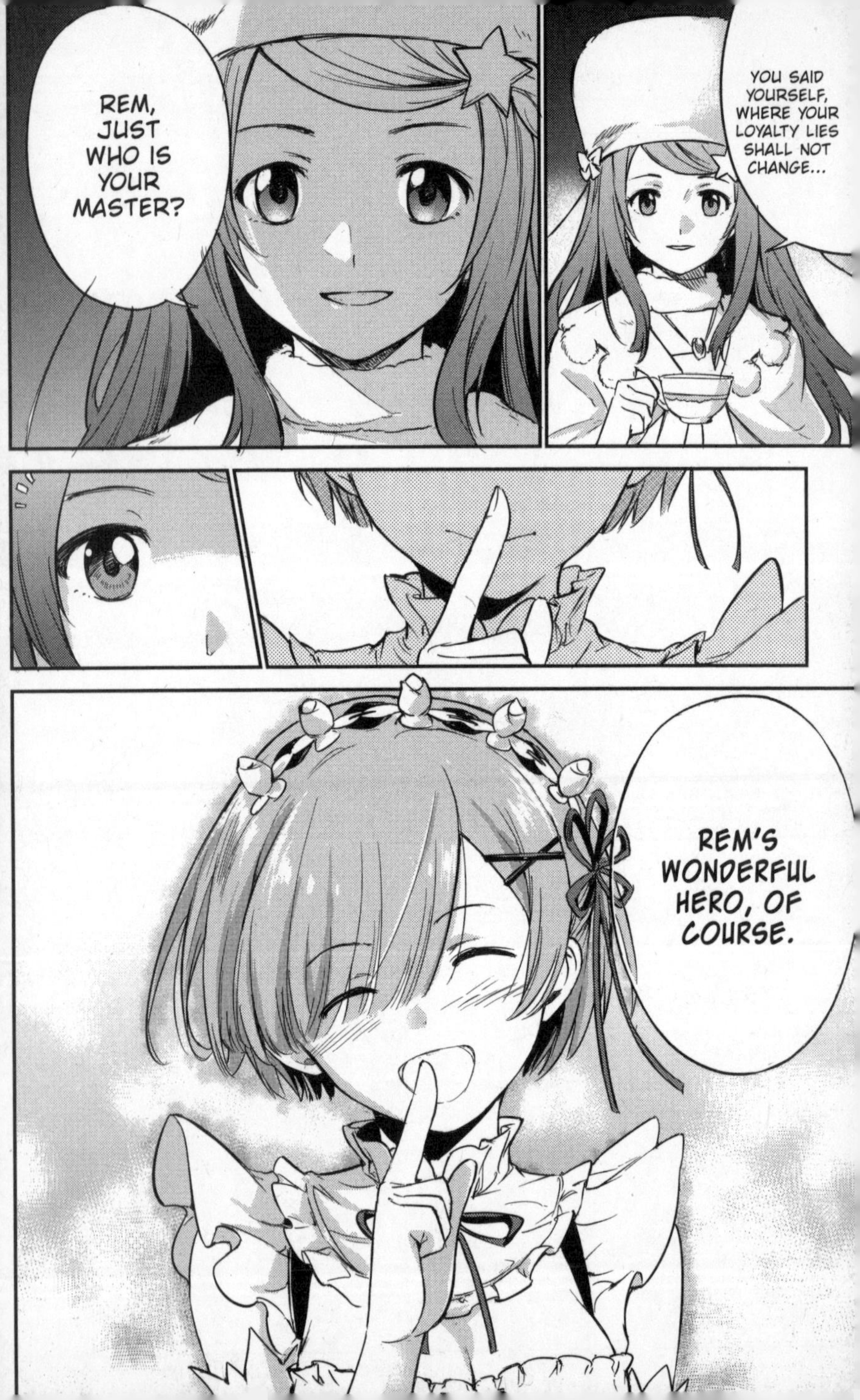
YOU SAID YOURSELF, WHERE YOUR LOYALTY LIES SHALL NOT CHANGE...
REM, JUST WHO IS YOUR MASTER?
REM'S WONDERFUL HERO, OF COURSE.

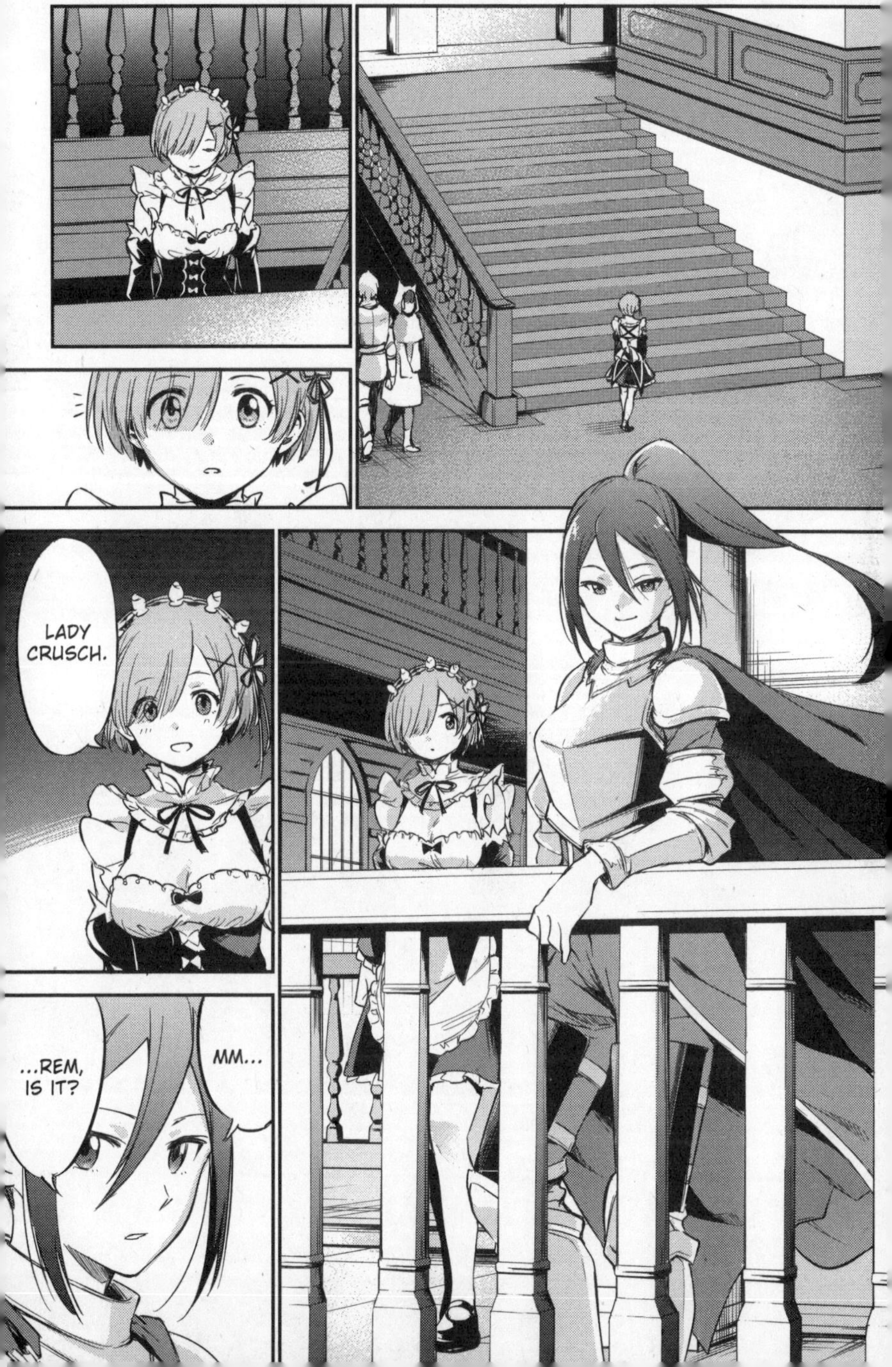
LADY CRUSCH.
MM...
...REM, IS IT?

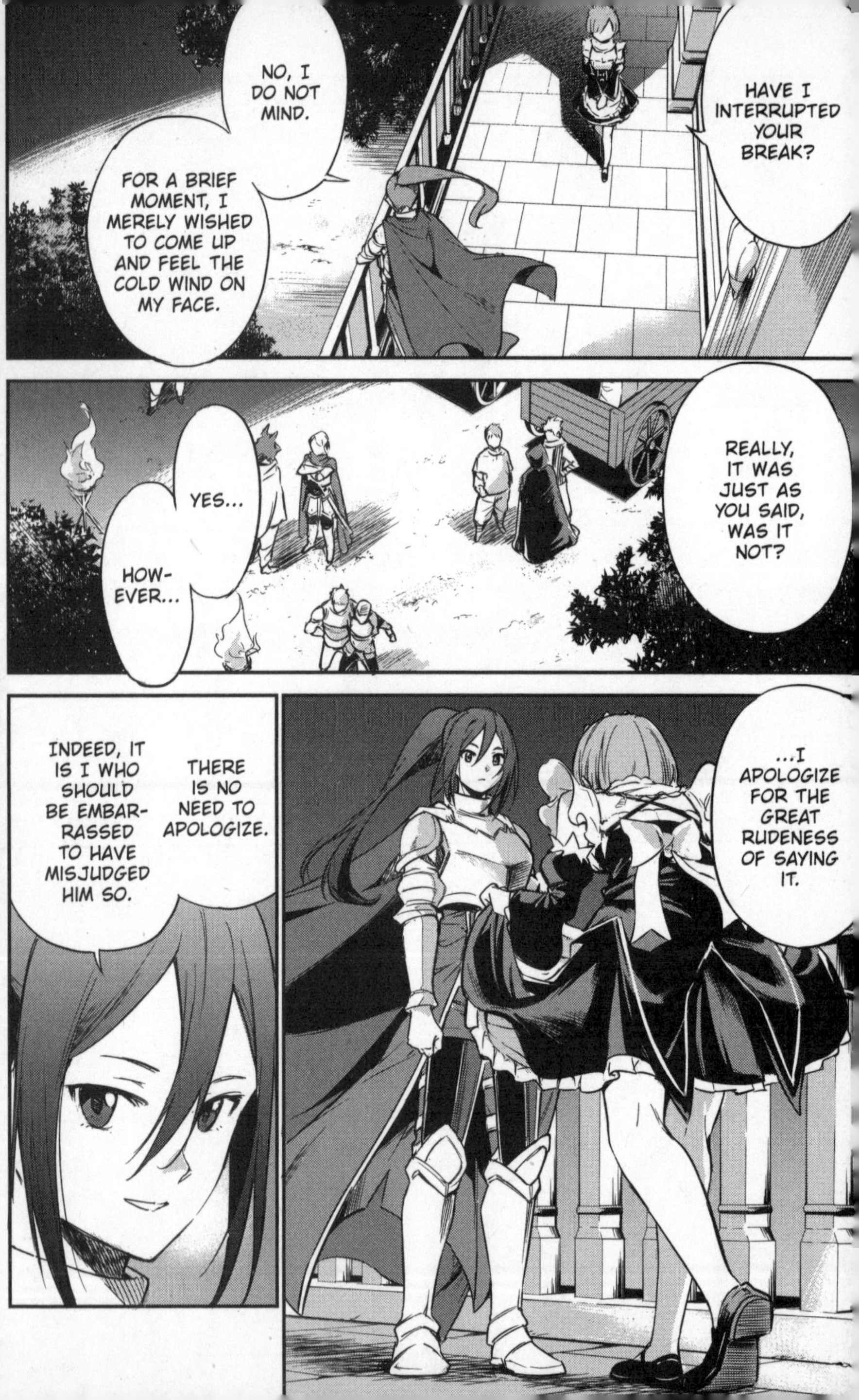
HAVE I INTERRUPTED YOUR BREAK?
NO, I DO NOT MIND.
FOR A BRIEF MOMENT, I MERELY WISHED TO COME UP AND FEEL THE COLD WIND ON MY FACE.
REALLY, IT WAS JUST AS YOU SAID, WAS IT NOT?
YES...
HOW-EVER...
...I APOLOGIZE FOR THE GREAT RUDENESS OF SAYING IT.
THERE IS NO NEED TO APOLOGIZE.
INDEED, IT IS I WHO SHOULD BE EMBAR-RASSED TO HAVE MISJUDGED HIM SO.

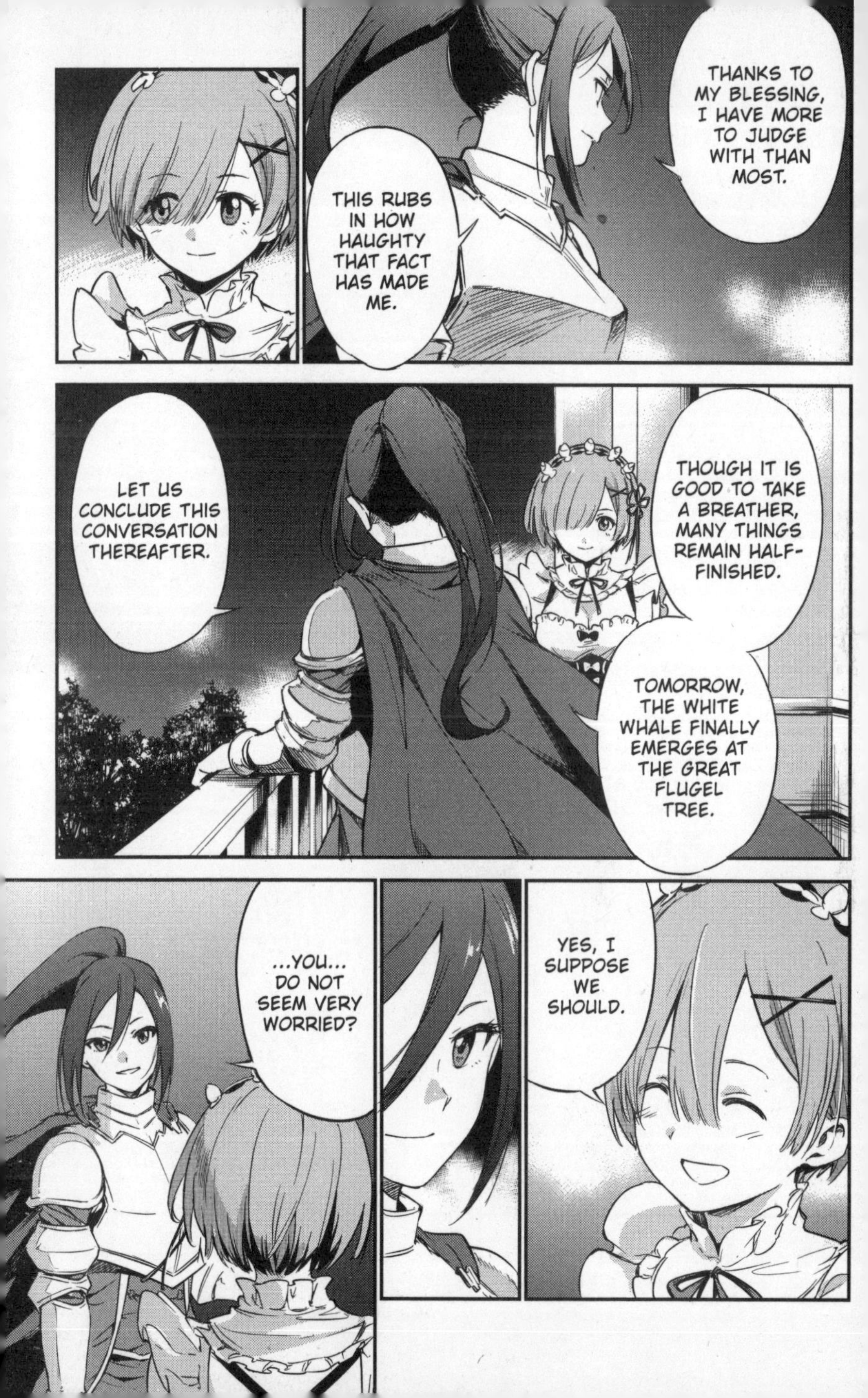
THANKS TO MY BLESSING, I HAVE MORE TO JUDGE WITH THAN MOST.
THIS RUBS IN HOW HAUGHTY THAT FACT HAS MADE ME.
THOUGH IT IS GOOD TO TAKE A BREATHER, MANY THINGS REMAIN HALF-FINISHED.
TOMORROW, THE WHITE WHALE FINALLY EMERGES AT THE GREAT FLUGEL TREE.
LET US CONCLUDE THIS CONVERSATION THEREAFTER.
YES, I SUPPOSE WE SHOULD.
...YOU... DO NOT SEEM VERY WORRIED?

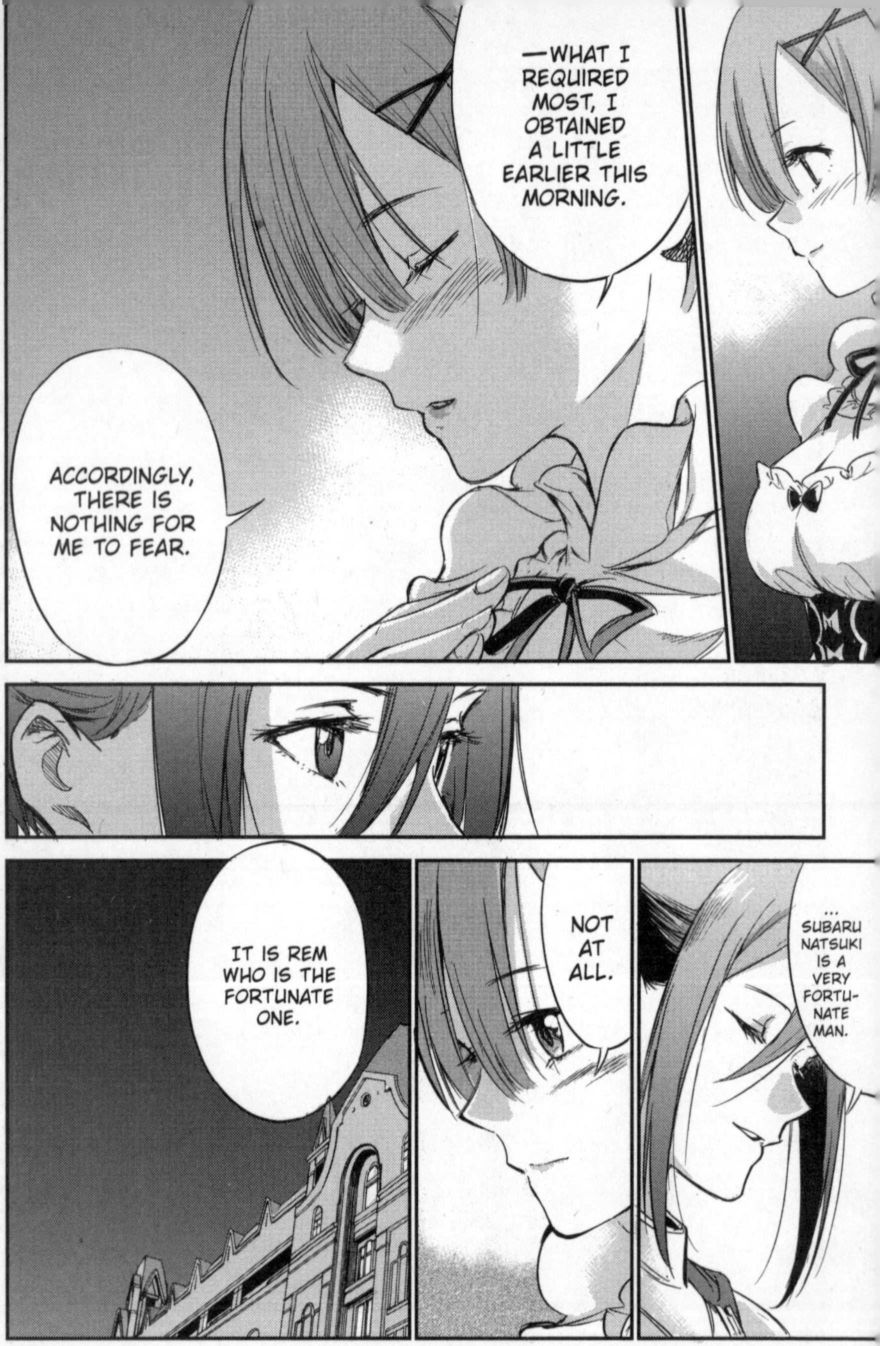

—WHAT I REQUIRED MOST, I OBTAINED A LITTLE EARLIER THIS MORNING.
ACCORDINGLY, THERE IS NOTHING FOR ME TO FEAR.
...SUBARU NATSUKI IS A VERY FORTU-NATE MAN.
NOT AT ALL.
IT IS REM WHO IS THE FORTUNATE ONE.

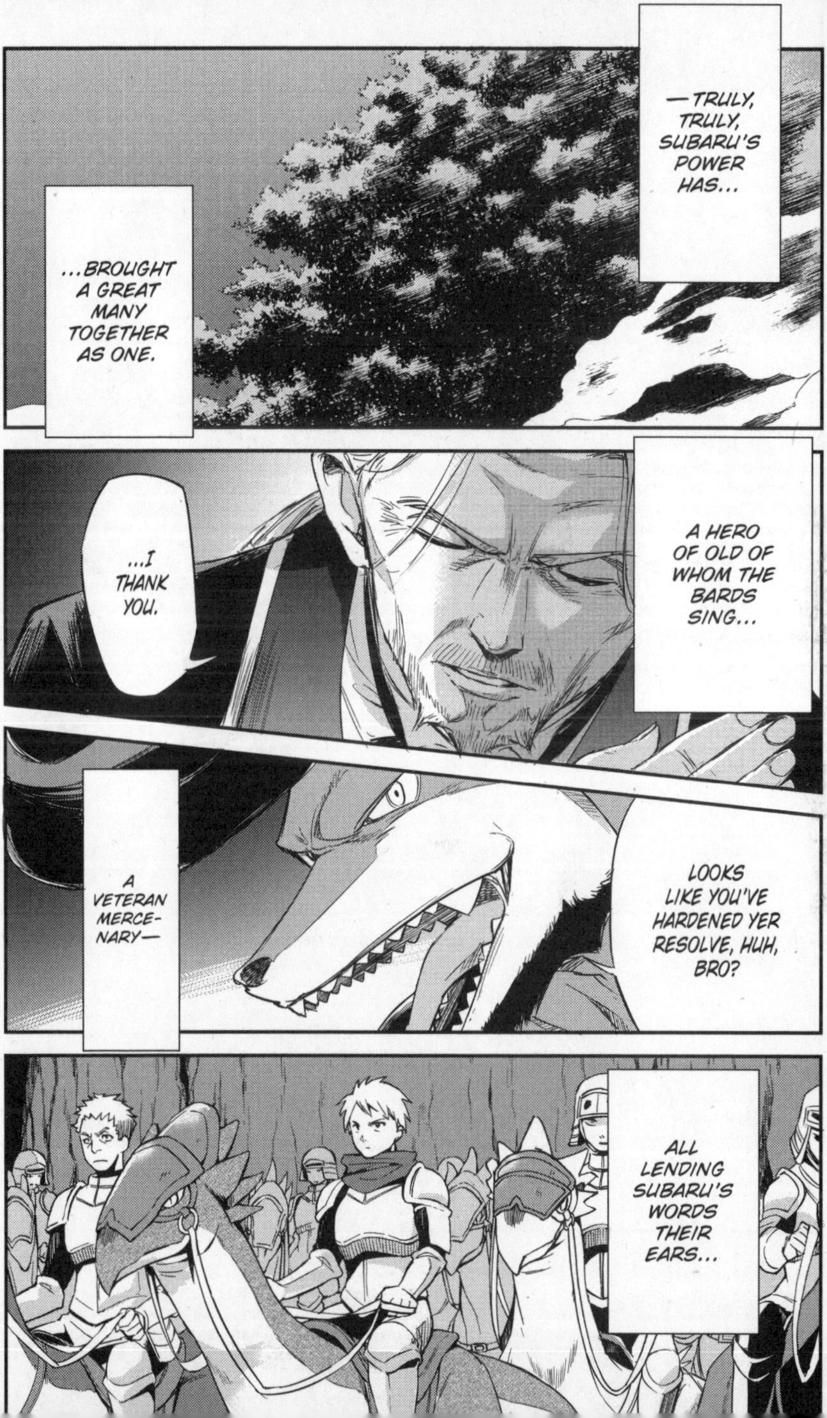
—TRULY, TRULY, SUBARU'S POWER HAS...
...BROUGHT A GREAT MANY TOGETHER AS ONE.
A HERO OF OLD OF WHOM THE BARDS SING...
...I THANK YOU.
LOOKS LIKE YOU'VE HARDENED YER RESOLVE, HUH, BRO?
A VETERAN MERCENARY—
ALL LENDING SUBARU'S WORDS THEIR EARS...

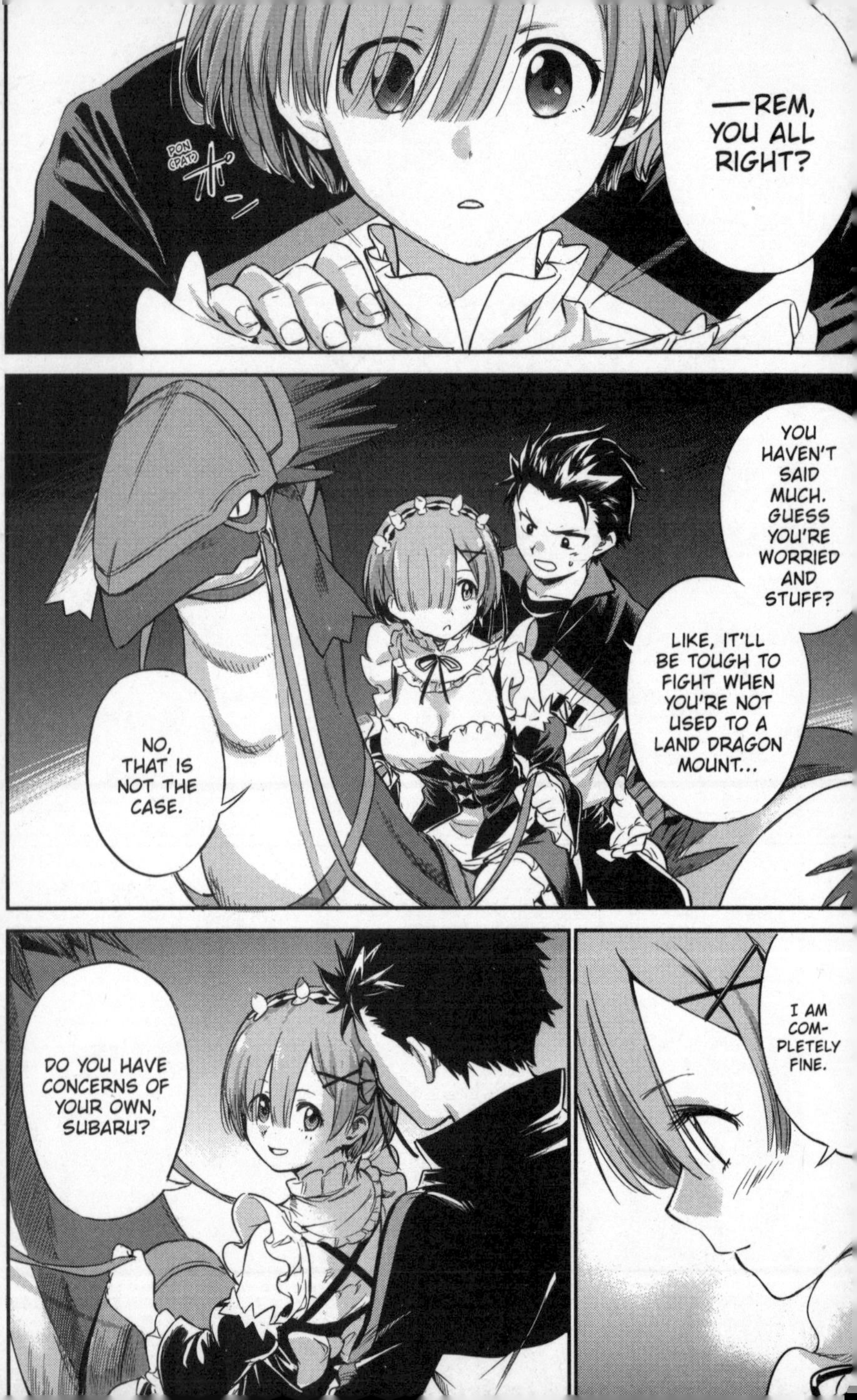
—REM, YOU ALL RIGHT?
PON (PAT)
YOU HAVEN'T SAID MUCH. GUESS YOU'RE WORRIED AND STUFF?
LIKE, IT'LL BE TOUGH TO FIGHT WHEN YOU'RE NOT USED TO A LAND DRAGON MOUNT...
NO, THAT IS NOT THE CASE.
I AM COM-PLETELY FINE.
DO YOU HAVE CONCERNS OF YOUR OWN, SUBARU?

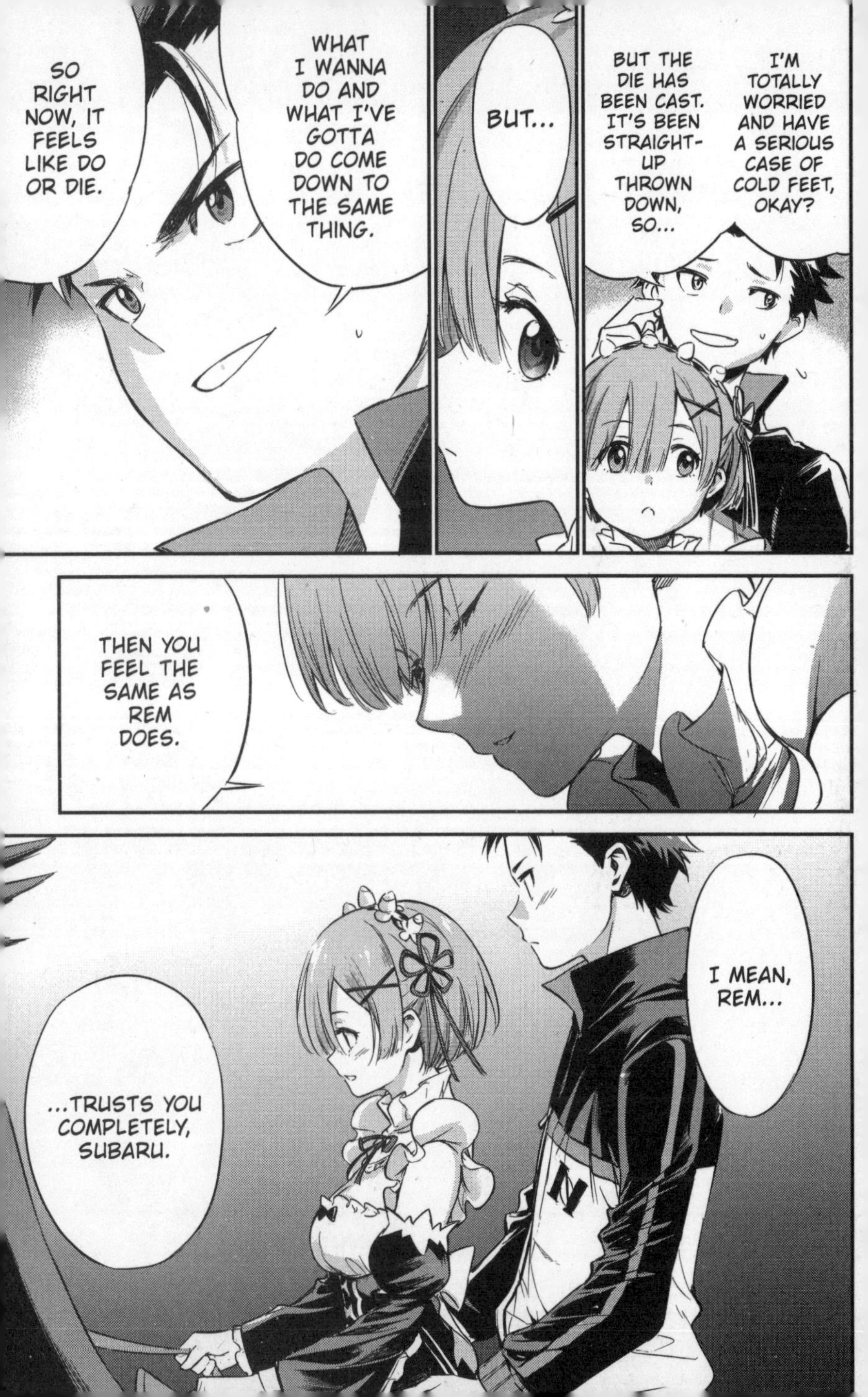
I'M TOTALLY WORRIED AND HAVE A SERIOUS CASE OF COLD FEET, OKAY?
BUT THE DIE HAS BEEN CAST. IT'S BEEN STRAIGHT-UP THROWN DOWN, SO...
BUT...
WHAT I WANNA DO AND WHAT I'VE GOTTA DO COME DOWN TO THE SAME THING.
SO RIGHT NOW, IT FEELS LIKE DO OR DIE.
THEN YOU FEEL THE SAME AS REM DOES.
I MEAN, REM...
...TRUSTS YOU COMPLETELY, SUBARU.

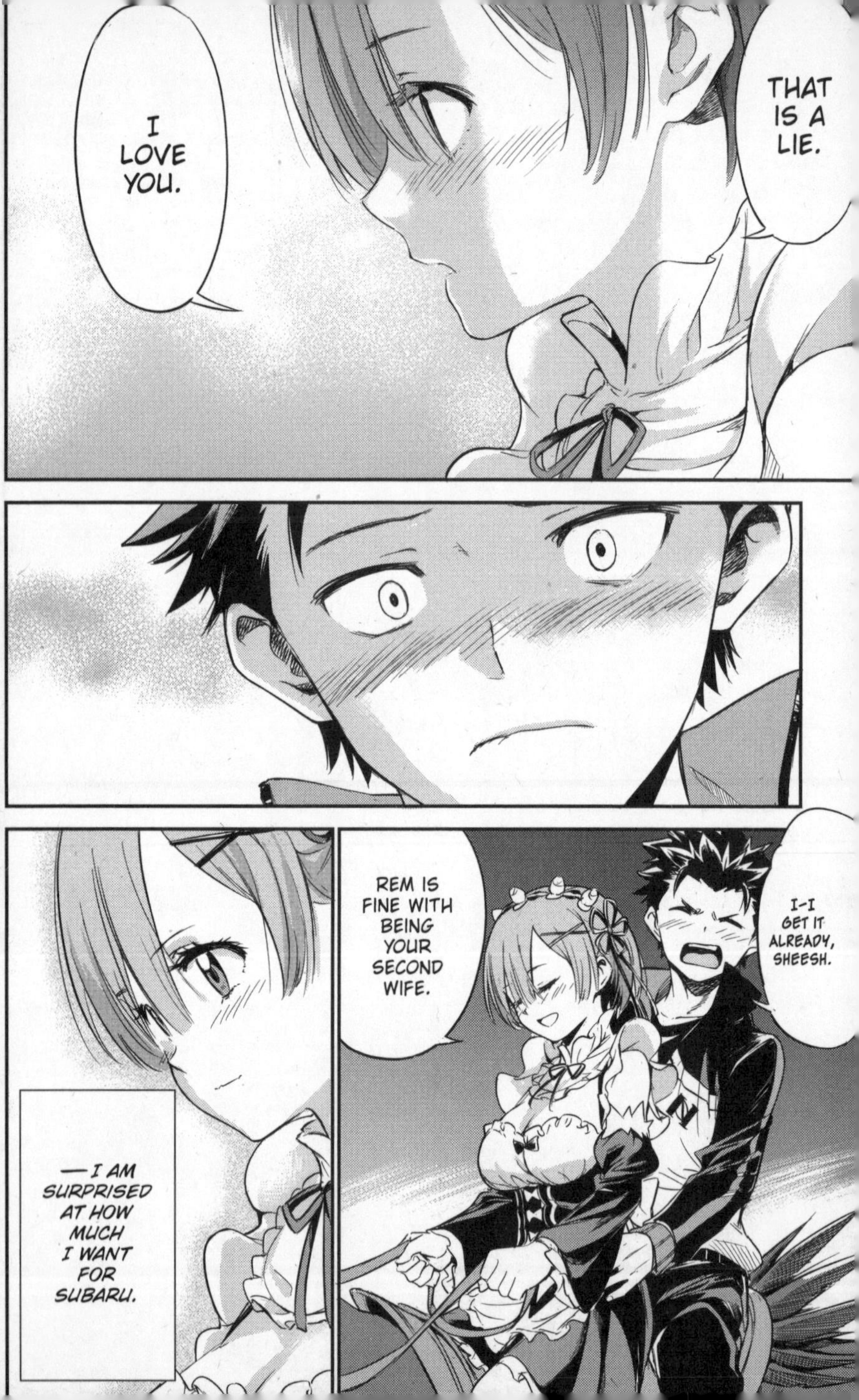
THAT IS A LIE.
I LOVE YOU.
I-I GET IT ALREADY, SHEESH.
REM IS FINE WITH BEING YOUR SECOND WIFE.
—I AM SURPRISED AT HOW MUCH I WANT FOR SUBARU.

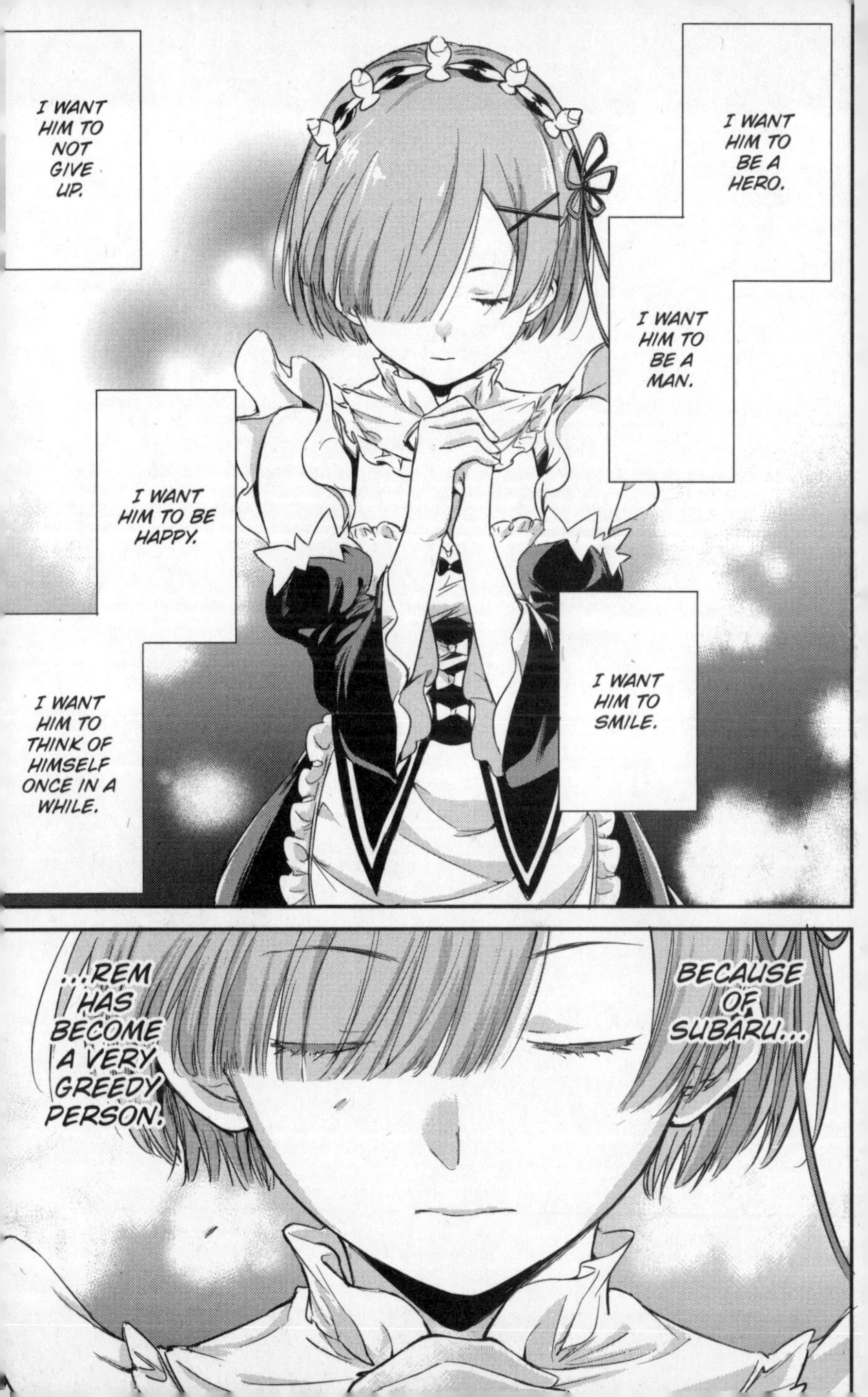
I WANT HIM TO BE A HERO.
I WANT HIM TO NOT GIVE UP.
I WANT HIM TO BE A MAN.
I WANT HIM TO BE HAPPY.
I WANT HIM TO SMILE.
I WANT HIM TO THINK OF HIMSELF ONCE IN A WHILE.
BECAUSE OF SUBARU...
...REM HAS BECOME A VERY GREEDY PERSON.

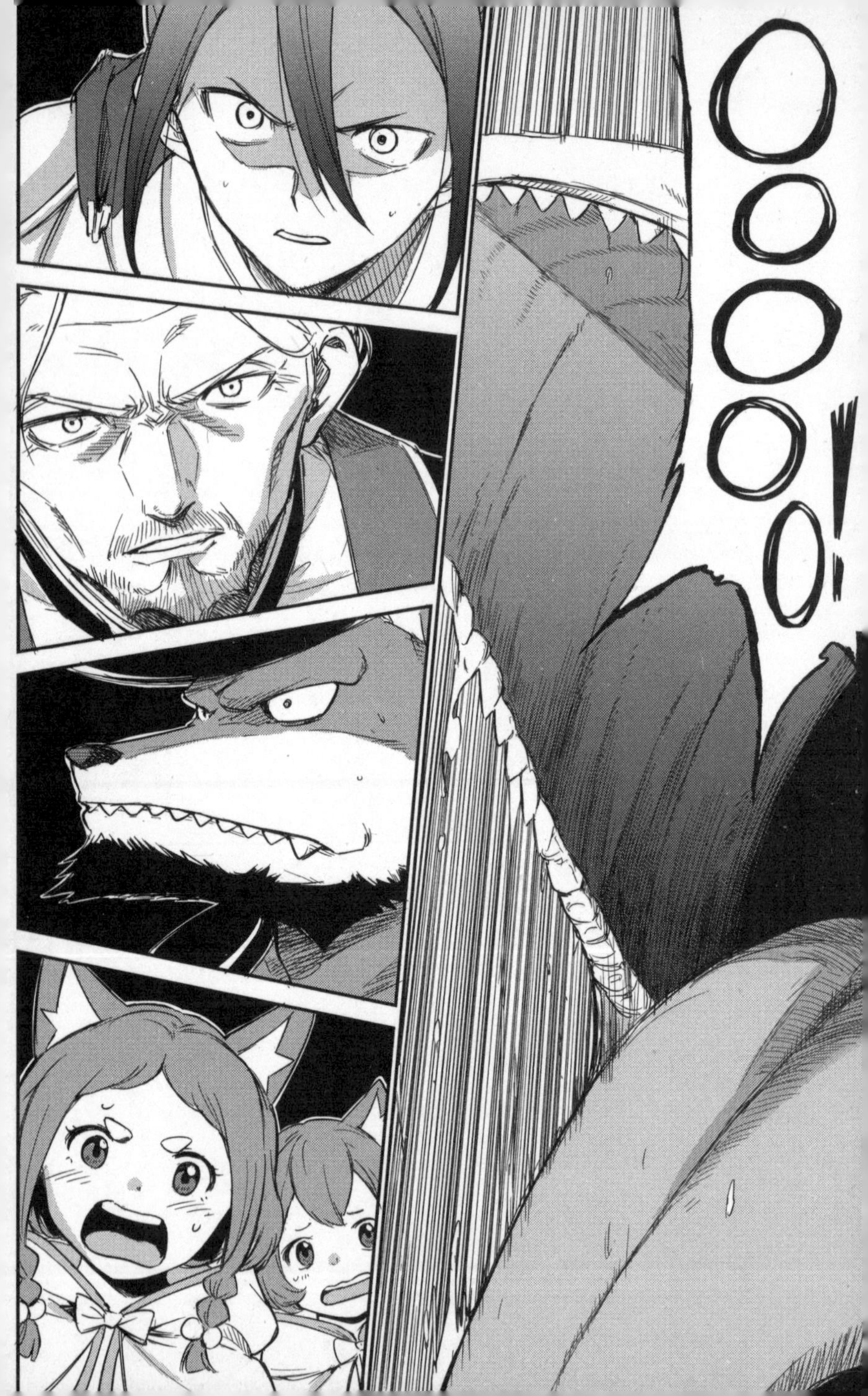
OOOOO!

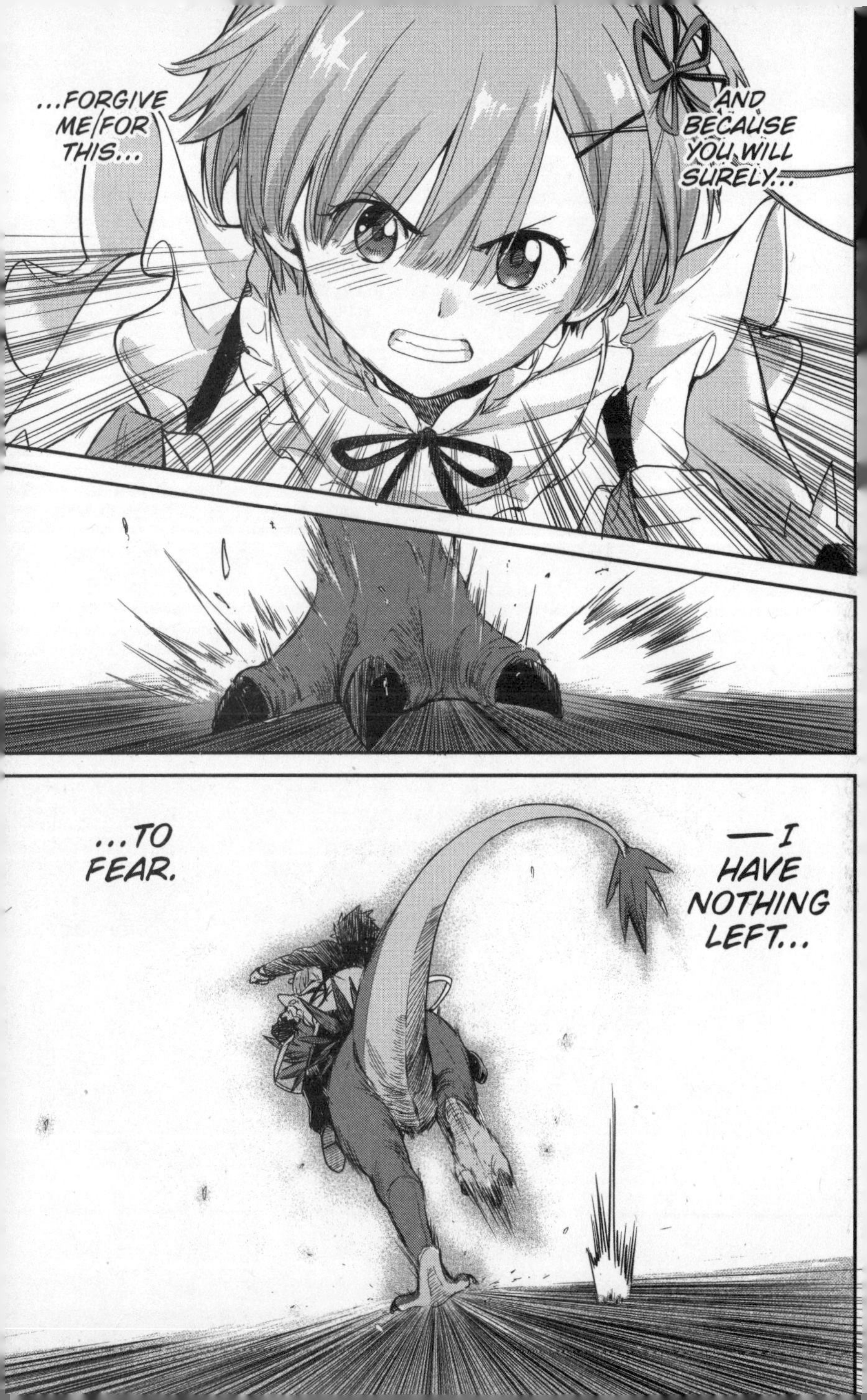
AND BECAUSE YOU WILL SURELY...
...FORGIVE ME FOR THIS...
—I HAVE NOTHING LEFT...
...TO FEAR.

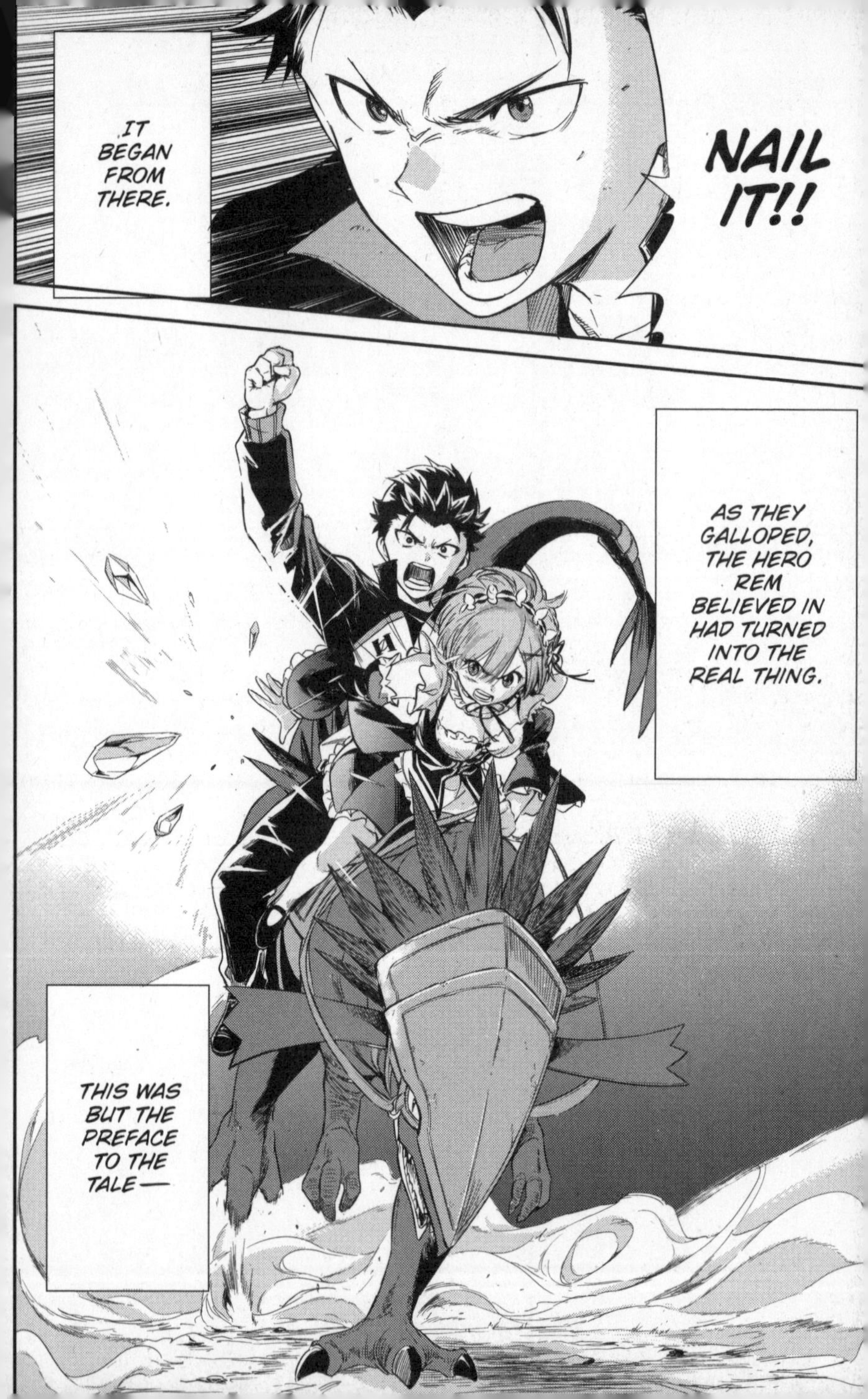
NAIL IT!!
IT BEGAN FROM THERE.
AS THEY GALLOPED, THE HERO REM BELIEVED IN HAD TURNED INTO THE REAL THING.
THIS WAS BUT THE PREFACE TO THE TALE—

Truth of Zero

The only ability Subaru Natsuki gets when he's
summoned to another world is time travel via his own
death. But to save her, he'll die as many times as it takes.

Re:ZERO
-Starting Life in Another World-

Illustration: Haruno Atori

CONGRATULATIONS ON THE RELEASE OF CHAPTER 3 VOLUME 11!

Re:ZERO -Starting Life in Another World- Chapter 4
The Sanctuary and the Witch of Greed

Supporting Comments from the Artist, Haruna Atori

Great job finishing Chapter 3! I am very reassured to have you as my comic version predecessor. Matsuse-sensei. It'll be a lot of fun taking over from Chapter 3 that you drew, so I'd better work hard...is what I'm thinking.

Supporting Comments from the Composition Supervisor, Yuu Aikawa

Matsuse-sensei, congratulations on finishing the manga for Chapter 3! It's been a lot of work over a long serialization.

Last year, when I was named as the composition supervisor for Chapter 4, I started by learning from volumes 1 through 9 of this series of yours. The tempo was great, and the manga you put together was straightforward and exciting, so I personally had enormous fun reading it. As a reader, I feel a little sad that a manga I've enjoyed each and every volume of is coming to an end. I will use it as a reference hereafter to carry on production with Atori-san, so best regards as we go forward with the comic version of Chapter 4.

Illustration by Shinichirou Otsuka
(Character Designer)

Re:ZERO -Starting Life in Another World-

Supporting Comments from the Author of the Original Work, Tappei Nagatsuki

Daichi Matsuse-sensei! Congratulations on *Re:ZERO* Chapter 3, Volume 11 going on sale.

And thank you very much for your hard work in completing the third chapter!

To be honest, I can't even describe the feeling of finally reaching the day that I could comment on Chapter 3 running its course. That's how long—truly, truly long—the journey has been.

With the previous, tenth volume of this chapter, we arrived at the TV anime's final episode, and this volume goes on sale in Japan in the run-up to the broadcast of the TV anime's second season. It is Matsuse-sensei, who has been with the *Re:ZERO* manga since the beginning, who has seen this tale to this point.

In times ahead, more tribulations and obstacles will assail the characters, and the delight and deep sentiments from overcoming them will continue. But for the moment, *Re:ZERO –Starting Life in Another World–* as admirably drawn by Matsuse-sensei, ends here.

However, *Re:ZERO –Starting Life in Another World–* continues onward, with the strength borrowed from Matsuse-sensei making it a much better work in the process.

Daichi Matsuse-sensei, truly, thank you very much for your long, hard work! I'm so happy to have had Matsuse-sensei drawing this! Let us both do our best henceforth!

Thanks!!

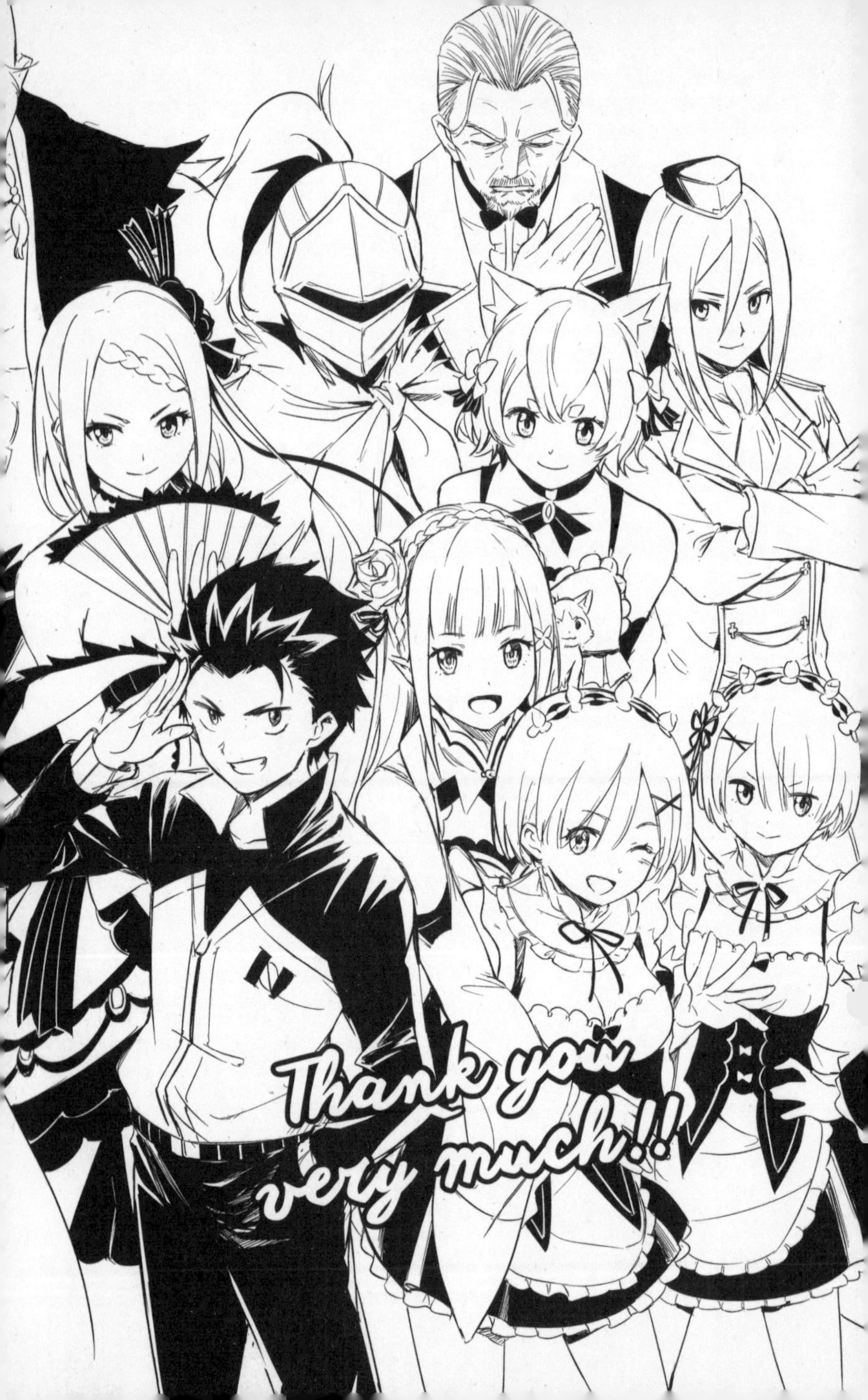
Thank you very much!!

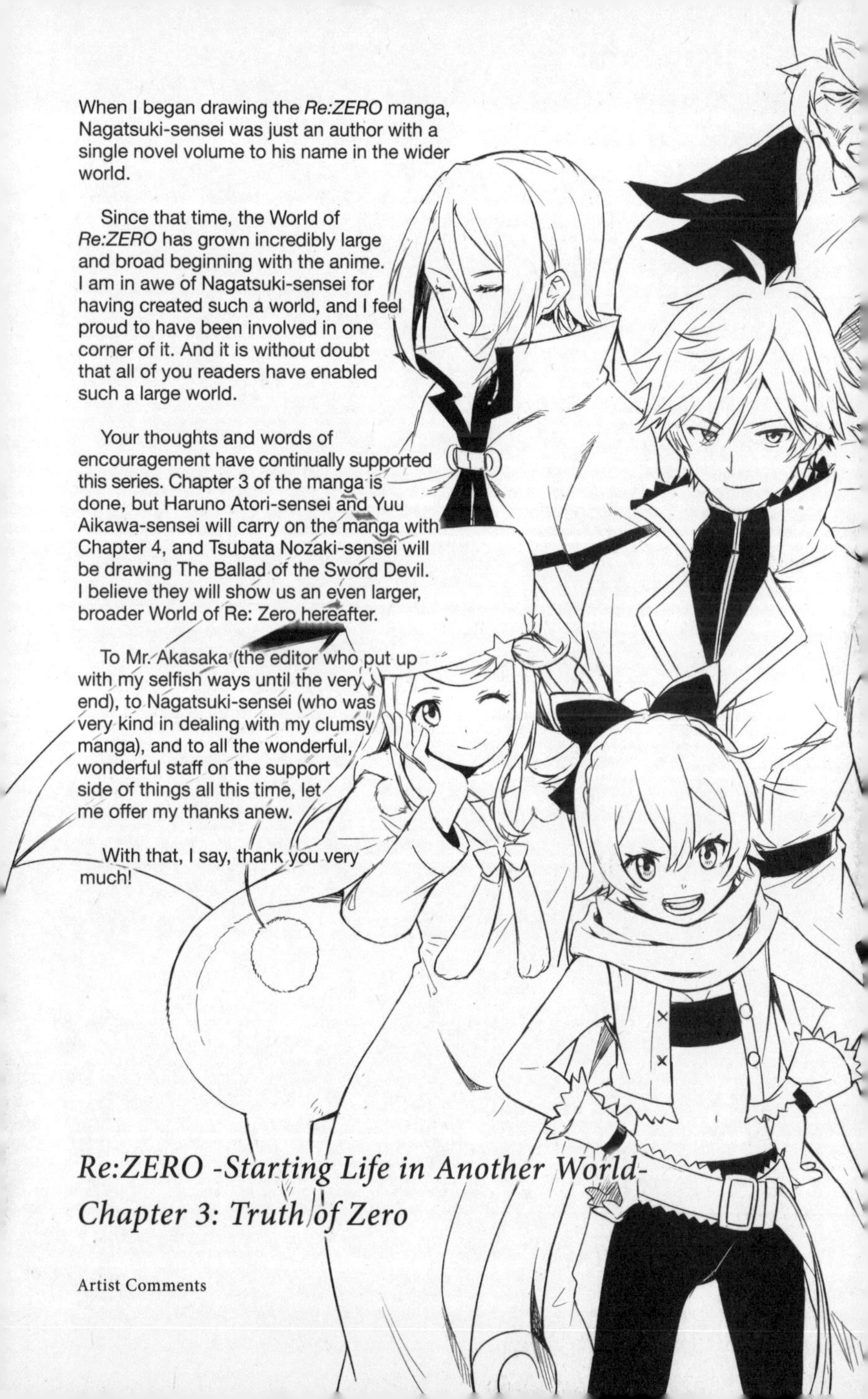

When I began drawing the *Re:ZERO* manga, Nagatsuki-sensei was just an author with a single novel volume to his name in the wider world.

Since that time, the World of *Re:ZERO* has grown incredibly large and broad beginning with the anime. I am in awe of Nagatsuki-sensei for having created such a world, and I feel proud to have been involved in one corner of it. And it is without doubt that all of you readers have enabled such a large world.

Your thoughts and words of encouragement have continually supported this series. Chapter 3 of the manga is done, but Haruno Atori-sensei and Yuu Aikawa-sensei will carry on the manga with Chapter 4, and Tsubata Nozaki-sensei will be drawing The Ballad of the Sword Devil. I believe they will show us an even larger, broader World of Re: Zero hereafter.

To Mr. Akasaka (the editor who put up with my selfish ways until the very end), to Nagatsuki-sensei (who was very kind in dealing with my clumsy manga), and to all the wonderful, wonderful staff on the support side of things all this time, let me offer my thanks anew.

With that, I say, thank you very much!

Re:ZERO -Starting Life in Another World- Chapter 3: Truth of Zero

Artist Comments

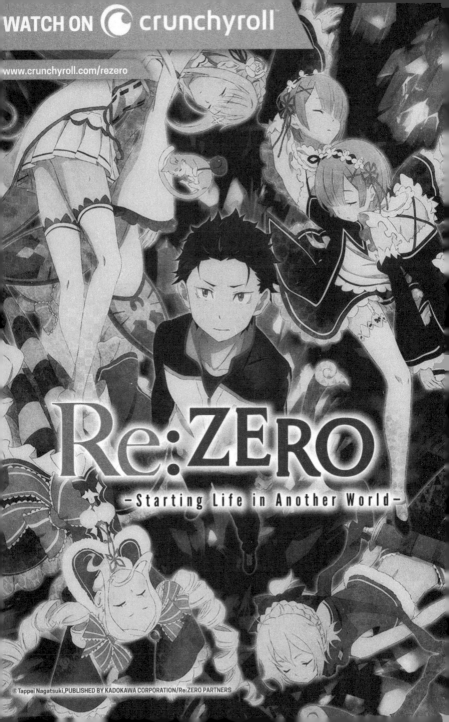

RE:ZERO -STAR[...]
IN ANOTHER W[...]
Chapter 3: Truth of Zero

3 9077 08974 8597

Art: **Daichi Matsuse**
Original Story: **Tappei Nagatsuki**
Character Design: **Shinichirou Otsuka**

Translation: Jeremiah Bourque
Lettering: Rochelle Gancio

This book is a work of fiction. Names, characters, places, and incidents are the
product of the author's imagination or are used fictitiously. Any resemblance to
actual events, locales, or persons, living or dead, is coincidental.

RE:ZERO KARA HAJIMERU ISEKAI SEIKATSU DAISANSHO
Truth of Zero Vol. 11
© Daichi Matsuse 2020
© Tappei Nagatsuki 2020
First published in Japan in 2020 by KADOKAWA CORPORATION, Tokyo. English
translation rights arranged with KADOKAWA CORPORATION, Tokyo through
TUTTLE-MORI AGENCY, Inc.

English translation © 2020 by Yen Press, LLC

Yen Press, LLC supports the right to free expression and the value of copyright.
The purpose of copyright is to encourage writers and artists to produce the
creative works that enrich our culture.

The scanning, uploading, and distribution of this book without permission is a
theft of the author's intellectual property. If you would like permission to use
material from the book (other than for review purposes), please contact the
publisher. Thank you for your support of the author's rights.

Yen Pr[...]
150 W[...]
New Y[...]

Visit u[...]
facebo[...]
twitte[...]
yenpre[...]
instag[...]

First Ye[...] First Yen Press Edition: December 2020

TEEN   Re: Zero:
RE: Chapter 3: Volume 11

12/15/20

Yen Press is an imprint of Yen Press, LLC.
The Yen Press name and logo are trademarks of Yen Press, LLC.

The publisher is not responsible for websites (or their content) that are not
owned by the publisher.

Library of Congress Control Number: 2016936537

ISBNs: 978-1-9753-1913-7 (paperback)
       978-1-9753-1914-4 (ebook)

10 9 8 7 6 5 4 3 2 1

WOR

Printed in the United States of America